Regency Christmas Spirits

Nancy Butler

Emma Jensen

Edith Layton

Barbara Metzger

Andrea Pickens

A SIGNET BOOK

SIGNET
Published by New American Library, a division of
Penguin Putnam Inc., 375 Hudson Street,
New York, New York 10014, U.S.A.
Penguin Books Ltd, 80 Strand,
London WC2R ORL, England
Penguin Books Australia Ltd, Ringwood,
Victoria, Australia
Penguin Books Canada Ltd, 10 Alcorn Avenue,
Toronto, Ontario, Canada M4V 3B2
Penguin Books (N.Z.) Ltd, 182–190 Wairau Road,
Auckland 10, New Zealand

Penguin Books Ltd, Registered Offices:
Harmondsworth, Middlesex, England

First published by Signet, an imprint of New American Library,
a division of Penguin Putnam Inc.

First Printing, October 2001
10 9 8 7 6 5 4 3 2 1

CONTENTS

v

The Merry Wanderer
by Nancy Butler

Thou speak'st aright;
I am that merry wanderer of the night.

It was the season that lured him down . . . down
from the airy reaches of a distant plane, where creatures of his own kind dwelled, unseen and unheard—
but not necessarily unfelt—by the mortals they observed. In the past, he'd been drawn by the festivity
and the song, the bright lights against winter's darkest
nights, the pungent greenery and the soothing fragrance of cinnamon and bayberry. This time, however,
he had been sent here with a task to accomplish. But
that didn't mean he couldn't enjoy himself a bit before
he got down to business.

As he made his way among the shoppers on the
cobbled High Street of this ancient and revered English city, he was compelled, childlike, to gaze beyond
the ice-rimed glass of a baker's window, eyes widening
at the delights displayed there—the colorful marzipan
animals, the sleek chocolate tortes, and the tiny
frosted fairy cakes.

Fairy cakes, Robin thought with a grin. *How very
apt.*

He was a creature without appetite in his normal
existence, but when he took on mortal form, he had
the same hungers as any man. And perhaps a few that
mortal men did not profess.

The tinkling of bells filled the air as a fair-haired
young woman, arms laden with packages, came

through the bakery door. Robin started at the noise, at a mere human heralded by that silvery sound. He realized the bells were set above the door, to alert the baker when customers entered his shop.

The young woman turned onto the pavement and nearly walked right into Robin. Her gray eyes flashed up in amused dismay as she neatly sidestepped him with a swift, apologetic grin. He caught a delicious whiff of nutmeg and treacle. And something else even his clever nose could not name. Before he could lean closer, she had hurried away down the street, the crimson feathers on her bonnet bobbing in time with her rapid pace. He followed in her wake, and though he merely strolled while she tripped briskly along, by some means he never quite lost sight of that bright beacon.

When she went into a toy shop, he lingered outside, only too happy to acquaint himself with the fabulous, frivolous creations of this modern age. Ah, such toys as he'd never envisioned when he was a young sprite six centuries or so ago. There were music boxes, mechanical drummers, dancing bears. He studied the model of a medieval castle, complete with portcullis and drawbridge, and was pleased to note that the toy maker had gotten it nearly right. Beside it sat a porcelain doll wearing a white satin gown and sporting a pair of gossamer wings.

"All wrong," Robin grumbled. Wings did not emanate from one's shoulders; where was the point of that? Upper back was more like it, where the good strong muscles lay. Not that he'd ever needed those troublesome things himself. His kind were not air spirits, but woodland spirits who stayed strictly on *terra firma*—or as *firma* as it got in his own sphere. There was a deal more a fellow could get up to down there than fidgeting about in midair, with only birds and bats for company. Mortals stayed on the ground, and since they were grist for Robin's mill, so to speak, he was quite happy with his lot.

The young woman eventually came out of the toy shop, and as she went past him, he was again beguiled by the commingling scents of nutmeg and treacle and . . . what was it? Oranges, perhaps, or wildflowers or summer hay. Something utterly delightful. Something he wanted to get close to again.

Fired by inspiration, he went immediately into the emporium across the street and soon emerged carrying a small parcel wrapped with ribbon. He then entered the toy shop, and since, in spite of being neither tall nor imposing, he gave off a combined aura of wealth and assurance, the elderly proprietor was at once at his elbow. "Good season to you, sir."

"And a good season to you." Robin touched the brim of his beaver hat. "I fear the young lady who was just in here, the one with the delightful bonnet, dropped this on the pavement." He held up the parcel. "I ran after her, but she was lost in the bustle of the street."

The shopkeeper's eyes narrowed. "She might yet come back for it."

"She appeared to be carrying half the High Street in her arms. I doubt she'll miss it until she gets home. However, I would be happy to return it to her. You don't happen to have her direction."

The man gave him a long, considering look. "You're not up to any mischief, are you?"

Robin nearly laughed. It was precisely what he'd been created for. But he schooled his face into sober lines and shook his head. "Indeed, I only want to see that her holiday is not blighted by the loss of her parcel." He shook it gently. "A Christmas gift, perhaps, for a sweetheart or husband."

"She has neither beau nor husband, more's the pity," the shopkeeper remarked. "It's probably for her brother. Not that he doesn't deserve her kindness, for a brighter, more charming lad I've yet to see. Her name is Julia Fitzwalter, the Lady of Islay."

Robin hid his elation and merely commented, "An odd title."

" 'Tis indeed, sir, an ancient one that's accorded little respect these days. Goes back before the Conquest, when the lords and ladies of Islay were given the responsibility of keeping the old lore alive." He grinned. "Though the lore's never gone out of fashion here in Glastonbury."

"Nor in some other, more distant places," Robin added softly.

He was halfway to the door, when the shopkeeper called out. "Don't you want to know her direction?"

Robin nodded. The charade had to be played out. "Tell me, then, where might I find this Lady of Islay?"

"Arden House," the man answered. "North of town, near the river."

She was the one; Robin had known it the instant he'd seen her.

There had been a sort of radiance in her face, a grace and purpose in her movements. It also helped that he had met both her parents on an earlier occasion—before she'd even been born. Julia Fitzwalter possessed her mother's hair, unruly waves the color of a fawn's coat, and her father's aristocratic profile as well as his fine gray eyes. It was Robin's hope that she also bore her sire's love of antiquity and his deep respect for tradition.

After retrieving his horse from the livery, he rode off across the winter-fallow fields that surrounded Glastonbury. The river sparkled off to his right as he made his way through a beech wood. As it thinned, he saw ahead of him the tall, freestanding buttresses and roofless retaining walls of Glastonbury Abbey, all that remained of the great cathedral after Henry VIII's soldiers had sacked it. Vines now twined their way up the golden towers, where once ceremonial banners had flown. Wild grass now covered the floor of the nave with nature's own verdant carpet.

A short time later Arden House came into view, sunlight gleaming off the pale ochre brickwork. The Elizabethan manor had been built upon the ruins of old Islay Castle and now housed over five thousand volumes of ancient text. But the lords and ladies of Islay were the keepers of more than the lore of Albion, Robin knew. They also guarded the keys to *his* kingdom.

Eleven months earlier, upon the death of Roland Fitzwalter, the faery council had been convened. Their chief concern had been preserving the *Book of Trey,* which resided in the vast underground library of Arden House. As long as there had been a man of principle watching over the precious volume, Robin's brethren had rested easy. Now, however, that responsibility had fallen—for the first time in centuries—to a callow young woman. The council had decided, after much twittering and flittering, that it was best if she were wed.

No one in the faery kingdom was as adept at matching up mortals as Robin, so the great queen, to whom he owed his allegiance, had sent him to assess this new Lady of Islay now that her year of mourning was nearly up. Titania had given him a week to get inside Arden House, discover the condition of the book, determine if the present lady was a fit caretaker, and if that proved not to be the case, find her a mate who would be.

A little daunting, to be sure.

It was a pity, he reflected, that Julia Fitzwalter hadn't found a husband and saved him the trouble of playing matchmaker. It seemed inconceivable that she was three and twenty and still unwed. Most Englishmen divested themselves of girl children the instant they were out of the schoolroom. But then her father had not been like most Englishmen.

Robin knew he could have shirked his task and risked Titania's anger; he had often enough in the past. But her punishments were always well thought out and rarely kind. Last time he'd failed to do her bidding, he had ended up exiled in Norway for fifty years, rubbing elbows with trolls and all manner of unpleasant mountain spirits. No, he'd take any action necessary to satisfy her. He wanted to stay in England. After passing so many centuries in this pleasant land, it felt like home.

He was abreast of the twin stanchions that flanked the drive, when he abruptly pulled up his mount. Strange inscriptions had been scrawled onto the stones. The words, which would be indecipherable to most people, were quite familiar to him—an ancient runic language, long dead. He shivered. Someone had been here before him, someone versed in the old ways. He studied the emblems, trying to gauge their meaning. It was a warning, he realized with disquiet, proclaiming that those who intended mischief to the house should stay away at peril to their lives.

"This is a fine kettle of fish," he muttered as he continued down the drive.

Julia caught the cake box with one hand as it slid off the pile in her arms. "I ought to get a job juggling in a street fair," she grumbled as she replaced the box atop her bundles.

She had managed to get halfway home without dropping anything, and perhaps had only slightly squashed the bag of honey buns, which were lodged under her left elbow. If she were a proper lady, she'd have had a maid to assist her. But servants cost money, and she might just as well wish for a band of angels to accompany her, as for a proper maid. Of course there was Lettie, their housekeeper and cook, but Julia had no intention of asking a woman of sixty-odd years to traipse up and down the High Street in her wake.

When Julia reached the drive to Arden House, her steps began to falter. It lacked only four days until Christmas, and she still hadn't told her brother about the letter from Sir John Fitzwalter. Distant cousin or not, the man had no right to foist himself upon them for the holiday. But that wasn't the worst of it—he had also informed her that he'd been corresponding with her father's lawyers, offering himself both as guardian to her brother and as overseer of Arden House.

She muttered a few unladylike oaths as she resumed walking.

It was tragic enough that Papa had succumbed to a wasting fever last January. But then, barely three weeks later, the elderly scholar he had chosen to be Harry's guardian had died in a carriage accident. Not one other of her father's wealthy, influential friends had come forward with an offer to look after the boy. At present, Harry was a ward of Chancery, pending some solution.

Julia prayed that it had not come in the form of Sir John Fitzwalter. She had met her cousin only once, at a family gathering a decade earlier, and had taken him in instant dislike. It had been difficult to feel charitable toward that unctuous, posturing young man, who was also unhappily afflicted with bad teeth, pop eyes, and a crow's beak of a nose.

What could her cousin want with Arden house, she

wondered for the hundredth time, when he possessed a prosperous estate in Yorkshire? She certainly couldn't fathom why he'd suddenly taken an interest in Harry when there hadn't been a peep from him since her father's death—at which time she'd received a coldly worded note of condolence.

And now this unsettling letter, which was at present tucked in her reticule. Harry was forever poking around in her desk, looking for quill pens and lost buttons, and she hadn't wanted him to find the missive, not until she'd had a chance to think things through.

It was, she realized, time to tell him the truth. About everything—not only about Sir John's letter, but about the state of the family finances. She had a gut-clenching suspicion that there was no money left in the family coffers. She'd sent off numerous inquiries to her father's solicitors in London, questioning the long-delayed settlement of his estate and had gotten only platitudinous nonsense in reply. This casual, if not downright disrespectful, treatment was making her angry. And afraid.

If she and Harry had truly been left penniless, the lawyers would be exultant over her cousin's offer to see to her brother. That was how Sir John had phrased it in his letter . . . *I'll see to the cub.* Except that *she'd* been seeing to him since he was seven, when their mother died. Julia had reached her own majority two years earlier, but the law did not consider her a fit guardian, being a mere female. She was resigned to this iniquity, but had little intention of handing Harry or the house over to a distant relation with fish eyes and a preening, oily manner.

Last night, in desperation, she had shared her concerns with Lettie. The older woman had offered a simple solution. "Marry," she'd said tartly. "Marry and let your husband set everything to rights."

As if it were that easy, Julia thought now with a sigh of frustration. As if cartloads of eligible gentlemen appeared at her doorstep on a regular basis. In her position as Lady of Islay she was accorded a measure of respect in the town, but she was also viewed as something of an oddity, the sort that young men obviously steered away from.

She had to tell Harry of their cousin's offer. He had a right to make his own decision. Even if he was only fourteen, he had a particularly fine brain and could often think rings around her.

Whatever her brother decided, it was going to be a difficult Christmas. Not only would there be unpleasant relations invading the house, but she still had to arrange the annual estate party—on an extremely limited budget.

She shook off her misgivings and went into the house. As she shrugged out of her pelisse in the chilly front hall, she tried not to notice the paintings and furnishings that were now gone from the space. Better to focus on the fine wainscoting and fan-vaulted ceiling. Such beauty needed no embellishment, she told herself sternly.

In contrast to the hall, the east wing was deliciously warm. Lettie somehow managed to keep the inhabited parts of the house toasty, in spite of the exorbitant price of coal. Harry insisted she was carrying on an intrigue with old Mr. Quince, the fuel merchant.

There were voices raised in lively conversation beyond the parlor door. Julia heard her brother's bright tenor, but did not recognize the second masculine voice. Perhaps one of Harry's friends from the vicar's school had stopped in. They'd make short work of her honey buns, were that the case.

She cracked the door open and peeked inside Harry was leaping about, flailing his arms, while t' young man perched on the threadbare sofa crowed with glee.

"And then what happened?" the man asked, leaning forward eagerly.

"Why, what do you think? Theseus lopped off the creature's head and carried it back to King Minos on a pike."

"Rather bloodthirsty, I'd say."

"Not a bit . . . that old minotaur had been gobbling maidens for decades. It was about time he met his match."

Julia gave a theatrical cough. Both heads turned to her. Her brother's face appeared more flushed than usual, his light brown hair tousled beyond description. But it was the face of the stranger on the sofa that arrested her breathing for an instant.

She'd feared at first that this might be Cousin John, come early to stake his claim on Arden House, but this bright-eyed man was the polar opposite of her sneering cousin. He was stylishly attired in a bottle-green coat and biscuit-colored inexpressibles, although his complexion was unfashionably tanned. The firelight caught ruddy highlights in his deep brown hair, which had been trimmed into tiny elf locks that capered above his brow.

"This is m'sister, Julia Fitzwalter," said Harry with a carelessly outflung hand. "Jules, this is Mr. Robin Goodfellow."

The stranger rose and gave a graceful bow. "It is a pleasure to meet you at last, Miss Fitzwalter."

She performed a small curtsy. And then cocked her head. "Do I know you, sir? You seem familiar to me somehow."

He grinned, and his lean face widened appealingly. "You nearly collided with me on the High Street. I believe you dropped one of your parcels." He took up a package from the sofa and held it out. "The toy maker gave me your direction. I hope you don't mind . . . it was a bit forward of me."

There was an unusual lilting cadence to his voice that made listening to it a pure pleasure. A touch of Ireland, she thought, or perhaps Wales.

"Not at all." She took the package from him with a smile. "I expect there are few mortals who would go to such lengths to perform a kindness for a stranger."

"Few indeed," he murmured.

Her expression of pleasure changed to one of puzzlement when she saw the name Spenser's Emporium imprinted on the wrapping paper. "Oh, but I fear this is not mine. It is from a shop that I cannot aff—that I rarely go into."

"Then it is yours by default. I doubt I could trace the owner." He paused and watched how her eyes lingered over the package. "Open it," he coaxed. "Perhaps the item is not of great value."

She undid the ribbon and drew aside the wrapping, pulling loose a patterned silk shawl in shades of cream and burgundy.

"It's lovely," she crooned, "but much too valuable to keep. You must take it back to the shop." She held it out to him, but he stepped back.

"Consider it a gift for your hospitality." He waved toward the tray of tea and scones on the side table. "I am a stranger in Glastonbury and have not had such a pleasant welcome before now. If it eases your mind, I will notify the shop and replace the shawl if its rightful owner should return."

Julia bit her lip. "That is very generous. However—"

"Oh, take it," Harry interjected. "You need a treat, sink me if you don't." His gaze shifted to their guest. "She's been blue-deviled all week. Moping about with

a full-fledged case of the megrims. Needs a bit of perk-
ing up, if you ask me."

"This season can be . . . trying," Mr. Goodfellow
responded. "In spite of all the merriment."

Especially if you are facing an oily usurper, Julia
added silently.

Mr. Goodfellow returned to the sofa, and Harry
launched into an enthusiastic retelling of the tale of
the Trojan horse. Julia settled on the padded window
seat and occupied herself by studying their guest.

He was not imposing, as some of her father's *ton*
connections had been. Nor was he precisely handsome.
Still, it was an attractive face, with an exotic tilt to the
cheekbones that contrasted nicely with the humorous set
of his mouth. He appeared fit, if a bit on the thin side.
Spare, she decided, rather like a whippet. She'd not been
able to determine the color of his eyes, but then he
turned to her with a question, and the light from the
window shone bright on his angular face.

His eyes were quite wondrous, a dappled blend of
green and brown and gold, each color distinct and
vivid. *Faun's eyes,* she thought, *like those of some
mythical woodland creature.*

"W-what?" she stammered, aware that he was regarding her with amusement.

"I asked if you would have the kindness to show me
the books in your vault." His slim-fingered hand traced
down the pristine fall of his neck cloth. "I am something
of a bibliophile, and I understand you have many rare
and interesting volumes here at Arden House."

Her mouth tightened. "So rumor has it. There was
a time when I also found the collection exciting."

"And now?"

She hitched one shoulder. "It has lost its allure, I'm
afraid. I refuse to make the place the center of my
life as my father did."

"Well, if it stirs unpleasant memories . . ." He rose and took up his hat. "Perhaps I'd best be off. It's been a pleasure meeting you both."

He bowed to Julia, then held out his hand to Harry, who clasped it firmly.

"Why don't *I* show you the vaults?" Harry said abruptly. "I've been down there a number of times this past year, attempting to put things in order." He worried his lower lip. "Papa left it in a bit of a shambles, I'm afraid."

"There's nothing I love so much as a shambles," Mr. Goodfellow pronounced. "You never know what treasures you might stumble across."

"More like black beetles and bookworms," Julia muttered.

Their guest turned to her and said in an undertone, "Try not to be too hard on your father. The work he did here is held in great esteem by those in distant places."

She looked at him coolly. "I did not intend to sound disrespectful."

He broke through her reserve by winking. "There's treasure down there, Miss Fitzwalter. I feel certain of it. I'm something of an expert on treasure."

"Very well," she said, rising from the padded seat. "I suppose I could spare an hour or so this afternoon. I haven't been in the vaults since Papa died . . . maybe it's time I took a look at my patrimony."

To her surprise, Mr. Goodfellow stopped her in the doorway and draped the silk shawl over her shoulders. He stroked one hand lightly along her arm to smooth the fringe, then said, "I imagine it's cooler down there than here in the house."

"Don't bet on it," Harry said. "It gets so cold in the front hall sometimes, I wonder it don't snow."

Julia sighed. "We've had to practice certain economies. Until the lawyers set the estate to rights."

Mr. Goodfellow merely nodded as he held the door for her.

He wasn't a tall man, she realized as she brushed past him, perhaps two or three inches above her in height. It allowed her a splendid view of his remarkable eyes, which had gone almost all gold. Most likely in anticipation of viewing the collection. Her father used to wear that same keen expression whenever he was heading into the vaults.

She led them to the kitchen, where the cellar door was located. Lettie looked up from kneading bread dough. She caught Julia's eye, then nodded meaningfully in Mr. Goodfellow's direction. "Very nice," she mouthed.

Julia pretended not to notice. She took down a large, ornate key from a pine shelf beside the hearth and unlocked the stout oak door.

"The key is kept out in the open?" Mr. Goodfellow asked in a low voice.

She drew the brass key from the lock and held it up under his nose. "As you can see, it measures nearly five inches in length. I am not about to wear it on a chain around my neck."

For an instant, his bright gaze flitted over the bodice of her gown. Julia was startled by the sudden heat that coursed through her. *How curious.*

"I was just thinking that anyone might come in here and find it," he explained, "and possibly get up to mischief down there."

She was about to dismiss this possibility, but then recalled what he'd said about treasure. It wasn't worth taking chances, not if the salvation of Arden House depended on something hidden in the vault. "I could lock it in my writing desk," she said.

"Yes," Harry drawled from behind them, "*that's* a safe place. She keeps the drawer key in a glass dish on top of the desk."

"I admire your trusting nature, Miss Fitzwalter."

She glared at Harry, and then turned to Mr. Good-fellow with a determined smile. "I'll think of a safe place. Now, Harry, if you would fetch a candle from the sideboard."

They went in single file down the wooden stairs. The first level of the cellar contained the usual house-hold overflow—hampers of linens, stone crocks, dusty glass jars.

"That's the wine cellar," Julia said, indicating a re-cessed oak door. "Papa never paid much attention to restocking it."

She wasn't about to tell Mr. Goodfellow that she had been forced to sell the majority of its contents to the local wine merchant to get through the planting season last spring. Even now that the crops were har-vested, she feared she would not be able to carry the estate through the winter without stripping Arden House of all its furnishings and paintings.

She led them across the floor, to where the outer wall of mortared fieldstone gave way to great hewn blocks of granite. "This is the oldest part of the structure, all that remains of Islay Castle. The Elizabethan masons who raised Arden House left the lowest level of the castle as it was, and built up from there." She opened an arched wooden door that hung on hammered iron hinges. "Watch your step—the stairs here have no railing."

They descended into an oblong chamber with a shallow, vaulted roof. The floor was paved with more granite squares, except at its center, where a mono-lithic round stone had been set. Robin read the chis-eled inscription aloud. "Kept safe for the ages."

A noble sentiment, he thought the first time he saw the stone.

Harry went at once to light the candelabrum that sat on a leather-bound trunk.

"Seven book rooms radiate off the central part of the vault," Julia explained. "My great grandfather added ventilation flues so that twice a year fires could be lit in a brazier."

"To burn off any moisture," Mr. Goodfellow said.

She eyed him approvingly. "Exactly. Though this cellar is dryer than most."

"Builders knew what they were about in those days," he said as he stroked one hand along the meshed stones of the wall. "Have you seen Chartres, Miss Fitzwalter? It's magnificent. Or Rouen? Well, of course you haven't . . . not with Bonaparte rampaging all over Europe."

"Perhaps I might see them one day," she said wistfully, "now that Napoleon has been sent to Elba." She cocked her head. "But how is it you've seen those places? We've been at war with the French for as long as I can recall."

Robin realized his error too late; he couldn't very well reveal that he'd not only seen those cathedrals, he'd watched them grow, stone by stone, century by century. "I . . . I visited France as a child. Well before Bonaparte was a threat."

He motioned to one of the doors along the wall and suggested they start there.

"I've done some cataloging in this room," Harry said as he pushed the door open and went to light a branch of candles on a pine refectory table. "But I'm afraid I've barely made a dent."

Robin stepped inside and was nearly forced to his knees by the sheer impact of all the ancient words bombarding him. The high shelves that ran along the walls were piled high with scrolls, bound books, loose folios, and leather boxes. He raised his face, eyes half closed, like a hound sniffing the air for game.

When he'd last visited here, again in mortal form, the *Book of Trey* had been lying on a shelf in this very room. At the time, Robin had warned Fitzwalter that a work of such antiquity was best kept hidden away. The man had obviously taken his advice, more's the pity.

"No, not here," he murmured softly, and then said, "Perhaps we should start our search in one of the rooms Harry hasn't gone through." He gave Julia a probing look. "When your father brought you down here, did he ever show you anything of particular value?"

"It was all valuable to him," she said a bit crossly. "Even the tiniest remnant of vellum, faded and yellowed, would excite him. During his last year, I fear he became obsessed with buying up any bit of old writing he could find. A peddler had only to show up with a tatty manuscript and Papa would empty his purse."

Robin nodded soberly. "He'd lost his sense of discrimination, perhaps?"

"He'd lost his mind," he heard her mutter. "But since you said you like a shambles, let's begin with what he called the mystery room."

The layout of this chamber appeared identical to the first, except that papers lay everywhere, scattered and heaped upon the shelves, the center table, even on the floor. However, Robin was not paying attention to the chaos around him, he was too busy fighting off a light-headed feeling of elation. It was here, somewhere in this room was the *Book of Trey*.

He swung to Julia and clasped her by the wrist. "It's much too dusty in here," he said. "You will ruin your gown and your pretty shawl. Let me sort through this room while you and Harry investigate the other chambers." At her apparent hesitation, he added earnestly, "I am not a thief, Miss Fitzwalter, only a devoted student of old lore. In Ireland, I once saw a shipmaster loading tattered manuscripts into his hold as ballast. It nearly broke my heart." He grinned at her. "I only want to view this collection and see if there is something here that might, er, help to pay the coal merchant."

"Amen to that," said Harry. "C'mon, Jules. We'll each take a room."

As the boy tugged her through the doorway, Robin breathed a sigh of relief, then let his gaze wander over the disordered shelves. He bit back his disappointment. The book was nowhere in plain sight—nothing visible was of the right size.

He spent half an hour tapping at the walls, listening for a hollow sound that might indicate a secret cache. He scraped his nails over the stones on the floor, pushing aside piles of paper as he crept forward, seeking a pressure-drive spring. Nothing was revealed to him. Yet the essence of the book was all around him, all but singing to him.

With a sigh he sat up and leaned back against one of the wooden uprights. Closing his eyes, he focused all his considerable powers on the book. Near, very near, and yet obscured. Not behind stone, he realized, but behind wood. Beneath wood.

He opened his eyes and stared at the pine table that sat not three feet from him. It was not much different from the table in the first room except that it had a deeper apron around the edge. And a sealed bottom.

"Clever, Fitzwalter," he murmured.

He scuttled up beside the table, swept away all the papers that littered the pine surface, and set the branched candlestick on the floor. He then ran his fingers along the foot-wide apron. There was a subtly raised area at one corner; he pressed it down and heard a faint snick. The top was now canted slightly.

Robin rose and dusted himself off. One wanted to be pristine in the face of such greatness. He held his breath as he raised the tabletop. Beneath it lay a large leather box, worked all around in intricate Celtic patterns. The box alone could have kept the Fitzwalters in coal for a decade.

He went to the door and poked his head out. Light shone from the two rooms most distant from his own. Good, he thought, they were both occupied. Returning to the table, he lifted the lid off the leather box, and his eyes brightened. The cover of the book beneath it was of the finest kidskin, a pure white that had not yellowed over the passing centuries. There were no words written upon it, only three entwined emblems worked in gold: a cloud, a tree, and a series of waves, representing air, earth, and water. The conjoined realms of the faery folk.

The pages were crisp beneath his fingers as he thumbed through them, the letters still a rich, inky black, the illustrations unfaded. The text was a mixture of Old English, Cornish, and Gaelic—the book predated the Norman Conquest, when French had, for a time, supplanted the native languages.

Robin knew much of what the volume contained, but found himself lost in the beauty of the words, skipping here and there, seeking a favorite passage or a well-remembered song. This was *his* patrimony, the stored history and lore of his brethren. Near the back of the book was a collection of spells and incantations for summoning faeries. And for controlling their power. It was what made the *Book of Trey* so dangerous, it was why the lords and ladies of Islay were so important to Robin's kin—they held the fate of the spirit world in their hands.

It was clear that Roland Fitzwalter had never told his daughter about the book—she'd hardly be so dismissive of his collection if she'd ever seen this exquisite volume. That omission puzzled Robin. Passing along the knowledge was a sacred duty; it had been for over eight centuries.

It would now fall to him to inform her of her role. But not just yet, he told himself. Julia needed to value the entire collection, not just the *Book of Trey*. A good start toward that end would be finding something rare down here to set her finances to rights.

He was about to replace the lid of the leather box, when he noticed a ragged thread at the bottom of the book's binding. He marked the spot with one finger and reopened the book near the back.

His sibilant gasp seemed to echo in the small room.

An entire section of spells had been removed, sliced neatly away from the spine, leaving behind that raveled silken cord. He stood in shock for several long seconds. With some relief he noted that the more potent spells, those for making spiritfolk do the bidding of men, were still intact.

But how had this happened? And when?

Then he recalled what Julia Fitzwalter had said about her father's final year, his obsession with buying every stray bit of old manuscript. If Fitzwalter had discovered the theft, perhaps he'd been trying to recover the missing pages. Such a faint, ridiculous hope, Robin knew. No wonder the man had died in a fevered delirium. He'd failed in his role of guardian, and he'd also failed to apprise his daughter of *her* responsibility.

Robin recovered the leather box and pushed down the tabletop until it latched. There was nothing he could do now. The missing pages were not in themselves a threat to his world. Without understanding the languages in the book or studying the lore, few mortals could use those spells.

However, his job was not over, not by a long shot. Julia was far too cavalier about her father's collection, still too angry at him to accept her role as his successor. Arden House needed a scholar with a deep core of moral fortitude to watch over it.

Julia Fitzwalter was going to have to find a husband. And soon.

Julia was sitting on the floor, leafing through a sixteenth-century volume on alchemy.

"Lead into gold?" Robin drawled as he peered over her shoulder. "I promise you, it's been tried before."

She looked up, swiping at a smudge of dust on her nose. He reached down and handed her his handkerchief.

"This is not going very well," she said as she wiped her face. "Harry's unearthed an illuminated missal that we can send to auction. But that's about it. All I've found are ledgers from an Irish monastery, books on astronomy—very outdated, I might add, since the earth appears as the center of the universe—and treatises on foretelling the future from owl entrails."

Robin shuddered as he settled one hip against the pine table. He'd been close to an owl or two over the centuries. "Did your father ever knock through any of the walls down here? The first lord of Islay is rumored to have brought back writings from the Holy Land; perhaps they were placed in a secret cache."

"I know my grandfather had a trunk of fragments written in Arabic and Greek, but Papa said they had deteriorated so badly they were nearly indecipherable."

Robin sighed. *Dust to dust.* The written word suffered that fate as inevitably as mortal man.

Julia pushed up from the floor, and he reached at

once to help her rise, catching hold of her elbows. "There you go."

He let his fingers linger for a moment, holding her there before him, and watched her pupils dilate. She blushed softly, adding a trace of rose to her cheeks, and he felt a resistance to this mild intimacy well up inside her.

Seduction had been the last thing on his mind this morning, but that was before he'd encountered the gray-eyed Lady of Islay. He quickly reminded himself of his mission and let his hands drop as he stepped back from her.

"It's very bad, isn't it?" he asked gently. "Your financial situation, I mean."

Her eyes narrowed. "We are still awaiting news from my father's lawyers on the settlement of the estate. This is merely an interim difficulty. And besides, we've only gone through three of the rooms down here. Something might turn up." She gave him a look of cautious expectation. "Did *you* come across anything valuable?"

"Nothing of worth to the general public, I'm afraid."

Her face fell. "Maybe I can find someone who will pay me for taking the whole moldering mess off my hands."

"No!" He'd spoken without thinking, his tone peremptory, almost angry.

Julia's fine mouth tightened into a thin line. "You presume too much, sir. Though it's true I haven't two guineas to rub together at present, I am still the Lady of Islay. Who are you to speak to me in such a way?"

So, the cat has claws after all, he noted with approval.

He leaned toward her, more amused than cowed. "If . . ." he said earnestly, "if you were truly the Lady of Islay, there would be no question of selling even one tattered page." His voice deepened. "Hades, woman, didn't your father teach you anything about your responsibilities to this library?"

She flung a hand out toward the disordered shelves. "Library?" she cried. "Midden is more like it. Trash heap. Rubbish pile."

He nearly bit his tongue to keep from shouting back. She was practically blaspheming. "You'd better go," she said with a bit more control. "We're having houseguests for Christmas, and the estate party is in three days. I have a hundred things to see to. Harry will show you out."

She put her chin up and crossed her arms.

Instead of moving toward the door, Robin set his hands behind him and leaned back against the nearest bookcase. He met her snapping, irritated gaze and held it, putting all his power behind that intent stare. "I could teach you," he said softly.

She shook her head, a small, rapid movement. "I have no desire to learn."

His expression darkened. "Then, you do not deserve your position, Miss Fitzwalter. This collection requires more than an ignorant, belittling, apathetic caretaker."

He heard her breath draw in. Then her expression shifted from one of affront to one of vexation.

"Would you please tell me what is going on here?" she demanded as she came toward him. "Who are you? Why have you come to Arden House with all your poking and prying? And what sort of name is Robin Goodfellow? Purloined from the Bard, quite clearly."

"It's my own name . . . a fine English name." He grinned slyly. "Perhaps Mr. Shakespeare purloined it from *my* family."

She gave a little huff of disbelief. "All I know is

that I never dropped that parcel in the street. It was a ruse to get you inside this house, inside this vault."

He bowed his head once in acknowledgment, eyes glittering gold.

"I never intended to let you down here," she continued. "But somehow my resolve was overridden. I never intended to start searching through these rooms, but that decision also was taken away from me. It seems you have made me do your bidding, against my better judgment." She poked him hard in the chest. "Who *are* you?"

"'Merely someone who knows how to be persuasive."

She said, "Devil take you," under her breath, and then looked up at him. "What do you want?" When he didn't answer, she added, "As you pointed out, we offered you our hospitality. You at least owe me an explanation of why you had to resort to trickery to get down here."

"Perhaps it's my nature to do things in a roundabout manner."

"Well, it is my nature to resent such underhanded dealings." She tugged the shawl from her shoulders, wound it into a loose heap, and thrust it at him. "I believe there is nothing more to be said."

She was out the door before he could frame a protest. He heard her slippers tapping on the stone steps as she fled to the upper level.

Harry was pouring over a book on falconry when Robin found him. He looked up with an incredulous grin and said, "Was my sister railing at you just now?"

"You don't need to look so cheerful about it."

Harry's smile faded and he said in a more sober tone, "Since our father died, I doubt Julia's raised her voice over anything. Not to laugh or to shout, not in joy or in anger. It surprised me hearing it, that's all. It means she's coming back."

Robin cuffed him gently on the side of the head. "Since when are sprats such astute judges of human behavior? And for your information, I deserved to be yelled at. I cheated my way into this house."

"I knew that," Harry said blithely. "Wasn't born yesterday, you know. I thought it was rather clever, pretending to bring her that shawl." He fingered the length of material that Robin held draped over one arm. "Pity she wouldn't keep it. It suited her."

"I can help her, Harry. I can help you both if you'd let me. But not if I am forbidden in the house. She has a great deal to learn about what it means to be Lady of Islay. If she turns her back on her responsibility to this collection, you have no idea what sort of trouble might arise."

Harry's eyes brightened. "Ah, a mystery."

Robin saw that he was still enough of a child to be intrigued by such a notion. "Yes, but I can't give you the particulars. Suffice to say, with this much ancient knowledge stored in one place, there are bound to be . . . emanations. Both dark and light."

The boy's face widened in delight. "Are you talking about magic?"

Robin's mouth tightened. "Maybe."

Harry crowed. "I knew it! Papa never let me down here. If there was anything I needed for my studies— the vicar is dotty on the Middle Ages, you know— Papa would fetch it to the upstairs library. And Julia's only ever been down here with him. Never alone. I think the place frightens her."

"She'll need to get over that right enough."

"Tell you what," Harry said as he returned his book to the shelf. "I will say that I need you to help catalog the collection. She can't refuse me. It's Christmas, after all. And Lord knows she hasn't the money to buy me a proper gift. I'll probably end up with stockings and handkerchiefs." He made a sour face. "So you will be my gift. That way, you'll have the run of the house and plenty of opportunity to teach her what she needs to know. From what I've seen, you're very persuasive."

"I'm beginning to have some doubts on that score."

"No, no," Harry said as they went from the room. "I think she likes you. I know she was railing at you just now, but she used to rail at me all the time, well, before Papa died, at any rate."

Robin stopped him with one hand on his shoulder. "Aren't you even curious about why I am here?"

Harry shook his head and then chuckled. "Papa always said that it's never a good idea to question Providence."

That evening Julia showed her brother Sir John's letter. Harry did not take the news of their cousin's offer with any good grace. After his initial protests, she told him in a forthright manner about their precarious financial situation, adding that Sir John might be their only hope.

"I doubt you will remember him," she said. "He visited here nine years ago with his mother."

"I do remember," Harry grumbled. "I may have been only five, but a child recalls being thrashed."

Her eyes widened in shock. "He hit you?"

He nodded. "I was playing in the stable yard when he came in from riding. I ran in front of his horse and made it shy. I didn't mean to, honestly. Anyway, off he came and fell right onto a pile of soiled straw. He leapt up shouting and clouted me on the head several times."

"And you never told anyone? Papa would have horsewhipped him for such a thing."

Harry lowered his eyes. "Cousin John said that if I

told a single soul, he would cut off my nose. He had a knife, Jules, in his boot. Small but very sharp. At five, that sort of thing stays with you."

She put her arms around him and gave him a bracing hug. "We'll make short work of him this time, Harry. He and his wife will be here in two days, but the minute Christmas is past, we will send them on their way. And I promise I will find you a proper guardian. I see now that Sir John is out of the question."

"This is nice," he said, rubbing her shoulder. "You haven't hugged me once since Papa died."

She tightened her arms around him and felt tears well up in her throat. He was right. She'd cut herself off from him in some way. From everyone, if truth be told. Out of anger at their father for leaving them, or anger at herself for resenting the responsibility that had been thrust on her for the house and the estate workers . . . for the wretched collection.

She reached out now and ruffled his hair. "Maybe you're getting too big for hugs. Lettie says she's had to let out all your coats."

"Growing bigger doesn't mean growing away, Jules."

"No," she responded gently, "it doesn't."

The next morning Robin was ushered into the hall by Lettie, who beamed at him openly. Harry came clomping down the stairs with an equally wide grin.

"It was rough going," he announced. "Julia swore she would not allow you back in the house. I had to cajole her for an hour. So you'd better find something really valuable down there, because we are pockets to let. Truly. And even though my wealthy cousin, Sir John, is coming tomorrow—he has designs on the place for some reason—we've decided to send him packing. But that will be difficult if we have nothing to back us up. He's the scabby sort who uses lawyers to get what he wants."

"Lawyers I can handle," Robin remarked dryly. "It's temperamental sisters who are my undoing."

"She'll leave us to our search, never fear. Got bedding to turn out and menus to plan to make the house ready for my cousin and his wife." Harry eyed him a moment. "You don't happen to have a toad on you? I fancy Sir John and his lady wouldn't appreciate finding one between their sheets."

"Fresh out of toads," Robin said patting his pockets. "But if you're so determined to see the back of him, I might be able to furnish a bit of help."

Robin spent the morning digging through one of the unexplored rooms. He wondered how Julia could dismiss the collection as worthless. It was true that many of the books were damaged and that most of the really ancient scrolls were so brittle as to be untouchable. But there was knowledge here and history. Academics from every part of Britain and Europe would flock to this place to do research, had they only known of its existence. But the lords and ladies of Islay did not open their doors to the public, only to a few trusted scholars. It was the *Book of Trey* that made this circumspection necessary. How ironic it was, he thought, that the most valuable item stored here required that everything around it, the accumulation of centuries, remain untapped.

Still, he had to make sure the Fitzwalters did not pilfer the collection to raise money. And since this Sir John's offer to play rescuer was about to be tossed in his face, Robin was back where he'd started, finding a husband for the Lady of Islay.

Fortunately, he'd already set things in motion toward that end.

*   *   *

Harry came in a bit after noon, rubbing at his belly. "If you're feeling reckless, you can come and have luncheon with us. Julia's table manners are fairly good, so I doubt she'll crown you with a gravy boat or anything."

He followed the boy up the stairs and through the house, noting that garlands of Christmas greenery had magically appeared in the front hall, dispensing the gloom, if not the chill. They found Julia teetering on a stepladder in the arched doorway between the drawing room and the parlor. She was trying to affix a thick strand of evergreen to the top of the arch.

"Perfect spot for mistletoe," Robin said, his eyes alight.

"We don't hold with the old pagan customs in this house," she responded.

"Pity," he said, and did not remind her that bringing greenery inside during the winter months went right back to the Druids.

He watched as she tossed the garland toward a rusted nail that protruded from the arch. She missed badly and nearly lost her footing.

"Here, you'd better let me do that," he said as he took hold of the wobbling ladder to steady it.

She cast him a look of annoyance and observed tartly, "You're barely taller than I am."

He grinned, unruffled by her barb. "Ah, but I've a much greater reach."

He raised his hand and set it against the small of her back, pressing slightly. He liked the way the anger quivered through her at this familiarity.

"Easy now," he murmured. "Let me guide you down."

She twisted on her perch and plucked his hand away. "I can do just fine on my own."

Harry chuffed once. "Then, I won't remind you of

the Christmas you climbed a ladder to hang holly over
the front door." He shifted to Robin. "Lost her balance and tumbled right down onto her—"

"Hush," she said quickly. "Mr. Goodfellow hardly
needs to hear that."

"Had to sit on a pillow until Twelfth Night," he
finished in an undertone.

Robin controlled his face while she came down the
ladder, then took the length of the garland from her,
and climbed the steps in her stead. He leaned up and
easily snagged the evergreen strand over the nail. Then
he looked down at her with a smug, triumphant grin.

Julia was gazing up at him, pale hair in flyaway
strands around her face, gray eyes now lit with amused
chagrin. She looked so much like her mother at that
moment that Robin felt the air whoosh out of him.
He'd been a little bit in love with Miranda Fitzwalter,
once upon a time. The warm, generous, beautiful Lady
of Islay. No faery queen was more graceful, no faery
maiden more lively or better humored.

Robin found he could not look away. The baiting
amusement in his eyes faded as a dawning awareness
overtook him. Julia's mouth opened slightly in bewil-
derment at his intense, fixated stare. And then an expression of startled recognition lit her face. The air
around them seemed to vibrate as they stood trans-
fixed, regarding each other with open wonder for several long, breathless moments.

And then Harry sneezed.

"Blasted dust," he muttered, tugging out his handkerchief.

Robin came down the ladder in a rush, fearful of
tumbling off himself if he remained up there. He
needed the solid ground beneath his feet, but even
the parqueted tiles felt shaky to him now. Jupiter, he'd

never been light-headed over a woman before. Not even over Miranda.

"Lunch, I think," Harry said, taking his arm and shooting him what Robin could have sworn was a look of concern.

Julia was already moving on ahead of them toward the rear of the house.

Goodness, she thought, as she paused to lean against the door-frame of the dining parlor, one fisted hand pressed to her middle. *That* had certainly never happened before. She'd looked up at the man and gone absolutely, stomach-tiltingly dizzy.

Well, what did she expect after climbing up and down ladders all morning? It was just a bit of exhaustion and had nothing whatsoever to do with that irritating, insinuating Mr. Goodfellow.

She heard the man and her brother coming along the passage, and quickly schooled her face into serene lines. He wanted her to play Lady of Islay and so she would. Gracious and welcoming—but with a spine of steel.

If Harry noticed that his luncheon companions were suspiciously quiet during the meal, he did not comment on it. He was too busy telling his sister about a book he'd unearthed on raising rabbits. "It sounds like a first-rate way to make money. Start with two," he said, waving his forkful of turbot about, "and you end up with two thousand. They apparently breed like, like—"

"Like rabbits?" Robin offered.

"I had a rabbit once," Harry continued, undismayed. "Fine little fellow. I'd let him run loose in the kitchen garden for a treat. I wouldn't mind looking after them, Jules. Truly."

She set down her fork. "I hate to be the one to tell

you this, Harry, but the only reason most people want rabbits is for the pot."

Harry gaped at the portion of fish on his plate as though it had suddenly grown long ears and a fuzzy tail. "Well, that's a dashed shame."

Robin elbowed him gently. "I think you'd better look for your fortune outside the hutch."

The boy's naïveté entertained him. It seemed to appear at the exact moment one had begun to think of him as very adult and very wise. He was intuitive, Robin realized. Attuned to those around him, which often made him seem more mature than his years.

When the meal was over, Robin sent Harry off to the cellar with a promise to join him shortly, and then turned his gaze on Julia, who was fidgeting with her dessert dish.

He said, "We need to talk, you and I."

Her face grew wary. "First . . . I want to thank you," she said haltingly. "For befriending Harry. He's been missing our father, and you've rather cheered him up."

"He said the same thing about you. Well, that I'd stirred you out of your grief."

"Not grief so much as incomprehension." She set her hands on the edge of the damask spread, fingers clenched. "There was no understanding it, Mr. Goodfellow. Papa was the sanest, the wisest of men. Then, for no discernible reason, he grew frighteningly disordered in his thinking."

"And when did this remarkable change occur, if I may make so bold to ask?"

"I know the exact hour," she said grimly. "The day before my twenty-first birthday he said he had a special gift for me. I was thrilled, as you might guess, imagining some beautiful gown or jeweled necklace. He spent that evening down in the vaults. It was nearing ten o'clock when he staggered into the parlor. I saw that he had been weeping . . . and his face—" She set one trembling hand against her mouth. "It was pale and drawn like a specter's, his eyes so hollow, so empty. I ran to him, but he held me away and wouldn't tell me what had happened. 'I have failed, Julia,' was all he said." She drew a long breath. "He spent the next week in his room . . . and when he emerged he was a changed man. He began ransacking the vaults like a lunatic and advertising great sums of money for any pre-Conquest writings. He had no thoughts for Arden House. I tried to take over the running of the estate, but I was ill equipped for such a thing. All my lessons in Latin and Greek, all my hours spent pouring over those wretched old books, they were of no help to me then." She gave him a look that pleaded for understanding. "I know you think I have neglected the library, but since Papa took ill, keeping Arden House afloat has consumed nearly all my time."

Robin had risen while she spoke, and he now went to stand beside her chair. "And so you never learned what his special gift for you was?"

She shrugged. "What care had I for gowns or jewels when my father was so distressed?"

Robin touched her shoulder and said softly, "It appears I've misjudged you both."

Her head snapped up. "I'm not looking for your pity, Mr. Goodfellow."

He bowed slightly. "Would you settle instead for my admiration?"

Her eyes grew less stormy. "I would settle for an explanation of why you are so intrigued by all this." She waited, but he made no response. "Well, since that doesn't appear to be forthcoming any time soon, I'd best get back to my Christmas preparations."

He stepped back as she rose from her chair and,

with a troubled expression, watched her sweep from the room. "You'll get your gift, Julia," he said softly.

When she learned why her father had come undone, she'd also receive the gift of understanding. Then, perhaps, the healing forgiveness could begin.

Robin rejoined Harry in the vaults, his thoughts only on books. By tomorrow his plans for Julia would be well under way. Today he would focus on sorting through eight or more centuries of writing. Somewhere in this monumental disorder, there had to be one real gem he could present to Julia to relieve her financial worries.

They followed Harry's plan of sorting the material by subject, rather than by chronology as his father had done, and each room had been designated accordingly—natural science, literature, philosophy, commerce, theocracy, and, in Harry's words, that romantic rubbish, by which he meant poetry and love songs. Robin had suggested they leave the mystery room alone for the present.

By midafternoon, Robin was stiff and aching, cursing the frailty of his mortal body, but feeling strangely satisfied. He could understand how monks of old had dedicated their lives to the ordering of vast libraries. There was great satisfaction in such a task.

Julia was coming down the stairs as they entered the front hall, laughing together like the best of chums.

Harry called up to her. "Hallo, Jules. I know Cousin John is arriving tomorrow, but is it all right if Mr. Goodfellow comes back?"

Her mouth pinched for an instant. She didn't need the distraction of that impish grin or those golden eyes. Or the heated memory of that breathtaking moment under the archway. "I'm sure the gentleman has other demands on his time."

The gentleman, who had just drawn on his great-coat, now tapped his hat idly against his thigh. "Actually, I find myself at loose ends. My business here in Glastonbury has been delayed until after Christmas."

Harry's face knit with concern. "You aren't spending the holiday with your own family?"

"I'm afraid I live a great distance from this place."

"That's a pity, to be so far from home," Julia said as she approached them across the tiled floor.

"Business." He shrugged carelessly. "A man has responsibilities. And I rarely mind being alone."

"You won't be alone if you spend Christmas Eve with us," Harry insisted. "We give a party every year for the estate workers and our friends in the neighborhood. It's quite merry. Mr. Goodfellow can come, can't he, Julia? And please let him continue helping with the books. We got a great deal accomplished today."

Julia wanted to tell him that it was impossible, that with Cousin John arriving it would not do to have a virtual stranger poking about in their cellars. But what if Mr. Goodfellow did discover something of worth down there, an old Bible, perhaps, or a Shakespeare folio? She wouldn't need her cousin's money then. He could take his interfering self back to Yorkshire and leave them in peace.

She put her chin up. "If Mr. Goodfellow wants to spend his time crawling about in the crypt, then he is welcome to do it. And of course he may come to the party; we open our doors to *everyone* in the district."

"Except our hermit," Harry grumbled.

Mr. Goodfellow's eyes lit up. "Never say Arden House has its own hermit. That is capital."

"I think so," Harry said. "But Julia keeps threatening to call in the bailiffs."

"An old vagrant has taken up residence in a rocky cavern near the river," Julia said. "He's been there nearly a year, since just before our father died."

"I used to go down there and talk to him, but Julia forbid me after she found out. He's quite old and wears Gypsy clothing." Harry glared at his sister for an instant. "He's not dirty or dangerous, as she claims. Still, there is something odd about him."

"Living in a cave, for one thing," Julia drawled. "And leaving all those strange drawings on the rocks and trees. He keeps writing things on our front gate."

Mr. Goodfellow leaned toward her brother. "Did he share his name with you, Harry?"

"Hereabouts they call him the Limner. Because he draws on everything, you see."

"Yes," Mr. Goodfellow said with a half smile. "I am beginning to see."

Robin set his horse in the direction of the river. The wind had come up sharp with the approach of darkness, and he shivered. This mortal body had few advantages that he could see. Well, perhaps one or two. There was, for instance, the pleasure of tasting food and on rare occasions, the delight of sampling women, even though such congress was risky for most of his kind. More than one blithe spirit had bartered away his faery existence after succumbing to human desire. And how each one had dealt with his fate afterward had never been known—those who strayed from the faery fold were as dead to their former brethren.

He informed himself sternly that such temptation was not going to trouble him in this case. Julia Fitzwalter was quite handsome, perhaps even beautiful. And as compelling in her complexities as her brother was in his. He knew she wavered between anger and vexation toward him, and yet, for one moment she had looked up at him with a lifetime of yearning in her eyes. But as often as he'd willingly played the fool for his master or his mistress, he had never yet played the fool for love.

That particular word hadn't ever been an issue with the earthy women of Tuscany and Provence, with whom he'd occasionally shared pleasure. Those stolen moments of human passion had been edifying, but hardly worth the price of forfeiting his powers and his immortality. A woman like Julia Fitzwalter, however, who could evoke feelings more potent than mere passion, posed a threat to him. In some ways she was far more dangerous than the book that lay hidden in her cellar.

The terrain began to grow rocky as he continued along the river. Great shards of stone thrust up to the lowering sky. There were drawings on them, Celtic shapes rendered in dark red paint. And more of those runes he'd seen on the stanchions in the drive. Something very odd was afoot here.

He came to a narrow opening in the rocks. After tying his horse to a bush, he continued forward on foot, holding onto the rough, weathered stone with both hands as he descended.

"Where are you, old man," he muttered under his breath. "And why have you come here now?"

It unnerved him, the notion that someone with this ancient knowledge had set up camp so close to Islay just as the current lord lay dying. He was sure there was nothing coincidental about it.

Robin peered around a jagged corner and saw before him a rocky clearing. A narrow-shanked old man was bent over a cook fire. The man stood up at once and looked straight at Robin.

"Oh, it's *you*." They'd both spoken at the same time.

"The Limner?" Robin said mockingly as he moved

forward. "Not much of a ruse. A child could unscramble those letters in a trice."

The old man rubbed one finger along his cleft chin. The last time Robin had seen him, it had been obscured by a long, silvery beard. "Good thing, then," the man stated, "that most people lose the child inside them before they reach the age of twelve. But not you, my spritely friend, eh? Eternally youthful."

Robin pulled himself up to his full height, still several inches below that of the man before him. "We do age, sir, just more slowly than most. I fancy I am just entering my prime. And speaking of aging, I'd have thought you long in your grave by now."

The Limner chuckled. "Wished it, you mean. You've never exactly been my ally, Robin, though we've sometimes fought for the same cause. As for my longevity, suffice to say I've dabbled with enough spells and such to ensure my existence for as long as I wish to retain this mortal coil." He stretched back, palms pressed to his flanks, "Although, I still haven't found anything to cure this perishing arthritis."

Robin held out his left hand enticingly. "Perhaps you would allow me to—"

The old man backed away, wagging one finger. "Oh, no, your power has more mischief in it than magic."

"And your wizardly magic's made more mischief than I could ever envision," Robin retorted sharply.

He uprighted a tumbled camp stool and sat down, dusting off the knees of his inexpressibles. The old man settled across from him on a fallen log, plucking at the hem of the green moleskin jacket he wore over dark breeches and soft crimson boots. Robin thought his clothing and the long, patterned scarf he'd knotted around his throat made him look like a damned, sneaking tinker. That impression was countered somewhat by the clean sweep of pure white hair that was brushed back from his brow and the expression of farseeing intelligence in his bright blue eyes.

"So tell me quick what you are about," Robin said. "I saw the runes at the gate. I read the warnings."

The Limner shrugged. "Those were just to keep out the bill collectors. Pity they don't work on wood sprites."

Robin merely smiled sweetly.

"I don't owe you any explanations," the old man continued. "But since you're here at my, er, hearth, I will tell you this—I believe the girl is in peril."

"Devil take the girl," Robin growled with more heat than was required. "My concern is with the *Book of Trey*."

The old man made a slight noise of surprise. "I thought that book a mere legend . . . I know *I've* never seen it."

"It exists, right enough. In the vaults of Arden House. But someone's been down there since my last visit and filched about twelve pages. Pages with spells for summoning spiritfolk."

The Limner considered this. "That might explain the danger to Julia Fitzwalter. Someone wicked is coming to Islay, and soon. I feel it in my bones. Can't say who exactly—I only ever get inklings about these things, very rarely precise details. But I do know that she stands between this person and what he desires. He is greedy for power. Well, that goes without saying for most men. We have avarice built into us, more's the pity." The Limner studied him a moment. "Perhaps you should destroy the book."

"It cannot be destroyed, old man. It represents our future."

The Limner arched one snowy brow. "How so?"

Robin frowned slightly. "The world has changed. You humans have lost touch with the old ways. In this age magic has become a commonplace . . . steam runs great ships and turbines, science has unlocked the unseen world beneath the outer fabric of life. My people, the faery folk, are a laughable anachronism now. Stories to lull children to sleep."

"And what of the book?"

"Without your kind to believe in us, my kind will cease to be. So as long as that book exists in this realm, then our future is assured."

"And how did such a dangerous book come to this mortal plane?"

Robin controlled his feelings of glee. So the old snoop didn't know everything after all. "It was Arthur's doing. You remember Arthur, now, don't you?" he purred.

The old man's eyes darkened. "I'll have none of your insolence, jackanapes. Or I'll turn you into a tadpole."

Robin grinned. "Been there already. Titania beat you to it back in the last century. It was dashed inconvenient, all that gulping about with gills. Anyway, you know that Arthur had traffic with our folk. The Lady of the Lake took a real liking to the boy. Wasn't only Excalibur she gave him, she also entrusted him with the book of our secrets. He hid it away and passed it to Sir Galahad, the pure. Who passed it to his great-grandson, Sir Gideon, the not so pure. Gideon lost it dicing, and it fell into the keeping of his cousin, Benedict Fitzwalter, the first Lord of Islay."

Robin wrapped his hands around his knees and leaned back. "Now, there was a man to admire. Crusader, visionary, philosopher. He brought a great many writings back from the Holy Land and began his collection. There are remnants of the lost library of Alexandria in the vault at Arden House. The knowledge of the ancients as well as faery lore. Pity you humans never availed yourselves of it."

The Limner scowled. "We haven't done too badly for ourselves, as you just pointed out. We've progressed considerably from the dark days of Arthur."

"Yes, well, you could have speeded things up a mite. But then you do need to learn from your mistakes, don't you. You're a dogged race, I'll give you that."

The Limner bowed in acknowledgment. "But help me understand this . . . Arthur received this book, which has the power to destroy your world, so that your world will not be destroyed?"

Robin grimaced. "It's a double-edged sword, to be sure. It was a symbol of trust between the faery folk and all humankind. The Lady of the Lake believed in Arthur's quest, believed he would establish a newer, more tolerant order that would sweep across the world, and then our realm and yours could become one. She was a bit naive, I'm afraid. She couldn't know that he would be betrayed and see his empire crash down around him."

The Limner shot a dark look at Robin, but he continued on. "She gave Arthur power over us, as we have power over you. A balance, if you will." He paused and sighed deeply. "But now I fear that the person who took those pages, if he is returning as you say, will use the book to harm us."

The Limner studied the fire. "Who might trouble to do that . . . a priest perhaps? Someone set on destroying the old ways."

Robin shook his head. "You'd be surprised at how many of the clergy still believe in us. And how many of my folk believe in the teachings of the man, Jesus. We're all branches on the same tree, in a way."

"Some might call that blasphemy."

"We also were created before recorded history, to

watch over you from our alternate sphere. Oberon insists
that he can remember that far back, but I take leave to
doubt it. Still, we were there, and now we are here. Who
am I to question that there is another realm, perhaps
even greater than ours, that has focused its intent on
saving your kind from their own worst impulses?" He
added slyly, "Headed up by a benevolent busybody."

The Limner ignored his wry grin. "I've never given
up my belief in that realm. It was what gave Arthur
his strength and his vision. And if I have tampered
with the passing of my days, well, I liken myself to
Methuselah, who lived nine hundred years."

"You're closing in on him," Robin murmured.
"Now, tell me, what has the Lady of Islay done to
deserve your concern?"

He shrugged. "I've often kept watch over Arden
House. For one thing, the first lord brought some troublesome texts back with him from the Holy Land. Old
Crookback, while still a prince, found several of those
manuscripts in the vault while visiting Islay Castle.
You know what happened after that. And then there
was the Earl of Essex, another visitor to the vaults.
Fortunately Queen Elizabeth had her head screwed
on properly and saw through his charm."

"Unfortunately, Miss Fitzwalter's head is not so well
placed. She resents the collection and wants little to
do with it. Which is why I need to find her a husband."

The Limner chuckled softly. "So the fate of your
people rests on some garden-variety matchmaking?
How droll."

Robin rolled his eyes and said nothing.

The next morning Julia was sorting through Harry's
Christmas gifts when Lettie knocked at the parlor door.

"Sir Percival Lancaster and Mr. Gareth Norfolk to
see you, miss."

Shoving the packages—predominately stockings and handkerchiefs—under her chair, she rose at once. And nearly goggled. Two impossibly handsome young men had come through the door: one tall and blond, with elegant, sculpted features, and the other brown-haired and broad shouldered. They were both dressed in the height of fashion and virtually shone with lustrous vitality in her small parlor.

Each of them bowed, and then Sir Percival said, "We were in the neighborhood, Miss Fitzwalter, and Mr. Norfolk remarked that it had been an age since we'd stopped by Arden House. Our fathers were both particular friends of Mr. Fitzwalter."

"We've come home from London for Christmas," Mr. Norfolk added. "We'll be in the neighborhood until Twelfth Night at least. We were so sorry to hear of your father's passing, but hoped that you had put off your blacks, now that this festive season is upon us."

"We'd like to know if you were free to attend a few small parties and seasonal celebrations."

"I . . . I . . ." Julia couldn't seem to make her brain stop spinning. She was quite sure she had fallen asleep before the fire and that these two gentlemen were nothing more than phantasms.

Fortunately, she soon regained enough of her composure to make coherent conversation with her guests. Then, not five minutes after their arrival, Lettie popped her head in the door and announced, "Sir Coriolanus Gloucester."

The gentleman who appeared in the doorway nearly cast the other two in the shade. Dark, he was, like a fallen angel, with pale skin and glittering black eyes. He came forward to clasp her hand. "Miss Fitzwalter. I am the new magistrate for this district, come out from Bath. Your late father was one of my favorite correspondents." He looked around at the other two men. "I hope I am not intruding."

Julia mumbled some platitude, still unable to shake off her bewildered incredulity.

Lettie came in with the tea cart, hard on the new guest's heels. She nudged Julia in the ribs and whispered, "Relax, child. I'll call Master Harry up from the cellar to sit with you, to keep things right and proper."

Julia sank down into her chair without a word.

After Harry had been summoned upstairs, Robin nearly wore himself out with lifting and carrying, arranging and sorting. He didn't want to think about what was transpiring in the parlor, even though he had set the play in motion. His solution would work, he was sure of it. Julia Fitzwalter had clearly spent little time in the company of personable young men. She would fall like a lightning-struck oak.

He worked right through lunch; afterward Harry came downstairs to report, with some awe, on the three men who had called on his sister. "Topping fellows," he proclaimed. "Sir Percival and Mr. Norfolk both graduated from Oxford; Mr. Norfolk's father teaches in Queen's College, as a matter of fact. Sir Corry attended Cambridge. And I nearly choked on my tea cake—every one of them received a first in classics."

"Amazing," Robin muttered.

He was glad that Harry didn't linger after that. Something inside him had begun to ache. Probably hunger, he assured himself. It couldn't be, wouldn't dare be, that he was sorry about letting Julia go. He'd never had her to begin with. You couldn't mourn the loss of something you'd never possessed. Perhaps it was the loss of possibilities that troubled him. He'd had no time to spend with her, to share a lighthearted, mutually satisfying flirtation. No, he'd had to get things moving posthaste.

He came across a small leatherbound diary at one point, and settled on the floor to read it, needing more than ever to distract himself. But Julia was there in all his thoughts. With a weary moan, he leaned his head back against a cedar post. He'd never before desired permanent mortality. His brief forays into human skin had always been a lark, a chance for making mischief. But now there was a yearning inside him to experience new things, human things. Julia had stirred him to discontent for the first time in limitless centuries. She needed looking after, required someone to lift the heavy burden of responsibility from her shoulders, and he resented that the task should fall to anyone but him. He wanted to stay here and bring her back to life. But how could he do that when he wasn't part of life, not the life she knew?

It was within his power to rip her from this sphere, to make her one of his own kind, but then Harry would be alone and the *Book of Trey* would be even more vulnerable. It did not bear thinking upon.

No, if he desired Julia—and recently that emotion had become second nature to him—he would have to enter her world.

Robin's thoughts drifted; he imagined his life as a man of flesh and blood. In the still darkness of night, he watched Julia asleep in the moonlight, his heart tripping with pleasure when she awoke and held out her arms to him with a murmur of passion . . . He strolled with her at a market fair, laughing as they sampled hot cider and pancakes drenched in clover honey . . . He heard a young boy cry, "Father," and was amazed as a flaxen haired sprite broke from a crowd of children and ran toward him with a lolling grin. He saw himself as an old man walking in a meadow, saw that Julia's hair had turned from pale gold to gray, her lovely face now lined and careworn. And he realized, as she turned her face up to his in the autumn sun, that her smile was unchanged, timeless, and only for him.

He came awake with a start and threw down the book that was still clutched in his hands. Muttering a string of ringing curses in Gaelic, he sprang up from the floor. Hades take the women! She was crusty and mistrustful and had barely said one kind word to him in three days. He was turned around in his head to believe there was any kindred feeling there, to think it was worth bartering his immortality for a parcel of alluring dreams.

She would be wooed and won by a mortal, just as the faery council decreed. And for insurance, he had one final task to perform. Then, he wagered, it would be wedding bells before the New Year.

Much better that things played out that way. He vowed he didn't need to form a foolish, pointless attachment to yet another Fitzwalter female. After one more minor manipulation on his part, Julia would be forever out of his reach.

He timed it precisely.

After calling out to Harry that he was off to the kitchen for a bit of late lunch, he went upstairs and made his way through the house. She was there in the parlor, tucked up on the faded velvet chaise, fast asleep. The afternoon had come on cloudy, and the room was full of shadows, save for the bright flames dancing in the small hearth.

He moved silently across the carpet, and then stood looking down at her. Her face was relaxed in sleep, one hand curled beneath her cheek. Her delightfully untidy hair had come partway down from its chignon; a narrow lock of it waved over her shoulder, reminding him of the provocative coiffures of the previous century. He reached out and touched the silken curl, then let his fingers trace up the warm, velvety contour of her throat.

He barely repressed the shuddering sigh that ached inside him for release.

Best be done with this, he warned himself. *Before you are made the fool.*

He drew out a tiny scattering of herbs from his vest pocket and pressed them gently over each of her eyelids. Then he knelt beside the chaise setting one hand upon the cushion and leaned forward until his mouth was nearly upon hers, crooning softly:

Sleep, fair Julia, and dream of thy love,
Be he dark as the night or pale as the dove.
Be he knight's son or don's son or dispenser of law,
Choose one, fair Julia, before the next dawn.
Then marry in haste, and repent not at all,
And all shall be merry in this Christmas hall.

He was about to rise and back away from her, when the door was thrust open. A tall, narrow-shouldered man in a dark cloak stepped into the room.

"Are there no servants in this household?" the man seethed quietly—and was all the more ominous for not shouting. "That a man and his retinue are kept waiting on the stoop."

Julia stirred beside Robin, gave a little groan at the sight of the man looming in the doorway. Robin instantly laid his hand over her wrist to soothe her. Her eyes darted to his face.

"Your guests are here, sleepyhead," he said softly as his fingers twined with hers reassuringly.

But she didn't appear reassured. She looked quite startled as she stared at Robin. Then her face softened into bemused amazement and the hint of a smile soft-ened her mouth. He had a fearful inkling that some-thing had gone very wrong. She wasn't supposed to be looking at *him* that way.

"Well?" the man said with a sneer in his voice. "Will someone have the decency to answer me."

Robin rose slowly and put his chin up. "Sir John Fitzwalter, I presume." He gave his most polished bow. "I am Mr. Goodfellow. A friend to the Somer-set Fitzwalters."

"Mr. Good-for-nothing," Sir John muttered under his breath. "And why are you closeted in here alone with my cousin?"

Robin shrugged. "I was making sure she had taken her nap. You can imagine how wearying it is to pre-pare a house this size for guests." He smiled urbanely.

"If she had servants to aid her like a proper lady," the man retorted, "then she'd not have had to trou-ble herself."

"Lettie's probably gone down to the home farm for stores," Julia said as she rose a bit shakily to her feet. Robin watched as she fussed with the stray tendril that refused to remain tucked behind her ear. He rather preferred it where it was. "I'm sorry there was no one to meet you at the door."

She went forward and gave the man a perfunctory kiss on the cheek. "Welcome, Cousin."

He gruffly returned the salutation and then turned back toward the hall, motioning to the woman who waited there. "This is my wife, Lady Alicia Fitzwalter. We were wed this September past. My dear, this is Cousin Julia."

"The Lady of Islay," Robin added intently.

"It's not really a proper title," Sir John said in a swift aside to his wife.

The woman looked at Julia over her elegant,

pointed nose, and, after waiting just long enough to border on rudeness, she sketched a brief curtsy.

"Miss Fitzwalter," she intoned with the barest hint of a smile, "let us hope that first impressions are not the ones we carry away with us."

"Please, you must call me Julia. We are cousins now, are we not?"

"Yes," said Robin. "Let us dispense with formality. It is Christmas, after all, when every one of us may run a little mad. Not the season to stand on ceremony, eh, Alicia?"

The lady's mouth pursed as her nose thrust even higher into the air.

Robin moved toward the couple, his arms held wide. "Come along now. Since Harry seems to have disappeared, I will play host and show you to your room." He virtually herded them out the door. "Lettie assures me the fireplace in there has stopped smoking, and that there's only the tiniest bit of soot remaining on the furniture."

He shot Julia one long, wicked glance over his shoulder, before he trundled her cousins along the hall, calling out in his lilting voice, "Just watch your step there. That floorboard comes loose at the awkwardest times."

Julia sank back onto the chaise and shut her eyes tight. This was a dream, she told herself. The whole day had to have been a dream. No, make that the past three days. Ever since Robin Goodfellow had tricked his way into this house, everything was off balance. But today had been the strangest of all. First those three gentlemen coming to call, each of them tripping over himself to gain her favor. Followed by the disturbing, enchanting dream she'd had while she napped—of blindingly bright spirits who shimmered and trilled in the air around her, filling her soul with such beautiful music that she couldn't bear to awaken.

And then . . . oh, she didn't know how to explain it, even to herself. Being rudely drawn from that sweet state by her cousin's harsh words and finding sudden shelter—and an echoing sensation of that beguiling dream—in a man's simple handclasp. A man she didn't think she even liked very much.

No, that wasn't true. He'd given Harry a precious gift these past days, the companionship of an adult male, something her brother had missed tremendously during the last eleven months. She had to like him for that alone. And for deflecting Cousin John and his odious wife.

Still, there was more to her feelings for Robin Goodfellow than mere gratitude. He made her warm inside. Oh, a deal of the time that arose from anger. But when she wasn't cross with him, she often thought of him with charity.

"That's a whisker," she muttered. She'd nearly swooned yesterday, when he'd set his hand on her back. Heat and chills had swept over her in equal measure. Gracious, the briefest look from those forest-gold eyes made her breathing alter. Worst of all, three nonpareils had walked into her parlor and been utterly engaging for an hour, yet all she had thought of the entire time was a roguish intruder with a whippet-lean frame and a sly smile.

She forced herself to rouse from this unsettling reverie. Lettie would require her help in the kitchen, and then she'd need to dress for supper. She wondered if she could prevail upon Robin to stay through the meal.

She set one hand over her mouth. When had she begun to think of him by his given name? Well, it was Christmas, as he'd said. When sane women could run a little mad and no one take notice.

She said it again, daringly aloud this time. "Robin."

It sounded almost as stirring as the vibrant singing in her dream.

Lady Fitzwalter had her own footman, a strapping fellow called Bottomfield. He stood behind her chair and waited on her as she dined, even to handing her her forks during each subsequent course. Robin wondered how much you had to pay a man to debase himself in such a way.

Not that Lady Fitzwalter was unhandsome. She looked every inch the aristocrat, from her sleekly coiled black hair, to her elegant satin gown, to the tasteful brilliants that glittered on her hands.

Her husband had also dressed to impress, and if clothing were the measure of a man, he might have passed for a lord. However, his face, with its protuberant eyes and unfortunate nose, had the aspect of a buffoon in an Italian farce. This impression was further fostered by his teeth, which appeared to have grown in every direction but up and down. To compensate for this, he spoke in a clipped, tight-lipped manner, one brimming with superiority.

Robin wanted to hurl the gravy boat at *his* head several times during the meal. But fortunately, for everyone at the table, he had more subtle vengeances at his command.

He'd not missed the way Lady Fitzwalter's footman watched her, with furtive, hungry glances. Bottomfield was not a bad piece of work himself—tall, as was demanded of his position, and possessed of a high, noble brow. Possibly some aristocrat's by-blow or perhaps just a well-favored Yorkshire lad, spared from the coal pits by his looks.

Robin's brain had begun to spin with delicious possibilities, when he was interrupted by Sir John's irritating voice. "And what is that, pray? A roast?"

Lettie had just set the platter for the meat course on the table. The item in question did appear rather meager for five people. The housekeeper had tried to obscure this lack by the addition of turnips to the platter. Some of them, unfortunately, were nearly as large as the cut of beef.

Sir John turned to his hostess. "I see no excuse for such poor household management. There are fields and cattle a'plenty on this estate, and yet your guests go wanting."

"They are dairy cattle, cousin," Julia pointed out. "We need every penny they earn us to pay the farmworkers."

"I see it's about time someone with a bit of business sense had the running of this place," he said. "Threadbare furnishings, patched bed linens . . . I am ashamed that my wife has to overnight here."

Julia's mouth clenched. "This would, I think, be better discussed after our meal."

"Meal?" he cawed softly. "I wouldn't give that roast to my hounds. If I'd known you were in such desperate straights, cousin, I would have come here all the sooner."

Robin set his chin on his palm. "Yes, and why did you come here, Sir John? I mean now of all times? What impulse drove you to suddenly look in on your southern cousins?"

"Duty," he said at once. "Not that it's any of your business, sir. I realized that I owed it to my departed uncle to look after his children and his estate."

"And his library?" Robin added softly.

Sir John shrugged. "I've some interest in books, just like any gentleman. And I have no aversion to increasing my library."

"Those books belong to me," Julia said suddenly

and with great heat. "That's one thing, at least, that was made quite clear in Papa's will."

Robin wanted to spring up from his chair and applaud her.

"They are what my father valued most in this world," she continued, "and so are without price to me."

"Without price to most people with a brain in their head," Sir John drawled. "Nine years ago I saw what was in those vaults of your father's. Most of it worthless bits of decaying parchment. It's no wonder you have to scrimp, if all your time and money goes to preserving that rubbish heap."

"We've discovered some very interesting things down there," Harry protested. "Illuminated missals . . . books of botanical illustrations." His gaze shot to Robin. "Mr. Goodfellow's an expert on old books. He'll tell you what we've found."

Robin flicked one hand negligently. "Just the usual second-rate monastery castoffs and the like. Nothing of museum quality, I'm afraid."

Lady Fitzwalter looked at her husband for an instant, and then said, "We do not enjoy seeing our cousins suffering from lack of even the basic necessities. Now, I am myself a devotee of old writings, an interest passed to me by my father, Sir Adair Crowley, who was a noted collector. Your library could not be in better hands than mine, I assure you. And to that end, I will prevail upon Sir John to pay you a fair price for what lies in the cellar vaults."

"It's out of the question," Julia said stiffly.

"But, my dear," said the lady with serene logic, "think of your brother's future, if not of your own. What chance will he have to advance himself without funds?"

Sir John leaned toward Julia. "From the sorry state of things hereabouts, I would say you have little choice, cousin. Once I am appointed Harry's guardian, you, miss, will have little say in the running of things. Not if you're living off my blunt." He tried to muster a benign smile. "At least selling off that collection will supply you with an independence of sorts."

"Nothing in this house is for sale," Julia proclaimed as she pushed back from the table. "Not books *or* people. You can take your money and go back to Yorkshire, for I will not take a penny of it." She drew in a ragged breath. "And now, you must excuse me."

Robin watched her hurry from the room, then motioned Harry to stay seated as he got to his feet. "Please, finish your meal. Miss Fitzwalter has had a difficult week. There is . . . an infestation of toads in the kitchen garden and her . . . her—"

"—rabbits have all had babies," Harry declared. "Hundreds of 'em."

Robin was nearly laughing as he made his escape. Harry, bless his fine boyish heart, had immediately launched into the grisly details of rabbit childbirth, and Lady Fitzwalter had been looking positively bilious.

He found Julia at the bottom of the stairs, clutching the newel post for dear life. He tugged her away and set her down on the carpeted stairs. "Listen to me, Julia." Her face tipped up at once at the urgency in his voice. "Where is the key to the cellar?"

She looked blank for a moment.

"I know now why he's come here. I will explain everything very soon. But for the moment, I need to know that the vaults are safe."

She nodded, then reached behind her neck into the round collar of her gown and pulled loose a gold chain. She drew on it until a long brass key slid free from the edge of her bodice.

Without thinking, he reached for it, feeling the heat of her body on the brass in his hands. Something equally warm thrilled through him at the thought of that key lying nestled between her breasts.

"You told me to keep it safe," she said in a small, sad voice. "Harry gives it to me after you're finished down there. And I always make sure the door is locked."

"Oh, sweetheart," he cried softly as he drew the chain over her head, "you're a trump!"

At that pronouncement, tears started streaming down her face. She clenched her hands and set them hard over her eyes. "What is wrong with me, Robin? It's nearly Christmas, but I do not feel merry at all. Not a bit. I miss Papa . . . and I am so confused by everything. Now those dreadful people have come here to my house." She thrust her fisted hands down in anger. "*My* house! And those wretched creatures have chased me out of my own dining parlor."

"Then, go back," he said evenly. "Don't let yourself be drawn into their game. Barrage them with small talk. Meanwhile, I'm afraid I need to go off for a time."

"No." Her eyes flashed at him as she stood up.

He reached forward and took her face between his hands, stroking his thumbs gently along her flushed cheeks. "An hour, maybe two. They can't hurt you, either of them. And you've got Harry at your back." He turned her and pushed her gently toward the passage. "Go now and be the Lady of Islay. Because that is what you are, Julia.

"Finally," he added under his breath as he went to fetch his greatcoat.

"He's here," Robin announced as he entered the clearing. The old man looked up from his crock of stew. "And I'm not sure how to proceed. I don't want to place either Julia or her brother in danger."

The Limner sucked at a front tooth. "Who is he?"

"Sir John Fitzwalter. His uncle showed him the vaults nine years ago."

The old man's face formed into a mirthless smile. "So it was the wicked cousin. How very literary."

Robin nodded. "He was an unpleasant customer even then—Harry told me the fellow thrashed him for scaring his horse. I have no trouble believing he found his way back into the vaults and damaged the book. And then perhaps he kept the pages to remind himself that he'd bested his uncle."

"A tricky situation, to be sure. And, no, we don't want to put the Fitzwalters at risk."

"We?"

"You're not the only one with a responsibility to the family. After their father took ill, I thought it prudent to stay here and keep an eye on them. Harry is delightful, though his sister is a bit more of a—"

"She says she's never met you."

"Not as a ragged hermit, no. She knows me as Mr. Quince the fuel merchant."

"Old busybody," Robin muttered. "Sneaking about."

"Oh, and you never sneak anywhere, young Puck?"

"Ssst," he hissed sharply. "That is not my name, not in this sphere. Not in any sphere if Sir John has his way."

"So you think he's learned to use the spells on the pages he stole? Even so, he can't know the true power of the book."

Robin preened a bit. He was about to unleash a bombshell. "Sir John took a bride this fall—Lady Alicia Crowley."

The Limner leapt up, scattering the remains of his stew. "The devil you say!"

"Close enough. Who better to decipher arcane texts

than the daughter of Adair Crowley—Dark Adair, supreme warlock of the Northern Kingdoms?"

"Mostly a supreme charlatan," the Limner said dismissively, regaining some of his composure. "But effective enough on occasion. This is not good news, Robin. Lady Alicia more than makes up for any lack Sir John may have in occult matters. Rumor has it she was stirring potions before she could walk."

"If she's been coaching her husband," Robin pointed out fretfully, "then the magic in the book will not be beyond his abilities."

"And if she's seen those pages, if Sir John described the book to her, then she'll want it for herself."

"She can't take it from Arden House. It's protected by an enchantment, remember? Only the lords of Islay and their blood kin can possess it. Which explains why Cousin John was able to take the pages away. I'm not sure he bears enough of old Benedict's blood, though, to make off with the whole book. Trouble is, if he or his wife get into that chamber, they can copy whatever passages they like. Anyone can read the *Book of Trey*. That's the whole point of it."

The Limner stood thinking for a time. "How potent are those spells?"

Robin shook his head. "I can only guess. Ultimately, they give you sovereignty over us. The spells are basic mortal magic, but they can unlock the more potent magic of my people."

"Rather like releasing the genie in the bottle."

"Exactly. Only Sir John will get a great deal more than three wishes."

The old man hunkered down again on his log. "I assume you need me around as a sort of human dogsbody, in case the fellow does have the skill to disable you."

Robin pulled the cellar key from his pocket. "I

thought you might want to hang about in the vaults tomorrow as insurance." He motioned toward the opening in the rock wall behind him. "After all, you'd only be trading one cavern for another. I'll even show you the *Book of Trey*."

The old man's eyes brightened. "That tempts me. And I am not averse to helping you. It's been awhile since I've really been able to flex my powers properly. However, we've a few old scores to settle between us, Robin. What do I gain if I aid you?"

Robin crouched in front of him and pulled a scorched branch from the edge of the fire. He tapped one end firmly against the ground. "Down here," he said, "is something you seek, but cannot find. It is why you return again and again to Glastonbury, to Islay."

"You're speaking nonsense."

"Am I? Try this on, then. What you seek disappeared in the time of Henry VIII."

The old man started. "You're snatching at phantoms, lad."

Robin shook his head. "I believe I have found it."

"In the book rooms at Arden House? You think I haven't been through them?"

"No," Robin said. "Not in there. But you must aid me before I tell you more. And none of your wizardly tricks this time to squeak out of your obligation."

The old man's cheeks drew in as he clasped Robin's hand to seal the bargain. "So speaks the king of mischief."

The house was quiet when Robin returned. A single candle burned within a glass chimney in the front hall, creating stark, eerie shadows on the papered walls above the wainscoting. He assumed the Yorkshire Fitzwalters had been weary after their journey and retired early. Which suited him fine.

He started up the stairs, his boots making a soft
footfall on the runner. By the time he reached the
upper landing, there were no footfalls at all. His cor-
poreal body had faded away, leaving only a glowing,
ghostly image in its place.

Since he himself had led the couple to their room,
he had no trouble locating it. He opened the door
noiselessly, for although he appeared spectral, he
could not pass through solid objects. He could, however, float. Which he did, right across the room to the
wide, raised bed.

Sir John was sprawled on his back, one bony leg
jutting from beneath the coverlet. His lady lay at the
edge of the mattress, facing away from him.

He hovered over her, got as close as he dared, and
again drew a tiny amount of the ground herb from his
pocket, pressing it lightly to each of her eyelids. And
in the softest of voices, he sang,

Behold the man who waits, my dear,
who waits and serves behind your chair.
Though low he be, his heart is true,
and care he carries for none but you.
Turn around and meet his eyes,
for your future within them lies.
I give you this gift to dream upon,
then awaken forswearing your own Sir John.

She stirred slightly and he wafted back, beyond her
range of vision if she should awaken. But she merely
grumbled something in her sleep, something that
sounded suspiciously like "toads."

Moving to the other side of the bed, he gazed down
at Sir John. Robin's eyes glowed red for an instant,
flashing like those of a jungle cat lurking in the shadows. There were spells a'plenty he could use to disarm

the man, but he wanted a face-to-face reckoning with this oily cur of a usurper.

He leaned close and whispered, *"Tomorrow just past midnight, leave revelry behind. If you seek the cellar vault, an open door you'll find."*

He was wearing a spectral smile as he drifted from the room. He had lured his enemy into the trap. With a little help from an old hermit, Sir John would be both thwarted and humbled. Robin could hardly wait.

He was fully substantial again by the time he reached Julia's room, though his steps were flagging. Rapid transformations always knocked the flinders out of him.

He scratched at the door, and when she opened it, her face lit up. At the same moment his heart sank. She really was not supposed to be looking at him like this, with affection and care brimming in her eyes. That privilege would go to one of three other men. *Mortal* men.

If something had gone wrong with his Julia's spell, what assurance did he have that he'd succeeded with Lady Fitzwalter? Then he recalled that Julia's spell would not become effective until the next morning. At dawn she would awaken and know her heart's desire.

She was now looking at him with concern.

"I just wanted to make sure you survived supper," he said lightly.

"Just barely. Afterward, Cousin John closeted himself with Harry and offered to send him on a Grand Tour of Europe."

"In return for a grand tour of the vaults?"

"Exactly. Can you believe how obvious those two are? An erstwhile Macbeth and his lady, full of plots and schemes." Her voice lowered. "Now, don't you think it's time you told me what it is they're after?"

She added slyly, "Since I fancy it's the same thing you're after."

He coughed slightly and tried not to flinch.

"Because I don't know what the women are like where you come from, sir," she continued. "But here in Glastonbury, we ladies know when the wool is being pulled over our eyes."

"I . . . uh, that is—"

She tapped one finger against her chin and observed him thoughtfully. "I imagine you've either found it already and are pretending to help Harry until you can think of a way to smuggle it out of here. Or you've not found it yet and need to keep searching."

"You are very bold," he said with a touch of anger, "to be bantering after dark with a man you think of as a thief."

She gave him an arch smile. "No, not a thief exactly. Merely a trickster. Harry says the Norse myths are full of them. It happens I could use such a fellow to outwit my northern relations. But a little honesty on your part would go a long way, Robin."

"I found what I sought on the first day," he confessed slowly. "And even though I can lay some legitimate claim to this object, I have no intention of removing it from the vaults."

"Why do I get the feeling you're not going to tell me what this treasure is?"

"I will, very soon. And then you will understand. You only need to trust me until that time." He reached out one hand to her, but she drew back. He sighed. "And the reason I have remained here is because you and your brother seemed so alone. So defenseless."

Her eyes darkened. "Not defenseless. More like unaware. I must thank you, I suppose, for shaking me enough to remind me of my duty to the collection."

"Have I truly shaken you, Julia?" he asked softly. "Now it's your turn to be honest."

A tiny smile played over her mouth. "You are a very tiresome man, Robin Goodfellow."

He managed to catch her hands this time. "But persuasive," he murmured as he drew her toward him. He couldn't help himself. He had only this night to steal a moment of closeness with her. By tomorrow she would be firmly bound to another.

His hands slid up her arms, settled on her shoulders. A wary expression briefly clouded her face, but then she tipped her head back and asked in a low, bemused voice, "Do you sing, Robin?"

He looked startled for an instant. "That's an odd question."

She set her hands on his chest. "It's just that being here with you . . . it reminds me of a dream I had while I napped yesterday. I heard the most hauntingly beautiful music, hundreds of voices singing within a shimmering light. I wanted to weep that I could never find such beauty again in this world."

He slid one hand beneath her hair, spreading his long fingers on her nape. "I could show you such beauty," he said in a low voice.

"I think you already have," she murmured, gazing spellbound into those remarkable eyes, at once earthy and gilded. It would be so easy to lose herself in them, and in the wonder of his lean face, the winning shape of his mouth, and the angular, exotic rise of his cheek. She ached for him to kiss her, to bring this moment of rare intimacy to its rightful conclusion.

She leaned toward him, letting him see the hunger and the need in her eyes. And then tried to hide her dismay when a combined expression of regret and resolve clouded his expression. She quickly turned her face from him in embarrassed confusion. Something brushed against her hair; she heard him speak her name once, a bleak, ragged whisper.

"Sleep now," he said as he gently disengaged himself from her. "And tomorrow you must behave with your cousins as though you suspect nothing."

"But won't you be here?"

"It's Christmas Eve," he reminded her. "You will be too busy with your party to miss me."

There was open disappointment in her face. "Harry will be quite put out if you're not there. You see, he's had the most splendid notion. Since the house is not at its best this year, we will hold our gathering on the grounds of the old Abbey."

Robin nearly smiled—he himself had made that suggestion to the boy. He wanted the merrymakers far away from the house. "It's not wise for me to come."

"Why not?" she asked with a touch of petulance.

"I think you know why not." His eyes, yearning but still full of caution, were the only explanation he dared offer. "But I won't be far off. I promise."

"You're up to some mischief, aren't you?"

He set one finger on her nose for an instant. "Eternally, Miss Fitzwalter."

Julia's first thoughts when she awakened were of Robin, but that did nothing to scotch her sour mood. How foolish was it, she mused crossly as she dragged herself from her bed, to give one's heart to a man who was awash with secrets and intrigues? A man who, furthermore, expected her to trust him, when he clearly refused to offer her the same consideration.

At least she had enough to keep her busy throughout the day so that she rarely thought of him. She spent the morning in the kitchen, helping the women from the estate prepare plum puddings and meat pies. In the afternoon she and Harry coordinated the setting up of tables and benches on the grounds of the ruined Abbey, which lay less than a mile from Arden House.

Sir John waylaid her at one point, as she was coming in the front door. "Christmas or no," he said, "I will set my case before you tomorrow. But I warn you, Julia, your lawyers have all but agreed to my petition. I expect they will be overjoyed to see the last of the Somerset Fitzwalters."

"I could say the same of the Yorkshire Fitzwalters, cousin," she responded.

Afterward, Sir John had retired to the upstairs library with her account books, claiming the estate party was "nothing but a blasted waste of time and money."

Lady Fitzwalter, on the other hand, seemed to have undergone a transformation and was almost giddy as she enlisted her strapping footman—whom she had begun to address as "Lambikins"—to help her carry food baskets to the party site.

It was growing dark when Julia went up to her room to change. She eyed her bed with longing, wanting only to lie down and sleep through the upcoming festivities.

Instead, she forced herself to change into her best gown, a soft merino in a deep rose color. She was adjusting the velvet collar when she realized that she no longer wore the cellar key about her neck. Her heart thudded for a moment, until she recalled that Robin had taken it from her last night. More mischief, she thought crossly as she tugged on her pelisse.

Harry was waiting in the front hall. He looked quite elegant in his beige greatcoat, topped off with Papa's finest beaver hat. He drew something from his coat pocket—it was the shawl Robin had brought her—and draped it around her throat. "Mr. Goodfellow asked me to give you this. A peace offering, he called it."

She raised a fold of it to her cheek and swore she could smell the crisp scent of woodland and forest. "You saw him today?"

He shrugged and said carelessly, "He's been about." He propelled her toward the door. "Cousin Alicia has gone on ahead of us in her coach. With her footman carrying a brazier, in case she takes a chill. I say, Jules, did you notice the way she's been ogling the poor fellow?"

She rolled her eyes. "And where has Sir John gotten himself off to?"

"He was in the kitchen earlier, ordering Lettie to fill his flask with a bit of Papa's brandy. But she got him back right enough," he said with a chuckle. "I caught her adding a dose of castor oil to his flask."

They started out across the lawns, to where one of the estate workers waited with a pony trap. It was a perfect night for the Christmas party, she thought as they cleared the gates of Arden House, the sky clear, the air nippy but without any trace of dampness.

Torches had been set up at intervals around the perimeter of the churchyard. Out of respect for the ancient Abbey, Julia had decided not to use the area of the nave, but only the surrounding lawn. Three dozen people were already milling about on the grass, and as the fiddlers struck up a tune, couples began to form.

An elegant carriage drew up beside their pony trap. "Miss Fitzwalter!"

Sir Percival stepped down from the carriage followed by Mr. Norfolk, who also greeted Julia with a crow of delight. "This is well met," he said. "You shall have two beaux to escort you to the ball."

"Three," she said, putting her arm over Harry's shoulder.

"I ain't dancing," Harry proclaimed. "Anyway, I see two of my friends from school—" He darted away before she could protest.

"Abandoned so quickly," she sighed melodramatically.

Both men assured her that they would not prove so fickle as they led her toward the lights. They stayed right by her side while she gave the traditional Christmas speech, and then raised their glasses high when the estate workers toasted her, calling out, "The Lady of Islay!"

She was soon light-headed from rum punch, and from being passed from partner to partner—she danced first with Sir Percy, then Mr. Norfolk, followed by Mr. Josephs, the curate. Then Sir Corry of the angel-dark looks swept her into his arms with a wide grin.

It was the grin that was her undoing. It made her think of another grin, one she'd been trying to forget all day. She forced herself to mind her steps as she was swirled through a lively reel—and then she saw him. Just the briefest glimpse of a lean face in the crowd and a flash of hair turned bronze by torchlight. Then Sir Corry spun her, and she lost sight of him.

Once the dance was over, she hurried away from her partner, insisting she had to check on Lettie, who was preparing the wassail punch. Midnight was less than an hour away, the time when everyone present would drink from the maple bowl.

Julia went past the long trestle where the food and punch had been set out. Harry was there with his friends, as was Lady Fitzwalter, smiling up at her tall footman. Julia sped past them, wondering if her uncle had ever made an appearance. She went swiftly along the outer perimeter of the crowd, determined to find Robin in this mass of people. He'd said he'd stay nearby; he had to be here somewhere.

A dark shape moving off to her right caught her eye. It drifted behind one of the Abbey's walls. With a determined frown she set off across the grass. It was the traditional right of the Lady of Islay to drink the wassail punch with the man of her choosing. And Julia was choosing him.

The sound of the fiddlers faded as she entered the nave of the church. The grass here was ragged and overgrown; it parted before her as she moved along the misted ground, keeping close to the wall on her left. When the wall crumbled away to a pile of mortared stones, she stopped, afraid to step into the open.

The wide sward before her was mostly in shadow; the torchlight from the party had barely infiltrated this part of the Abbey's interior. But then she gasped as a flickering light drifted down from the open sky, a soft luminescence that swirled slowly at the center of the nave. She heard singing then, the same haunting voices that had beguiled her in the dream.

The dark figure of a man stood amid that shimmering cloud, arms stretched skyward, head thrown back. While she watched, the outlines of his lean body began to blur. Slowly he transformed, until he appeared to be a translucent copper flame in the center of that swirling light.

"No!" she cried out. "Please, no!"

The light instantly vanished.

She spun and flung herself against the wall, shutting her eyes, trying to force away the image of what she'd seen. A moment later, his hands were on her shoulders. "Julia?"

She turned, pushing at him roughly. "Who are you?" she sobbed raggedly. "*What* are you?"

He shut his own eyes for a long moment. When he looked at her again, they were full of pain. Even in this sullen darkness she knew that. "What do you think I am?" he asked softly. "What do you know in your heart?"

"You . . . you are . . ." She couldn't speak the words, even though they were ready on her tongue. She reached out to him, grasping the lapels of his coat. "I didn't see it," she whispered frantically. "I drank too much punch. It was a trick of the light. Please tell me that is so. A trick of the light."

He set his hands over hers, warming them. "You know what you saw, Julia. I didn't mean for you to . . . but this night, this rare night when spirits break the bonds that separate your world from mine. You see, my kin are all about us. They called to me, and I was powerless not to respond."

"What do they want of you?" she asked weakly. "You are not like them." She pressed her hands hard against his chest. "You are real, solid . . . you are here, in this world."

He pulled her closer and rubbed his chin over her cheek. "Yes, for now."

"It's not enough."

"It has to be. It's all we have, sweetheart."

She mustered a severe frown. "Don't call me that. I won't be the sweetheart of such a deceitful, sneaking—"

"Insinuating?"

"Horribly insinuating." And then her voice broke, "Oh, Robin, tell me this is a dream and that when I awake you will be just a commonplace man with boring hobbies and a tidy income. One who will stay with me and—"

He dropped his arms from around her and swung

away. "This is no dream, Jules. I am what I am, and I haven't the power to change it."

"Or the desire to?" she asked sharply.

"Can you change the color of your eyes or the shape of your sweet mouth? I am only a specter here, for all that I appear solid to your eyes. That other is my true mantle, my true life."

She reached out and touched his face. "Is it as beautiful, that life, as I imagine it to be?"

"It was . . . for many centuries it was."

"And now? Will it be beautiful for you now?"

He swiped her hand away. "It doesn't matter, damn it." He took her shoulders and turned her roughly toward the distant lights. "Out there are three men I found for you. Good, steady, intelligent men. To help you with Arden House, to help you with Harry . . . to care for you and nurture you . . . and if you are so blind that you can't see that I did it out of—"

She threw herself at him, twisting her fingers in his hair to pull his head down. "You, Robin," she cried intently up against his mouth. "Only you. And if not you, then no one. Not ever."

He drew his head back, even as his arms were encircling her. His eyes bore into hers. "I can offer you no tomorrows. But will you take me as I am? For one short, precious interlude?"

She drew in a deep breath to stop her trembling and nodded. "It's Christmas, Robin. When sane women may run mad."

He leaned his head down to nuzzle her ear and sighed against her skin, *"Then spirits may cast off their cloak of night, and dance within the mortal firelight."*

She tugged at a lock of his hair. "Dance with me, Robin Goodfellow. Dance with the Lady of Islay."

"It would be my greatest pleasure."

He spun her around and around the great open

space, moving to a lilting inner music that filled both their hearts. He swung her off her feet so many times that she was breathless and giddy when they stopped. The next instant, she found herself thrust up against one of the retaining walls, his body capturing hers and holding her there.

"And now," he said hoarsely, "we will both run mad."

He slid one hand along the curve of her jaw, tipping her head slightly to one side, and then with truly maddening slowness he lowered his mouth over hers. He stroked his lips along the span of her mouth, sighing out a deep, shuddering groan when she arched against him in response.

Her arms slipped around him beneath his greatcoat, her fingers seeking purchase along his spine. He was whipcord lean, so cleanly muscled. And when he set one arm around her waist and drew her tight against him, she felt his true strength—in the implacable flex of his wrist at her back and in the tensed muscles of the thighs that now cradled her.

His other hand was drifting along her throat, fingers splayed, fingertips questing, and when it stroked down the velvety surface of her bodice, the heat erupted inside her. He kissed her harder as she moaned. She opened her mouth to those kisses, savoring his touch with every pore of her body and tasting him down to her toes.

Off in the distance, the church bells of Glastonbury began to sound the twelve strokes of midnight.

"I must go," he said breathlessly as he tugged back from her.

"Let me come with you," she cried. "Wherever you are going . . ."

He cradled her face tenderly and mused, "If it were only that easy. But don't fret . . . I am not bound for other worlds at the moment. There's something I need to do. Something that might be dangerous."

Her eyes flashed. "As if that would keep me away."

He gave her a rueful grin. "Very well. I did make a promise to show you true beauty. I suppose it's about time I kept it."

He led her through the kitchen to the cellar entrance, unlocked the door, and left it open behind them. Julia was far too bewitched to notice. He took her hand and guided her down the stairs into the darkness.

"I can't see," she protested softly.

"No, but I can. Keep close beside me"—he slid his arm about her waist—"and I swear you will come to no harm."

They crossed the upper level, then went down the stone steps that led to the vault. Robin coaxed her across the floor and into the mystery room, then shut the door behind them.

"It's rather like blindman's buff," she said. "Moving about in the dark."

He released her hand and heard her sigh of dismay. "I'm right here, Jules. Just stand there for a moment until I . . . ah, there it is."

A snick sounded loudly in the still, dark room.

Robin guided Julia closer to the table, and then reached around her to lift the top off the leather box. The darkness above the table was suddenly lit with a blossoming of shimmery light. It danced and sparkled in every color imaginable.

She cried out, reeling back against him. His arms closed around her.

"This is the real treasure of Arden House, Julia," he whispered against her ear. "The rare book that your family has guarded for centuries."

"It's the same light, the one I saw in my dream. But what does it mean? What new enchantment is this?" She pressed farther into his chest. "I'm frightened, Robin."

"No, don't be. It's not meant to frighten but to awe. With its power and its majesty. It is called the *Book of Trey,* and it contains the lore of my people."

She set one trembling hand upon the embossed cover. "Why didn't Papa tell me of this? He surely knew it was here."

In answer, Robin opened it to the pages that were missing, then touched the base of the book. "See here, where the binding is raveled. Someone got in here during your father's lifetime and damaged the book. I don't believe he discovered the vandalism until two years ago. And after he did, I expect he was ashamed to show you. That is why he was buying up any old bits of manuscript; he was trying to find the missing pages."

"This was to be my gift," she murmured wistfully. "Oh, my poor father." She turned to gaze at him. "And where are those pages now? Do you know?"

"Your cousin has them. Nine years ago, he"— Robin looked over his shoulder—"Ah, but why not let him tell us how he came to possess them."

Julia gave a stuttering gasp.

Sir John was now standing in the doorway, holding a lit candle. He set the pewter holder on the nearest bookshelf and moved toward them. "Having your own little party?" he drawled. "In your haste to be alone with each other down here, you neglected to lock the cellar door."

"How convenient for you," Robin said. "And I gather we have led you to what you seek. Most thieves are not that fortunate."

Sir John's mouth twisted. "Thieves? Ah, no. I have

as much right to that book as she does. More, perhaps, since I know what it contains."

"My father showed it to *you*?" Julia asked, her feelings of betrayal writ plainly on her face.

"Hardly. But when Uncle Roland took me through this room, I noticed the way his gaze kept darting to that table. So I filched the key from his desk, came back down here that night, and managed to spring the hidden catch. What I found was . . . impressive."

Her voice shook. "Then, why did you damage the book?"

He shrugged. "Because I could? I was angry that your precious father didn't trust his own blood kin enough to show it to me. I suppose I could have taken the book, but I thought it a bolder stroke to leave the evidence of my handiwork behind."

"It ruined him!" Julia cried in outrage. "And then it killed him."

Sir John scowled. "It was his own fault for not sharing it with me. At the time I could only guess what such a book meant. Then I began delving into the dark arts and studying the old lore. But I still didn't know the true value of the book or those pages until recently. Until I wed."

"You still don't have a clue to what they mean," Robin said softly.

Sir John's eyes glittered. "You think not? Then watch, Mr. Goodfellow." He began to intone in a low, singsong voice words that only Robin understood. *"Arcane spirits of earth and sky, spirits of stream and sea, all those spirits who dwell close by, speed you now to me."*

Sir John stood waiting, expectant. His smug expression began to fade a little when nothing happened.

The truth was that in spite of the man's rather amateurish delivery, Robin had indeed felt himself begin to transform. It had taken all his willpower to retain his mortal shape. It was clearly time to bring in reinforcements.

"Your wife's lessons in magic apparently did you little good," Robin said.

"What do you know of magic?" Sir John muttered.

"You might be surprised." Robin then called out in a loud voice, *"Magus magnus, great sorcerer of the sacred cave, I summon you!"*

There was an explosive flash in the doorway, followed by a billow of smoke. A tall man in a flowing purple robe appeared there, bearing a golden wand in his hand.

Julia recognized Mr. Quince, the fuel merchant, and nearly called out his name.

"What paltry trickery is this?" Sir John scoffed. "Parlor magic!" He peered at the old man. "Pah! I've seen better actors on the stage in Leeds."

The Limner stalked toward him. "Do you want me to turn you into a ferret?"

Sir John refused to be cowed. "Someone's already turned you into an old goat."

"Mind your tongue, rascal," the Limner growled. "Or you will see the sharp side of my wand."

Sir John set one hand on his chin, and then looked up with an evil smirk. "Here's something I recall, good for ridding the home of pestilential emanations—*spiritus malefactorum, banished be by my decree*—"

"Oh, piffle," muttered the Limner. "You're hardly worth my effort."

Sir John grit his teeth and uttered a few dark syllables. To the surprise of everyone, the *Book of Trey*, weighty as it was, flew up from its box and landed on his upraised hands.

"It's mine now, Julia," he proclaimed, clutching it to his chest. "The rest of this moldering heap can fall down around your ears, for all I care. But the book is mine." He backed away from them toward the open door.

Robin made no attempt to stop him with magic—the book's enchantment protected whoever held it. Instead, he threw himself at the man, intent on wrestling it away from him. A small, sleek knife appeared in Sir John's hand and he sliced twice at Robin's arm, up and back, cutting deeply through the fabric of his greatcoat.

Julia cried out as she ran to pull Robin away. She quickly scanned his tattered sleeve, but there was no blood, in spite of her cousin's fierce strike.

"Let him have it," she implored. "Let him take the book."

Robin spun to her, gripping her shoulders, and said under his breath, "You don't understand. It could mean the end of my world."

She drew in a ragged sob. "Then, you can stay here with me."

"No," he said grimly. "Not at that cost, Julia. He will have unimaginable power. If he can control *my* people, your kind won't stand a chance against him."

Sir John was leering at them from the doorway. "Very touching. Am I to take it, Mr. Goodfellow, that you are one of the faery folk? I see my summoning spell worked after all." He tucked the book more firmly under his arm and shot Robin a twisted smile. "And I gather it was you who beguiled my wife away from me. Well, she served her purpose, withal. Now, sir, I need to take my leave, but I'm not through with you . . . or your kind."

He snatched at his candle, then disappeared through the door. He was crossing the outer chamber at a run as Robin snarled, "Do something!" to the Limner. The old man went striding from the room, with Julia

and Robin in his wake. Sir John was already halfway
up the stone steps.

The Limner raised his wand and swept it through
the air just as Sir John was reaching for the door latch.
He was sent reeling back from the portal—as though
lightning struck—and landed on his knees several
steps down, still clutching book and candle.

"You cannot take the *Book of Trey* from this
place," the old man pronounced. "Not while someone
with a greater claim stands close by."

Sir John glared down at them, crouched like an animal ten feet above their heads. His eyes appeared to
glow amber in the gloom. "She'll not live to take it
from me."

Robin shifted Julia behind him and heard her muffled protest. "You dare not harm her," he said evenly.
"She is protected by my power."

But the man perched on the ledge of stone was not
heeding him, instead he was riffling through the pages
of the book. When he stood at last, he looked directly
at Robin. "Don't be so sure." Then his voice soared
out above them as he read from the book. *"Spirit heed
you this command, do my bidding with thy hand. Make
your master well content, and remove this earthly im-
pediment."* He pointed one long, bony finger at
Julia. "Now!"

Even though she could not understand the words,
from the expression of shock on her face Robin saw
that Julia clearly understood their intent. He closed
his eyes against the intense pain that was coursing
through him. For a neophyte, Sir John had a mighty
grasp.

"Run, Julia!" he groaned, thrusting her away from
him. But there was nowhere she could run except up
the stairs, straight into her cousin's arms. Once Sir
John had her, he could easily pass through the door.

Julia cast one horrified look at Robin's face, saw the murderous intent growing there. She swung to the Limner. "Help us."

Robin's eye entreated him. "Yes, please."

The old man smiled grimly. "There is only one way to place you beyond his power." He held Robin's gaze and his expression spoke volumes. "You won't like it."

Robin's face twisted as he fought against the urge to harm Julia. *Damn the Lady of the Lake and her pernicious gift to mankind.*

Sir John was now moving cautiously toward them, down one step, then another. "Come, Robin," he coaxed. "Come and finish your work."

Robin forced Julia back against the wall, his bright eyes now dull and dead. "No! Robin, no!" she cried, as his hands slid around her throat. His gaze met hers; the dead look gone now, replaced by one of unutterable regret.

"Do it, old man," he uttered hoarsely over his shoulder. "Do what you must."

A fleeting smile of satisfaction crossed the Limner's face. He nodded once and began to chant in Gaelic, slowly at first and then more rapidly.

"What the devil is he up to?" Sir John snarled.

"Protecting Julia," Robin gasped as his hands dropped away from her throat. He sagged to his knees on the stone floor.

Sir John came down the final few steps, moving swiftly toward Julia now, the sleek knife again in his hand. Whether to harm her or force her up the stairs with him, she never knew.

The chamber had begun to vibrate, a low, thunderous humming that echoed off the vaulted ceiling. The walls appeared to move, the floor to buckle, as if the great hewed stones were waves upon the sea. Robin reached up for Julia, pulling her down beside him and cradling her in his arms—while the vibrations grew ever stronger, the chamber shifting and rocking like a ship's cabin during a storm.

"What are you doing!" Sir John wailed to the Limner. "Stop it, I say! Oh, God, make it stop!"

He careened back, dropping his candle and clutched the *Book of Trey* to his chest, one hand clasped over his horror-struck face. The candle sputtered out, casting the tilting chamber into darkness.

A shaft of fire flared up from the center of the chamber, a fierce, soul-piercing light that gradually took on human form, revealing a gilded warrior in helm and tunic.

"Who disturbs my Winter's rest?" a voice boomed. *"Who dares to intrude on my peace?"*

The glowing countenance shifted to Sir John Fitzwalter, one bronzed hand raised toward him. "You, foul insect, festering worm, shall go from this place and never return. By the grace of the Lady of the Lake, the book is mine. Mine!"

The *Book of Trey* was snatched from Sir John's trembling hands and sent tumbling through the air until it was caught up by the flaming figure. A sheaf of papers flew up from the pocket of Sir John's greatcoat and fluttered across the chamber, neatly reinserting themselves in the back of the book.

The gilded warrior bent and laid the book gently in Julia's lap, then gave a mighty yawn, stretching his brawny arms over his head. He smiled at the Limner. "I always hated being awakened, especially by rude upstarts."

He slowly disappeared, the flame around him dying down as his shape grew ever more faint. Once he was gone completely, the rumbling vibrations ceased.

Sir John was now a gibbering puddle on the floor of the chamber.

The Limner stared bemusedly at the spot where the apparition had been, then sighed deeply. He bent down and retrieved the candle, lighting it with a snap of his fingers. Then he dragged Sir John to his feet by the scruff of his neck. "That'll teach you to dabble in things over your head. Now, I'm going to march you upstairs and watch you pack . . . just to make sure you didn't pilfer anything else from Arden House."

"There was something in the brandy," Sir John was muttering under his breath. "It tasted strange . . . something in the brandy."

Julia had her arms around Robin now, holding his head against her breast. He was still conscious, but barely.

"Are you dying," she cried softly.

"It feels like it," he gasped, and then winced as another tremor shot through him. He knew there were tears coursing down his cheeks; he felt her fingers brush them away.

"What can I do?" she entreated him.

"Leave me," he said raggedly. "Please. I don't want you to see me like this."

She laid his head gently down, bundling her silk shawl for a pillow. "I'll never forget you," she said softly. "Never."

"You will forget," he said. "I've already seen to that. Tomorrow morning this will all seem nothing more than a dream."

She lifted the book, shaping his trembling fingers around the kidskin binding. "Isn't there something in here that could help you?"

"Not any longer. But that doesn't mean you should forsake it."

"I won't," she said. "I vow on my father's grave to protect it as long as I live."

He raised his head and managed a feeble grin. "Miss Fitzwalter, you're a trump. But please go . . . there is no purpose in staying—"

She bent down and kissed his mouth, stroking her fingers over his cheeks, where their tears now mingled. "You can't make me forget, Robin," she sobbed. "Not what you did for me tonight."

She pushed away from him then, and fled up the stairs. The door above him closed with a resounding thud.

"You have no idea what I did for you," he rasped out to the empty chamber.

The Limner brought him a glass of brandy and a blanket, then hunkered down beside him on the floor.

"I don't suppose it's reversible?" Robin asked, his voice barely audible.

The Limner shook his head. "You knew that when you asked me to do it."

Robin chuckled weakly. "So you've gotten back at me after all."

"It's your own fault for leaving me down here with the book. I learned some very illuminating spells."

Robin rolled his eyes. "Illuminating is hardly the word I'd choose. How long do you think before I'm done?"

The old man laid a hand on Robin's forehead. "Not much longer."

Robin grimaced. "That was an impressive showing you provided . . . your gilded warrior king with all the trappings. When you flex your power, it's quite something to behold."

The old man gave a terse laugh. "I didn't do it. Sir John roused the specter when he tried to harm Julia."

He grinned wanly. "And now I have my answer . . . he *is* buried here in Arden House."

"He and his queen."

"Good thing Sir John didn't rouse my Gwennie," the old man mused. "She had a fearful temper. So tell me, how came they here? I gather the Fitzwalters rescued the bodies from the crypt when the Abbey was looted by King Henry's troops."

Robin's nod was barely perceptible. "Found an account of it . . . hidden in an old diary. They're buried . . . beneath the round stone."

"Kept safe for the ages," the old man quoted.

But Robin was beyond hearing.

When Julia awoke on Christmas morning, there was a strange muzziness in her head. She couldn't seem to get her thoughts around anything, and her heart ached with some deep sadness she could not name.

Lettie met her in the hall and informed her that Sir John had left Arden House abruptly in the middle of the night. "Proper strange he looked, miss. His hair all gone white in the front and his cheeks sunken in. Guess he took it hard . . . I mean that Lady Fitzwalter ran off with her footman directly from the party."

Julia muttered some comment—she could barely recall her cousin and his wife. She clasped the housekeeper by one arm. "Have I been ill, Lettie? Did I miss the Christmas party?"

Lettie clucked over her. "Not a bit of it, you was in the thick of things, dancing with this young gentleman and that. No wonder your head is still spinning. You go on and have your breakfast. And don't bother to wait for Master Harry. He sneaked a few glasses of punch last night and went riding out this morning to clear his head."

Julia made her way to the breakfast parlor, wondering how much rum punch she'd drunk herself, that she couldn't put two thoughts together. The whole previous evening seemed a blur . . . well, except for the certain recollection that she'd danced inside the Abbey walls with a man who had nearly kissed her into a swoon.

She heard someone on the other side of the door, and wondered, as she pushed it open, if Harry was already back from his ride.

A lean-cheeked, golden-eyed man was sitting at the table coring an apple.

Her heart somersaulted once in her breast. "Robin!"

He looked up, startled, and the knife slipped, leaving a thin bloody ridge on the edge of his index finger. She flex across the room to kneel beside him—as everything that had occurred last night came back to her in a rush.

"Oh, Robin, you're alive. And you're bleeding!" she crowed.

"The first of many inconveniences," he muttered as he sucked on the edge of his finger.

"But I thought you were dying last night."

"Not dying, merely changing. The old man made me mortal, Jules." He sighed. "For all time, I'm afraid. Otherwise I might have injured you . . . he had to place me beyond your cousin's power. It was the only solution."

She set her hand on his sleeve. "I'm so sorry."

"Don't be." His eyes met hers, and she saw that beyond the overlay of sadness there was a measure of acceptance.

"But to give up all that beauty. . . . It's nearly unthinkable."

"There's beauty here as well," he said gently, stroking his thumb over her cheek. "And magic. It occurred to me last night that I've spent a great deal of time over the years playing at being mortal. Maybe it's what was meant for me in the end."

"But you didn't have a choice," she protested softly.

"Ah, but I did. I knew your cousin couldn't actually force me to kill you. Few spells are strong enough to make mortal or faery go against their true natures. But I couldn't bear the thought of hurting you, not in any way." He took her hand, raised it to his mouth. "Besides, there was one moment at the Abbey when I absolutely ached to stay here with you. So don't blame yourself, Jules. Not overmuch."

Her expression darkened. "You intended to go away last night, though, didn't you? That's why you put some horrid forgetting spell on me. Well, I can tell you it didn't work."

"No," he said with mock regret. "I'm discovering that you are strangely immune to my spells. Maybe that's why I decided to stay on . . . to see if I couldn't find some way to enchant you after all."

She wrinkled her nose. "I've always seen through your mischief, sir. Right from the start." Then her eyes narrowed. "Except for last night. I can't believe you intentionally confronted my cousin with only that old man to aid you."

Robin grinned. "That old man—who happens to be Harry's hermit—has more power in his little finger than a dozen Sir Johns. I'd never have allowed you down there otherwise."

"Then, why didn't he stop my cousin from overpowering you?"

"He was letting things play out. You see," he added with a frown, "there's a very old score between us. I . . . er . . . introduced a French knight to a Cornish queen many centuries ago. A *married* queen." He tugged slightly at his neckcloth. "World's have changed on such chance happenings, I'm afraid."

"Lancelot and Guinevere," she said in a faraway voice. "And it all came undone after that."

"So you knew who our spectral visitor was, then?"

She nodded. "Yes, I knew. I'd heard rumors that he and his queen had been reinterred in Islay Castle, but no one was ever able to prove it. It appears I've discovered all the secrets of Arden House in one night."

"Not all of them," he said as he drew a small volume from his coat pocket and handed it to her. "The money from this should get you through the next decade or so."

She opened the worn leather cover. "It's a diary," she said. And then her mouth gaped. "Good heavens! It appears to be written by Elizabeth Tudor, dated three years before she came to the throne."

"Yes, the Faerie Queen," said Robin with a sigh. "I found it in the vaults several days ago. Consider it my Christmas gift to you." He added teasingly, "I hope you've one for me. Harry says that all you ever give him are stockings and handkerchiefs, but I am not dismayed. I believe mortals can never have enough of those."

She looked thoughtful for a moment, and then her face brightened. "I do have a gift for you," she said as she rose. "Come and see."

She led him to the parlor, to where the garland hung over the doorway. "There," she said, pointing to the highest part of the arch.

He looked up at the spray of grayish berries amid the evergreens and grinned. "Ah, the old pagan custom."

She set one hand on her chin and said musingly, "I've been at my wits end deciding which of my three beaux I will allow to lure me here. Sir Percy is quite handsome and Mr. Norfolk is very amusing. I expect it will be Sir Corry, though, since he is divinely dark, and I have always favored dark—"

Robin muttered a soft curse and swung her hard up against his chest. Then he was kissing her, arms strong, mouth hungry. She sighed and wrapped her arms around him, around that supple, steely back that felt so very real and solid under her hands.

"Beware," he murmured against her mouth. "My spells may not work on you, but I can inflict all sorts of nasty things on your suitors—boils, bedbugs, odious cousins from Yorkshire."

She pulled back from him, her eyes bleak, her voice laced with sadness. "Have you forgotten already? You can no longer use your spells, Robin."

"Oh, piffle," he said carelessly. "Your hermit's promised to teach me mortal magic. Well, once he gets back from his latest quest. Now, come here, sweetheart . . . I fear I've still not gotten the hang of this kissing business."

Julia thought he'd gotten rather more than that. But she wasn't going to tax him on where he'd learned to kiss like an earthy peasant instead of a properly re-strained gentleman. His kisses made her feel both cherished and inflamed. Not a bad combination.

She still couldn't wholly envision what it would mean for him to give up his life, his true mantle. But in time she believed there would be other compensa-tions—children of his own to love, a large estate to challenge him, a vast library to set to rights. And who, after all, would make a better guardian for the *Book of Trey* than Robin Goodfellow?

He was holding her now, his head on her shoulder, murmuring sweet endearments against her ear. She pulled back a little and set her hands on his chest.

"I never thanked you," she said. "For coming here and bringing life back to this house. And for making me understand my father's behavior that last year. Remember when I said it didn't feel like Christmas? Well, it does now . . . there's light and joy everywhere." She looked deep into his forest-gold eyes. "Can you feel it, Robin?"

He paused and his lashes fluttered on his cheek for an instant. "Does joy sort of rush over you and steal your breath?"

She nodded slowly.

"Then, yes, I do feel it. That and a hundred other wonderful sensations. And a bit of hunger," he added slyly, rubbing his lean belly. "I never did get to eat my breakfast."

He tucked her hand under his arm and turned her back toward the dining parlor. Julia paused in the archway, her head tipped to one side. "Did you hear that just now? It sounded like singing, distant merry singing.

The old gods laugh, he thought. Oberon and Titania and their train of faery folk having a fine chuckle at his expense. Well, let them. For many long centuries he'd believed mortals to be the most foolish of creatures. But in all that time, in spite of the beauty and magic of his world, he'd never once experienced the pure, exhilarating pleasure of loving another being.

Maybe he'd been the fool.

"It's my heart you hear," he whispered against her hair. "Just my heart."

"Where are you off to on Christmas morning?" Harry asked from the mouth of the cave. The old man was inside, stuffing his ragged clothing into a tapestry bag.

"It's hard to tell exactly," the Limner said as he

emerged, sniffing the wind like a keen-nosed old hound. "Somewhere in Belgium, I believe. Not too far from Brussels."

"And what will you do there?"

The Limner's brows furled. "My, you are full of questions this morning."

"It's no wonder," Harry said darkly. "Some havey-cavey things have been going on at the house . . . Sir John left in the middle of the night, his wife ran off with her footman, and when I came in after the estate party, I heard Jules weeping in her room. Then this morning, when I asked Lettie what was toward, she just smiled and said, 'Providence.'"

"A wise woman," the Limner remarked. "And now I must be off. It's many days' walk to Dover." He fidgeted with the sleeve of his tattered greatcoat and made a noise of annoyance. "This isn't going to work," he muttered and then, to Harry's complete astonishment, he drew a fine fat rabbit out of his sleeve.

"Here, you'd best take him. Rumor has it you've a fondness for the beasts."

Harry clutched the pied rabbit to his chest. "How on earth did you do that?"

"Parlor magic," the old man responded, and then chortled. "Some might think it's all I'm capable of these days."

He turned and waved once to Harry when he reached the end of the rocky path. There would be more rocky paths ahead of him, he knew. But as ever, he would do what he could. For this country he loved, for the gilded warrior whose memory he kept alive. And for another warrior who bore the same name, who would soon face a terrible foe in a small village outside of Brussels.

He would do what he could. For Arthur.

The Wexford Carol
by Emma Jensen

1

County Wexford, Ireland

The Honorable Elizabeth Fitzhollis had dirt beneath her fingernails. She also had a bruise on her chin and bits of dried plaster in her hair. She didn't think Mr. Dunn, the family's aged solicitor, had noticed. He was glancing nearsightedly at the paper in his hand, beaky nose nearly against it. Lizzie did, however, believe he had noticed the not very pleasant smell emanating from her person. He'd wrinkled his nose upon entering the room, squinted at her, then emptied the contents of his bulging leather satchel onto the already concave desktop.

There hadn't been much Elizabeth could do about the smell. She had been knee-deep in a clogged drainage ditch when Dunn had arrived unexpectedly. She'd only had time to clamber inelegantly from the hole and bolt upstairs to don a worn but appropriate dress before joining him in her father's study. A bath had been out of the question. There hadn't been time. And she was just going back into her discarded clothing and the ditch, shovel in hand, within ten minutes of his departure anyway.

The bruise was from the pantry door. It had been

sticking for months, but fixing it hadn't been anywhere near the top of Lizzie's list. Having yanked it open into her own face the day before, she'd moved it up a few notches. The collapsing ceiling in the Lily Room had been much more pressing, hence the plaster in her hair. Had it been the ballroom ceiling, she could simply have closed the door and forgotten about it for the time being. But the Lily Room was where she spent what scant quiet time she had, usually battling with monetary figures that wouldn't budge no matter how many times she rearranged them.

The patch job she'd done on the ceiling was just that. Until the west wing had a new roof, there would be leaks and damp, and sagging plaster . . .

". . . will be arriving in a fortnight."

Lizzie dragged her attention away from the crumbling roof tiles to what Mr. Dunn was saying. He did tend to prattle on about debts—nothing of which Lizzie was not well aware, so she tended to listen with only half an ear. "Who will be arriving, sir?"

The solicitor peered at her over the paper. "Captain Jones."

Lizzie ran through the list of creditors. To be sure, there were quite a few, but that name rang no bells. "And who is Captain Jones?"

"Why, the agent for the new owner, of course."

Oh, no. Please, God, no. Lizzie's stomach did a dizzying flop. She'd been waiting for this day, dreading it, but never quite believing that Cousin Percy would actually sell her home, her beloved Hollymore.

"Captain Lawrence Edward Jones," Mr. Dunn read, squinting at the missive, "representing the Duke of Llans. His Grace plans to set up a hunting estate here, and Captain Jones will be supervising the demolition and subsequent development."

"D-demolition?"

"Mmm. He has no use for the house. Far too large and"—Mr. Dunn cleared his throat apologetically—"er . . . not, shall we say, in the best of repair. He will replace it with a smaller lodge. Now, Captain Jones will expect a room . . ."

Lizzie had stopped listening. Replace Hollymore. Knock down stones built upon the stones that had sheltered Henry II in 1171, break out the stained-glass windows in the Long Gallery that had been a gift from King Charles mere months before he lost his head. Rip out the wooden paneling in the dining hall that bore the carved names of the twenty-two Fitzhollis men who had died at the Battle of the Boyne.

Yes, the house was tumbling down around her ears. Yes, her father had died without a son to inherit or anything to leave his only daughter. Yes, as the new baron, Percy had every legal right to sell the house. Lizzie simply hadn't expected him to do it. All in all, she thought miserably now, she shouldn't have been surprised.

She loved Hollymore, every damp stone and rotting panel. Percy loved his title, money, and his horse, in that order.

"I am correct in that, am I not, Miss Fitzhollis?"

Lizzie blinked at the solicitor. "I am sorry, sir. I did not hear you."

Dunn clucked his tongue, not unsympathetically. "I was referring to your father's aunt. You will have a home with her, will you not?"

"I will, yes."

Oh, yes. A home in pinch-faced Aunt Gregoria's over-warm little cottage that smelled of cats. A home where each morsel of food was weighed before it went onto a plate and candles were only used for a half hour each evening.

Lizzie practiced economy. Gregoria had turned it into a Holy Crusade.

"Well, then." Dunn began to gather up his belongings. Several papers stuck to the decaying leather blotter, still more had been impaled on the decidedly ugly sculpture of a hedgehog that squatted atop the desk. Lizzie gave the thing a careful pat as she freed the papers. The bronze hedgehog had been part of her great-uncle Clarence's "natural" period. Not one of his more successful sculpting endeavors. But it remained in its place of honor because both Lizzie and her father had been very fond of Uncle Clarence. And because it couldn't be sold as nearly everything else in the house had been. No one in their right mind would buy it.

Lizzie herself retrieved Mr. Dunn's hat and stick from the coatroom. O'Reilly, the ancient butler, was busy replacing the paper stuffing in the first-floor windows, and both maids were doing their best to rescue the parlor furniture. Lizzie peered carefully into the solicitor's hat before handing it over. The coatroom was a bit dark and cobwebby, and the Reverend Mr. Clark had been understandably unhappy on his last visit when he'd donned a very large spider along with his hat. Pity, she'd thought at the time, that it hadn't been her cousin. But Percy kept all of his belongings near to hand when he paid his unwelcome visits.

After a quick check to make certain he wasn't standing on a crumbling bit, Lizzie left Mr. Dunn on the front steps and went off to summon his carriage. Kelly, the groom, was still trying to capture the pair of owls that had flown into the Gallery two nights before. So far, they had been impressively clever at avoiding his net.

Eventually, she got Mr. Dunn into his carriage and waved him down the weedy drive. Only when he was out of sight did she allow her shoulders to slump. It was a brief break, though. She knew the staff would gather at teatime—they always did after his visits—and would want the report. Usually, it was merely the news that their wages would be delayed again. Since none of them had been paid in more than six months, they left those meetings cheerful. This time would be so very different.

And so Lizzie found herself in the warm kitchen two hours later, bathed and better-smelling but exhausted from her moderately successful second round with the ditch, facing her loyal staff over their tea. She studied the beloved faces as they sipped the strong, sweet tea or gnawed on O'Reilly's biscuits. The butler-cook-general factotum was cheerful as ever, eyes bright in his seamed face. But Lizzie knew his rheumatism was acting up again. As hard as he'd tried to hide it, she had seen his grimace as he sat down at the table. Meggie, the ginger-haired maid, had plaster dusting her young face; black-haired, motherly Nuala had a bigger bruise than Lizzie's on her right cheek. And Kelly, who tended the single horse and overgrown gardens as best he could, as well as being resident house wildlife trapper, had a face so red from his exertions with the net that it rivaled the brilliant hair he shared with his sister Meg.

All were regarding her with trust, loyalty, and hope familiar enough to warm Lizzie's heart, and powerful enough to break it.

"It isn't good," she began, and determinedly kept her voice from cracking as she repeated the solicitor's news. That done, she assured them, "I'll find you better posts elsewhere before I leave. I promise you that."

No one spoke for a long moment when she'd finished. Then O'Reilly, undisputed leader of the pack,

growled, "Don't you be worrying about us, missy.
We'll be just fine." There was a chorus of nods and
ayes around the table. "We've all places t'go. 'Tis you
who needs the caring for. Stuffed away wi' that bitter
old bat. 'Tisn't right, no more than you slaving away
at this old pile. Beautiful young girl needs beaux and
balls and a house wi'out falling walls."

Lizzie smiled. "You know you love this old pile as
much as I do." And they all did. O'Reilly's father
and grandfather had been in service to the Fitzhollises
before him, as had Nuala's mother and both of Kelly
and Meggie's parents. "Besides that, it has been so
long since I attended a ball that I wouldn't know
where to put my feet, at present all the walls are
standing splendidly, and if I wanted a beau, there is
always Persistent Percy."

It had its desired effect. There were snorts and
smiles all around. Lizzie was grateful for the unbend-
ing support. Grateful, too, if amused, by the familiar
compliments. She supposed she was young enough; six
and twenty was hardly an advanced age. And enough
men had called her beautiful. She had inherited her
father's rich gold hair and Irish-green, thickly lashed
eyes. Along with her mother's heart-shaped, high-
boned face, willowy frame—a bit hardened, perhaps,
by all the shoring and shoveling and plastering—and
quick, wide smile, it was a pleasant enough picture.
But her beauty had, for good or ill, not been quite
enough to surpass her want of fortune. One after the
next, her youthful swains had taken themselves off to
wealthier climes. Lizzie suspected that her forthright
nature and frank intelligence had something to do
with the matter as well, but for whatever reason, no
man had come courting in the two years since her
father had died. Except Percy, of course, and she
would marry his horse before she would have him.

"I will manage perfectly well with Aunt Gregoria," she announced to her staff now. "I will still be close to the good company of the area. And, if I am very well behaved, and manage to remember the names of all eight cats, she will take me to Dublin with her when she performs her good works."

There were more snorts and smiles. Gregoria Fitz-hollis's idea of good works consisted of distributing scratchy woolen gloves and sermons on resisting the drink to Dublin's unsuspecting poor. That she herself was rather partial to sweet sherry was a source of wry amusement to her acquaintants. But a weekly half bottle of genteel after-dinner sherry consumed in the presence of her vicar, Gregoria steadfastly asserted, was as different from whiskey in a tavern as orange and green. She'd never commented on the other five half bottles she consumed during every sennight.

"I still don't like it," Kelly muttered, hunching and bristling in the protective mien he'd always used for Lizzie despite the fact that she was several years older. "Sure, and this captain's a dog for coming to shove you out of your rightful home."

"And just after Christmas, too!" was Meggie's indignant addition. "Couldn't be bothered to wait 'til the holidays had well passed. They're all just the same, they are, the fancy. Sensitive as turf bricks." She gave Lizzie a sweet smile. "We don't count you among them, o' course, Miss Lizzie."

"Thank you." Lizzie took the compliment with a smile of her own. With the exception of her beloved if ineffectual sire and the gentle mother she'd barely known, her opinions of the aristocracy were much the same. Most she'd met were just like Percy. "But I do not suppose we can blame Captain Jones. I imagine he comes and goes at the duke's bidding."

"You're too kind, *cailín*," Nuala scolded. " 'Tisn't

this captain having his heart broke during what should be the kindest time o' the year. Bad business for holy days, I say, and may they know it."

Silently Lizzie agreed. It was a sorry thing indeed to conduct such business just after Christmas week. But despite the fact that both Captain Jones's name and the duke's title were Welsh, it was likely that the duke at least was more English than anything and, like members of the English High Society in which he no doubt lived, just didn't care whose holidays were inconvenienced as long as they weren't his own.

As it was, there had been little holiday spirit at Hollymore for a very long time.

"Poor Miss Lizzie," Meggie sighed.

"Poor Miss Lizzie," the others echoed, a mournful toast.

Lizzie shook her head, tried to shake off the weight of sadness. "Don't be shedding any tears for me." Her brave face lasted only a moment. She whispered, "Save them for Hollymore."

Four heads bobbed dejectedly. "Is there naught we can do?" Kelly demanded.

"Aye, Miss Lizzie." Nuala leaned forward, sweet face furrowed. "Can your cousin be made to change his mind, do you think?"

"Oh, Nuala." Lizzie gripped her chipped earthenware mug tightly and willed her lips not to tremble. "I'm afraid not. Even if he hadn't already sold Hollymore to the duke, it would only be a matter of time before he took the next man's gold."

The older woman harrumphed. "I'd like to see him show a shred o' decency just this once."

"Like to show him the business end of a musket, I would," O'Reilly muttered.

Lizzie fully agreed with both. But any time spent thinking of Percy was wasted time. She had something else in mind. "There's nothing to be done for my future here," she said firmly, "but I've had an idea to save Hollymore."

Her staff all leaned forward eagerly. "Well, go on, miss," O'Reilly prompted. "What would that be?"

"We've at least a sennight before Captain Jones arrives, perhaps more. I know we've had quiet Christmases here since Papa died . . ." The first had been spent in mourning, the next two in the sort of penury that precludes all but the most modest of celebration. ". . . but this year can be different."

"A last hurrah in Hollymore?" Kelly inquired bleakly.

"Well, yes, that. But there's more." Lizzie took a deep breath. She didn't want to sound too hopeful. Didn't want to feel too hopeful. "Perhaps, just perhaps if we can show Hollymore at its best . . . Yes, yes, I know," she murmured when four sets of eyebrows lifted. "The best it can be in its present condition. Perhaps then Captain Jones will see how very wonderful a house it is and will persuade the duke to keep it, to restore it rather than raze it. His Grace could use it as a hunting lodge. At least then . . . well, at least then it will still be here, and there might well be places for all of you in it."

"As if we'd take money from them as put you out," O'Reilly snapped. The others nodded.

"I won't have you even considering making any such foolishly noble stand for me," Lizzie said fiercely. "But you can do this: Help me save my house. Here is how I think we should begin . . ."

Later that afternoon, garbed in an old pair of her father's wool trousers and one of his warm coats, Lizzie stood on the sweep of rear lawn that was more crabgrass than anything, surveying the holly maze below that had been planted in honor of her family

name. Dense and glossy green with red berries, the
branches growing thickly from ground to top, the holly
was a cheery sight. The shrubs had been planted
among the maze hedge and, when left untended, made
navigating the maze a prickly business. Needless to
say, they had been left untended.

Lizzie planned to go at them herself with hedge
shears. If she and Kelly put their minds and backs to
it, they could make the maze passable—if not perfect—and supply the house with ample decoration all
in one day. The problem, of course, was which day.
The parlor ceiling wasn't finished, Kelly still hadn't
captured the second owl . . .

She jumped as a hand landed heavily on her shoulder. "Bidding it all a fond farewell?"

She shrugged off the hand and turned to face her
cousin. It was difficult at times to reconcile the character with the appearance. Short, round-faced, with the
blond curls and pink cheeks of a cherub, Percy Fitzhollis—Baron Fitzhollis now—could have modeled for
Raphael, and done service to Lucifer.

He was garbed as always in his idea of London fashion. Today it was an azure jacket over an orange-
spotted waistcoat and white pantaloons. To Lizzie's
eye he looked like a tubby bullfinch. In her mind, she
thought of him as more of a reptile.

"Percy, you are a snake," she said wearily. She
never bothered mincing her words around him, but
neither did she expend more energy than was absolutely necessary.

"No such thing in Ireland," he drawled back as he
sidled in to stand much too close. "Can't say the same
for temptation, though."

Lizzie crossed her arms over her chest. If he were
going to loom and slobber, she wanted at least eight
inches between them. "You sold my house."

"My house, actually. Soon to be the Duke of Llans's house."

"Until he knocks it to the ground," Lizzie said bitterly.

Percy grinned, rosebud-mouthed and forked-tongued. "Plans to build a hunting lodge. Invited me for grouse season already. Splendid fellow, the duke."

"And where on earth did you manage to meet a duke?"

"Didn't, actually. Put an advert in the *Journal*. Apparently Clane saw it and passed it on."

Percy had never met the Earl of Clane, either. Lizzie had. They had danced together at several balls, even had a moonlit walk in Phoenix Park once. Lizzie had liked him, even indulged in a few romantic reveries. But she'd been so young, barely seventeen at the time. Then Clane had gone off to serve in the army, and by the time he had returned, Lizzie's father had died and she had been long gone from Dublin Society events. Clane was married now, she'd heard. He'd probably thought the same of her when he'd seen that Hollymore was for sale.

Lizzie had told herself sternly not to cry. She told herself again. It wasn't working. "Oh, Percy," she snapped, cursing the catch in her voice, "how *could* you?"

Her cousin shrugged. "Why wouldn't I?"

"Perhaps because this land has been in the family for eight *hundred* years? Perhaps because you know how much it means to me?"

She knew that was a mistake the minute she'd said it. But emotion had softened her brain and loosened her tongue.

Percy's eyes sparked. "Isn't too late, y'know, Lizzie."

"And what is that supposed to mean?"

"Haven't signed all the papers. Told you before: have me, have your beloved house."

Yes, he'd told her more than once, usually when he was foxed on second-rate Madeira. Even had Percy not been a fool, not been a reptile, and not always spoken in half-formed sentences—only to be expected, Lizzie thought, for someone with half a brain—she wouldn't have had him. Only now, with Hollymore at stake . . . She shuddered at the thought of seeing Percy's face first thing in the morning and last thing at night.

"Makes perfect sense," he was saying now. "Always did . . ."

Had Lizzie seen it coming, she would have been ready with knees, nails, and teeth. But she only had time to gasp in surprise as Percy grabbed her by the upper arms and thumped her into his orange-spotted chest. Her sharp protest was lost to his soft lips and jabbing tongue.

Her first thought was that she was going to be ill. Her second was that if he didn't release her immediately, she was going to box his ears until they rang like Christmas bells.

"Pardon me."

At the sound of the deep voice, Percy released her so abruptly that she nearly went down onto her bottom. She stumbled back, furiously wiping at her mouth with the back of her hand.

"I say," Percy muttered at the man standing not ten feet away, "ain't sporting, that. Interrupting a fellow when he's at play."

A single black brow winged upward, but all the man said was, "I do not mean to intrude, but no one answered the front door. Perhaps you can tell me where I can find Lord Fitzhollis."

No deferential lackey this, Lizzie thought. From the top of his towering dark head to the soles of his booted feet, he exuded arrogance and command. He wasn't a handsome man; the blue eyes were too cold, the jutting nose and jaw too hard, but he was certainly an impressive figure in his naval uniform coat.

At the moment he had his ice-blue gaze fixed on her.

"Captain Jones, I presume," she addressed him. He continued to stare at her. "Captain Lawrence Jones? Oh, dear."

Everyone present jumped as metal clanged loud and hard against the stone terrace. A piece of the gutter had come loose. It wasn't the first. Lizzie gave the two-foot long section a mournful look. It had shattered the slate tile beneath it.

Captain Jones, when she turned to address him again, was scowling fiercely enough to frighten what stone gargoyles remained on the ramparts. Lizzie sighed. "Forgive me for saying so, sir, but your arrival really is atrociously timed."

2

Captain Lord Rhys Edward-Jones studied the almost startlingly beautiful woman who was wearing breeches and had, until a moment earlier, been in the arms of a fussy little cherub, and wondered why the favors he did for his brother never seemed to involve ordinary specimens of humanity. He sighed.

"I am looking for Lord Fitzhollis."

The cherub gave a regal nod that was diminished somewhat by the ridiculous arrangement of his cravat. "I am Fitzhollis."

"I am—"

"Yes, yes," the lady interrupted, briskly brushing the man's lingering pudgy fingers from her waist, "we know. You are Captain Lawrence Jones, representing the Duke of Llans in his purchase of Hollymore. Mr.

Dunn told me. He also told me you were scheduled to arrive a fortnight from now."

As Rhys watched, a young man with brilliantly red hair and a bulging sack came trotting into view from the house. The sack seemed to be alternately swelling and deflating in his grasp and, if Rhys wasn't mistaken, was emitting an odd, muffled sort of shriek. Neither Fitzhollis nor his companion seemed to notice. Only when the fellow opened the sack and released a large, screeching owl did the lady turn. She gave a cool, satisfied nod, then swung her emerald gaze back to Rhys.

"I am afraid, Captain," she announced, "that we are not quite ready for you."

Before Rhys could reply, or inquire just who she was to be ready or not, the man on the lawn gave a dismayed yelp. As the party on the terrace watched, the owl did a slightly clumsy turn midair and flew back toward the house, where it abruptly vanished from view. Shoulders slumped, the young man tucked the sack under his arm and shuffled back up the lawn.

"Splendid effort, though, Kelly!" the woman called to him. He gave a dispirited wave and disappeared through a stone doorway.

Rhys waited for an explanation. Instead, the cherub shoved an overlarge pinch of snuff up his button nose, sneezed, and demanded, "Do tell me, Captain, how the duke is faring. Well, I trust, marvelous fellow. Anticipating a smashing grouse season."

Rhys was not aware of his brother Timothy ever anticipating anything about grouse. He was, however, well aware of the fact that Fitzhollis's sole dealings with the marvelous Duke of Llans had been through Timothy's able man-of-affairs. Fitzhollis wouldn't have known the duke if the duke had walked over him. Rhys was spared the necessity of reply, however, by a crash that resounded through the open door behind him. It was followed by several smaller crunches and one pained squawk. Human, he thought.

The lady promptly stepped forward. "I daresay you would like a tour of the grounds, Captain Jones."

What he would like was for her to get his name right and offer her own, along with an explanation of sorts. He had no idea who she was; she clearly had some bungled idea of who *he* was. After that, he wanted a bath and meal. The journey from Wales across the Irish Sea had been uneventful but long. The experience of trying to hire a coach and get to County Wexford had been long and extremely trying. In the end, it had involved a crowded public conveyance containing a ripe and motley collection of travelers, an equally uncomfortable ride from Wexford town in a farmer's wagon, and a long walk up Hollymore's sweeping drive. His valise was still at the bottom, by the listing stone gateposts.

Nor had the sight at the end of the long and bumpy drive improved Rhys's mood. Hollymore was, to put it mildly, a crumbling monstrosity of countless different architectural styles and tastes, a squat, sprawling beast of a house. If his brother were wise, he would raze the thing before setting foot on Irish soil and build himself a nice, solid hunting lodge without a headless medieval gargoyle or frill-less Elizabethan frill to be found on it.

"What I would like, madam," he began, and was interrupted by a discreet cough from behind him. "Ah, yes, of course," he muttered. "We mustn't be unmannerly. Allow me to introduce my nephew, Vi—"

"Andrew Jones, at your service." Seventeen-year-old Andrew, otherwise known as Viscount Tallasey, gave him a small jab in the ribs as he pushed past.

The cherub sneezed again and huffed into action.

"Ah, yes. Of course. M'cousin and fiancée, Miss Fitzhollis."

"Oh, Percy," she snapped, "I am not—"

"Of course." A light had gone off in Rhys's head. "The late Lord Fitzhollis's daughter."

"Well, yes," she said with an exasperated sigh, "I am that. Elizabeth. This is my house. But I am not—"

"*My* house," her cousin corrected, winking at the other two gentlemen as he spoke. "Ladies and their notions, you know."

From the mutinous set of Elizabeth's jaw, Rhys decided that statement from her fiancé had not gone over well. He also decided that Timothy's efficient man-of-affairs was not quite as efficient as he seemed. *Aging spinster,* the man's report had read. *Merits little or no attention in the matter.*

If this was anyone's idea of an aging spinster, Rhys was the King of Connaught. He also had a strong suspicion that Elizabeth Fitzhollis would merit at least a little attention. She could not possibly be ignored.

"An honor and a pleasure, Miss Fitzhollis." Andrew, flashing the Edward-Jones smile that made him look exactly like his father and sent most ladies and scullery maids alike into moon-eyed sighing, bent over Elizabeth's hand. She went neither moon-eyed nor breathy. She didn't even smile. Then Andrew announced, "Allow me to say how extraordinary your home is," and suddenly Rhys found his own eyes going a bit crossed.

An irritable-looking Elizabeth Fitzhollis was beautiful. A smiling one was absolutely dazzling. Her cousin, Rhys noted, was nearly slobbering at her side and even his own, ever-poised nephew was goggling slightly.

"Isn't it wonderful?" she breathed, turning that astonishing smile onto the crumbling pile behind them. "There is not a house standing in all the isles to equal it."

There might not be, Rhys agreed silently, making a determined effort to drag his eyes from the lady to the pile of stones behind him. But he'd seen any number of abandoned ruins that were quite on a par with Hollymore.

"So, Miss Fitzhollis," Andrew was asking now, "may I take you up on your offer of a tour?"

"Pushing young pup, ain't he?" the increasingly less cherubic baron demanded.

Andrew's brows went up, but he continued to smile pleasantly at Elizabeth. She, for her part, rolled her eyes. "Oh, Percy. Really. I would be delighted to show you Hollymore, Mr. Jones. And Captain Jones, of course," she added eventually, almost as an afterthought.

This time, the shriek from the house was definitely human, certainly female, and it was followed by a new series of crashes and thumps.

Elizabeth sighed. "Perhaps we ought to start with the grounds."

"Perhaps we ought to set a matter or two straight," Rhys muttered.

He was drowned out by Andrew's, "Splendid!"

And Fitzhollis's dismayed, "But my boots, Lizzie!"

Elizabeth ignored Rhys entirely, but smiled at Andrew as she stalked across the terrace on—Rhys couldn't help but notice, considering her garb—very long, very nicely shaped legs. She stepped over the fallen gutter and pulled the French door closed with a rattling thump. There was paper jammed into several cracked panes.

"Yes, the mud would most certainly ruin the gloss on your boots, Percy," she said matter-of-factly. "I suggest you go home."

"But, I could—"

"You've done more than enough already, thank you. Go home. Come for dinner if you must."

Fitzhollis's mouth pursed in a defiant pout. "Won't have you ordering me about, Lizzie."

"No, of course you won't." She smiled, but it was not even close to the blazing smile that had lit the very air. "I wonder, do you think Aunt Gregoria would care to discuss the state of her sherry reserve?"

Whatever that meant, it had a quick and notable effect on the man. Fitzhollis flushed a bright pink and took himself off so quickly that he nearly left his highly polished, high-heeled boots behind. His fragmented farewells trailed in his wake.

Rhys, watching this display with some amazement, felt a distinct if fleeting surge of pity for Fitzhollis. By all appearances, the pair were a match made somewhat south of heaven. Despite the fact that Elizabeth Fitzhollis was easily the loveliest sight he'd seen in aeons, she seemed a bit scatty. And officious. There was little question of who would be running the household. And judging from what Rhys had seen so far of this household, the lady was not much of a manager.

He ignored the following thought: that there was something under Elizabeth Fitzhollis's surface, something deeper than beauty, that should have been well above the touch of anyone like her cousin.

Rhys thrust away that foolish sentiment and turned his attention back to the matter at hand. "Miss Fitzhollis, I really must inform you—"

"Come along, *Uncle Lawrence*," Andrew interrupted. The little sod was grinning like a fox. "I am all eagerness to see what the duke has done this time. One can always be certain of a surprise or two when he decides to toss his money about."

It was on the tip of Rhys's tongue to reply that it was ultimately part of Andrew's inheritance that Timothy was tossing into this ramshackle heap of stone. Tim had always enjoyed a good jest, and he had passed that unfortunate quirk on to his son. For the first time, Rhys wished this was one of those jests. Pity he knew better. His brother had taken it into his head that he needed an Irish hunting box. Apparently it would be here.

Rhys had willingly enough undertaken the task of overseeing the preparations. Timothy and his wife were visiting friends on some godforsaken little Hebridean island, and Rhys had little to do now that he was in the process of selling out of the navy. His years on the seas had left him wealthy, a bit weary, and heartily sick of salt water. So when his brother had declared the need to visit the Wexford property, Rhys had offered to make the journey. He had sailed from Cork countless times, and had developed an appreciation for Ireland. The landscape, once one got away from the coast, was refreshingly green, the people were pleasant, and the whiskey was exceptional.

He could use a stiff shot now.

What he had on hand was a disapprovingly stiff golden goddess in attire that, against all his good sense and inclination, was making parts of his own anatomy go taut. He tugged his greatcoat closed.

It seemed Andrew's glib comment about tossing money had struck an unpleasant chord. "I hadn't meant to say this quite so soon," Elizabeth was saying crisply, "But since you've caught us unaware, I don't suppose I have a choice." She turned to face Rhys fully, hands on nicely rounded hips. "I don't mean to speak ill of the duke, especially since I do not know him and he *is* your employer, but he is making a terrible mistake with Hollymore."

"Is he?" Rhys replied. Judging from what he'd seen so far, he was inclined to agree. He suspected, however, that he and the lady of the house would have very different opinions as to why.

"I do not blame His Grace. Or I am trying not to. Men of his ilk are seldom bothered to attend the smaller details of business transactions. I suppose it simply did not occur to him to come see Hollymore himself. He really ought to have done so. Seeing the estate would almost certainly have changed his plans."

So far, they were still in agreement.

"Had he seen the house," she went on, "he would not possibly have considered tearing it down."

And there was the divergence. Had Timothy seen the house, he would most certainly have insisted it be razed before allowing his son anywhere near the place.

"A moot point, I am afraid, Miss Fitzhollis," Rhys said blandly.

She gave a vague hum, then asked, "How long do you plan to stay?"

"A fortnight at most." In fact, he thought it would be somewhat less than that. He'd seen just about all he needed to see.

Elizabeth tilted her glossy head. "Forgive my impertinence, sir, but your idea of a fortnight and mine seems to be different."

Rhys bit back his own sarcastic retort. "I assure you, Miss Fitzhollis, that your Mr. Dunn was informed of my anticipated arrival date in the letter that was posted nearly a month ago."

"A month ago?" She sighed. "Ah, well, that would explain that. Mr. Dunn is not as sharp of mind or eye as he once was. Still, Captain, I confess I find it odd that you would arrange to be here over Christmas."

Andrew, who had expressed much the same sentiment more than once, gave a not particularly discreet snort. Rhys shrugged. "It is just a day, Miss Fitzhollis. I assume we will find a Church of Ireland Christmas service just as long and hymn-filled as one at home. Perhaps you will be so kind as to allow us to accompany you."

"You are assuming I am not Catholic, Captain."

"Are you?"

"No, as it happens, I am not. But most of the nearby residents are. And they take the holidays quite seriously. There is a great deal more to the next fortnight than one long and hymn-filled church service."

Andrew snorted again. "Don't expect him to understand, Miss Fitzhollis. My uncle was off practicing military drills when they handed out holiday spirit."

"Watch your tongue, puppy," Rhys muttered resignedly. In a family that possessed an overabundance of every sort of spirit, he stood alone in his preference for contained emotions. And said family delighted in reminding him of that fact at every opportunity.

"No one is immune to an Irish Christmas," Elizabeth announced. Then, with a decisive nod, she gestured toward the muddy expanse before them, broken only by an oddly shaped copse of spiny holly bushes. "Shall we walk?"

She strode off down the rocky slope on her long legs, Andrew grinning at her side. Rhys followed with less cheer than his nephew, but with a far better view of Elizabeth's pert bottom as it flashed in and out of view. The man's wool coat she was wearing looked to have been mended one too many times. The split above the tails appeared destined to stay split.

Cursing under his breath, he dragged his gaze away. Of all the views he should be studying, Elizabeth Fitzhollis's posterior was not among them. With luck, she would complete her tour and take herself off to wherever she was residing and out of his sight. Rhys recalled something about a maiden auntie. He pictured a tidy, rose-covered cottage with a profusion of lace doilies and china shepherdesses. God only knew what sort of havoc Elizabeth would wreak on bric-a-brac with her brisk, arm-swinging movement.

"There," she announced, pointing to a listing stone bench, "is where Jonathan Swift is reputed to have first conceived of *Gulliver's Travels*."

"Attacked by resident leprechauns?" Rhys muttered under his breath.

She heard him. "So he said, apparently," she shot back smartly, "but I expect it was my great-grandfather's whiskey."

Here was the remnant of the moat into which King Henry II had taken an unexpected tumble. "He made a great joke of it," Elizabeth informed them, as if the event had taken place last month, rather than seven centuries earlier, "demanding that a stone tablet be placed to mark the spot of Henry's downfall." She'd then glanced around bemusedly. "I have no idea where that went. The largest piece used to be around here somewhere."

Andrew earned another brilliant smile when he promised to have a look around for it in the coming days. Rhys silently wished him the best of luck. There were enough treacherous looking stones lying about to make one seven-hundred-year-old fragment feel right at home.

Here came the brackish fountain where the pirate Grace O'Malley had sailed a model of her ship and *there* the oak tree under which Wolfe Tone had planned his rebellion. Elizabeth's father, as she explained it, had been instrumental in the strategy, but prevented from participating by her mother, who would not countenance the shedding of any blood, no matter how noble the cause.

A fortunate decision, Rhys thought, as the blood would no doubt have been the baron's.

As they passed Wolfe Tone's oak, Rhys shoved a moss-laden branch from in front of his face, and was promptly forced to scuttle forward in a hurry as the whole thing detached itself from the tree and crashed to the ground. Elizabeth gave him a brief backward glance. "Mind yourself," she murmured, leaving him with the impression that she was scolding him for having attacked the precious tree.

By the time they had done a circuit of the impenetrable maze—Elizabeth had insisted they just have a peek inside the entrance, and Rhys's coat had suffered greatly from the brief experience—of rocky flower gardens and spectacularly muddy ha-ha, the winter light was all but gone and they had met the figurative ghosts of just about every late, illustrious Irish personage.

"The outer grounds will have to wait until tomorrow," Elizabeth announced as she guided them back up the hill, her stride as brisk as when they'd begun. "I shall see to readying a set of rooms for you."

Rhys hoped she would then take herself off and leave them to whatever peace the house offered. "Are you in residence near here, Miss Fitzhollis?"

She stopped and regarded him with obvious surprise. "Not near," she said. "Here."

"You *live* at Hollymore?"

"Of course I do," she said, starting off again. "Where else would I live?"

Where else indeed? Rhys wondered wearily as he pulled a holly spine from his lapel. And vowed to give Timothy's incompetent man-of-affairs a good dressing-down when they got back to Wales.

He had expected a skeleton staff. He most certainly had not expected a lady of the manor, especially not one with an angel face, racehorse legs, and rapier tongue. As far as he was concerned, matters could not get much worse.

Of course he was wrong.

"I think it marvelous," Andrew announced two hours later when they had been settled into their respective motheaten chambers and completed their respective lukewarm baths. "Rather like having a holiday in a moldy old Highland castle."

Rhys, eyeing the sagging tester bed on which he was supposed to sleep later, thought of the ancient Highland castle in which his brother and sister-in-law were having their holiday. He doubted it was half as moldy as this place. Nor could he find anything marvelous about the idea.

Other than the faded bed drapes, which he could only hope did not house any owls or other unwelcome creatures, the room had little decoration. It didn't have much in the way of furniture, either. But there were telltale marks on the floor and walls where various objects had once been. Sold off, he decided, like the contents of so many other estates. All that remained was the bed, a wardrobe that probably would have been sold—or fallen—had it not been firmly attached to the wall, a rickety washstand, and a single painting above the mantel. It depicted the front of the house itself, and was every bit as ugly as the subject.

"God help us," Rhys muttered as he wandered over to study the scraggy white dogs painted into the foreground. It took him a minute to realize they were meant to be sheep.

"Are you still determined to correct them as to our identities?" Andrew asked from across the room. He was testing the back of the behemoth wardrobe for a secret door. He enjoyed such pursuits.

"Why are you so determined that I not?"

Andrew tapped away. "Oh, I don't know. I suppose there's something very pleasant about being plain Andrew Jones for a change. Being Lord Tallasey, heir to the Duke of Llans, does get so heavy sometimes. Don't you ever tire of being the ever-formal, ever-proper Captain Lord Rhys Edward-Jones?"

Rhys grunted. As a matter of fact, he was quite happy being the ever-formal, ever-proper Captain Lord Rhys Edward-Jones.

He leaned in to have a closer look at the painting. Yes, definitely sheep.

"A beloved family heirloom, no doubt," his nephew suggested, joining him in front of the painting. "Stop scowling. It is merely old and lacking in taste."

A bell rang faintly from the depths of the house.

"For our sakes," Rhys growled as he and Andrew headed from the room, "let us hope the same cannot be said of our dinner."

3

Dinner was awful. The leek soup was cold, the roasted chicken singed to crispy. O'Reilly had done his best, Lizzie knew, but the fates had been working against him. The Joneses had not been expected, his rheumatism was giving him the devil of a time, and his help had been slightly incapacitated.

In the absence of holly boughs to decorate the mantels, Meggie and Nuala had rushed out in search of an alernative. The pine and yew they'd gathered were certainly attractive, bringing a lovely green scent into the rooms. But they'd inadvertently brought home an army of tiny spiders as well. Both women had been bitten from wrist to neck, necessitating salves and compresses and, in Meggie's case, a large glass of restorative wine. The poor girl had still looked a fright as she moved wide-eyed and ointment-spotted around the table to remove the plates.

Beyond all that, Percy had returned, and he had brought Aunt Gregoria with him. The two had not even taken their seats in the drawing room before they proceeded to do untold damage to Lizzie's plan.

"We nearly had our necks broken as we were coming up the drive," Gregoria had snapped as she'd stalked into the drawing room, trailing yards of graying crocheted shawl and pinched disapproval. "Disgraceful, the state of it, all hillocks and holes!"

Scarcely had all the introductions been made when the lady continued sourly, "Honestly, Lizzie, your staff is robbing you blind and doing not a jot of the work for which you pay them their exorbitant wages!"

Nuala, to her vast credit, did not pour the lady's sherry over her tight gray topknot. Nor did she so much as blink when Gregoria snapped, "You have barely covered the bottom of the glass, stupid creature! Lizzie might not be aware of her portion going down your throat, but I am on to you!"

Upon arrival, Percy had promptly settled his rotund bottom onto the settee beside Lizzie. "What are we doing in here?" he asked, gesturing around the drawing room with his own glass, and slopping a generous amount of his own sherry onto one of Lizzie's two semi-fashionable white dresses. "Thought you'd closed it up."

She had, the winter before. There was no use, after all, in maintaining rooms that were never used. But shabby state aside, the Grand Drawing Room, with its Chinese silk walls and painted ceiling, was one of Hollymore's gems. In honor of the Joneses, Meggie and Nuala had swept, scrubbed, and dusted, and laid a fire in the pine-festooned hearth. Lizzie tried to be optimistic. No spiders and no chimney fires. She couldn't recall when last there had been a fire in that grate. Certainly not since last autumn when Kelly had opened the flue and nearly been brained by a pair of falling bricks.

"This is a lovely room," young Andrew announced sincerely.

"What is that noise?" his uncle demanded.

Lizzie listened. All she could hear was Kelly whistling outside the window. "That," she replied tightly, "is the 'Wexford Carol.' It is one of Ireland's most famous Christmas tunes."

Captain Jones looked down his long nose. His nephew chuckled. "Christmas, Uncle Lawrence. You know, the season to be jolly. A very pretty tune indeed," he said to Lizzie.

What would have been her warm reply was forestalled by Gregoria, demanding, "What wine are we to have with dinner, girl?"

"A nice Burgundy from Lambe's," Lizzie answered. She'd sent Kelly quietly haring into town with a few precious shillings they could scarce afford to spend on something so frivolous as wine. But the Joneses needed to be impressed.

Gregoria snorted. "Washed up on the beach, no doubt, and sold at a tidy price by that reprobate of a wine merchant. Nasty, watery stuff, Burgundy," she remarked to Captain Jones. "Never take it myself, if I can possibly help it." Before the Captain could respond, Gregoria turned on Lizzie again. "Your father had some very nice claret put by. I cannot imagine why you would not be serving that to your guests. Burgundy," she huffed. "An insult, I say."

The truth of the matter was that the very last of the late baron's reserve—which really had been no more than several dozen bottles rendered unsalable by the loss of all means of identifying their type or vintage— had been lost three weeks earlier when the ceiling of the wine cellar had collapsed. Lizzie had no intention of revealing that in front of the Joneses.

Percy did it for her. "Gone under a pile of rubble,"

he sighed. "Whole bloody ceiling came tumbling down on m'head. Could've done me serious ill."

Unlikely, Lizzie thought. Her cousin's head was hard as marble and just as dense.

And so it had gone on, Gregoria and Percy doing their best, intentional or not, to reveal the state of all but Lizzie's undergarments. Captain and young Mr. Jones had sat politely through it all. Even had he been able to get a word in, Captain Jones seemed disinclined to chat. His nephew had made a few charming efforts to engage Lizzie in stories of Hollymore's less-damaged days. Percy or Gregoria had been there each time to spoil the moment. So the story of the Charles I windows, the mahogany paneling, the Parma marble had gone untold. Instead, the Joneses heard about Percy's unfortunate encounter with a falling window-sill and the time a trio of mice had scuttled from behind the dining room wall and across Gregoria's feet.

Lizzie had resorted to a second sherry. And she loathed sherry. She might have had a third had Gregoria not effectively drained the bottle.

The meal itself had been worse.

The picture of the polite gentleman, Captain Jones had waited, stiff and expressionless while the ladies had taken their seats around the table. Lizzie felt a surge of pride at the sight: several chairs had been scavenged from around the house to make five, the remnants of her mother's china and Kerry lace table-cloth had been laid—with various candlesticks and dishes covering the holes. There were tapers in all the remaining wall sconces and among the pine and yew boughs.

It was a lovely, cheery scene. Until Captain Jones sat down.

His chair collapsed under him with the speed of a blink. There was a crack, a thump, and there he was, seated perfectly upright against the intact chair back, his own legs straight out in front of him and the four chair legs sticking out from beneath him like the limbs of one of Meggie's spiders.

He didn't say a word, merely sat for a long moment, staring stonily in front of him. Then, slowly, he gathered in his long legs and started to lever himself off the floor. At the sound of the crash, Kelly had rushed into the room. He hurried forward to help, and there was a tense minute as he appeared to wrestle with the captain. Then the wooden splat broke away with a crunch, and Captain Jones was flat on his back.

"Thank you," he muttered upward to the hovering Kelly, sharply waving away the younger man's extended hand, "but I believe it will be best if I manage this myself."

He rose as elegantly as the situation allowed. Kelly, red-faced and wild-haired, rushed off to find another chair. When it arrived, Captain Jones lowered himself rather gingerly. Everyone present held their breath while this chair creaked, shifted, but remained intact. Everyone, that is, except Andrew, who was making faint gasping noises. A quick glimpse in his direction told Lizzie he was making a valiant effort not to laugh. For her own part, she was ready to cry.

"Captain," she managed, voice tight, "I am so very—"

"Miss Fitzhollis." He met her gaze with hard eyes. "Do not mention it."

Just then, Meggie and Nuala bustled in with the cold soup. Percy and Gregoria started flapping their tongues again. Lizzie felt her heart sinking inch by desolate inch.

It didn't take long for both Joneses to give up on their meal, the captain with a deepening scowl and his nephew with an apologetic smile in Lizzie's direction.

Then, charming creature that he was, he tried again to engage her in conversation.

"I have been admiring the artwork, Miss Fitzhollis."

Lizzie didn't need to look at the pair of hunting scenes on the wall. Both were atrocious. She didn't need to answer, either.

"My brother's work," Gregoria announced. "It's all over the house."

"Ah," Mr. Jones said. "A family tribute."

Percy let out a braying laugh. "Not half. Stuff ain't good for anything but covering the holes in the walls. Good stuff's all been sold."

Lizzie's heart took another sad little dip.

"I . . . er . . . I see." Poor Andrew really was doing his best, she knew. What could he possibly say? He cleared his throat and turned to Gregoria, who was tapping an irritable finger against her empty glass. "I understand Miss Fitzhollis will soon be residing under your roof, madam. That must be a comfort to you."

Gregoria snorted. "As if she'll be with me for any length of time. No, no, off she'll go to take her place in Percy's home, leaving me all alone."

Lizzie closed her eyes for a weary moment. Gregoria didn't want her, never had. Nor was she at all in favor of Percy throwing himself away on his cousin. The splendid boy, she'd declared more than once, could do far better. Meaning, of course, that he ought to be wedding a quiet, malleable heiress. But then, his choosing Lizzie would save him having to make any settlements of his own, so Gregoria had grumblingly resigned herself to the match. Which, of course, was not likely to happen if Lizzie had anything to say about it. If he set his feeble mind to it and was very, very fortunate, Percy might be able to find a woman willing to trade her money for his title. Heaven help her.

"When is the happy event to take place?" Andrew inquired politely.

"Next spring," Percy replied, puffing out his new waistcoat, this one a striped yellow and turquoise.

When swine fly, Lizzie thought. "I do not—"

"Boy!" Gregoria bellowed. She'd never bothered to learn Kelly's name.

He had been standing at rigid attention near the door, no doubt waiting to catch the captain should the second chair go the way of the first. He stepped forward. "Yes, ma'am?"

"My glass is empty."

"Yes, ma'am."

Gregoria's ever-pinched face grew more so. "Well, bring me more wine!"

Kelly drew himself up regally. "There isn't more, ma'am."

Gregoria stared him down fishily, but Kelly stood firm. "Hmph." She slapped her napkin onto the table. "Thieves *and* liars, Lizzie. You are a stupid, stupid girl."

And with that, the meal was over.

Now, with her relatives long gone and her guests abed, Lizzie quietly let herself out the back of the house and onto the terrace. She donned yet another of her father's worn coats over her dress and pulled it closely around her as she stepped into the cold Wexford night. In the dark, the maze didn't look quite as overgrown, and it was almost possible to believe that the fountain statue still possessed its head. Almost.

Lizzie crossed the terrace to sit on a cracked step. "Oh, Papa," she whispered, rubbing her cheek against the soft wool of the coat's collar. "I am afraid this is all going very, very badly." Then, unable to stave off the tears any longer, she rested her head on her arms and wept.

She did not see the male figure looking down from the empty window frame above.

4

Rhys rose from his slanting and lumpy bed the following morning to find first a cold hearth and thin film of ice on the wash water and later, evidence that some rodent had temporarily nested in one of his stockings. There, too, was a vivid and itchy path of red bumps across his torso where he'd been bitten by some small insect. He added several more red marks to his own face shaving with the icy water.

By the time he descended the creaking staircase, he was in a grim mood, and it was not yet eight o'clock. He assumed his nephew and hostess would still be abed. With any luck, he would be able to order something palatable to eat. After that, he intended to do a quick tour of the house on his own. If Elizabeth insisted on accompanying him around the grounds, so be it. But he didn't need her pointing out each notable nook and cranny inside this decaying monstrosity. Hollymore's days were numbered. Rhys was not going to let Elizabeth make him feel guilty for that. He made a point of never doing anything for which he might later feel guilty. And as he'd had nothing whatsoever to do with either the house's decline or sale, he could do without its mistress's sad little recriminations, silent though they might be.

He would find the entire task considerably more comfortable if he didn't have to look into that lovely, heartbreaking Madonna's face at every turn. Damned if he knew where his well-honed detachment had gone. Elizabeth Fitzhollis was hardly the first beautiful woman he had disappointed in one way or another.

And this was just a house. It wasn't as if he had en-gaged her heart. He didn't owe her anything save some courtesy. There wasn't a reason on earth for the strange, restive feeling in his gut.

He made his grim way to the dining room to find it empty. All the pieces of the broken chair had been cleared away, but Rhys could still hear the crunch and crack echoing around the gloomy space. His jaw tightened. No doubt Andrew would gleefully report the event to the family, who would get endless joy from making Rhys relive it. He would have to remember to sit down carefully for a while. He wouldn't be surprised if his brother had a few chairs altered to collapse.

After an irritable glance at the empty sideboard, he decided he would have to go in search of one of the house's bumbling servants if he wanted to eat. Recall-ing the meal of the previous evening, he decided he didn't especially *want* to eat, but probably needed to. Hoping the cook couldn't do anything too terrible to several eggs and some toasted bread, he returned to the hall.

The squat little butler with a face like a walnut and an impressive scowl was standing just outside the door. "Can I be of help to you, sir?" he fairly grunted.

"I would like some breakfast, as a matter of fact."

The fellow darted a quick glance at a nearby stand-ing clock. It read, Rhys noted, ten past eleven. Judging from the still pendulum and cracked case, it might well have ticked its last on the night of seventeen De-cember, 1750. The message, however was clear. He was being chastised for rising so early.

"This way." Without waiting to see if Rhys fol-lowed, the man stomped off.

Rhys followed. After several halls and turns, the butler tugged several times at a small paneled door.

It creaked outward. Rhys gave a sardonic glance at the little sprig of mistletoe suspended from the lintel. He ducked under it—and felt his jaw going slack in surprise.

The little room was a solarium of sorts. The entire rear wall and part of the ceiling were glass. Cracked glass, certainly, and a few panes seemed to be covered with oilskin, but everything was sparklingly clean and bright. There were vases of winter foliage dotted about, the walls were a sunny yellow with a pattern of plaster lilies, and the graceful marble fireplace was festooned with red ribbon and ivy. The sideboard was loaded with shiny silver serving dishes that were dented and mismatched. And in the midst of it all sat Elizabeth.

She was dressed in a forest-green wool dress, some years out of fashion and visibly mended in spots, but striking nonetheless. The light coming through the windows brought a glow to her fair skin, and picked out fiery lights in her neatly coiled golden hair through which she had whimsically threaded a red ribbon. Titania, Rhys thought, momentarily sorry that he knew the names of no winter holiday faeries, and something warm and wholly unfamiliar wreathed through his chest.

Dear God, she was lovely.

Her glorious smile dimmed somewhat at the sight of him, going cool and polite. "Good morning, Captain."

"Uncle Lawrence!"

Rhys glanced in disbelief at Andrew, very awake, fully dressed, and lounging in his seat across the table. Remnants of breakfast littered his plate.

"Andrew," Rhys said dryly. "You're up a bit early." A good three hours early, as a matter of fact.

"What, sleep through a morning such as this?" His nephew quirked one brow until it nearly met his shock of earth-brown hair. "Perish the thought. Miss Fitzhollis and I were just about to go out for a stroll. Now you can join us."

"Perhaps the captain would like to eat," Elizabeth suggested. "Help yourself, sir. You will find what you need on the sideboard."

Minutes later, he was settled at the table with a surprisingly appetizing breakfast in front of him, and a cup of marvelously strong coffee in hand. "It appears I am the late riser."

Elizabeth shrugged. "I expect you are accustomed to Town hours."

He wasn't, actually, not of late, but neither was he accustomed to farm hours. "You are not, I see."

"I prefer the morning light," she replied, then blinked as Andrew pushed himself away from the table.

"Back in a tick," the young man said cheerfully. "Then we will go at your convenience, Miss Fitzhollis. Do try the black pudding, Uncle."

He strode from the room, closing the door with a solid thunk behind him. Rhys suddenly found himself alone with Elizabeth in a room that, surprisingly charming as it was, suddenly seemed far too small.

She broke the long silence. "Do you care for black pudding, Captain?"

He did not, but debated fetching some to be polite. He quickly decided against it. There were limits to courtesy. "Perhaps later," he demurred.

Elizabeth delicately wiped her mouth, then set her napkin aside. She propped her elbow on the table and rested her chin in her palm. Her eyes, Rhys noticed, were holly green this morning, and fixed intently on his slightly achy, certainly itchy person. He shifted in his seat.

"Are you married, Captain Jones?"

He blinked at the unexpected question. It was one he loathed as it was usually asked by mothers with marriageable daughters lurking nearby. But as far as he knew, no one lurked, and the question was being asked by a woman with her own nuptials looming.

"No. I am not."

"Why?"

This startled him even more. Women never asked that bit. It just wasn't . . . proper? It was certainly personal. He gave the terse, stock answer. "I have been at sea for the better part of ten years."

"Mmm." She hummed thoughtfully. "That sounds rather lonely."

"Hardly" was his dry retort. "It tended to be among several hundred other men in very cramped quarters."

"Yes, I know that. I meant that being away from home, away from the people who care for you would be lonely."

It had been expected. Rhys shrugged. "Home was always where I left it. Whenever I was on land, it was waiting for me, the same brick and stone, filled with the same faces."

"That," Elizabeth murmured, "is what matters." She shook her head with a small sigh, pulled a holly sprig from a small vase, and played with it absently. "I suppose I ought to apologize, Captain. You certainly did not see the best of Hollymore, or of me yesterday."

"You were not expecting me," he said graciously.

"I was wishing you to Hades, actually."

So very blunt. And so very, very pretty. For some odd reason, Rhys smiled. "You would be far from the first."

"Be that as it may, I was discourteous. You see, Captain Jones, this is my home—"

"Miss Fitzhollis, I . . ."

She waved her free hand. "Yes, yes, Hollymore is Percy's to sell. An unfortunate quirk in the entail. The property could only go to the male heir, but there was nothing to make him keep it."

"Most inconvenient." He hadn't meant to sound glib.

"Indeed." Elizabeth lifted a bronze brow. "Most inconvenient. My father tried to have the matter altered to no avail." She shrugged. "The first Baron Fitzhollis had eight sons, so he saw no need to make any provisions for female inheritance of property. But that is neither here nor there now. Percy had a right to sell Hollymore, and he exercised that right. What I need to say is that it broke my heart."

Curious behavior for a besotted finacée. But then, Rhys mused, the man would not want to be second in his wife's affections to a pile of stone. There was also the strong possibility that the new Baron Fitzhollis simply did not have the funds for the upkeep.

"I am sorry for that, Miss Fitzhollis." He hadn't meant that to sound glib, either. Especially not when he had seen her crying on the terrace the night before. He hadn't been able to hear, but he hadn't needed to hear to know the sobs were wrenching ones. Heartbroken ones. "I am sorry."

"You don't need to be." Elizabeth removed her face from her hand and sat up very straight. "But there is something I would like from you."

"And that would be?"

"Give Hollymore a chance."

"How?"

"Get to know it. Allow me to show you its great value. Then tell the duke that he mustn't tear it down."

Rhys paused with his coffee cup halfway to his mouth. "Miss Fitzhollis. I simply cannot—"

"Try." Elizabeth faced him squarely, chin up. "The first stone was laid at Hollymore seven hundred and eighty-six years ago. That is a tremendous amount of history to eradicate for little more than sport."

They sat in silence for a long minute. Then Rhys set his cup down. "I don't think I can help you, Miss Fitzhollis. But"—he raised a hand when she started to speak—"I will keep what you've said in mind."

She nodded. "I know that is all I can ask, Captain." Then, rising to her feet, she announced, "I'll see if Kelly can prepare the cart. We'll be able to cover more ground that way."

Rhys hastily set his cup down and rose. There was no servant to open the door for her, so he reached smoothly around her to do so. As his hand closed around the doorknob, his arm brushed warmly against hers. He could feel the soft friction of wool against wool, could smell the clean, honey scent of her hair. "Elizabeth."

"Yes?"

He hadn't realized he'd spoken aloud. And to be so forward as to speak her name . . . She didn't seem to mind, didn't even appear to have noticed. Rhys shook his head and tried to think of something more appropriate to say. She waited, a slender golden beam in the sunny room.

"For what its worth," he said gruffly, "this is a lovely room."

"Yes" was her simple reply. "It is."

Rhys turned the knob to open the door. It didn't budge. He pushed. The door still remained resolutely closed.

"It sticks." Elizabeth sighed. "Some of the doors have a tendency to stick . . . every once in a while.

Rhys raised a brow and tried again. When nothing happened, he stepped back and, putting his weight behind it, thumped his shoulder firmly against the paneling. The door groaned, but opened.

"Thank you." Elizabeth stepped past him into the hall. "I—"

The plaster bouquet that decorated the space above the door frame missed Rhys's head by an inch. It fell heavily past his nose and shattered against the floor. He lifted his eyes from his plaster-dusted ankles to Elizabeth. She was staring at him wide-eyed. For a long moment, neither said anything.

Then she sighed, a small, desolate sound. "Oh, dear."

"Yes," Rhys said tersely, pulling the sprig of mistletoe from where it had landed on his shoulder. Mistletoe. *Ridiculous,* but . . . He jerked his gaze away from Elizabeth's soft, mobile mouth, and tossed the sprig away. Then he stepped back into the room.

As he walked stiffly back to the table, he heard her footsteps receding down the hall. "Good God," he muttered, and poured himself more coffee.

Andrew bounded back into the room several minutes later. "Well?" he demanded, dropping solidly into a chair. It, of course, stood firm.

"Well, what?"

"Well, did you kiss her?"

Rhys frowned and shifted in his seat. "That is a ridiculous question."

Andrew looked at the doorway, took in the sight of the fallen plaster ornament and discarded mistletoe. "*Christmas,* Uncle," he sighed. "*Carpe diem* and all that. Oh, well. Did you and Elizabeth at least have a nice chat?"

"*Miss Fitzhollis,*" Rhys said pointedly, "and I . . ." He paused. "What *is* that noise?"

Andrew listened. "Kelly," he said, "singing outside the window. I believe Elizabeth called it the 'Wexford

Carol.' Pretty. I'm certain Kelly would gladly teach it to us."

"God forbid."

Andrew shrugged. "*Christmas*, Uncle. So, what did you and Elizabeth discuss?"

"Nosy brat," Rhys muttered with more affection than rancor. "As it happens, our lovely hostess and I don't have a great deal to say to each other."

"Mmm. She wants to save her house and you want to reduce it to rubble."

Rhys glanced at the shattered flowers near the door. "I don't *want* . . . Oh, for pity's sake. It hardly needs any help in that quarter. And lest you forget, puppy, it is your dear father who wants to raze this behemoth. Even if I cared, it is not my decision."

Andrew appeared to ponder this for a moment. When he opened his mouth, Rhys expected an argument. Instead, his nephew demanded, "Do you know what time Elizabeth gets up in the morning?"

"That is hardly my concern."

"Five o'clock. Do you know what she does at five o'clock in the morning?"

"Of course I don't. Andrew—"

"She does a candlelight tour of the house to see what has broken, disintegrated, or fallen during the night. After that, she fixes what she can. It rained last night."

"And?"

"And this morning when it was barely light she was on the *roof*, Uncle Rhys, trying to nail down loose shingles. After that, she cleaned out the gutters. And yesterday morning, before her solicitor arrived to tell her that her house had been sold, she was trying to dig out a blocked drainage ditch."

Rhys slowly digested this information and found himself growing angry. The image of Elizabeth shoveling out a drainage ditch sent his hackles up. He couldn't even begin to contemplate her clambering around three stories above the hard earth. "What are they thinking," he growled, "to let her do such things?"

"Not *let* her?" Andrew gave a short laugh. "From what I understand, she threatens to sack the lot of her staff—all four persons who are left, that is—every time one of them tries to stop her. And that is nearly every day."

"I suppose you're going to tell me that she doesn't pay them quite enough to climb the roof themselves."

Andrew snorted. "She can't pay them at all, hasn't been able to in more than half a year. They love her," he added quietly. "She loves them. And she loves this place. Desperately."

"How did you learn all this?" Rhys demanded. "Did she pour it out along with the coffee this morning?"

Andrew's handsome face hardened uncustomarily. "You know, Uncle Rhys, sometimes you are hard as nails in a frozen pail."

"I refuse to take that as an insult. And a bit of respect wouldn't be amiss, puppy."

"I respect you, Uncle. I simply do not always understand you."

"You are your father's son," Rhys muttered.

"So I am." Andrew tapped long fingers against the tablecloth. "As it happens, Elizabeth talked about the building of Hollymore. She didn't say a word about how she spends nearly twenty hours of every day trying to keep it from tumbling down. No, I heard the story from O'Reilly."

"Who?"

"The butler—and cook and window fixer. Joseph O'Reilly. I've just cornered him in the hallway. Surly fellow until you get to know him; he's really quite charming. Poor man suffers terribly from rheumatism. Ghastly this time of year. And Kelly says—"

"Who?"

"Kelly. Corcoran. The footman, groom, and gardener. And owl trapper this week, as it happens. Elizabeth would never have told me any of this. So they did."

Rhys closed his eyes wearily and leaned back in his chair. A creak made him think better of it, and he lowered the chair legs carefully to the floor. His nephew always got to know people—the names of spouses and children and family dogs. Rhys barely knew the Christian name of his butler. He had no idea if the man had children or a dog.

"What is it you want me to do, Andrew?"

Andrew opened his mouth, then closed it again. After a moment he announced, "Christmas is next week. Bad enough that we're here at all, but far worse the reasons. Can we simply not spoil the holidays for Elizabeth and her household?"

Rhys knew he'd done that already, just by arriving. And he could hardly be expected to traipse around decking the halls and wassailing, or whatever it was these people did at Christmas.

Mistletoe. *Ridiculous.*

"Andrew . . ."

"Please, Uncle Rhys."

Rhys reached for his now-cold coffee. "I will not sing," he muttered.

"Fair enough," his nephew shot back, and began whistling as he checked the sideboard for hidden drawers.

5

Lizzie cleared the top of the desk with a dejected sweep of her arm. The sheaf of bills thudded heavily into the waiting drawer, which she shoved closed. It hardly mattered anymore. In the six days Captain Jones had been in residence, he had not shown so much as a smidgen of interest in saving Hollymore. He had strode about the house and grounds on his long legs, militarily stiff and forceful, taking notes and occasionally muttering to himself or his nephew.

He had been polite. Too polite, really. Lizzie had found conversing with him rather like talking to a very well-trained parrot. He fixed her with his cool blue gaze, tilted his head as she spoke, and repeated back the occasional phrase. He had not appeared in the least impressed by the Charles windows or the Boyne paneling. Lizzie's spirits had lifted somewhat when he'd stood thoughtfully in front of the green marble fireplace in the Great Hall. Massive and ancient, it had the family symbol: the holly bough, carved into its surface. Now, in honor of Christmas, the top was festooned with entwined holly and ivy. It was a beautiful piece, saved from sale by the simple fact that removing it would have been impossible without destroying the entire hearth and chimney.

Captain Jones had soon dashed Lizzie's hopes by announcing, "Perhaps my brother will want this salvaged for the new lodge."

Small blessings, she tried to convince herself. At least the marble wouldn't be reduced to rubble with the stone surrounding it.

She'd caught the captain watching her often, sometimes with surprisingly—and, she had to admit, appealingly—softer eyes. Each time, he had glanced quickly away, and for that Lizzie was grateful. She couldn't have borne seeing the pity she knew was there. Captain Jones was a hard man, but not, she'd come to believe, a wholly unfeeling one. There was certainly an abundance of affection for his nephew in those ice-blue eyes. He might try to cloak it, just as Lizzie did her anguish over her home, but as she saw the flashes of emotion in him, she expected she wasn't any better at hiding hers.

She didn't want his pitying glances. She didn't really want him looking at her at all. It made her feel skittish and slightly warm and came with the inexplicable and absurd urge to check her reflection in the nearest tarnished mirror.

Lizzie glanced up now as the bells from the local church sounded faintly in the distance. It was noon on Christmas Eve. No more work would be done outside today in the county. Inside, even here at Hollymore, kitchens would be filled with the smells of the holiday, and the last of the decorations would be laid.

Her hopes for her house were all but dashed. It had been the hardest admission she'd ever had to make, but she had been forced to silently acknowledge that beneath the greenery and candles, behind the red of holly berries and scent of cloves, Hollymore was still a slowly crumbling pile of stone, beloved as each stone might be.

She had one last hope. It wasn't a great one, but it was all she had.

After that . . . The day after Christmas was St. Stephen's Day. She would hand over the house to Captain Jones and, while the festivities of the day went on through Wexford County, she would slip quietly into her place in Gregoria's house. No fuss, no dramatic farewells. She would just as quietly start perusing the Dublin newspapers she would borrow from the Reverend Mr. Clark—Gregoria refused to pay so much as a penny for something so frivolous as the printed word—and if she were very lucky, would find a post as a companion or governess by the new year.

"Well," she said aloud, standing and patting Uncle Clarence's bronze hedgehog on its misshapen head, "enough of that."

Her staff would see to most of the traditional Christmas Eve activities, but there was one she insisted on doing herself. Propped just outside the French doors was a stack of small holly and yew wreaths, twenty-six of them to be exact, strung together with twine. She gathered them up, ignoring the prick of holly spines through her worn wool coat, and set off through the gardens. The little family chapel hadn't been used in decades, since its roof had collapsed, but the ground was still consecrated, still the resting place of departed Fitzhollises.

Lizzie placed the first wreath on the grave of the first Baron Fitzhollis. The marker had long since been lost to the earth, but each generation had taught the next where the right spot was. Lizzie's father had brought her, year after year on Christmas Eve, to lay the wreath. Now she wondered who would take on the hallowed task. She couldn't bear to think that the precious Christmas tradition would be lost. Perhaps she could tell Andrew. Or Captain Jones. Strange as it was, she had a feeling that he would understand.

No, she thought. He might understand, but there was no more reason for him to care about her long-gone Fitzhollis ancestors than for their house.

"I'm sorry, my lord," she whispered to the first Baron's headstone. "I . . . I tried."

The next twenty-two wreaths went carefully, reverently one by one onto the graves of the Fitzhollis men who had died at the Battle of the Boyne. "I'm sorry," she offered to each. And, as she went, found a precious and growing comfort in the task and in the quiet around her.

Of the last three wreaths, the first went to her great-uncle Clarence. She didn't apologize to him. He'd been a jolly little man who'd lived for his art, and for the next day of eating, drinking, and being merry. "Happy Christmas, Uncle," Lizzie offered to the stone marker he had carved himself. It depicted him as a sort of cheery Irish Bacchus, wearing a holly laurel and holding a chisel, a paintbrush, and a bottle of wine. *"Sláinte."* She had surreptitiously saved a little vial of claret from the previous night's dinner, and tipped its contents now onto the earth at the base of the stone.

The second wreath was for her mother. And the last, the fourth she had placed on its spot, was for her father. She sank down beside it, not caring about the cold or damp and pulled her legs up to her chest, wrapping her arms tightly around them.

"I've done nearly all I can, Papa," she told him. "I wish I could have done more or better—but that's neither here nor there now. I love Hollymore with all my heart, but then, I loved you, too, and I've managed to carry on without you, hard as it has been at times."

She rested her chin on her knees. "I'm thinking I'll go to Dublin, if I can find a post. Or England, perhaps. Yes, yes, I know what you think of England, but I've never been out of Ireland and I should like to see London. And you never know. Perhaps I will find a family with a well-stocked library and constant fires in the hearths." She smiled as a brisk breeze lifted the curls around her face. "Fair enough. I don't mind a bit of cold. But I cannot stay with Gregoria. You wouldn't want me to."

She fell silent for a long moment, listened to the wind rattling in the trees and whispering through the cracks and crevices of the fallen chapel. "It isn't much, Papa," she continued softly, "but I will say a prayer, make a wish tonight. I've never wished for something so big as a house before. It was always for candy on Christmas, or new puppies in the stable. I suppose I was afraid of being disappointed if I asked for something larger." She recalled the mountains of sweets she and her father had shared every Christmas, gorging themselves until they were both ill. "Oh, Papa. Well, they say no wish made on Christmas Eve in Ireland goes unanswered."

She patted the hard earth. "There's never any harm in trying. You taught me that."

A crunch from behind her made her start. She turned to find Captain Jones not twenty feet away and wondered if he'd heard her conversing with her father. Not that it would matter if he had, she supposed. He was the one who was intruding.

He seemed to realize that. He cleared his throat. "I am sorry. I am interrupting a private moment."

Elizabeth shrugged. "I was nearly done." She patted the earth again, and made sure the wreath was centered. "Happy Christmas, Papa," she murmured. "I love you."

Then she rose to her feet and brushed some lingering dirt from her heavy skirts. "Can I help you, Captain?"

He was looking, she noted, rather less starched than he had during his first several days at Hollymore. Living without a valet, she assumed. Much to his credit and amid much grumbling, O'Reilly had surpassed himself in the kitchen, but had adamantly drawn the line at acting as manservant to the guests. "I'll feed him," he'd muttered of the captain, "but damned if I'll put my hands on his things. Let him wear dirty drawers. It'll serve him right enough."

Lizzie had no idea about the state of Captain Jones's drawers, but the rest of him had become appealingly rumpled of late. His cravats had wilted, softening the line of that formidable jaw, and his buttons and boots had lost their sharp, almost painful gleam.

It was clear he'd been out walking in the cold. His midnight hair was wind-tousled, his skin given a virile glow. He might not be a handsome man, but Lizzie, try as she might, couldn't help appreciating the sight of him. She busied herself rewinding her father's fraying old muffler about her neck.

"I have been having a last stroll around the grounds," Captain Jones remarked. "Andrew and I will be leaving on Monday."

The faint flare of disappointment startled her. She decided she would miss young Mr. Jones's genial presence. It had been so long since there had been infectious cheer in the house. She certainly would not miss his uncle's stern, stolid presence. Of course she wouldn't.

"You'll be leaving on St. Stephen's Day," she said.

"Is that significant?"

"The day," she replied. "Not your leaving. It commemorates the day that a wren betrayed St. Stephen to his enemies by singing loudly in the bush behind which he was hiding."

Rhys raised a brow. "Interesting event to celebrate."

Elizabeth tucked the last errant strand of wool into her collar. It should be ermine, he found himself thinking, or the finest, softest kasimir. Not that the dun-colored wool detracted in the least from her beauty. She was glorious, shining gilt and ivory in the cold winter air.

"It is a day for song and mummery," she replied. "Boys dress up in costume and traipse through the villages, collecting money and gaming. I thought Andrew might enjoy it."

"Yes," Rhys said automatically, "he probably would. But we'll be on our way back to Wales."

"Mmm. Pity." She glanced around. "Where is Andrew?"

Rhys knew she wouldn't ask the same question should Andrew be present and he himself nowhere to be seen. He promptly quashed the twinge of regret. "He is in the house somewhere, tapping and prying at the paneling, looking for hidden passages. Foolish boy."

"Oh, not at all."

"Ah. Should I take it you have been encouraging him in this endeavor?"

Elizabeth smiled. "I haven't actually, but only because I wasn't aware he was searching. I hope he finds something."

"Do you expect him to?"

"Well, I have been searching all my life and have found nothing more exciting than a secret drawer in my father's desk." She smiled again. "It was full of spare quills, or rather, the remains of them. Papa and I decided the drawer had last been used by Great-Grandfather Seymour. He hoarded everything except gold, more's the pity. When he died, my grandfather found three hundred forks stashed away in various parts of the house. Heaven only knew what sort of entertaining my great-grandfather was planning on doing . . . Anyway, Andrew ought to find what he's searching for if he tries hard enough. Hollymore is like that."

Apparently it occurred to her that she'd belatedly hit upon one more of Hollymore's charms: its mysteries. She launched into, "There are priest holes from the fifteenth century. And certainly some passageways

used by various Fitzhollises in smuggling activities. I'm
certain if Andrew explored that part of the old dungeon that hasn't caved in, he might find an oubliette
or two . . ." She broke off at the sight of Rhys's scowl.
"Oh. Oh, dear. I do not mean to say he is likely to
fall *into* an oubliette . . ." She gave up. "I believe I
will return to the house. O'Reilly will be needing help
in the kitchen."

"Allow me to escort you."

He offered his arm. She took it—with some reluctance, he thought, but she took it. He could see a hole
in the thumb of one woolen glove, and he found the
sight oddly charming, even as he found himself cursing
the wastrel men of her family for allowing such a prize
to be reduced to wearing much-mended clothes and
holey gloves.

As they started back to the house, he pondered the
scene upon which he had clumsily intruded. The sight
had first stopped him in his brisk tracks, then had had
him literally creeping closer. He didn't think he had
ever actually crept before. But she had been so beautiful, heartbreakingly so, first settling the wreaths carefully on the graves with a quiet word or two, then,
seated like a child on the cold earth, legs tucked up,
conversing with a headstone and little green twist of
holly and yew. He hadn't meant to eavesdrop. He
wished he hadn't.

It isn't much, Papa, but I will say a prayer, make a
wish tonight. I've never wished for something so big as
a house before. It was always for candy on Christmas,
or new puppies in the stable. I suppose I was afraid of
being disappointed . . .

"What are you going to wish for?" he asked, and
was startled by his own question. Embarrassed, too,
that he had given himself away.

Elizabeth, however, glanced up and gave him one

of her stunning if fleeting smiles. "You overheard me talking to my father," she remarked, seemingly not angry in the least.

"I didn't mean to eavesdrop, Miss Fitzhollis. I certainly—"

"Elizabeth."

"I beg your pardon?"

She stopped beside a particularly ugly little statue of a cherub, pulled her hand from his arm, and turned to face him fully. "It is Christmas Eve. I think such formality seems wrong somehow, when we should be thinking of peace and goodwill, and can be suspended for two days. Don't you?"

She rubbed a bit of grime from the cherub's head with her sleeve. Then she removed a cluster of holly berries from her pocket and deftly arranged them on the stone curls. That done, she looked expectantly back to Rhys. He fought the urge to rub a faint muddy smudge from her cheek.

"Well?" she demanded pleasantly.

He'd never spent much time contemplating peace on earth and goodwill to men. After all, he'd been a naval officer at war for so many years. "That is an appalling cherub."

"Isn't he?" she answered, fondly patting the thing's fat cheek. "My uncle Clarence's work."

"Ah. I should have known." Then, without thinking, he said, "Rhys."

Her smooth brow furrowed. "I beg your pardon?"

He was not going to have *Lawrence* falling from those inviting lips, not if Andrew and St. Stephen and all the heavenly hosts demanded it. Not when he could hear her saying his proper name. "If I am to call you Elizabeth, you will call me Rhys."

"Rhys." She pondered that quite seriously for a moment, then laughed briefly, a wonderful, silvery sound.

"It suits you. Far better than Lawrence, if I may say so without giving offense to your parents."

His late father hadn't given a damn what his second son was called as long as he responded and the first son stayed healthy. His mother, Rhys decided, would find the entire story vastly entertaining. He might even tell it to her when he got back to Wales, although he wasn't much of a bard. That was yet one more of Tim's talents.

"No offense at all. Elizabeth." He felt his hand lifting of its own accord toward a loose gold curl. He clenched his fingers into a fist and shoved it into his greatcoat pocket. "What are you going to—" He broke off and shook his head, wondering where his impeccable sense of propriety had gone. "No. I should not even think of asking."

She laughed again. "I rather like that you did. And I am glad that you overheard that particular tradition. Everyone should know to make a wish on an Irish Christmas Eve. You included, Captain. It might very well come true."

"Ah, the simplicity of superstition."

She gave him an exasperated glance, but didn't take umbrage. "They could be far worse," she chided mildly. "Another says that if you die on Christmas Eve, you go straight to Heaven."

"Is that what you will wish for, then? My speedy demise?"

"Goodness. A jest. Very good, Captain." As he watched, surprised, charmed, and increasingly warm, she removed another sprig of holly from her pocket, tucked it into a buttonhole on his coat, and briskly patted his chest. "As you could easily guess, I will make a wish for Hollymore."

With that, she stepped back, draped an arm around

the cherub, and surveyed her handiwork on Rhys's coat. She gave a satisfied nod.

In that brief moment, Rhys was enchanted to his toes.

And suddenly angry. "Did you inherit nothing at all?" he heard himself demanding harshly. "I cannot believe your father left you with nothing . . ."

This time her smile was slow and sad before it turned blithe. "Of course I did." She patted the stone shoulder. "I inherited all the remaining artwork at Hollymore. And that is something worth more than all the gold in the world to me. Now, I really must see how O'Reilly is getting on with our dinner."

She hurried off. Rhys followed. As he went, he noticed something he had not before: There was mistletoe hanging from a good many of the scrubby trees that lined the scrubbier lawn. Sighing, he continued on his way. He caught up with Elizabeth in the Great Hall where she appeared to be supervising the maneuvering of a better part of the local woods. Andrew, the young footman, and the elderly butler were wrestling with a massive, slightly feral-looking log. They were trying to cram it into the fireplace, which, despite its own mammoth proportions, seemed to be resisting the intrusion.

Rhys studied an arm-sized twig that jutted from the log and was sticking out from under his nephew's elbow. "What," he demanded, "is that?"

"It's the blockna . . . blockna . . ." Andrew replied, panting somewhat as he hefted his end in a different direction, trying to make it fit. "One more time, if you please, Kelly."

"*Bloc na Nollag,*" the footman grunted from his side.

"The Yule log," Elizabeth explained as she, too, joined in the fray. "Now, Andrew, if you lift there,

and Kelly, you turn it there . . . O'Reilly, at the risk
of having you snarl and snort at me, might I suggest
that this is not the best activity for your rheumatism.
Perhaps you ought to relinquish . . .'' The butler did,
just as Rhys stepped forward to help. The behemoth
of a log landed squarely on his booted toes.

Andrew would later report that the responding long,
lurid, and decidedly inventive curse had been heard
all the way to Wexford town. By the time he had
hobbled up the stairs to see how many of his ten toes
were intact, the unfortunate *bloc na Nollag* had been
relegated to the woodshed. When Rhys hobbled back
down several hours later on ten unbroken but com-
plaining toes, it had been replaced by a much smaller,
much less interesting specimen. From the po-faced
looks the staff gave him as they served the meal, he
surmised that it all had been a sad disappointment,
the responsibility for which landed squarely on his uni-
formed shoulders. Elizabeth, at least, inquired after
his feet. She then cast a mournful look at the Hall
hearth as they passed on the way to the drawing room.
It was almost a relief to retire.

Once settled in bed, Rhys stared grimly into his
own fire. Thirty-six hours. In thirty-six hours, he and
Andrew would be safely on their way back to Wales.
By the time Rhys returned, demolition should have
begun. He wouldn't have to set foot in Hollymore
again. He wouldn't have to suffer the recriminating
glares of the scowling O'Reilly, or endure Andrew's
silent but potent opinions on the matter of his empty
rib cage. He had a heart, damn it. It simply refused
to bleed on demand. Not even for someone like
Elizabeth.

Thirty-six hours, and he would never have to face
Elizabeth again. Only, he found himself thinking as
his eyes drifted shut, a man could do far worse than

face Elizabeth closely and often. For a fleeting second, Rhys wished that once, just once, she would look at him with the same dreamy eyes she had for her sad if splendid ruin of a house . . .

His own eyes sprang wide as the door to his bed-chamber creaked open. Andrew stood in the doorway, candle in hand, eyes wide. "I think," the young man announced without preamble, "that you'd better come with me now."

"Andrew—"

"Please, Uncle Rhys. It's important."

Rhys couldn't have refused the plea if he'd tried. Sighing, wincing, he climbed from the bed and donned his dressing gown. He followed Andrew into the hall. There were candles lit everywhere in the house, and they were being allowed to burn all night. Another Irish tradition, Elizabeth had explained. A fire hazard, Rhys thought, but certainly an attractive one. With their light, Andrew didn't need the single taper he carried. Not, Rhys realized, until he entered an empty bedchamber down the hall.

It was one they'd seen briefly during their early tour of the floor. Apparently Andrew had been back. The wardrobe door stood wide, and Rhys watched as his nephew disappeared through it. "Well, come along!" came impatiently from the depths. Rhys poked his head in. Where Andrew should have been was another door—or rather several panels standing open. A scuffling echoed from the space behind it.

"Andrew," Rhys growled, "come out of there now. You cannot know if it is safe—" He then grunted as a heavy, sheet-shrouded object came sliding out to thud into his shin.

"Take that into the room," Andrew commanded, "and come back. There are three more."

Several minutes later, uncle and nephew stood staring at the four paintings they had uncovered and propped against the bed. Rhys had collected more candles from the hallway. He leaned in close to the first painting and couldn't stop himself from letting out a low whistle.

"Is it . . . ?" Andrew whispered.

The face of a not especially pretty young girl looked back at them sourly. Yes, Rhys thought, an ugly child, but a very distinctive style. "Gainsborough," he announced.

"I thought so. And that one."

There was little question that the long-faced Madonna was El Greco. The dark supper scene could only be Rembrandt. But it was the final piece, the delicate lady in silk and ermine with the unmistakable emblems of English royalty surrounding her, that had Rhys's jaw going slack. It could have been Elizabeth, but he suspected that he was looking at the ill-fated Catherine Howard, fifth wife of Henry VIII.

"Holbein," he murmured.

"Valuable?" Andrew whispered.

"Extremely."

It appeared Christmas had arrived early at Hollymore. *Allelujah*, Rhys heard in his head. In chorus. Elizabeth Fitzhollis was about to become a very wealthy young woman. She would be able to give Timothy every penny he'd paid for her home—and more. *Allelujah.*

Then it occurred to him that perhaps this gift of some quirky magi was not something to celebrate.

6

On Christmas morning, Elizabeth gave herself the ultimate luxury and stayed in bed past seven. Then, after a quick and chilly wash, she donned the one wool dress, the soft green, she possessed that had neither stains nor mended spots, and headed downstairs.

"Happy Christmas, Miss Lizzie!" Meggie chirped as she hurried by with an armful of holly.

"Happy Christmas." Lizzie lifted a brow at the maid's departing back. Such a hurry.

The Lily Room was empty, but breakfast was laid out on the sideboard. There was chocolate this morning, a rare treat, and Lizzie stood for a moment, steaming cup held to her face so she could breathe in the rich aroma. She noted with a smile that someone had replaced the mistletoe. It might have been a silly gesture, but it was a charming one.

Now, if only a knight would come along, tall and strong, armor shining, for one sweet kiss . . .

"Happy Christmas, miss." Kelly poked his face into the room. "Is there anything I can fetch for you?"

"No, Kelly. Thank you. Happy . . ." But he had already gone. "Well," Lizzie said to the empty doorway. There would be no knight, shining or otherwise, on this day, she thought, and resolutely pushed the image of aquamarine eyes and a poet's mouth in a warrior's face from her mind. She would settle for old friends.

She took her time with breakfast, doing her best to savor what would be her last Christmas in her beloved home. Somehow, though, it didn't seem to be working. It was, she decided, being alone that was dampening her festive mood.

She nearly sighed with relief when Andrew bounded in a half hour later. Seeing the mistletoe, he grinned and blew her a saucy kiss from the doorway. He had a sprig of holly tucked into his lapel and a winning smile on his handsome face. He stopped at her side and bowed with a charming flourish. "Good morning, Elizabeth, and a very happy Christmas to you!"

Feeling much better, Lizzie returned the greeting. Then, "Will your uncle be joining us soon?"

Andrew rolled his eyes. "Oh, Uncle Lawrence. I doubt we'll see him for some hours yet."

"But it's Christmas morning."

"So it is. And a glorious one at that. There is frost on the ground and a glimmer in the air."

Yes, Lizzie had stood at the window, drinking in the sight. But the glimmer had dimmed. "Captain Jones will not be joining us for church, then?"

"Unlikely." Andrew tucked cheerfully into his sliced ham. "I, however, am very much looking forward to it. When do we leave? And can we walk?"

She always had, but had assumed they would take the dog cart. "If you don't mind a mile in the cold."

"Mind? On the contrary." Both glanced up as O'Reilly stomped into view. "Ah. Good morning, O'Reilly, and a happy Christmas."

"Happy Christmas, Miss Lizzie. And to you, young sir." The butler appeared to wink. But no, Lizzie thought. He never winked. She worried that the poor man might be developing a palsy. No one knew precisely how old O'Reilly was, but he certainly would not see sixty again. "We'll be off to Mass, miss. Is there anything you'll be needing afore we go?"

"No, thank you, O'Reilly. Happy . . ." And he was gone, too. "Hmm. Curious."

Andrew shoved a last forkful of eggs into his mouth, then jumped to his feet. "Shall we be off, then?"

Bemused, Lizzie rose. "Certainly. But—"

"Splendid. Now you go fetch yourself something warm to wear. It's frightfully chilly out there. I felt it right to my toes."

Lizzie couldn't imagine what he had been doing outside, but didn't have the chance to ask. Andrew was hustling her out of the room and into the hall. A few minutes later, booted and cloaked, Lizzie joined him on the front steps. A distinct crunching sound caught her attention. Andrew didn't seem to notice.

"What is that noise?" she asked. It seemed to be coming from behind the house. But when she started toward it, Andrew grasped her hand and tucked her arm through his. "Oh, Kelly puttering about before they go," he commented cheerily. "Come along now, before I freeze on the spot."

He whistled a tune as they headed down the drive. Lizzie recognized it. "That is the 'Wexford Carol.' "

"Indeed. Lovely piece. Now, do tell me, will I be allowed to sing very loudly in church this morning . . . ?"

He did, much to the disapproval of Aunt Gregoria and to the vast delight of most of the congregation. Lizzie was grateful for his genial presence by her side as she said her fervent prayers. And when she, along with the rest, chose a wisp of straw from the manger—a symbol of blessing and luck that she so needed—Andrew tucked one of his own into his pocket.

When the service was over, he did a charming social circuit, pumping the hand of a bemused but delighted Reverend Clark, chatting with Josiah Lambe, tickling the Kinahan's baby under the chin, and sending pretty young Ann Dermott into a blush with his cheeky grin.

He even offered his hand and merry greetings to Percy, who was sporting a truly ridiculous combination of purple-striped waistcoat and green coat. "And may I say that is a very fetching hat, ma'am," he complimented Gregoria on her storm-gray bonnet. Whether because the milliner had sewn it on too tightly to remove or in honor of the day, the thing sported a rather prickly looking collection of black feathers.

To Lizzie's astonishment, Gregoria actually grunted a thank-you. Followed, not surprisingly by, "I trust you have managed to obtain something potable to serve with dinner, girl."

It was only more Burgundy, actually, but Lizzie smiled and replied, "Of course, Aunt." In truth, she hadn't been expecting her relatives for dinner, but she probably should have. They always came when they were least wanted. O'Reilly could be counted upon to prepare more food than was necessary on Christmas. With luck, Percy would leave some for the rest of the party. "We shall see you this afternoon, then?"

"Not a bit of it." Percy thrust his familiar snuff up his nose and sneezed onto Andrew's coat. "Coming now, of course."

"Of course." Lizzie swallowed her sigh. "Well, shall we go?"

Gregoria's beady eyes slewed around. "Where is the carriage?"

"We walked, Aunt."

"Walked?" was the disbelieving response. "Good heavens, why? Has that good-for-nothing groom of yours driven the cart into the ground?"

"We walked," Andrew cut in with his winning smile, "for the sheer pleasure of it. I would be honored if you would take my arm, madam, or I will certainly run and have your carriage readied."

Lizzie could almost see the wheels turning behind her aunt's eyes. To subject her ancient carriage to the winter roads . . . "Give me your arm, young man," the lady said imperiously. "We shall walk."

It was not a particularly merry group who arrived at Hollymore an hour later. Gregoria had carped about the state of the roads, the wear on her shoes, and the paucity of the fires at Hollymore. Percy, for his part, had snorted and sneezed, and spent the entire walk trying to slip an arm around Lizzie and suggesting various dates for a spring wedding. Through it all, Andrew maintained his goodwill and charm. Lizzie wanted to cry.

Nuala greeted them just inside the door. She cheerfully accepted coats and cloaks, not so much as batting an eyelash when Gregoria snapped, "And don't you be going through my pockets! I know precisely what is there."

"Has Captain Jones come down?" Lizzie asked quietly.

Nuala nodded. "And up again. Now, Kelly's got a fire going in the blue parlor, and there's cider and eggnog ready. You just go have a nice sit, miss, 'til he's ready."

"He . . . Kelly?" Lizzie began, but Nuala was bustling off. "Well."

"Marvelous. Eggnog!" Andrew was all but pushing Gregoria across the floor.

"Yes. Eggnog," Lizzie murmured. "Very nice. But we haven't any brandy . . . ."

Percy got a grip on her arm just as Kelly appeared briefly in the facing hall door. Elizabeth knew she was mistaken, but the objects in his arms looked just like champagne bottles. That was quickly forgotten when Meggie scuttled through a far archway, a steaming basin in her hands and what appeared to be the medicine basket tucked precariously under her arm. She disappeared through the door leading to the back stairs.

"Really must insist on speaking with you, Lizzie," Percy insisted, casting a nervous glance toward the grand stairway. "Matters to be settled, y'know."

"Oh, Percy!" Lizzie blew out an exasperated breath. "There is nothing to be settled. Now, if you would let go of me . . ."

He didn't, and tried to pull her right past the parlor door. Sighing, she tugged her arm free of his grasp and followed Andrew and Gregoria into the room. The holly decorations seemed to have multiplied overnight. There were bunches and garlands and little wreaths with bright candles in them on every surface. There was a large fire burning merrily in the grate and, as promised, mulled cider and eggnog on the side table.

"Mistletoe!" Percy cried. Lizzie elbowed him smartly in his well-padded ribs.

"Eggnog." Gregoria plunked herself down in the seat closest to the fire. "And don't be stingy, young man!" she commanded as Andrew hurried to fill a cup for her.

"No later than April, Lizzie." Percy rubbed his rib cage as he made his own quick way to the refreshments. Lizzie closed her eyes for a weary moment, then smiled as Andrew pressed a warm cup into her hands.

"Have a little faith in this blessed day," he murmured, then was off again to refill Gregoria's waving cup.

A long quarter hour later, footsteps sounded outside the door. Kelly opened it with a flourish and stepped aside to admit Captain Jones. Lizzie's heart, heeding no message her brain was sending, gave a cheery little thump at the sight of him. His coat shone richly in the light, his boots gleamed with new polish, and he'd combed his hair back so it gleamed like ebony above his brow. Where, Lizzie noticed, he had several angry-looking scratches.

His eyes met hers, warm blue, and he smiled. It was a smile like his nephew's: swift and startling in its power. This time, Lizzie's heart did a dizzying flip.

"Happy Christmas," he announced huskily. "I think, Elizabeth, that you should come with me. You need to hear the decisions I have come to regarding Hollymore."

He held out an arm, over which was draped her cloak. His hand, she noticed as she rose a bit shakily to her feet, bore more scratches. Confused, pulse skittering, Lizzie met him halfway and allowed him to help her into her cloak. "Where are we going?"

"Outside," he replied. "This needs to be done outside."

"Now, see here"—Percy hauled himself to his feet—"Can't just be taking m'fiancée off like th—"

"I can and I will. Elizabeth?"

She did not protest as he guided her out the door. In fact, she didn't say anything at all as they left the house. Rhys kept his eyes on her as they reached the terrace steps. He wanted to see her expression every step of the way. His determination almost had him going tip over tail when he stepped on a loose slate. But it was worth it, worth the stumble and every painful scratch on his body, when she saw the maze.

"What . . . ? Who . . . ?" Her eyes were wide, brilliant as she surveyed the dramatically if not particularly neatly trimmed hedge. "Did you do this?"

"I had help." And he had. Every member of the staff had pitched in, working by his side. "When were you last inside?"

She shook her glossy head. "I don't quite recall. Years."

"Do you remember the way?" He guided her through the entrance.

"I . . . I'm not certain."

"Trust me." Tucking her arm firmly through his, not feeling a single one of the deep holly scratches that the little maid had carefully bandaged, he walked until they met the first turn. "Now, first, you must allow me to introduce myself before we go any farther."

She stared at him, brow furrowed. Damn, but she was beautiful. It was all Rhys could do to keep from hauling her into his arms there and then. "But I know who you are," she insisted.

He smiled and stepped away. Bowing low before her, he said, "Captain Lord Rhys Edward-Jones at your service, Miss Fitzhollis."

"Lord . . ." She blinked. "Oh, dear. Truly?"

"Truly. Your solicitor's eyesight is apparently rather poor."

"Oh, dear. Yes, it is. But why did you—"

"Never mind that." Rhys took her arm again and guided her to the next turn. "My brother is the Duke of Llans."

She pondered this for a moment. Rhys half expected her to rail at him. Instead, she sighed. "So Andrew . . ."

"Andrew is Viscount Tallasey. He will someday be the Duke of Llans." Before she could speak again, he changed the subject and demanded, "Why on earth would you even think of marrying Percy Fitzhollis?"

This earned him a small, heartbreaking smile. "Have him, have my house," she answered quietly.

Rhys muttered something rude. Elizabeth shrugged.

"If I said yes, he would not sign the final papers selling Hollymore to your brother."

"He lied. All the papers were signed, sealed, and delivered."

Once more, to his surprise, Elizabeth did not rail. Instead, she sighed again. "Yes, I rather thought so."

"So?"

"So, I was *never* going to marry Percy. Not even for Hollymore. I am selfish, perhaps, Captain . . . er, I beg your pardon. Lord Rhys."

"Rhys," he said gruffly. "And you are not selfish. You are a splendid, brave, clever woman." They walked to the next turn.

"Now what?"

"Now this." He reached into his pocket and withdrew the sprig of mistletoe that Andrew had pushed into his hand early that morning. All four members of Elizabeth's staff had had spares on hand in the last hour.

He gently tucked the mistletoe into Elizabeth's braided coronet. And finally, at last, not a moment too soon for his liking, he hauled her into his arms, up onto her toes, and kissed her. She gave a small, surprised squeak. Then she was kissing him back, sweetly, sensually, and every inch of his taut body went to flame. "God," he murmured against her lips. "Dear God, Elizabeth."

It seemed an aeon later, yet far too soon, when he gently held her away from his chest—where, he noted, his heart was pounding strongly enough to burst free. "I have a gift for you."

Her eyes were slightly unfocused as she replied, "That wasn't it?"

He gave a pained chuckle. "No. No, this is something far better."

"I don't think it could be," she said hazily, and Rhys almost grabbed her again.

"Trust me." He satisfied himself by holding her hand this time. "Now, this isn't really from me. I would say it is a gift from Hollymore. I am hoping, of course, that you'll allow me to take care of the matter of the house, but if you'd rather, this ought to more than pay for all you wish."

"What *are* you talking about?"

"Wait," he commanded, and used his free hand to cover her eyes as they approached the final turn.

He'd had Kelly build makeshift easels for the paintings. It had occurred to him that a half hour in the winter air wouldn't precisely be good for a Rembrandt, but he'd needed to have things just this way. There were blankets to cover the paintings as soon as Elizabeth had seen them, and no doubt all of her staff was lurking nearby. They could haul off the art. He intended to have his hands full of Elizabeth.

"My lord . . . Rhys," she protested as he kept his hand over her eyes.

"Hush." He guided her into the center of the maze and directly in front of the paintings. "Miss Fitzhollis, allow me to present Hollymore's salvation: Misters Gainsborough, El Greco, Rembrandt, and Holbein. Happy, happy Christmas, Elizabeth."

He removed his hand.

Elizabeth stared. "Oh. Oh, my." He heard her breath catch. "Where on earth did you find these?"

"Andrew discovered them, actually, behind a secret panel in one of the bedchambers. I assume one of your ancestors tucked them away for some reason, and they've been waiting for you to find them."

He stood back, heart swelling for her.

She glanced up. "You're whistling."

She was right. "So I am."

" 'The Wexford Carol.' " Elizabeth reached up and stroked her hand quickly down his cheek. Then she stepped forward to the Holbein queen and gently touched a fingertip to the face that was so much like hers. "Oh. Oh, Rhys."

He thought she was crying. He was wrong.

To his utter amazement, she began to laugh. It started as the light, lovely, silvery sound he knew. A minute later she was gasping and holding her sides. In the end, as he watched slack-jawed, she was forced to grope for the broken stone bench in the center and perch precariously on the edge.

"Oh, Rhys," she gasped. "I love you!"

"I am very glad to hear that," he muttered, "as I am rather alarmingly in love with you, too. But perhaps you will tell me just what is so funny."

She drew an audible breath and wiped at her eyes with the hem of her cloak. "Those." She pointed to the paintings.

"I fail to see the amusement in four masterworks of art."

"No. No, I don't suppose you would. They're very good, aren't they?"

"Very."

"And not worth a penny." Elizabeth rose and waved at the Gainsborough. "Don't you recognize her?"

Rhys scowled at the unattractive young lady. "Should I?"

"The pinched lips? The little eyes?"

Now that she mentioned it, there *was* something familiar in the face. "It is . . ."

"Aunt Gregoria! Of course, I didn't know her then, but I daresay it's a spitting image."

Rhys made the calculations in his head. He supposed a young Gregoria could have sat for the famous painter. He didn't know precisely when the family's fortunes had turned.

"And this one." Again, Elizabeth gently touched the lovely blonde.

"An ancestress?"

"My mother." Her eyes were soft when they met his. "My great-uncle Clarence painted these. All of them."

Rhys felt his jaw dropping. "Uncle Clarence of the cupid and the god-awful hunt scenes?"

"The very same. He was a very skilled copyist, you see, but it never gave him half the satisfaction of letting his creative impulses run wild. And you thought . . . Oh, dear." Shoulders shaking again, she returned to the bench. Rhys lowered himself to sit beside her. "Are you very angry?"

"To be honest . . ." He lifted her chin and stared sternly down into her heartbreakingly beautiful face. "I am bloody delighted."

"Good heavens, why?"

"Because," he replied, "this means you are still poor as a church mouse."

"And that makes you happy?"

"Deliriously so." He kissed her again, a quick, light touch, and grinned when she hummed with pleasure.

"You see, I cannot imagine you having me otherwise. Now I can offer my fortune along with my humble person."

"Oh, Rhys."

"You will have me, won't you, Elizabeth? I am rather disgustingly rich."

"I would have you," she said softly against his lips, "if you hadn't a shilling to your altogether too-grand name."

This time, it was she who pulled his face to hers.

"What did she say?" came sharply from the hedge behind them. Kelly.

There was a rustling and shushing. "Get yourself off my shoulder, you daft eejit," O'Reilly muttered. "Are you after flattening me?"

"Hush!" Nuala hissed. "I want to hear how she answered."

"Sure and she answered yes!" came Meggie's pronouncement.

There was a loud scuffling and a yelp from the other side. "Ouch. Can't go this way." Percy. "Lizzie? Won't wait forever for your answer, y'know."

"Oh, shut up, boy!" Gregoria snapped. "Just push through. And stop whining. It's only a little scratch. *Lizzie*? You come out right now! Do you hear me? Oh, give me your flask, Percy. I feel faint . . ."

Just then, Andrew's grinning face appeared around the corner. "Well?" he demanded. "Did you kiss her?"

"Go away, puppy," Rhys muttered.

His nephew didn't budge. "*Christmas,* Uncle. So, what did she say?"

The rustling grew louder on all sides. Rhys sighed. Then grinned. "She said yes," he shouted.

"That's the spirit!" Andrew crowed, coming to give Elizabeth a resounding kiss on her cheek. Then he poked Rhys solidly in the chest. "*There's* the spirit.

And merry well about time, too. Now come and have some champagne. Mr. Lambe's finest."

"Champagne?" Gregoria's voice carried stridently through the hedge. "Washed up on the beach, no doubt. For God's sake, Lizzie, when *are* you going to have some decent spirits in this hovel? Oh, do stop sniveling, Percy. It is merely a scratch . . ."

EPILOGUE

Letter from the Earl of Clane to the Duke of Llans, November 4, 1813:

My Dear Llans,

Call me the worst of meddlers, but I have a scheme brewing in my head and, as it will not go away and I cannot figure how to manage it myself, I am appealing to your sense of friendship and your brotherly devotion.

The enclosed is an advert from yesterday's paper. As you will see, it is for a Wexford estate. It belongs to a family I knew in my youth. The daughter, Elizabeth Fitzhollis, lives there now. She is a lovely girl; I fancied her madly for a bit in my much younger days. I have only recently learned that her father died several years ago and, due to the typical nasty legalities, left her virtually nothing at all. Everything—lock, stock, and her beloved, crumbling pile of a house went to a perfectly awful cousin who is advertising it for sale.

I would offer my assistance in a heartbeat, but it would look rather dodgy and Elizabeth wouldn't accept it anyway. She is proud and lionhearted and, I have learned, so determined to keep her moldering Hollymore standing that she shores and mends and digs herself. A mule shouldn't have to work so hard.

Now, generous a soul as I know you are, still let me assure you that there is something for your family in this as well. I know how fond you are of your brother, as are we all of Rhys, despite his damnable starchy deportment. I also know that you, Susan, and the rest of the realm have despaired of his ever finding a woman to suit him. I think Elizabeth Fitzhollis just might be that woman.

Buy the pile; send Rhys to look at it. If all goes as I expect it will, not only will you have a lovely sister-in-law and a happy brother, but he'll insist on taking said pile off your hands quicker than you can say "felicitations."

If all does not go as I expect, and that is a very rare occurrence indeed—oh, cease with the guffaws, sir—I will buy Hollymore from you at a profit. If Rhys does not come back with Elizabeth, perhaps he will come back with some Christmas spirit. Heaven knows he could do with a bit.

Ailis sends her love to you and Susan, and thanks you again for the marvelous Welsh hospitality during our honeymoon. She cannot abide England and is vastly relieved whenever I reveal a close acquaintance in a Celtic clime. She also bids me inform you that if you do not bring your sorry selves to Dublin in the new year, she will feature you prominently in her next set of caricatures. Trust me, my friend, you do not want that.

A Happy Christmas to all.

Clane

Good people all, this Christmastime, consider well and
bear in mind
What our good God for us has done, in sending his
beloved Son.
With Mary holy we should pray to God with love this
Christmas day;
In Bethlehem upon that morn, there was a blessed Mes-
siah born.

The night before that happy tide, the noble Virgin and
her guide
Were long time seeking up and down, to find a lodging
in the town.
But mark how all things came to pass; from every door
repelled, alas!
As long foretold, their refuge all was but a humble
ox's stall.

There were three wise men from afar, directed by a glo-
rious star,
And on they wandered night and day until they came
where Jesus lay,
And when they came unto that place where our beloved
Messiah was,
They humbly cast them at his feet, with gifts of gold and
incense sweet.

Near Bethlehem did shepherds keep their flocks of
  lambs and feeding sheep;
To whom God's angels did appear, which put the shepherds in great fear.
Prepare and go, the angels said. *To Bethlehem, be not
  afraid,*
*For there you'll find, this happy morn, a princely babe,
  sweet Jesus born.*

With thankful heart and joyful mind, the shepherds went
  the babe to find,
And as God's angel had foretold, they did our savior
  Christ behold.
Within a manger he was laid, and by his side the vir-
  gin maid,
Attending on the Lord of Life, who came on earth to
  end all strife.

High Spirits
by Edith Layton

Lovely young Arabella Danton was having a wonderful time at the party. She had an abundance of Christmas spirits. She'd even had some before she got to the party. It made her very happy. She'd hated the London Season until she got into the spirits. Then she discovered she could be everything she always wanted to be in company: witty, breezy, charming, light-hearted—and light-headed. So what if that pretty little head ached in the morning? It was the night before that counted.

It was the secret of her unexpected success this Season. Her biggest secret. Her only secret.

It was a wonder that she needed one.

A glance could show even the veriest dolt that she was adorable. She had a head full of cinnamon curls, made even more piquant by the boyish crop the stylist in London had recently given her. Only her fine gray eyes could meet the exacting standards of the Season, because no face graced by such a tiny nose and possessed of such full lips could be called classically beautiful. Much that mattered, the gentlemen didn't even seem to notice. They said she was winsome and then some, which could also be because her little body was such a symphony of curves.

She was a mad success even though she wasn't an Incomparable, because she was that rare and delicious thing: a young woman with everything a fellow ever dreamed of, with a kind heart, too, so that a fellow knew she'd never deliberately hurt him when she refused him any of the things he'd be likely to want of her. She was approachable, conversable, and not a bit threatening even to the youngest, least-experienced suitors. She had a delightful sense of humor, and took nothing seriously. When she wasn't laughing, she was smiling. When she was in public. And she never went out in public anymore unless she was well fortified for it. Which was why she was the rage, why she had so many gentlemen in the *ton* panting for her, and why she was having difficulty remembering just who was so smitten with her, and why.

It hadn't always been that way.

Arabella arrived in London for the first time in October, and immediately attended four *ton* parties. Then she refused to go to another, though she knew the only reason her stepmama had gone to the expense of sending her all the way from Surrey was because she wanted her to find a likely gentleman, marry, and then never go back to Surrey again.

"Aunt Fanny says you don't want to go to Almack's tonight," Arabella's brother Pace remarked. He'd run her to earth after having sought her on his aunt's explicit instructions.

She was sitting, or rather, huddling, in the window seat of her aunt's back parlor, doubled in a tight knot, arms around her knees. She seemed to be staring sightlessly at the tiny garden. There certainly wasn't anything to look at, for their aunt didn't decorate places company couldn't see.

"You have to go, you know," he said, without much sympathy.

"No, you have to tell me to go. Or Aunt will tell

Iris, and Iris will have Father cut off your allowance," Arabella said bitterly. "Too bad. I'm not going to one more of those . . . cattle markets, even if it means you won't have the blunt to buy yourself a new handkerchief, or neck cloth, or—or whatever new fribble you decide a gentleman of fashion needs this Season."

Her brother restrained himself from a hasty retort. What he needed money for wasn't a thing he'd confess to his sister.

"I never knew you were so poor-spirited, Midget," he commented. That was the sort of dare that always sent her up a tree—or into the water—or right to their stepmama, Iris, with an outrageous request he wouldn't risk making himself. But now she only curled into a tighter knot, her chin sinking to rest on her knees.

"I won't go, I won't be humiliated again," she said. "I refuse to be—on sale, in public. If Iris wants to barter me, she'll have to put me up on a real auction block. Or have pirates kidnap me and do it in Madagascar, or somewhere. Or the Orient," she added vaguely.

That gave her brother confidence. When Bella was silent she was dangerous, when she got fanciful she was vulnerable.

"Almack's an auction block?" He hooted. "Huh! Females would give their back teeth to be presented there. *Crème de la crème* of the *ton,* my short lady! You should go if only so that you can tell everyone at home you were there."

"She doesn't want me at home anymore, that's why she wants me to go there," his sister said in a hurt little voice. "And have you seen the girls there? They're beautiful, and they all know each other, and all they talk about is the gentlemen they want to attach. And those men? Ha," she said mournfully.

"They're so full of themselves. Oh, Pace! I want to go home, but I know I can't. Father won't say boo to Iris. So I'm exiled until I find a husband. I don't want one! At least I don't want any of the ones I've seen."

"Well, there's the problem. You can't have a husband," he joked. "You need to find a single fellow and turn him into a husband."

She didn't laugh. She only sniffled and swiped the back of her hand under her little nose. That touched her brother as no tears could have done.

"This place would give anyone the dismals," he said gruffly. "Nothing to see out that window but—nothing. Come on, let's go for a walk. I'll buy you an ice," he said when she hesitated.

She grinned. It was like the sun coming out, even for her brother, who was sure he was immune to all her wiles. "I'm not a child anymore," she said with some dignity. "A grape ice?" she asked, peering up at him from beneath uncommonly long lashes.

"Two of them," he said handsomely. "Go get your bonnet, I'll wait."

Ten minutes later, Mr. Pace Danton and his younger sister Arabella were promenading down the street toward the park, her hand on his arm. They were a charming couple, both with cinnamon curls and fine gray eyes. Both were dressed in gray, Pace in a charcoal-gray jacket and slate pantaloons, his sister in a storm cloud gray wool pelisse to protect her thin muslin gown from the autumn breeze. They looked like a pair of wide-eyed Pilgrims: Pace, tall and straight, with refined features and a ready smile, Arabella, obviously his kin in miniature.

Pace had finished his last year at University and was in London looking for a position with some likely politician because he fancied a career in public service. He might have preferred staying home, learning how to manage the estate he'd come into one day, but the thought of sharing that estate, all thirty rooms of it, with his stepmama, sent him out into the wide world looking for something more pleasant. Taming wild animals, he often said, would be that.

"You never had any trouble with the boys at home," he finally remarked, when he thought enough time had passed.

"I never had anything with them," she said on a sniff. "They wouldn't dare court me; Father wouldn't have it. He's not very aware of the world, but he didn't want his daughter marrying a farmer. But these fellows are seeking fortune or fame, and the girls here know it. They spend all their time choosing their clothing, trying to be named 'Incomparables,' so the men who marry them can feel they've won some sort of lottery. It's all about appearances; no one gets to *know* anyone else. I suppose because they all know each other already. But you understand that," she said sadly. "You've been here before."

He refrained from commenting that the girls he'd passed his time with in London were not for marrying.

But his sister knew him. "I suppose you weren't looking for a wife." She sighed. "You don't have to yet. Men are so lucky."

"Point is," Pace said, "you're taking it too seriously. You were never like that at home. You look so glum and angry only a madman would ask for a dance with you. Be more lighthearted."

Another sigh gave her opinion of that. They walked on into the park. Pace hoped he'd meet some respectable London friend he could introduce his sister to. She wasn't a beauty any more than he was an Adonis, but it was amazing how her mood influenced her looks. She'd been shy and uncomfortable at the parties they'd gone to, and had looked drab and uninteresting. She looked like herself again today, and he felt she could dazzle any man in the city, if she—and he— could only keep her spirits up.

But he didn't cross paths with any friends, respectable or not. It was only early afternoon, so most of his cronies must still be abed. Pace nodded to a mere acquaintance, a fellow dressed especially fine, and felt Arabella, at his side, withdrawing again. He was about to try to cheer her, when her steps faltered.

"Pace!" she breathed, coming to a standstill. "Who is *that*?"

She was staring at a woman in an elegant high-perch carriage stopped by the side of the road. The woman was surrounded by a group of gentlemen on horseback, and she was jesting with them and some other gentlemen who had hailed her from the path. From their loud delighted laughter, they were being royally entertained. The woman was plain, but well dressed, she looked like she might be a celebrity Arabella could write to her friends at home about, but Arabella had never seen her before.

"No one," Pace said quickly, guiding her forward. "Let's move on."

"Oh," Arabella said as she resisted and stood absolutely still. "You mean no one I should know. Then she must be a demirep? But she couldn't be."

He turned so he stood in front of her. "You're not supposed to know about such things, can we leave?"

She moved a step, but only so that she could see clearly again. "I *do* know about such things, so it would be stupid to pretend I didn't. But she can't be!" she went on in a whisper, so there was no chance the woman could overhear her. "She *funny-looking*. Her hair's frizzy and her eyes are too close set, she has a long nose and she's skinny. I thought a prostit-, a demirep, had to be beautiful."

"That's *Harriet Wilson*," Pace whispered in an agony of discomfort. "She's clever, that's more important than looks. And she's famous, too. That makes her even more desirable, no matter what she looks like. Can we go?"

"*That* Harriet Wilson?" his sister gasped. "But that blond fellow is your friend Lieutenant Reardon," she said in scandalized tones, "and there's Mr. Montgomery. Oh, my! He's engaged to that dreadful Elizabeth Spears! And . . ." She fell silent.

One of the gentlemen on horseback who had been listening to the others with banked amusement, chanced to look around, and saw Arabella. He was a large, dark gentleman, impeccably dressed, with ebony hair showing under his high beaver hat. He had an angular face, a hawk-like nose, and bold dark eyes. He paused, pinned Arabella with that black stare, then his wide mobile mouth curled in a slow smile. An evil, knowing smile, Arabella thought, catching her breath. Fascinating and terrifying.

" 'Gads!" Pace said in an under voice, "Aldridge has seen us. Can we leave now instead of standing here, gaping like country mice?"

Arabella quickly lowered her gaze and nodded, letting her brother lead her away.

But as soon as they'd gone out of sight of the group, she tugged on Pace's hand. "Who *was* that?"

He didn't ask who she meant. "Rupert Aldridge is rich, clever, and influential; he knows everyone, and everyone wants to know him. He's got a killing sense of humor, and they say the same of his fencing and boxing skills. A very dangerous man, Midget. His tongue's sharp as his sword. He saw us gaping like fish; he'd make sport of us if he knew our names, and we'd be ruined—or at least, laughed at, which is the same thing."

"He's Harriet Wilson's protector?"

"No, I don't think so, he's much too discreet to take up with someone that famous—or infamous. But of course he'd be wherever anything interesting was happening."

"I've never seen him at Almack's or any party I've been to," Arabella said thoughtfully.

"Of course not," her brother said without thinking.

His sister giggled. He turned to look at her. If she only looked like that when she went out on the Town, he thought, she'd have a bigger crowd around her than Harriet Wilson did.

"Iris would kill you if she heard you," Arabella said. "You just admitted Almack's is no-account, and all those parties Aunt drags me to are the same."

He reluctantly grinned. "Well, I suppose they are, but you can't go to any other kind if you're looking for a husband."

"I'm not!"

"Well, you'd better. You're one and twenty now, Bella. That's a dangerous age, at least to still be unwed. It made Iris realize you weren't going to take the hand of any of those dismal relatives of hers. And that, however weak-willed he is, Father isn't going to force you to. But this! She finally opens the purse to get you out of her hair. Do you dare go back home empty-handed?"

They walked along in silence, thinking of their step-mother's reaction to her money being wasted.

Arabella sighed. "Empty-fingered," she corrected him. "I suppose not."

"Do you so dislike the thought of marrying?" he asked, frowning.

"Oh, no. I think I'd like to find someone and set up my own household, if only to get away from Iris. I wish Father hadn't given her his spine along with his hand." She frowned. "He's a nice man, but he doesn't do a thing unless she agrees. I wish she'd had some children, too, so she'd have some sympathy for us. But all she ever wanted was us out and gone."

"Never fancied a fellow?" Pace asked curiously.

Her color rose. "Oh, of course. Mr. Gifford, and Francis Young, when I was a girl."

He hooted. "Gifford? Don't tell me you liked him? He was just a farmer and couldn't even speak the King's English! And he had a nose like one of those turnips he grew!"

They engaged in a spirited argument that built higher and higher, then collapsed into ripples of mutual laughter, the way their arguments often did. Two children brought up on a remote estate by a stepmother who didn't like children or entertaining them, they'd learned to rely on each other. When Pace had gone off to school, Arabella had been bereft. The only thing she liked about her present sojourn in London was that she could see him again, though that wasn't often. He kept her away from his care-for-nothing friends and hated to go to the *ton* parties she had to attend. His absence was one of the reasons she was so shy at them.

Another reason was that she felt out of place. But the most important one was that in spite of vague romantic dreams and certain tingling feelings that embarrassed and intrigued her, she wasn't sure exchanging her stepmother's rule for a husband's absolute control would be much better. She'd been happy with her single state, her pets, her books, her dreams. Well, perhaps not "happy." Content. Maybe not "content," she admitted. In waiting. Yes, that was it. Now she was in action. She hated that.

"But I don't like the men I'm meeting," she said

plaintively, "and I don't enjoy the parties, either. What can I do, Pace?"

He straightened his shoulders. "I'll come along with you next time. We'll face it together, like in the old days. It will be better, you'll see."

He'd helped her face the woman their father had brought home as a new bride, a stepmama straight out of the better fairy stories—or worse ones. Pace had survived his stepmother's wrath because he seldom took anything seriously, except his responsibility to his sister. His mother had asked that of him on her death-bed. Though he was only three years older than his sister, he never forgot his oath. He was a very good brother, if not the most responsible one. But he was great fun and a firm friend. Arabella had looked up to him since she'd been able to focus her eyes. She nodded.

"Done," she said.

Pace inspected his sister with a critical eye the next evening. "Turn around," he commanded.

Arabella spun on her heel in the little salon. "Good," Pace said, watching her. "White's the color for young girls, but it don't do a thing for you. That green thing does."

"Lime, with strawberry stripes," Arabella said, looking down at her new gown with pleasure. "So. I look well, I suppose."

The gown was charming, but her brother wished her face matched it. Instead, she looked pale and worried.

"Now you have to introduce me to charming young men, remember? And keep the bores away. And," she said, her spirits falling, "keep me from shaking in my slippers."

He frowned. Then marched over to the sideboard. He picked up a decanter of brandy, poured a half glass of it, and handed it to her. "Drink it up," he said. "Dutch courage," he explained to her puzzled look. "Look, whenever a fellow has a hard course ahead, he takes a good jot of this stuff, and it gives him fire and nerve. Must work the same for females, I'd expect. Go ahead."

She put her nose on the rim of the glass, and her head reared back.

"It smells awful," he agreed. "And at first, it tastes worse. But it does the trick, you'll see. Makes you feel warm to your toes. You'll like wine better. Maybe we'll use that next time, but tonight you need instant courage, and believe me, it sits in that glass. Now, one, two, three, drink it back like one of Nurse's vile medicines."

"But it isn't medicine," she protested.

"The deuce it isn't! Every fellow I know takes it when his spirits lag or when he needs to relax. Everyone does. You can't go to the clubs here, but I have, and let me tell you, there's more drinking than eating or gambling going on. And these are important men who run the government. The Corinthians, too, top of the trees fellows everyone admires. They all drink and they're not a bit ashamed of it, because a chap who can't handle a bottle can't control himself, everyone knows that. And everyone drinks. Ale at breakfast, wine at luncheon, brandy before dinner, and all the wine they can hold all night. Why, there's no greater compliment than to call a chap a 'three bottle man.' "

"That's just wine, and I'm not a man."

"And what's this? Just a jot of brandy. You always claimed you were smart as any fellow, didn't you?"

She looked dubious.

"You're no coward, are you?"

That did it. It always did. She drained the glass in one gulp.

Then there were a few minutes of coughing, wheezing, and gasping to be got through, which was why he'd asked her to come to the little parlor alone. But a few minutes later she looked up at him and grinned. Her eyes were still tearing, her face was still red, but she looked like his delightful madcap sister again. He hadn't seen much of that Arabella since she'd come to London. She threw back her head and picked up the hem of her skirt as she took his proffered arm.

" 'Lead on, MacDuff,' " she misquoted, " 'And curst be he that first cries, 'Hold enough!' Ah, will there be more of that where we're going, if that wears off?"

There was rataffia where they went. Arabella paused in her dancing for a moment, and reported that to her brother. "Phoo," she whispered, "it has no bite. It tastes like candy. Can you get me some more brandy?" She giggled at her inadvertent rhyme.

"Oh, no. Brandy's tricky, it's a delicate balance. Too much and you fall on your face, and get sick as a dog. Just a bit does the trick."

"But if it wears off?" she asked nervously. "Because, you know, I'm feeling just a bit anxious again."

"I'll bring you a glass of wine. Meet me behind those potted palms after this set. Now, be off. Richardson has the next dance, and he looks anxious because you're not ready."

She smiled and turned, beaming at the young man who had come up behind her. He looked dazzled. As did her next partner, and her next, and her next. She danced the night away, laughing, joking, teasing, captivating every man there. And she only had to sneak two more glasses of wine to do it.

That never happened again. Pace got her a small silver flask to hide in her fur muff, so she didn't have to rely on him at any other parties, and she went to every one she was invited to, and shone like the new star in London's social firmament that she'd become.

The gentleman looked pained. He leaned forward slightly, with a too charming expression that made his guests uneasy. "I take it to mean that you think I should drown the girl for you? Or, failing that, at least abduct her and sell her on an auction block, somewhere in the Far East or farther afield?"

"Fiddle!" his sister Anne said gruffly. "Just talk to her and discover what she's up to."

She eyed her older brother narrowly. Except for his extraordinary physique, there wasn't a trace of the hardworking boy she'd known left in Rupert. He had easily fit into London Society after he'd left their country home. More than that, now he led it. He had everything but a title, and he could have bought two of them from his grateful prince if he wanted. But he seemed to want nothing but amusement now.

He was tricked out in the latest fashion today, as usual, his jacket stretched perfectly across his wide shoulders, waistcoat hugging his broad chest, seamlessly snug pantaloons showing every hard muscle in his thighs. His crag of a jaw was closely shaved, his thick jet hair barbered by the best valet in town. He'd never be thought of as handsome, except in a certain light and at certain moments, when anyone could see he was much more than that.

Rupert's deep smooth voice commanded attention no matter how softly he spoke, and his words were honey sweet. One only noticed how wicked they were when his voice fell still. His manners had always been good, but now his sister feared they were too polished—he didn't seem to take anything seriously anymore. Except for his family, and that was why she was now here.

Still who would have thought her rough-and-ready

brother could look like such a tulip of the *ton*? She
granted he wasn't exactly that. His strength and size
made him a very outsize tulip, most men of fashion
were Narcissi. Rupert was built along the lines of an
Atlas. Big as he was, he was definitely complete to a
shade, and one of the most influential fellows in Town,
because of that acid wit, she supposed.

He hadn't been like that when they were young.
But after their parents died and he'd completed his
obligations, repaired the family fortune, educated and
married off his younger siblings, he'd gone on to enjoy
himself. He deserved that after raising his younger
brothers and herself. But she couldn't like the way
Town had soured him. Only thirty, he was jaded
enough for a man twice his age—a man twice his age
who'd been disappointed in life, at that.

"Don't jest, dear Rupert," their aunt said with a
worried frown. "She's angling for our Walter. Angling? She's making a dead set at him, and everyone
knows he's promised to Catherine Steele."

"Indeed, but does Walter know that?" Rupert
asked sweetly.

"Since he could toddle," his sister said. "And looking forward to the day, Rupert, I swear he was. Until
that Danton girl started in on him."

Rupert thought about his cousin, a pleasant young
man, but it was difficult to think of him being any
maiden's dream. Walter took after his father and
would look exactly like that kindly, if dull, gentleman
in a few years: spare, pale-eyed, wan, his fair hair already thinning. But who knew what kind of Gypsy
heart beat beneath that mundane exterior? Well, good
for him if that pallid organ was finally causing a fuss.

"If a little flirtation set him off course he's better
off not marrying Catherine," Rupert said in bored
tones. "And so is she. These cradle engagements are

passé. They were fine for our parents and grand-parents, but this is the nineteenth century. Modern men marry for love, they tell me."

The silence that met this remark was eloquent. Rupert knew many things, but his sister and aunt were sure he didn't know a thing about the workings of the human heart. The human body, definitely, to judge from the many high flyers he'd had under his protection and the women of fashion he'd had discreet liaisons with. But love had never come into it. The rumor was that Rupert's own heart had been broken when he'd been young and poor; at least that was the tattle spread by those who were willing to concede he had one. No wellborn girl would give him the time of day when he'd been young. Now they were eager to give him all the days of their lives. His relatives had to ruefully admit that would sour anyone.

His aunt clutched her teacup tightly. "The chit told him she'd fly with him to the Antipodes, or the stars."

Rupert's dark eyebrows went up. "You heard this?"

"Everyone did," his sister said. "Arabella Danton sparkles, people hang on her every utterance."

"She's that beautiful?" her brother asked, thinking, of course, she had to be to cause such a stir.

"No," his aunt said sadly. "She's just . . . watchable, there's no other word for it. She sparkles. You simply *have* to look at her when she's in the room. She enchants the gentlemen, there's no other word for their reaction, either."

"There is," Anne sighed. "They're ravished. She's winsome, with a lively sense of humor and radiant eyes. And a remarkable form, of course."

"And this radiant creature said she'd fly to the stars with *Walter*?" Rupert asked, his brows going even farther up.

"Yes. Only not just yet," his sister reported glumly,

"because then she said she had tickets to the opera, and didn't know what kind of theater she'd find in the Antipodes or on the star of his choice, so she feared she couldn't go with him just yet. Then she laughed and danced with him again."

The dark brows went down, a white smile slashed across her brother's dark face. "Hardly a serious comment."

"She danced with him three times, Rupert."

The smile faded. No lady took three dances with a fellow without having had or accepted a proposal from him. Rupert sat back and spread his hands as if in surrender. "If Walter wants her, you'll just have to accept that. Her father's acres don't march with yours, but the girl is of good family. Unless you want me to kidnap him, too?"

"She's toying with him," his aunt said, ignoring his jest. "If she wanted him that would be one thing. This is quite another. When he asked to take her to the opera, she laughed in his face and said she didn't want his snoring to ruin her evening. Then she danced off with another man."

"So then the situation is not serious," Rupert said with a trace of annoyance.

"But it is! Catherine invited Walter to her home for Christmas; he goes every year for their house party, but this time he turned her down! We thought he'd be announcing their engagement there. Catherine's a sensitive girl and of marriageable age. If he slights her, she'll find another, if only to save face. This Danton girl will marry another, too, and then where will Walter be?"

"He'll be free, which is a very pleasant state, denied to many men," Rupert said in a tone that implied he was not one of those lucky men.

"We thought that if you spoke with the Danton girl,

you could find out which way the wind blows," his sister said.

"Really?" Rupert answered slowly. "I'd have thought you'd want me to close the door against the wind. Do you expect me to corner the chit and ask her intentions? Surely another female would be better suited to do that."

His sister and aunt exchanged a look. "I did try, that's why we're here this morning," his aunt said. "I asked her at the Merriman's soiree the other night. She obviously thought I was joking, because she laughed and said, 'My intentions? Oh, dear lady, I haven't any! Except for one—to have fun.' Then she waltzed off again. You have such a way with women, we thought you could find out more and maybe persuade her to let him be."

"Oh, I see," Rupert said mildly. "You expect me to confront her at Almack's? Perhaps at the theater?"

"We thought you'd pay a call on her," his sister said patiently. "She's impossible to get alone at a party because she's always surrounded by men."

"Oh," Rupert said again, digesting that. "Then, once in her home, you'd want me to charm her, appeal to her better nature, saying that if she doesn't really want Walter, in all conscience she ought to leave him alone. And perhaps hint that I can offer her entrée to more distinguished circles? Or would you rather I make an outright attempt to steal her heart away?"

"No," his sister said quickly. "Just see her, and speak with her."

"You don't think that my paying a call on her might look like I was smitten by her? Or do you think that *would* be the perfect deception?"

"Oh, no," they both protested, weakly.

"Interesting," Rupert mused aloud. "Now, I thought you'd come here this morning to continue nagging . . . ah—urging, that I be home in plenty of time to get the house ready for our family's Christmas festivities. Instead, you'd rather I stay in Town in order to lure some female away from Walter?"

"Don't be difficult," his sister snapped, then added more ingratiatingly, "We only want you to see how the land lies. You're so good with people, you can do that better than anyone we know."

"I see," he said with a curling smile. "You just want me to try flattery, bribery, and coercion to get her to cut line, is that it?"

"Exactly!" his aunt said with relief, "Just so!"

"No," he said.

No one else was waiting in the salon. Rupert was relieved: the fewer people who knew of this, the better. He'd deliberately come after the polite hour for callers. He hadn't come only to please his sister, he found himself wildly curious. But he was startled when Arabella Danton finally came into the room to see him. He remembered her instantly. He'd been bemused by the wide-eyed young woman in the park, so obviously agog at seeing the notorious Harriet Wilson. Most London ladies would have scurried away, refusing to so much as be seen clapping an eye on such a disreputable female.

But this young woman had been refreshingly scandalized by what she saw. At least he'd felt refreshed seeing such an honest reaction. He remembered how vivacious her shock had made her look, the way her eyes widened as she'd maneuvered around that youth who must have been a brother as she tried to get a better look. Elfin and adorable, he'd thought then. Small and undistinguished, he thought now.

Now her animation was gone. Everything about her seemed muted. She didn't wear gray this time, she was even more subdued in a lavender gown. Her complexion was pale, her eyes dull.

"Good afternoon," she said as he bowed over her hand. "To what do I owe the honor of your visit, sir?"

At least she was straightforward, Rupert thought. But why in God's name was Walter so ravished by her? His sister and aunt had wildly exaggerated. That incident in the park must have been a trick of the light. This girl had no sparkle, no zest. Maybe she was ill. She certainly looked pained. But beyond that?

She did have a delicious figure. High breasts jutted out over a narrow waist and gently rounded hips, and from what he could see, small as she was, she was perfectly proportioned. On another woman that shape might have been spectacular. She tried to conceal it. Her gown had a high buttoned neck, and she carried herself as though she were tiptoeing around a sickbed. No wonder they let her interview him alone, with only the door to the salon left open as a bow to propriety. Who'd attempt this poor subdued miss?

It would have been amusing to try to trick a cold-hearted flirt. Rupert could only assume that this little creature was Walter's natural mate, so he might actually even try to foster this match for his cousin. Walter was the dullest young man Rupert knew; this was obviously a case of like calling to like.

"Good morning, Miss Danton," he said, taking the seat she indicated. "I imagine you wonder why I'm here?"

She sat opposite him, and winced at his question. "Is it because my brother and I were rude, staring at you and Harriet Wilson the other week?"

"Miss Wilson and me, and a dozen other men," he corrected her, pleased that she remembered him too. "But, no. I'm surprised you'd even mention her name to me, it's not at all the thing."

"I'm not good at talking around things, sir. And I can't imagine any other reason you'd pay a call on me." She pressed two fingers to her temple. "Pardon me, I have a bit of the headache this morning."

"I'll make this brief, then. I've come because *I'm* rude and presumptuous. Forgive me in advance, but please hear me out. This is embarrassing for both of us, but my aunt, Mrs. Browning, asked that I speak to you. It appears she noted her son Walter's interest in you. He appears to be besotted. She wonders if you reciprocate his feelings. She has nothing against you, but she believed him to be on the verge of offering for an old friend and near neighbor, and is understandably surprised by his sudden change in plans. He won't discuss the matter with her, so she asked me to discover your intentions in regard to him. I'm the family cat's paw, it seems," he added with a smile calculated to win her sympathy.

It didn't. It only seemed to shock her out of her torpor. Her eyes opened wide, showing them to be rain-cloud gray and very appealing. Her figure *and* her eyes were noteworthy, Rupert thought, thinking better of his cousin's taste.

"Walter Browning?" she asked incredulously. "I haven't the slightest interest in him above being his dancing partner. He's an excellent dancer," she confided. "Not too good and not precisely bad. You see, gentlemen who fancy themselves fine dancers demand a lot of their partners, and those who can't dance at all tread on your toes. Walter knows just enough not to mind the fact that I'm always forgetting my steps, and that's a great comfort to me. But I assure you I don't think of him in any other way."

Rupert cleared his throat. "Ahm, but you were heard to tell him that you'd fly to the stars with him."

She looked genuinely puzzled. "It must have been

a jest or something misheard. I assure you I have no
designs on your cousin. Except on the dance floor, of
course. And if that upsets Mrs. Browning, you can tell
her for me that I won't so much as tread a quadrille
with him again. He can marry his old friend tonight
for all I care."

"I thought it was blown out of proportion, forgive
me for bringing it up."

"Well, but you had to, I suppose," she said with a
tiny frown.

He had to contain a smile. She was more than
charming when expressions played across that winsome face, she was utterly delightful.

"If my brother took up with someone I didn't approve of, I'd worry," she added.

"It's not that they don't approve, it's merely that
they were surprised. Almost as much as you were in
the park the other day. I don't think I've ever seen
anyone so surprised, come to think of it."

She smiled. "But you see, I thought a famous cour-
tesan would at least be pretty."

He laughed. "My dear girl, now *I'm* shocked. That's
a most improper comment."

"Isn't that absurd?" she asked, her brows swooping
down. "You can prance around with her in public,
and heaven knows what in private, and I seeing that,
can't even mention it to you?"

"I assure you I don't prance. And only heaven
knows what I do with the woman in private, because
I don't, having never known her in that fashion." He
winced. "Gads! *This* is most improper, should I expect
your brother at dawn, with pistols?"

"Yes, only if you let him in, he'll probably ask you
to give him some instruction. He positively carols about
your expertise with them, and swords and such."

"Especially 'and such,' " he said. "I'm very good at that."

They smiled at each other.

He was very good at small talk, too, and so was she. The permitted half hour flew by, and later he couldn't recall what they'd talked about to make him laugh so much. By the time he took his hat from a footman and left the house, he thought much better of his cousin. Of course the boy was attracted to Arabella. She'd attract him the same way a comb attracted lint on a cold morning, the electric luring the inert. Set her cap for him? As if she had to, his aunt was daydreaming. The only problem Rupert could see was that Arabella Danton was much too good for Walter. Rupert decided he had to find a way to tell the lad without hurting his feelings and then speed him to that Christmas party and the girl he was supposed to marry.

As to who would be good enough for Arabella? Rupert envisioned that delectable body, that adorable face, and admitted he, too, was attracted to the fey little woman. And here he'd always fancied the most ostentatious types. But he wasn't getting any younger, and she was unique. Quietly alluring, charming without being pushy, bright, demure, but adorably so, seductive without halfway trying. Perhaps . . .

Instead of giving his mistress a bracelet this Christmas, Rupert decided it was past time to give her a severance payment. And shop for a ring? Perhaps. Maybe he'd bring a surprise home for Christmas this year. A surprise and the greatest gift of all—for himself. After all, what better time to introduce a fiancée to his family than at their usual gala holiday festivities? He'd inherited the Hall and kept up the old traditions there. The house would be decorated to the eaves. His sisters and his brother would be there with their families, and all the other relatives, too, except for Walter, who'd hopefully be pledging his future somewhere else. What better time? Thinking of time . . . Rupert hesitated, amazed at how far he'd got in his thoughts and how little progress he'd made in reality.

Early days, he thought, shaking his head as he strode back to report to his worried aunt. But some nights at parties where Arabella was might give him a better notion of what to do next.

He'd look through the pile of invitations that always accumulated on his desk, and reason out where a dewy young woman would be taken to of an evening. Better, he'd just ask Walter where he was going tonight. And then tell him not to.

The musicians were earning their keep at the Swanson party that evening. But even so, the stir Rupert made as he entered the room was audible. The hasty babble that ensued when he was sighted sounded like a henhouse after the fox had got in.

Aldridge? Here? At a party for ingenues and marriage-minded gents?

But it was past time for him to settle down, suddenly everyone remembered that. It was more exciting than the prodigal son's return. The mamas stared gimlet-eyed at him as he sauntered in, the prodigal bachelor in their sights.

He danced with his host's daughters, every unfortunate-looking one of them. But he certainly didn't need money, so no one put any construction but good manners on that. He stepped in time with several Incomparables, too, his face betraying nothing but his usual amusement and easy charm. Then he stood at the sidelines, chatting with some gentlemen. Watching the Danton chit, of course, the unexpected star of this Season.

The mamas stared, nervously, the other bachelors watched and worried. Could Aldridge capture her attention for longer than a few sets? Few men had this Season, and those few didn't seem able to recapture the glory of her company at the next parties where she reigned.

The music stopped. Arabella returned to the sidelines. Rupert nodded to the gentleman he was talking with and began ambling over toward her. She looked up, saw him, grinned—and turned and accepted Walter Browning's hand for the next dance.

Rupert stood still for a moment, an unreadable expression on his dark face. It was only unreadable because no one had actually ever seen him surprised, certainly not angry, and they could scarcely believe it. By the time they decided it must be that, his usual bland expression was back in place. But he remained still as he watched the dancers swirling in a lively polka, his dark eyes intent. Arabella and Walter seemed to be having a wonderful time. She laughed as she danced, and once or twice stole a glance at Rupert, and laughed some more.

When she immediately took Walter's hand for the next dance as well, the only people not watching them were watching Rupert. He went to the punch bowl, accepted a cup of the ruby-red stuff, and drank it down fast. And watched the dancers over the rim of his crystal cup. The reflection from his punch must have accounted for the increased color on his dark face.

But though it looked rich, the punch was poor stuff, more fruit juice than wine. Gentlemen who wanted to drink something with body either went to the salon where other men were playing cards, or left the place altogether. Rupert bowed over his hostess's hand, and left. Drinking wasn't on his mind. Murder was.

Rupert stalked through the night. *Early days?* he thought savagely, remembering his thoughts on the

way to the party. It was early *hours* for him to be
going home; the moon hadn't even begun to set. But
he couldn't go to his club, for he didn't want company.
He'd had quite enough of women, he didn't want to
visit his mistress, either. And he didn't choose to look
up any friends. He simply didn't trust his emotions
tonight. He felt like hitting something or running it
through, any perceived slight would wind up in a duel,
or worse. No, he was best off by himself because anything said to him now would be taken wrong. Damn
and blast the conniving little witch! How she must be
laughing at him.

He stalked through the night streets with such a
feral expression that passersby shrunk back when the
moon showed his face clear. He felt as much cheated
as enraged. He was furious at himself for having believed her. That was easier than hating her. It was
hard to hate anyone so lovely. He remembered how
she'd looked as she'd danced. His sister was right: Arabella Danton did sparkle. She'd worn a golden gown,
and whatever she'd said about her dancing, she'd
moved lightly as the elf she resembled—a very curva-
ceous elf, he thought, and scowled. Her face had been
sunny as a child's, filled with mirth and easy laughter.
Her glances at him had held more mischief than
malice . . .

His lips grudgingly quirked. He had to admire her
spirit, though. As he thought about that his fit of black
anger lifted for the first time since she'd granted his
cousin a second dance. After all, he'd come to her
house without invitation to ask her intentions concerning Walter. She might have been insulted, certainly he
would have been if the same sort of questions had
been asked of him. And what could a young woman
of breeding do in that case? Especially when the gentleman who offended her had a position in the Society

she was trying to fit into. What were her options? Throw him out? Call him names, challenge him to a duel? Send that young brother of hers after him to do it? Rupert's pace slowed.

No, he'd left her no option but to swallow her annoyance and pretend to agree, then show him she was her own woman after all. Spectacularly. He liked courage, he admired pluck. Helena hadn't had any, he remembered. She'd been eminently squashable. When her father announced he had a richer husband for her than newly orphaned and impoverished Rupert Aldridge, she'd bowed her head meekly and let herself be led to the altar without a backward look at 'poor Rupert,' leaving only a note saying they must never meet again. Rupert's scowl reappeared, he didn't like revisiting his past.

But his mood brightened. Courage? He almost smiled. Arabella Danton certainly had that—and everything else, in plenty. She'd turned the tables on him, hadn't she? Fixed him properly, in a place and at a time when there was nothing he could do about it but stand, watch, and seethe. How she must have enjoyed that. In retrospect, he could see it was brilliant retaliation, which he doubtless deserved. Lucky Walter, he thought grimly, his unborn smile dying.

He stopped in his tracks, struck by a horrible idea. *Walter?* Had he chased her into Walter's arms? Willowy, reticent Walter? Rupert had watched him tonight, wondering at Arabella's delight in his company. The fellow looked so dumbfounded with joy, he couldn't squeak out a word as he'd danced with Arabella. And she'd laughed up into his face as though he was the greatest raconteur in Town—and slid a triumphant look that said volumes more to Rupert, on the sidelines. No, he couldn't see anything between that mismatched pair but the dances she said she'd so enjoyed—and a chance to revenge herself on her tormentor, her dance partner's presumptuous cousin.

Rupert started walking again, head down, muttering to himself. Gads! He hoped he hadn't sealed lucky, dull Walter's happy fate for him. There was nothing for it. Rupert gritted his teeth. But he felt his heart leap up. He'd have to see her again.

Rupert was taken aback. He'd come into the salon expecting frowns, and received a shy but dazzling smile. She looked pale and weary this morning, but that might have been because she was wearing a soft blue gown instead of the gold that had flattered her so last night. He gazed at her wan face and realized she must be a night bird, one of those people whose mornings were bleary and difficult, their personalities only blooming in the moonlight. He'd known a few women like that. One of his mistresses had actually shied a teapot at him for whistling when he dressed. He turned his thoughts, feeling marginally ashamed of even thinking such a thing while Arabella's mild and inquiring eyes were on him.

He took the seat she indicated, sat back, and smiled at her. "Too much dancing last night?" he asked, trying to ease into the thing he had to say before he could say more. He hoped she'd be the one to admit how she'd defied him, so they could laugh about it.

She nodded, then looked sorry that she had. "Too much everything," she said, pressing a hand to her head. "I have to stop keeping such hours. Mornings are so much easier in the countryside, we go to bed at reasonable hours. But if you want to know anyone in London, you have to go to bed when the birds are waking up. I don't recall ever hearing birdsong as I fell asleep at home. Unless it was their night songs."

He quirked an eyebrow.

"Oh, you're not from the country, I expect. Well but birds do have different songs for night and morning. Night songs are what they use for gathering in their fledglings. Morning songs are much louder. Or so it seems to me," she said with a slight grimace.

"I know what you mean, I'm not only a creature of Town. My estate *is* in the countryside. But surely most of the birds in this district are served under glass. The rest are sparrows and pigeons. They don't sing, they gabble or chatter. That might be what bothers you."

She smiled. "Maybe so."

"But I haven't come to discuss birds this morning," he said, to get the thing over with so he could relax and enjoy her company. "I actually came to congratulate you for a brilliant bit of payback. All I want to know is if it was that—or something more that I should tell my aunt about."

She looked puzzled.

He sighed. Whatever her answer, she was certainly making him walk the extra mile. He was surprised at himself, it was an indication of his respect for her that he allowed it. "My dear Miss Danton, all that dancing with my fortunate cousin Walter! Was it in effect telling me that you're your own woman, and don't like anyone dictating to you? Or should we expect an announcement from him soon?" He paused, hoping no emotion but curiosity had showed in his voice, even though he discovered his question made him nervous as he awaited her answer.

She looked aghast. "Oh!" she said. "I danced with him, did I? Yes, of course, I did. And you didn't want me to, but you see . . ." She hesitated, then went on, her eyes fixed on his, "I couldn't hurt his feelings, could I? I'd promised the dances to him . . . Yes," she said with more liveliness, "so I did. But as for a declaration of anything, no, it was never that, please believe me."

She was flustered, she was surprised, she wasn't laughing. A joke was a joke, but she seemed terrified lest he'd actually think she had a serious thought in her head about Walter.

Rupert was content. No, he was delighted. No, he realized, as he deftly changed the subject, he was thrilled. He hadn't been thrilled in a long time.

He remained so for the rest of his visit to her and became more so the next day when she went riding with him. He was even more so when she took tea with him three days after that.

It astonished him, it delighted him, but Arabella Danton appeared to be everything he'd been looking for, and he hadn't even known all the things he'd been seeking. She was warm and friendly, bright and charming, many of their interests dovetailed. And he lusted for her, absolutely. Though she shone in the moonlight, she was a different woman by day. *Both* women appealed to him. The gay and vivacious flirt he'd seen at the party. The sensible, reticent young woman he met by day. He wanted more. He wanted both. And any other thing she might reveal to him when he finally had her in his arms.

But he went carefully. He saw her only by day. He customarily avoided the places she went to by night, and continued to do so, because he was now in this game to win. Let her go to Almack's and *ton* parties by herself, let her dance with others and chat with them—and, he hoped, miss his company too. He wanted her to compare him with the halflings and old men, the starchy and foppish, those in the market for a wife, looking for birth and fortune instead of personality. Let her meet men who thrived in such deadly dull and correct settings and find them wanting.

It would certainly stir up nothing but gossip if he competed directly. Let her miss him, then he'd make his move. If he chose to, that is. He had her days, let them butt heads with each other vying for Arabella's nights. For now.

So they strolled the streets and rode through the parks, investigated national treasures, met in art galleries and historic sites, and took tea in her aunt's parlor. And talked. And talked.

She seemed as enthralled with him as he was with her. Though he wondered if that were possible. In little more than weeks, he both thought he'd known her all his life, and had never known a woman like her. He was, he discovered, as foolishly in love as a boy, and the boy he'd been would have loved her too.

Rupert knew his reputation as a caustic wit, but curbed his acid tongue with her and found he liked himself better that way. He realized his heart had become soured, preserved from harm in purest vinegar. But Arabella slipped past his defenses, luring him with that charming face and form, laying siege with fascinating conversations and a battery of shy smiles that had quickly escalated to contagious laughter. She'd finally captivated his wary heart when he realized the honesty of her own. He was eager to surrender.

Still, he bided his time. He wanted to make no mistakes this time. Christmas was coming, a wonderfully sentimental time. The new year approached, a very auspicious time. Sophisticated as he was, jaded as he'd become, a joyous season was coming and he hoped to make it more so.

"A masquerade tonight?" Pace asked his sister when he saw her pacing in the parlor, waiting for their

aunt to come downstairs. She wore an ornate powdered wig that somehow suited her piquant face, making her look like a little china figurine. She wore an
antique pink gown with a cinched waist, low neckline,
and wide-belled skirt graced by darker pink panniers.
But she was overshadowed by her gown's vivid colors
because her face was nearly the color of her wig. She
was far too pale and wan-looking.

"The Howards are giving a masquerade ball; Aunt
says they're all the thing."

Pace nodded, eyeing her. "You saw Aldridge
again today?"

"Yes," she said, looking down and fingering the lace
at her sleeve.

He whistled. "No wonder you look racked. Flying
high, Midget. Take care you don't get your wings
burned."

She shrugged one white shoulder.

"Speaking of flying," he said carefully, "he's more
famous for seeing high flyers than escorting young ladies. But I suppose he *is* courting if he sees you by
day and minds his manners. Or does he?"

She nodded, looking regretful.

"But you don't see him at night?"

"He can't take Almack's," she said quickly, "or any
of those deadly places Aunt keeps dragging me. You
can't blame him. Lord! *I* can't take them."

"Well, it's a peculiar way of courting a girl, but
there's nothing shady about it. Couldn't be, since he
always sees you in sunlight." He laughed at his own
jest. "And no one sees him in his usual haunts by
night anymore. He's said to be growing sober as a
judge, reclusive as a monk. Strange way to woo, but
he's a singular fellow and it seems to be working," he
added, watching her color rise. "Tell you one thing, it

would be something if you attached him. You really like him?"

She ducked her head, then looked straight at him. "Really. At first, he terrified me. But now? Pace, I feel like I've known him *forever*. I'm so comfortable with him. Well, not exactly 'comfortable,' " she admitted, thinking of the way her breath caught when Rupert looked at her with warmth in his dark eyes, the way his velvety voice made her skin tingle as though he'd touched her with more than words, the way she couldn't sleep at night for wondering. . . .

"But much more comfortable than going to all those parties Aunt keeps dragging me to," she complained. "She says I can't put all my eggs in one basket. As though men were eggs!" she said indignantly. "But that's just how all the ladies at those parties talk, which is why I can't deal with them. She also says I oughtn't to put any serious construction on Rupert— Aldridge's—seeing me, because if he *was* serious, he'd take me to parties. Do you think that's true?"

"He must be," Pace answered, buying time. He couldn't resist her imploring look. He'd lie about anything when she looked like that. If he had to, he'd even confront Aldridge and ask his intentions—if this went on too long.

"Well, we'll see," she said sadly. "In the meanwhile, Aunt says Stepmother doesn't take any chances with her money and so neither can I. I won't marry to please Iris, so that's that, but until I go home, I have to go along with Aunt, and that's usually to the parties where she thinks I'll find an 'eligible' gentleman. Not that she thinks Rupert isn't eligible! But she can't believe he means marriage. Truthfully, neither can I. At any rate, I can't like the gentlemen she thinks are eligible, or those parties, the way everyone looks at you, how they weigh your rank and bank account.

They don't see you, they judge you; they don't hear you, they rate you. They still terrify me. That reminds me, have you got what I asked you for?"

He frowned, reached into his pocket, and handed her a package. "That's an awful lot of bottles, little sister. How much are you drinking?"

"Count how many deadly parties I have to go to, and you'll have your answer. Oh, bother. Can you open this for me?"

He hesitated. "It hasn't become a habit, has it?"

She looked exasperated. "I'm not drinking that much. Look how tiny that bottle is! And I don't need any when I'm happy. I never take any during the day. But at night? Soon as the sun sets and Aunt reminds me where we're going, I start to shiver. It's a godsend, Pace, it *does* give me courage to go on.

"If I could take some from Aunt, I would," she said as she unwrapped the bottle and struggled with the seal. "But when she saw the level in her precious decanter shrinking, she blamed poor Alice, the downstairs maid, and I couldn't have that, could I? So, open it, do. I have to go to the Howards' ball tonight, and masquerade or not, you know what bores they are. It will be such a squeeze. They've hired a hall, but it will be filled with the same dreadful people, only dressed like other people more interesting than they are. Who wouldn't be? How I wish Rupert would be there! But he's too clever to subject himself to them.

"I only have enough brandy to take the edge off my boredom anyway, you know that," she told him. "Boredom, and terror. You know Walter Browning is *still* pursuing me? And that horrid Mr. Cantwell? And Lord Peter?"

"Not that fading flower?" Pace yelped. "What did you do to deserve his attentions?" He used his pocket-knife to loosen the seal on the bottle, then handed it to his sister.

"Breathed, I suppose," she said, thanking him with a sunny smile.

They joked about the unfortunate Lord Peter and made sport of her other suitors until Pace realized how late it had grown. "I have to be off, short lady," he said carelessly, putting a finger to the tip of her nose. "The cards wait for no man. Have a good time."

As soon as he'd sauntered from the room, Arabella closed the door behind him. She quickly poured the contents of the bottle into her silver flask, slipped it into a hanging pocket under the panel of her skirt, and sighed with relief. Then she went to the decanter on the sideboard and poured herself a half glass of brandy. She drank it down quickly, one hand still on the bottle. She drew a deep breath and replaced the stopper. After a moment's pause, she lifted the stopper, poured herself another jot, and drank it down before replacing the top again.

The door to the parlor swung open.

"Are you ready?" her aunt asked.

Arabella nodded.

"Good—tsk! Would you look at that?" Aunt said, going directly to the sideboard and staring at the decanter. "That scoundrel of a brother of yours was just in here, wasn't he? Every time he comes in, the level goes down. The boy must be a sponge!"

Arabella smiled.

"Young men!" Aunt said with a mixture of exasperation and amusement. "Well, come along, we don't want to be late. My, you do look well tonight, the color suits you, your cheeks are glowing."

Arabella's radiant smile grew wider.

Rupert's eyes narrowed under his eye mask as he watched Arabella cavorting with her dancing partner.

Cavorting? She was romping, larking, tossing back her head, and laughing with glee every other minute, no matter who she danced with, and she seemed to be dancing with every man at the masquerade. She claimed to hate *ton* parties. Yet here she was, looking deliriously happy.

The mask was the reason why he'd impulsively decided to come here tonight to try his luck at last. No one could see him until midnight, which was when he'd hoped to remove his mask in all ways and ask Arabella to be his wife. It was time.

They hadn't known each other very long, but Society made it difficult for a man to get to know a well-bred woman much better than he knew her now. He knew his heart and mind, both were filled with her. No woman had made him feel this way, except for Helena years ago. But he'd been a boy then, and she a girl lacking the courage to love him, and now he was grateful for that.

This way, too, should Arabella choose to refuse him, no one would see his grief. It would be nothing less than that, he'd realized, which was why he'd determined to ask her tonight.

He wanted the disguise because he was that unsure of her. And it looked like he was right to be, he thought uneasily, hearing a peal of silvery laughter. At least he fancied he could hear it above all the gabble and music as the party goers in their fantastic costumes revolved around him. The hall was crammed. He knew most of the guests and many bored him, but they were all transformed tonight, making them almost interesting. Tonight they weren't vain or foolish or dull, they were ancient kings and temptresses, ogres and fairies, foxes and hounds, and dozens of other clever or clichéd whimsical and beautiful characters.

It had been a brilliant stroke for the Howards to rent a hall for their masquerade. Christmas was almost upon them. Dressing up was always part of Christmas revels, so all the wealthy ladies and gentlemen were sure to have some sort of costume in a trunk in the attic. Many of the guests used their costumes other times, too, because public masquerades were all the rage. Anyone could pay a nominal sum and go to one. And anyone did.

This was an elite affair, but the upper classes went to public masquerades, too. They mixed with the rabble and felt safe doing it. Gentlemen slummed in secret, seeking what they could find under other party-goers costumes. No real lady would admit attending a public masquerade; still, Rupert recognized costumes from the last time he'd escorted his mistress to one. It had been the last time, she was now his past mistress, he'd already sent her a generous gift for Christmas, along with a note of farewell.

He'd given up his present for his future, but when he looked at what he'd hoped his future to be, his heart sank. Arabella was dancing as though she hadn't a care in the world. He knew it was Arabella, he'd thrilled her aunt by asking and had got a prompt description of her costume. Arabella shimmered and shone in her pink panniered gown. Though she wore a powdered wig and an eye mask, there was no doubting who she was because of her exquisite figure, so artfully displayed in the ancient gown. And also because she was dancing with cousin Walter, dressed very aptly like a frog prince, the same costume he always wore to pantomimes at family celebrations at Christmastime.

Rupert was miserably aware of Christmas celebrations tonight, because he knew he ought to have been on his way home by now. Instead he was at a masquer-

ade in London, trying to understand what he—and the
lady he'd thought to ask to be his wife—was doing
there. It was clear to see she was having a wonderful
time. He wasn't. He was a glowering pirate instead of
a jolly one tonight. His outfit was complete with a
slouched hat, bloused shirt, cutlass bound to his sashed
waist, and high cuffed boots. He'd felt like a perfect
buccaneer, but seeing Arabella's glee, suddenly didn't
feel like swaggering anymore. He was crestfallen and
confused. How could she be so different from day to
day and night to night? Candlelight was supposed to
change a woman's looks, not her mind.

She looked perfectly at ease, confident, radiant, actually giddy. But she said she detested these parties.
And she was with Walter again, the man she'd said
she had no interest in. She looked interested now.
Rupert was at a loss to understand it. Had she been
making sport of him? But to what end? He didn't
think he was infallible, but he'd swear that look he'd
surprised in her eyes lately matched the one he was
helpless to conceal in his when he gazed at her.

When the dance ended Rupert strode to Arabella,
now fanning herself and laughing up at Cousin Walter.

"My dance, I believe, my lady?" he said with a
sweeping bow.

A respectable young woman would never dance off
on the arm of a stranger, the glory of a masquerade
was that it was the one place where she might. He'd
reveal himself when he danced with her, then find
some time to speak to her alone. He didn't know what
to make of her this evening, maybe she had an
explanation.

"Of course, how could I have forgotten?" she said
with a laugh, giving him her hand.

"Ah, good, a waltz," he said, and led her to the
dance.

They didn't speak for a few minutes, in which time he realized she'd lied about her skill and was as good a partner as any man could expect. She didn't show any concern about finding herself alone with a stranger. But she was a stranger tonight, too. The Arabella he knew would have been talking all the while. Surely she'd be shy and somewhat stiff in his arms at first. This Arabella's eyes glittered behind her mask, she was languorous and relaxed in his clasp, moving to the music with sensual ease. He began to wonder if this was really Arabella. But her scent was lily of the valley, as always, her skin looked white and pure as the complexion he couldn't forget, and her petite size and delicious shape were unmistakably her own.

It wasn't hard to dance her through the thicket of celebrants. It was simple to lose sight of her aunt and Walter. And it was a little more difficult to sidle out of the vast ballroom and into the shadows of the back hall, all while keeping in step. But he'd been here before with women who weren't ladies, women who knew the night and the pleasures it could hold. Another few steps to the now distant music and he'd led her out a back door and onto the balcony. Other couples were in the shadows, but Rupert knew where there was a niche in the wall; a few steps farther, and they were there. Then he stopped.

She looked up, as though suddenly awakened. He thought it might be the chill of the night. So he folded her into his arms to warm her, and brought his lips to hers to warm himself.

She didn't struggle. She merely said, "Oh!"

It wasn't the correct reaction to a stranger's embrace. If he thought about it he'd be alarmed. But he ruthlessly banished criticism and surprise, took advantage of the moment, and deepened the kiss—and lost himself. This was Arabella as he'd only dreamed of

her being. She felt tiny in his arms, but she was more
than enough woman for him. He sipped at her, drew
back, and kissed her again. Her lips were full and
sweet, and when they parted her mouth was warm and
welcoming, generous, without inhibition. She nestled
deeper into his embrace, her arms wound around him,
her hands at his neck, her breasts pressed against his
chest. Her elaborate gown thwarted his questing hand
as it slid down her back, but he soon had it on her
slender waist, the other at her breast. He pulled her
closer and drank her in with wonder and grateful joy.
She tasted of dark sweet wine, of welcoming woman,
of heady liquor, of brandy, a lot of brandy actually . . .

His head jerked back. He dropped his hands. "How
much have you had to drink?" he asked.

Now he could see her eyes were half-closed. Her
hands twined at his neck, she tried to draw him closer
again. "Just a sip, a nip, hardly a bite." She giggled.

He frowned. "A sip? You walked out with a
stranger after only a sip?"

"You're not strange at all, Rupert," she said, snug-
gling into his body, for warmth, he expected, because
now her attitude was more childlike than enticing. "I
knew it was you, silly." She patted his chest with one
open hand. "Your voice," she said dreamily, "How
could I mistake that? It sends chills down my back.
And your size," she added, her nose on his chest now.
"Who else is your size? And your hands. You have
such wonderful hands: so big, so strong, so capable."

"Capable of many things," he agreed. None of
which he'd allow himself now, he thought with deepest
regret. He tilted her chin up with one of those strong
hands. "Capable of wringing your neck—or Walter's.
You're drunk as a sow, Arabella, my dear."

"All I had was a sip or two," she argued without
much force. "Or three, perhaps. After all, how am I

to face such an evening without my friend Brandy?"
She giggled again, then looked up at him and complained, "You didn't say you'd be here. I thought I
was going to have to face it alone. I was *so* happy to
see you, I can't tell you. But I'm telling you, aren't I?"

She looked puzzled, but all her emotions were fluc-
tuant, flickering across her face as she felt them. "Why
are you frowning? Are you angry with me?"

"No," he said, firmly putting her at arm's length
because he knew his limits. Having her closer would
definitely make him forget her condition. "I may kill
Walter, though, for plying you with drink."

"He didn't ply me with anything. I plied myself."

"Certainly," he said, admiring her gallantry and not
willing to risk an argument. Drink made tempers hot-
ter and more vocal, he didn't want her drawing attention. "Wait here. I'll see if there's a way I can get you
to your carriage without meeting anyone. They may
not see your face, but we can't risk them not recogniz-
ing your costume. Doubtless, you showed it off. Then
I'll get word to your aunt, so you can go home. You
came in her carriage?"

"No," she said, seeming a little more sober. She
stepped back, crossed her arms, and hugged herself
hard. She stared up at him. "Walter took us in a hack-
ney. Are you angry about that? You look *very* angry."

"I'm very angry," he agreed, gripping her shoulders
and maneuvering her back into the shadows of the
niche. "Now, stay! Or I'll be angrier still."

He went to the door they'd left by to see what traffic was in the hall. No one. Good. He turned back—
in time to see Arabella in silhouette as she withdrew
a small silver object from beneath a pannier of her
gown. It flashed in the moonlight as she squinted at
it, shook it, tipped it up, and drank down whatever
was in it.

He stood stock-still. Then strode back and snatched the flask from her now nerveless hand as she stood arrested, staring up at his hard and angry face. He sniffed at the flask.

His sneer was clear to see even in the half-light. "A *nip*? A sip? This is your own flask . . . So it wasn't Walter."

"I *said* so," she said, nodding.

"Good God, Arabella, how long have you been . . . ? Of course!" he exclaimed, stunned and appalled. "The two Arabellas, the day lady and the night drunkard. That's it, isn't it?"

"I—I take it for courage," she explained, stepping back. "Pace said all the fellows do it. Is there any left?"

"So you think you need courage now?" he said, his lips tightening.

"Oh, no!" she exclaimed, then thought about it. "Well, but you looked so savage. But I do need some in order just to go to these things, and a drop more to get through them."

He stared at her for a long moment. "Of course," he said slowly. "You're right. You know?" he added with a twisted smile. "I think I'll prove you *do* need courage. Come with me."

He didn't give her a choice. He began to steer her out into the hall, stopped, and asked, "Where's your wrap?"

"I gave it to a footman," she said in confusion, fumbling in her bodice and extracting a card. "He gave me this for it."

"Good," he said, snatching it from her. Without releasing his grip on her arm, he walked to the front of the hall and called for the lady's wrap. He kept Arabella to the shadows, beyond the light of the flickering gaslight high on the walls.

"Are you taking me home?" Arabella asked meekly, standing a little straighter, sounding a little more serious.

"Eventually," he muttered.

It was a clear cold night. Rupert had taken his open phaeton in spite of it, preferring speed to the dubious comfort of sitting cooped up at the mercy of another driver. He handed Arabella up to the high seat, nodding in silent appreciation of her enveloping cloak. It concealed her shape and the voluminous hood hid her face. He'd lost his temper, but while waiting for the footman to come with her wrap, he'd almost lost his resolve. When he saw her cloak, he was determined to go ahead with his impulsive plan. He picked up the reins.

"Are we going home?" she asked again, but in a smaller voice.

"Yes, after I take you to meet some of your friends. If not now, they will be later. You have much in common."

She frowned, trying to puzzle that out.

"You'll think more clearly when the night air clears the fumes from your brain. What you see will do the rest, I hope," he said curtly. "How long have you been swilling liquor, by the way?"

"I don't. It's just when Aunt insisted I go to a ball last month. I think it was, the other month, at least, Pace saw I was frightened, so he gave me some and told me it was Dutch courage. It helps, Rupert, it really does," she said, imploring him to understand. "I'm not a sot. I just use it."

"It uses you," he said grimly, and flicked his whip to set the horses trotting faster down the freezing streets.

The night was growing colder, and Rupert's temper began cooling along with it. He glanced at Arabella, because now that the blood was no longer buzzing in his ears, he could hear her silence. Was she terrified? Or so drunk she'd fallen asleep? Her hood covered her profile—he might as well be looking at a specter inside the enveloping folds of it.

"Don't be afraid," he said suddenly as that terrible thought occurred to him, "I won't hurt you or let anything else harm you."

"I know that," she said softly, in a solemn voice. "It's just that you're so angry with me."

"I was. But for good cause. You'll see."

They'd been in the heart of Town in a district with theaters, taverns, restaurants, thronged with merrymakers out for an evening. It wasn't a long ride to his destination, though, and in a few more minutes they were there. Here, the streets were as crowded, but with men, women, and packs of children, some merry, but most not. The roadway was filled with dirt, garbage, and manure. No street sweepers plied their brooms here, but there were people picking through the rubbish, looking for what few items they could sell. There wasn't much of that. Arabella's hood swiveled as she looked around. She sat straighter, very still.

Rupert pulled the phaeton up beside a ramshackle building with the sign *The Waltzing Mouse* hanging over it. He tossed a coin to one of the shabby men standing outside. "Hold them a few minutes, and there'll be double that for you," he promised, then climbed down, went around to Arabella's side, and reached up for her hand. "Come with me, please," he said gruffly. "But keep your hood up."

She entered the tavern with him warily, but didn't hang back. She did stop and stare once her eyes became accustomed to the low light and thick smoke that filled the place. Rupert's hand at her back propelled her to a table in a corner. He held out a chair for her, then said nothing as she sat and stared around the room.

He couldn't see her expression. But he saw her hands clench in her lap.

"I know," he said wearily, drumming his fingers on the sticky tabletop, "I shouldn't take a lady to such a place. Young gentlemen come here when they're slumming, though. I begin to think young women should, too. Some of these poor creatures are afflicted by poverty, that's true," he said with a gesture to indicate the others in the room. "But more of them are more beset by their friend, 'Gin.' They haven't the funds to keep company with your friend, Brandy, you see." Then he was still, watching her look around the room.

The drabs in the opposite corner were the worst, he supposed. Old women with few teeth, less clothing, and no dignity at all. They sat or rocked precariously on their chairs, trying to keep their balance. Some shouted conversations at the others, some cackled, some had toppled to the floor and slept in the straw where they lay. It wasn't pleasant seeing an old woman naked to the waist. But Arabella had seen a woman's breasts, he supposed. It was important that she see more.

The women at the tap were younger, and harsher, but most were just as drunk and scantily dressed. Some sat in men's laps. They were all drinking, some laughing, some weeping. The men were enjoying themselves in various ways that made Rupert begin to rue his decision. But still, there was some discretion in public, even here. At least, there'd always been before. If there were none tonight, he'd take Arabella and leave in an instant. He watched, tensed to bolt if he was wrong.

"This is a bawdy house?" Arabella whispered, finally turning her face toward him.

He saw how white she was. His voice was gruff. "No. This is just a low tavern, like many others in London. Some of these women sell themselves, but most are just enjoying themselves. They get gin—Blue Ruin, Strip Me Naked, Flash of Lightning, Mother's Milk—they have a dozen names for their beloved—a penny a glass. And they must get it. Maybe they started drinking for courage, but, believe me, they continue for life.

"Don't think it's just the poor," he added bitterly. "I was going to take you to elegant gaming hells, where you could see ladies and gentlemen losing their money at cards, dice, and the roulette wheel. Drunken ladies and gents. Only we call a fellow who drinks 'A three bottle man' and congratulate him for it. And we pretend the lady doesn't drink at all, though we watch her down a dozen glasses 'for her heart' or 'her stomach's sake.' It's our disease as well as theirs," he said, gesturing to the patrons of the Waltzing Mouse.

"But I begin to think this was a bad idea. How can you think of yourself as one of these poor creatures? Or as any of the more fortunate sots at the gaming hells, either? Every drunkard thinks he's above it, each one thinks he's not one." His face grew tight. "My father," he said, "thought he was a connoisseur of fine wines, brandies, cognacs, and champagne, if only because he could afford to get drunk luxuriously. He did, though the price was higher than he bargained for. It meant he didn't leave a penny for his children, and his antics helped put paid to his wife's life years before his own premature death. Enough," he said harshly, "I'll take you back. This was a bad idea. A very bad idea."

They drove back to the masquerade in silence. "I

won't ask you to forgive me," he finally said as the hall came into view. "What I did was unforgivable. I presumed. I had no right. I know it, and begin to rue it, but ask you to understand. I kidnapped you. You might press charges against me, you know. But I care for you, Arabella, and seeing you—how you could be two women, one bright and charming, the other just as bright, but much less charming; upset me. I had no right to, I'll trouble you no more."

He stopped the carriage in front of the hall, and swung around to look at her. Her eyes were opened so wide he could see the whites of them shining out of the recesses of her hood. "I'm not a prude," he said gently. "Certainly not a man without faults. I drink sometimes, too. But I drink *sometimes*. And for the pleasure of it, in company—not for courage. I eat, too," he said with a small sad smile, "but never for solace, as I suspect our prince does, hence the shape in which our prince is. You see? Good things can be done for the wrong reasons. And overdone for them, too. Well, consider what I just did," he said sadly. "But spirits, once overdone, can become so necessary that nothing else is. I just didn't want to see you wasting yourself. But I'd no right."

He looked at her for another long moment, then leapt from the seat and handed her down to the ground. They went into the masquerade ball again. He took her down the hall to a dim recess before helping her off with her cloak.

"I'll give this back to the footman and have it put with your aunt's wrap," he said, taking her cloak over his arm. "There's such a press of people, I doubt you've been missed. If you were, you must send word to me immediately, and I'll tell your aunt it was my fault—if not why it was. Don't worry, no harm will come to you from this night, except that which I have

done. For that . . . I'm not sorry, but I do regret it if
only because it was not my right. Good-bye, Arabella,
I wish you joy and luck, and above all, courage."

He bowed. And left her.

Missing someone was worse when everyone else was
celebrating, Rupert decided. He couldn't be sure, he'd
never missed anyone so much before. It hadn't been
that many weeks since the masquerade and his lunatic
abduction of Arabella, but he'd suffered every day of
them. He hadn't gone home, the family revels would
go on without him. He hadn't had the heart to face
them without the centerpiece of the celebrations he'd
planned to present to them. London was no better,
though. Now the streets were all holiday, crammed
with shoppers and carolers giddy with expectation of
great joy. He brooded and expected only greater
regrets.

He'd no right, he reminded himself again and again.
He'd been presumptuous and cruel. He hadn't gotten
any promises from her, his own expectations had been
at fault. He'd written her a note to that effect. She
hadn't answered it. He didn't blame her. If he was a
drinking man, he'd have finished off several quarts by
now, and wouldn't that be an irony? But his father
had at least cured him of that excess. Instead he suffered an excess of regret.

Rupert sat in his study and sifted through all the
invitations he'd received, all fine ways of celebrating
Christmas—if a fellow hadn't a family, or a beloved
to share the holiday with. He absently shuffled
through the invitations. His hand stilled at the name
on one of them. He opened it and stared.

She was inviting him to her Christmas party?

How could she? How could he? Would she dance
by on Walter's arm and laugh at him? Or worse, de-

clare her engagement to Walter? Rupert realized he deserved that, even if she didn't. But perhaps it wasn't that. Was it that she would accept an apology from him after all? Did she want one? His breath stilled at a terrible thought. Had her aunt found out? Would he be forced to ask for her hand, which as a gentleman he'd have to do to preserve her reputation? His spirits lifted, then fell. Could he bear to marry her and watch her defy him by drinking her life away, as his father had done?

Rupert stared into the fire. He supposed he could just get up, saddle a horse, and leave right now. That way he'd spend Christmas on the road, where there was no one he knew and no way to be hurt, except by highwaymen. And they'd only take his purse or his life, not his heart.

Arabella's aunt's house was ablaze with lights, and carriages were in line at the curb. Evergreen wreaths were draped over the lintel, the frosted windows glowed rosy red. It was a warm and welcoming place on a chill December night, but Rupert was reluctant to come in out of the cold. Still, he faced his fear, as always, gave his phaeton to a footman, and went into the house—apprehension in his heart, no trace of it on his face.

He gave his coat and hat to a footman and strode forward, but was halted at the door to the grand salon, where the party was being held.

"Good evening, Mr. Aldridge," Pace Danton said stiffly. "Happy Christmas. I'm glad you could come tonight."

The lad was excessively formal. Rupert tensed with the horrible thought that he meant to offer a challenge. His thoughts went scrambling. How could he evade a duel? How could he fire into the air or drop his sword without injuring the boy's feelings? How could he duel without harming him physically?

"I thank you for pointing out what I failed to see," Pace went on quickly. "I can't say what she'll do, but you'll see."

Rupert nodded, vastly relieved. He hadn't an idea of what to say. But he looked up and saw for himself, and was repaid for his momentary surge of hope.

Arabella was having a wonderful time at her party, clearly imbued with an abundance of Christmas spirit. She was in the center of the grand salon, wearing a silver gown, a wreath of silvered holly twined in her curls. She shone in the midst of her throng of suitors like the moon in the dark of the night. A punch bowl with sizzling apples bobbing in ruby-red wassail was at her elbow; she held a cup in her hands, and she was laughing. She was radiant. She sparkled. *Lord*, he thought sadly, how she shone. This was the Arabella of the spirits, he saw it and knew it, and wanted to turn around and leave.

But she glanced at him then, and he was pinned to the spot by the sudden delight he saw flash in her eyes. He had at least to go bow over her hand before he left. He had that much courage. Hers might come from a bottle, his came from years of training. It would cost him more days of regret and nights of sorrow, but he had to face his fears and live with them.

He went to her and bowed over her hand, to the annoyance and resentment of her doting court of enthralled suitors. "Miss Danton," he said, "how good to see you in such great spirits."

"How good to see you, too," she said vivaciously, putting her cup down on a tabletop. "I'm *so* glad you haven't left London yet, I did *so* want to wish you a glad holiday and a prosperous New Year."

"It would prosper better if you'd grant me a dance,"

he answered without meaning to, mustering a smile from somewhere, though his heart ached. She was so lively, so charming with the color high in her cheeks and a smile hovering at the edges of those lovely lips. It was clear that her friend and his foe, Brandy, was with her tonight. But good, too, in a way, for him at least. Now he could leave her knowing his hopes had been impossible ones. Still, his sorrow for her outweighed his personal relief.

"Why, I will!" she said. "The third dance is a waltz, and I begin to believe there won't be room for so much as a sidewise sidle by the fifth dance. All our guests will have arrived, and it will be so crowded there'll scarcely be room to *comment,* much less dance."

Her court laughed at her witticism and gazed at her fondly. Rupert winced. She was so merry, so bright, so free, so absolutely addled, he was glad she'd given him the third dance. He wondered if she'd be upright by the fifth.

He stood apart and watched her flirt with her suitors. He stood on the sidelines, his shoulders against the wall, and watched her dance the first two sets. He marveled that she didn't miss a step, but remembered there was a line of drunkenness a person could tread without failing, it was only when that line was crossed that they staggered. From her exaltation he realized she was nearing it. No wonder she'd hinted there'd be no fifth dance for her.

She felt so good and so right in his arms when he claimed his promised dance that he forgot his resolve and grieved again for the loss of her. She'd been right, though. Her aunt's grand salon was clearly too small for dancing. Soon the waltz might become as obscene as its critics claimed, since the dancers were already pressed so close they could scarcely move, much less twirl. Arabella made a charming moue, and looked over her shoulder.

"Tsk! Can't swing a cat in here, certainly not a partner," she exclaimed with outsized exasperation. "Come, let's move in that direction, shall we?" Her eyes twinkled up at him, indicating they should maneuver to the left, where her little chin was pointing.

He obeyed, letting her steer him by her expressions, following her lead by watching her eyes and her tilted shoulder. After a few turns and "your pardons" as they bumped into other dancers, he found himself suddenly standing outside the crowded salon.

"Good!" Arabella exclaimed. She snatched up his hand, and giggling madly, tugged him quickly down the hall and out a door.

He found himself standing with her in the cold at the edge of her aunt's deserted garden, the door swinging shut behind them.

"Better!" Arabella giggled. "Alone again at last!"

"Arabella," Rupert said wearily, "This is not at all the thing, you know." Likely she didn't, not anymore, he thought. But so much as he wanted her, he wanted no drunken groping, no brandy-stoked kisses. There had to be a better farewell than this. He looked down at her and took her hand to lead her inside again. She saw his intent.

"Oh, drat!" she said, and took a deep breath before reaching up, tugging his head down, and putting her lips on his.

It would be ridiculous to struggle, he thought, prepared to endure it for a moment before he firmly put her aside and brought her back to her party.

But her lips were sweet and her mouth so warm, and she flung herself close and clung to his shoulders. His arms went around her instinctively, and he found he couldn't let her go to save his soul or hers. It was like embracing fire. She wore such a flimsy gown and her body was pressed so agonizingly close and she tasted so deliciously of ginger snaps, cinnamon, and spices, and Arabella and . . . Nothing else.

He jerked back and held her at arm's length, the question burning in his suddenly darker and amazed eyes.

She mustered a tremulous smile. "I'm not used to accosting gentlemen," she said in a shaky voice. "I thought to find some mistletoe, but couldn't wait. Oh, Rupert—I had to show you. I—I'm me. Just me. I haven't had a drop of anything more enlivening than fruit punch since you spoke to me. It wasn't enough to tell you, I had to show you. The flask went into the Thames right away, and by the time I dared take a sip of brandy to test myself the other day, I didn't need another! I understood, you see. The brandy made me courageous, but I realized that if I could be brave with it, I certainly could try to be so without it.

"I pretended I was soused one evening, and I behaved with just as much bravado," she said with rising excitement. "I realized all spirits did was give me permission to be brighter and happier. I gave myself that permission, and it worked! Oh, Rupert, you were right!" she cried. "I wasn't drinking brandy for courage anymore, it was drinking up all of mine."

Her stormy eyes were starrier with unshed tears now. "I *didn't* want to be sprung all the time, you know, swiggered, foxed, bosky—there are more names for being drunken than I knew! I talked to Pace and he told me."

She took another sustaining breath. "But mostly, I thought about it." Her eyes searched his face, her own now deadly serious. "I wasn't worried about being like those women I saw, after all, more than three glasses makes me vilely ill. Still, three glasses every night is too much for me. It made me careless and foolish enough, Lord knows. Still, that wasn't it. The thing was that I was terrified of losing you as well as myself.

"But I presume," she said, looking down. "I don't know if you wanted me or were just being a Good Samaritan. Whatever your reasons, you were just that," she said, raising her eyes to his again. "So tonight I had to let you know that you did a good thing. And I found the courage to do it without drinking a thing. What you said made sense to me and made me see that. I thank you from the bottom of my heart for caring enough, at least, to let me know."

"Not want you?" he asked, dumbfounded. "By God, Arabella, I wanted nothing else." His wits came storming back. He took her by the shoulders and looked down at her, his expression grave. "I kidnapped you. I compromised you and myself, and knew what I was doing. In fact, I was surprised no one caught us, and you didn't insist—but, of course, you wouldn't. Surprised, then disappointed. Arabella, I do adore you, you must know that. Even when I grieved for you, I wanted you."

He grasped her two hands in his. "I was the one who lacked courage. I should have stayed with you, helped you. Can you forgive me?"

She smiled. "You should know better. Only I could help myself. I did. You told me. I listened. I thank you."

"Is that all? What now?"

She lowered her lashes over her eyes. "What would you?" she asked softly.

"I would marry you," he said fervently. "Will you have me?"

"I'll have no other."

It was cold in the little garden—it was December after all. But neither of them felt it. In fact, when

Rupert got so overheated he decided to remove the top of Arabella's gown in order to cool her off, and she wordlessly and enthusiastically agreed, he finally realized their embraces had made it far too warm.

"Here, now," he said with a sheepish grin that Arabella thought sat surprising well on that dark rakish face of his as he drew back, drawing the neck of her gown up, "no more of this, at least out here and right now. But let's go back and let the world know we'll be married by Christmas, shall we?"

She giggled as merrily as any besotted female. "We can't, silly. That's tomorrow. But, Rupert, now I can raise a wassail to you, and not have to have another. Isn't that grand?"

He nodded. "A wassail and a wedding toast."

She smiled with regret. "There's not enough time. But by next Christmas, surely."

"By the new year, with a special license?" he bargained.

"You're clearly befuddled by holiday spirits," she said tenderly, brushing back the disordered hair from his high forehead with an air of fond possession.

"Intoxicated by the very best vintage," he admitted as he took that hand, brought it to his lips, and sighed with the air of a man coming home at last. "Pure Arabella."

"Impure Rupert," she said with a matching sigh as she rested in his embrace again. "That's my favorite libation now, and forever." She stirred in his arms. "May I have another sip?"

"My own dear little sot," he said with a crooked smile as he lowered his head to hers, "of course, let's toast our incredible good luck. Happy Christmas to both of us. Come fill your cup, my love, because mine is overflowing."

The Christmas Curse
by Barbara Metzger

CHAPTER ONE

" 'Struth, Christmas just is not what it used to be."
The old knight looked around his Great Hall
with its banners and tapestries and suits of armor. He
shook his bearded head.

"You aren't what you used to be, either," his fond
wife replied with a tongue that could cut a haunch
of venison.

"Faugh. In my time, we had ribbons and pine
boughs, mistletoe and holly. Good honest revelry, with
minstrels and mead, after we got down on our knees
and prayed, of course."

"In your time, you old tub of tin, you had knees."

Sad but true, Sir Olnic was a mere shadow of himself. He was, in fact, a shade, a specter, a spirit, a
ghost. His beloved Lady Edryth, as beautiful in his
eyes as ever, appeared to other, mortal eyes as a wisp
of smoke, a dust mote in a moonbeam, a wafting of
lilacs.

She drifted now through the Great Hall of Worth
Keep, her long red locks flowing behind her, held off
her alabaster cheeks by a simple gold fillet. A summer's day would have burned that fair complexion,
but Lady Edryth had not been kissed by the sun in a
long time, a very long time. She had not been kissed

by her husband in ages, either, and was not like to permit such license in the near future.

With her richly embroidered blue velvet gown making a soft swishing noise—or was that the wind whispering through the cracks of the ancient pile?—Lady Edryth floated past the long rows of antique armor that lined the smoke-darkened walls. Only one suit of metal was currently occupied, the one in which Sir Olnic currently sulked. It had been the knight's second best chain mail, his finest one having suffered irreparable damages, although not as irreparable as Sir Olnic had suffered, that long-ago, curse-causing Christmas Day.

"Sir Olnic the Worthy," his lady-wife muttered now. "Hah. You are not even worthy of a good polishing, not after you frightened off all the servants. Again. My home is going to wrack and ruin, no thanks to you."

"Oh-ho, so now it is my fault? You did not chivvy the maids about their mopping?"

"Lazy creatures, all of them. But I never had a flock of angry geese attack the poor cook."

"They were looking for the ring, by all the saints. Your blessed ring."

"And what about the mad squirrels, or the bellowing cows? Was that before or after the wild boars or the whirlwinds? No one will come next or nigh the place, not at Yuletide."

"Saints above, I was trying to move the ring. 'Sooth, it is getting closer, isn't it?" Sir Olnic crouched lower in his armor, clanking the cuisse piece at the thigh. He jangled it again for good measure, not that anyone was listening. Servants rarely entered this area of the old castle, and never near Christmas, if they could avoid it. There was, the knight knew to his abiding regret, no avoiding his beloved's recriminations.

"Closer?" his dulcet-voiced darling shrilled. "Three

miles in three centuries? At this rate, the Keep will collapse around our ears, if we had ears, of course, and our heirs will be living on the moon, before we dissolve your wretched curse."

Sir Olnic rattled the heavy sword at his side. "Your memory plays you false, madam wife, the same way you betrayed your marriage vows."

"I never did, you maggot-minded old fool!"

"Prithee, 'twas not I who called the curse down around our house."

"Well, 'twas not I lost my temper on Christmas Day."

They had been entertaining the neighborhood at a Yuletide feast, with suckling pigs and stuffed partridges, venison and smoked oysters. There were musicians and mimes, ale, mead, and wassail. Spirits rose and, with them, tempers.

"I still say that cur Rostend insulted me and my house," Sir Olnic declared.

"Sir Rostend paid me a compliment on my dress, by all the heavens."

"His eyes were prying you out of it, I swear."

Alas, Sir Olnic lost his head, challenging his long-time foe to a duel. The joust turned into a melee between their armies of followers, a bloody pitched battle. Sir Olnic lost. He lost his head, indeed, but also his arm, a leg, and various and sundry suddenly unnecessary appendages. Worst of all, he lost his wife's wedding ring.

Jousting on Christmas Day, breaking the king's truce, would have sent both men to the gallows. Taking a life, even one so unlamented as Sir Rostend's, on the day of the Nativity would have sent Sir Olnic straight to Hell, except for his beloved's parting words. As she angrily crammed her gold ring onto his little finger, her favor to wear at the joust, Lady Edryth had declared: "If you lose this ring"—which Sir Olnic would only do, of course, if he lost his life—"then your soul will walk this hall through eternity. You will never find rest, as God is my witness and by the love I bear you, until the ring is back in this castle, on the finger where it belongs."

Lady Edryth had died shortly after her husband, defending her home and her son's patrimony from those who saw her lord's death as an invitation to increase their own holdings. She succeeded in preserving the succession, but was doomed to join Sir Olnic's eternal limbo by that very curse. Taking the Lord's name in vain, on Christmas, no less, and usurping His authority, kept her from the Gates of Heaven. Instead, she bided in the Great Hall of Worth Keep, keeping her spouse on his ghostly toes and the housemaids on theirs.

As far as Sir Olnic could figure, with centuries to consider the dilemma, he needed to get that blasted ring onto the finger of the bride of one of his descendants. Lady Edryth could no longer wear it, for certain, and simply placing the gold band in the hand of an heir could not possibly satisfy the terms of the curse. No, that would have been too easy for his lady-wife. She needed true love, besides. Oh, and he soon discovered—after a decade or two—that he could only be truly effective, have the slightest bearing whatsoever—besides a few moans and metallic clanks—on the solid world, during the twelve days of Christmas. His lady love did not do things by half. Nor did she have half the effect on the mortals who shared their castle.

Unfortunately, Sir Olnic's descendants, who had taken the family name of Nicholson and who had risen, by that same pigheaded valor, to the title of Barons of Worth, seldom wed for love. They made advantageous marriages, increasing land and wealth and power at whichever court held sway at the time. They also took up residence elsewhere for most of the year, for which Sir Olnic could not blame them. Hell, the Keep was haunted, wasn't it?

Aside from having neither heir nor beloved bride to hand, the ancient knight had not yet retrieved the ring, but he was getting closer. The jousting ground was a torn-up mud pit by the time all the bits and pieces of the combatants had been gathered for burial. Who knew who ended up in which mausoleum? No one cared, except for Sir Olnic, who was, to his— literally—everlasting regret, missing his left hand's little finger, with his wife's ring on it.

The tilting field was seeded for grass; he sent in squirrels to dig it up. The grounds keepers replanted; he called forth whirlwinds. They sowed wheat; he sent crows. They let it go fallow, he followed with rooting pigs. Finally, finally, many Christmases later, he managed to loose a herd of goats in the acreage. One of them actually uncovered the ring, but the blasted nanny ate the thing before Sir Olnic could get anyone to retrieve it. He was working on the milkmaid and her beau, but too late. The next effort was certainly beneath a knight's dignity, surveying the grass beneath a goat. Still, he was rewarded. The ring ended in a pile of manure, that much closer to the Keep. Some years later, nicely rotted, the mound was gathered by the gardeners and placed around the rosebushes.

Sir Olnic tried hens and hedgehogs. He tried killing the rosebushes, but the gardeners merely replanted in the same spot. Geese, snakes, a small boy once—Nothing had brought the ring to the surface. Now the knight was desperate. For the first time in decades, the Nicholson heir was in residence at Christmastime . . . the bachelor Baron Worth.

Lady Edryth shook her head. "Forsooth, you'd do better trying to marry off one of the goats."

"Christmas is not what it used to be, is it, Salter?"

"No, my lord," the old butler agreed. "But then Christmas is never quite what one expects, at Worth Keep."

Nick had to raise his glass to that. This would be the first Yuletide Oliver Nicholson, Baron Worth, had spent at the family seat in over a decade. This was not, however, the first glass he'd lifted since his arrival. The two facts had more than a passing acquaintance, although the dismal old place currently suited his dismal old mood. Still, the lack of decorations, the pervasive chill in the air despite the fires in the hearths, the absence of any reminders of the festive season, were vaguely disturbing to the baron on this Christmas Eve. He stretched his long legs closer to the fire in the book room of the newer wing. "Are there decorations in the servants' quarters, at least?" he asked.

"There are hardly any servants in the servants' hall, my lord, not at this time of year. Most take their holidays to visit family. Or accept temporary positions with whichever of the neighbors are entertaining." He did not say that the few staff members with responsible positions or nowhere else to go were cowering in the gatehouse, the gardener's cottage, or the estate manager's house, as far from Worth Keep as they could get. "Mrs. Salter and I do have a red candle in our sitting room. If we had known of your visit, my lord, we would certainly have seen the family rooms decorated for the season, with a pine bough or such in your valet's chamber, and a sprig of holly for your groom over the stables. Mrs. Salter does have a goose ready to cook for tomorrow's dinner, however, and her special Christmas pudding."

Which were undoubtedly meant for the loyal old retainers' meal. "My apologies, Salter. It was a sudden decision. Still, I am sure you must have prepared a wassail bowl for the carolers who will be arriving any moment."

The butler straightened a figurine on the mantel. "No carolers will be coming, my lord."

"Ah. The Worth wraiths, I suppose?"

The butler nodded his gray head. "And the Christmas curse."

"Do you and your good wife not believe in ghosts, Salter?"

Salter believed that no one but Master Oliver, now Baron Worth, would keep on such an elderly couple to run his residence. The butler's eyes were bad. His wife's hearing was worse. "We've neither seen nor heard any disturbances, my lord."

"Well, I've ghosts enough of my own without counting the family phantasms. Why don't you go make us some mulled ale or punch, then, that we might toast the holiday ourselves, and to the devil with curses and craven servants."

When the butler left, Lord Worth poured himself another drink and relaxed back against the worn leather cushions of his chair, remembering other Christmases. He recalled house parties and balls at other people's homes, services and children's Nativity reenactments, at other people's churches. Gaiety and gifts, mistletoe kisses and sleigh rides, rich foods, familiar carols, friends. The joy of the season echoed in his mind like a distant church bell. Why, he'd even made his first and only proposal of marriage at a Christmas ball, and had been turned down, right under a kissing bough. Nick barely remembered the young lady's name, only that she'd laughed to think he expected her to follow the drum. With so much champagne and punch, and a promising military career ahead of him, he'd hardly regretted the refusal.

He regretted it now. If the pretty little blonde Julia had accepted, he could have children at his knees tonight, helping to light the Yule log, reading the Gospel. She could be playing the pianoforte while neighbors joined them in song. She could be warming his vast, cold bed upstairs.

Instead Oliver Nicholson was well past thirty, with a cousin as heir and a chill that never went away. He was more alone than he had ever been, with only his memories as companions. Ghosts, indeed.

Was he cursed? Nick wondered, fingering the scars that sliced down his cheek and kept his left hand from wielding anything heavier than a fork. He'd been a good officer, keeping his men alive under horrific conditions, keeping them armed and fed, half at his own expense. No, he was not accursed, unless surviving when others had fallen was a malediction, except . . .

Except that three years ago, his troops had been decimated when he'd been sent away from them, behind enemy lines, on Boxing Day.

Except that two years ago his best friend Gregory had given his life to save Nick's, two days after Christmas, as soon as fighting had been resumed after the holiday peace.

Except that last year, the French cannon shot would have killed him, if the saber wound had not leveled him seconds before, on New Year's Day.

Coincidences or some quirk of the family curse that kept Worth Keep in chaos at Christmastime? Nick did not know, any more than he knew what he was supposed to do with this life he'd been granted. He was useless to the army, although they had offered him a desk position. He could take his seat in Parliament, if he had a mind to be bored beyond endurance. His estates had competent managers, and his investments were in wiser hands than his. He had no taste for the *beau monde* and its frivolous pursuits, where the crucial decisions involved the color of one's waistcoat or the height of one's shirt points. The succession was assured with his cousin's brood, so Nick did not even have the excuse of needing a bride as a mission for his sorry life. Besides, no female but the most arrant fortune hunter or blatant title seeker would have him, not with his scarred phiz and mangled hand.

Lord Worth did have one goal, though, other than getting as drunk as a dockhand off duty, a goal that had brought him to this benighted building at this season of goodwill: somehow, he was going to make amends to Gregory Rostend's family. The baron raised his glass now, with his good right hand. "Here's to you, old friend. May one of us believe that the life you saved is worth the cost."

He drank the brandy as the hall clock struck midnight, then tossed the empty glass into the fireplace just as the bells of the distant church rang in Christmas Day. The noise was considerable, so loud even Mrs. Salter was sure to hear it. The sound was too loud, Nick considered in his brandy haze, for a mere shattered crystal goblet. The Worth ghosts must be stirring. Happy Christmas.

2

"What have you done now, you gormless gaby? You could have killed those old ladies with your puerile pranks."

"Bosh, I merely waved a greeting in passing."

Lady Edryth threw up her hands in dismay and disgust. "Merely? Merely? An armored knight suddenly appearing at the side of the road is merely? By all the saints, you sent one coach into the ditch, and the other into a stone pillar. Why, you could rot in Hell for such an evil deed."

Back in his suit of armor, where he would not have to look into his wife's angry green eyes, Sir Olnic muttered, "How bad could Hell be, after an eternity with a nagging woman?"

"What was that, husband?"

"I said I bade them good e'en, not boo. Asides, if that other driver hadn't been cup-shot, he could have avoided the mishap."

"Now you are foisting the blame off on others? Fie on you, you rusty old relic. You took ten years off the lives of those old ladies, and neither had ten years to spare. To say nothing of what palpitations or permanent injuries you might have caused them."

"Tough old birds, those sisters. They'll live to dine out on the story for another score of years at least."

"Ah, now you've taken to soothsaying? What's next, divination from entrails? Why, if I could wield my dagger, I'd show you entrails, I would."

Sir Olnic rocked back and forth, rattling his metal mouthpiece but keeping his own lips shut. After a century or two, even a hardheaded warrior learns a lesson or two.

"What were you thinking anyway? That you'd fetch the ladies to the Keep for the heir to choose a bride? They're both old enough to be his mother, by the sword of St. George. Nay, if maidens still married so young, they could be his grandmother! Would you have the dolt take a wife too old to bear children, much less his weight in bed?"

Not willing to admit that he'd wished to see the women in the carriage for himself, to ascertain their ages and availability, Sir Olnic blustered: "You go too far, madam. I intend to find the heir a fitting bride, when the time is ripe."

"The time has rotted on the vine, and those two plums have withered to prunes. Meanwhile, what is your jackaninny namesake supposed to do with two spinsters having heart spasms?"

"He'll manage. Competent lad, our boy. A soldier, don't you know."

"Another bloodthirsty barbarian, more like." She did not say, like father like son, but she was thinking it, Sir Olnic knew. "He'll be too busy caring for the old maids to go courting this Christmas season, that is certain. If he does not drown himself in the bottle. Heaven alone knows when we'll get another chance."

From the depths of his armor, and the depths of despair, Sir Olnic swore: "I have a plan."

Lady Edryth curled her lovely lip. "So did Genghis Khan."

"And I'll wager he's not roaming his tents, trying to marry off his descendants to satisfy some romantic woman's foolish curse, getting a lost ring on a Worth bride's hand."

"Give it up, prithee. Your baron will not find a wife."

"What, do you think that his scars are so dire no female will look on his suit with favor?"

Lady Edryth waved her handkerchief at Sir Olnic's visored helmet. "Those are honorable scars, won in battle. My scion sons have always served their kings and their countries, and no decent woman would turn her back on such a noble paladin. But a gentle lady will look inside." She tapped on the steel breastplate. "And your gallant's heart is as hard as your armor. Your heir carries far more wounds than meet the eye."

"The boy is your descendant, too, you know. He's got your green eyes."

"But he has your black hair and broad shoulders. And your love of wine."

Sir Olnic wished he had a drop of the spirit right now. "He's brave. None but the stouthearted would take up residence here at Yuletide."

"He's thickheaded, just like you. Hiding away in a moldering castle, the way you hide in your armor. I do wonder where he got that nose, though." She touched her own smooth, straight nose. "I always suspected that Lady Christina, the one who was married to Sir Buspar, had played her husband false. Perhaps this Oliver Nicholson is not our heir at all, not the one meant to end the curse."

Just then they heard voices from the doorway. Lady Edryth stepped behind her husband's suit of armor. One voice was louder than the other cries and screams and whimpers.

"Salter, fetch hot water. James, you ride for the doctor. You there, light more candles. And you, madam, had better stop shrieking in my ear or I'll bloody well toss you in the castle's dungeon for the rats to eat, if the ghosts and ghoulies don't get you first."

Sir Olnic nodded, which would have caused the woman in Nick's arms to faint, if the baron's threats hadn't already. "That's my boy, all right."

Pandemonium, that's what it was. For a moment Nick thought he was back at the front, in the thick of battle. Men were shouting, horses were screaming, bodies were strewn about. But there was no cannon fire, no pall of gunpowder hanging over the midnight, moonlit scene, just someone bleating: " 'God rest ye merry, gentlemen.' "

Was he foxed? Trying to recall how many glasses he'd consumed, Nick shook his head, but the sight still remained. Without another thought, he began to free the frightened horses from their traces. With his one good hand, he managed to shift the light gig enough to make sure no one was trapped underneath, but the sole occupant must be the singer, propped against a tree, bottle still in hand. " 'Let nothing ye dismay.' "

The other coach was smashed to pieces against one of the pillars that held the bridge leading to the castle. Another foot or so and the carriage would have landed in the water that surrounded Worth Keep. By now Salter was tottering across the bridge with a lantern, and a few servants peered out of the gatehouse door. Lord Worth, recently Major Nicholson, started bellowing orders, over the caterwauling.

One old lady was passed out cold, her head against a rock. At least she was quiet. Nick quickly ascertained that she still breathed, and no bones appeared broken. The other was screaming fit to wake the dead. If one believed her yammering, the noise was unnecessary, and too late. She was clutching her bony chest, though, which worried the baron worse than her hysteria. The women's driver was babbling about bogeys, but Nick could smell the spirits on the man's breath, so he ignored that, too. With luck the fellow was cast-away enough that he wouldn't feel his broken leg being set.

"There are no such things as ghosts!" Nick shouted over all the noise, for the benefit of the victims as well as his reluctant helpers. The grooms and the gate-keeper kept looking over their shoulders while they led the horses away and pulled the doors off the carriage, to use as stretchers. "The drivers were both drunk, is all."

"Returning from the party at Rostend Hall, I'd wager," the butler offered.

"Lady Rostend was entertaining?"

"As she has annually on Christmas Eve, except the years she was in mourning, of course."

"Of course." Nick used his neck cloth to wipe at the blood streaming down the bosky caroler's forehead, trying to determine how badly the fellow was injured.

Salter held the lantern closer, although he looked away from the gory sight. "I, ah, am certain your lordship would have received an invitation if Lady Rostend knew you were in residence."

Pigs would fly first, Nick knew. Then again, the way events transpired at Worth Keep, flying pigs would be an improvement. "Leave this old sot for last. The gash looks worse than it is; head wounds bleed a lot. A few stitches should be enough to fix him up, though."

He lifted the unconscious woman onto the coach door himself, while her companion, her sister, according to Salter, screeched her refusal to set one foot inside Worth Keep. "If you will not walk, madam, I shall have to carry you, for you cannot stay out here, and your sister's injury appears too serious to undergo another bumpy carriage ride. I have seen enough concussions in the army to recognize the symptoms." The old lady only screamed louder, so Nick picked her up without a by-your-leave and started striding across the bridge to the Keep. The others followed, bearing their burdens and their qualms.

Inside, Mrs. Salter had placed sheets over the facing couches in the morning room, since none of the guest rooms had been prepared. The unconscious woman, Miss Henrietta Mundy, was carefully transferred to one, with a blanket hastily thrown over her to protect her modesty. Nick deposited the other lady, Miss

Charlotte Mundy, who was now equally as unconscious, onto the other. The driver was laid on a blanket near the fireplace, before his litter bearers left to
see to the horses. The other drunk was helping himself
to the newly made wassail, serenading them all with
his fourth or fifth chorus of " 'Comfort and joy.' "

If the man weren't already bleeding like a stuck pig,
Nick would have drawn his cork. Comfort and joy,
indeed! The place looked like a field hospital. "The
doctor is going to need hot water and bandages," Nick
instructed Salter and his wife, "and the Misses Mundy
will feel better for some hot tea when they wake up.
I suppose we'll have to ready chambers for them, too.
The driver can bed down in the stables, and this sorry
excuse . . ." He nodded toward the bloody but cheerfully off-key caroler.

"Mr. Bidlaw, my lord."

"Mr. Bidlaw can be sent home as soon as the doctor
has stitched his head." He noticed the footman James
standing by the door. "Why the devil are you still
here? I sent you for the doctor at least an hour ago."
That was what it felt like, at any rate.

James coughed and studied his feet.

Salter cleared his throat. "My lord?"

Nick had that prickling at the back of his neck, the
one that had saved his life more than once, the niggly
twinge that warned of danger ahead. "Salter?"

"Ah, Mr. Bidlaw is our local physician."

The dawn of Christmas Day was almost breaking
when Nick was finally finished. By the time the coffee
had been made, Bidlaw was fast asleep, but the others
were moaning or weeping or wailing, as was their
wont. Nick would have joined in, but he was too busy
giving directions. As the only moderately competent
person in the Keep, he knew it was his duty to do the

necessary, so he did it. With the grooms' help, although their nervous hands were none too steady, he set the driver's leg. With Mrs. Salter's help, the only female employee on the premises, he loosened the stays of both thankfully unconscious Mundy sisters. With his valet's help, before the clunch cast up his accounts at the sight of all the blood, he stitched the doctor's forehead. Never had Nick missed the army more, or at least his knowledgeable batman, who was more skilled than any battlefield surgeon. When he had done what he could, the baron saw the patients carried to bedchambers and sent old Salter and his wife to bed before they collapsed. Then he saw to the horses. And made sure the debris was off the roadway lest the broken carriage cause another accident. Then he checked again on the old ladies, not liking how Miss Henrietta was still unconscious, or how Miss Charlotte's complexion was grayish, or how upset they would be to find out he was the one who had helped the housekeeper remove their outer layers of clothing. Almost as upset as they'd be to wake up with his pasty-faced gentleman's gentleman in their bedroom. Nick could almost hear the shrieks now.

Finally, with the candles guttering and the fires burning out, he dragged his weary body through the cold, silent halls until he faced the rows of armor.

"Damn you!" he shouted, almost shaking the broadswords and sabers that lined the walls. With his right fist raised, he swore again at the empty-eyed visors. "Damn you, I say! I am your target, not innocent people. If you have laid a curse on this house, I am lord here, I am the heir, I am Worth. On your honor, attack me, you fiends, not old ladies or drunks, or valiant soldiers like Gregory Rostend. Come at me, by God, or else be gone."

3

"Now you've done it, my lord sovereign of the scrap heap. Now he's cursing at us! Our own flesh and blood is trying to exorcise us out of our own home. By the heart of St. Hildegarde, the heir is challenging you to a duel of wills."

Sir Olnic puffed out his metal chest, no mean feat for a phantasm. "The boy's got ballocks," the old knight proudly declared.

"He's got your blather for brains, arguing with astrals. In case you have forgotten, husband, you were to see that he fell in love, not into a distempered freak."

"I am working on that, jewel of my heart."

Lady Edryth turned her back on her spouse's armor, and on his endearment. If the old fool thought he could turn her up sweet with honeyed phrases, he was a few years too late. A few hundred. "Well, he will not be receptive to Cupid's darts, not with a houseful of invalids to care for on his own."

"I am working on that, too."

"How? No maids will enter the castle, not at this time of year. After this day's work, I doubt any of the footmen will return from holiday. None of the villagers will take employment here; they already cross themselves when they pass the bridge. Or were you thinking he could send for some London doxy to play at nursemaid, then make her his baroness? It will not serve! I tell you now, I will not have a trollop taking my place here!" Lady Edryth stamped her foot, but since she hovered a foot above the marble-tiled floor, no sound disturbed the early morning air.

"Be patient, my love. I know what I am about."

If looks could kill—and if he were not already dead—Sir Olnic was about to be melted down into a decorative tea caddy. What choice did Lady Edryth have, after all, but patience?

Lord grant him patience, Nick prayed.

Miss Henrietta Mundy had awoken to find him at her bedside, with his dark, scarred visage made more gaunt and shadowed by lack of sleep. She'd cried out something about the devil. "Not quite, ma'am, merely Oliver Nicholson. You are safe at Worth Keep." At which she'd gone off in another swoon. Nick did not have to worry about her wits being addled from the accident, he was relieved to note. Any sane person would have fainted, too.

Miss Charlotte Mundy had half risen to find herself half dressed. Her screams were drowning out the church bells. At least she was not suffering an inflammation of the lungs.

Mr. Bidlaw had wakened with a pounding headache. "Too much celebration, what?" he'd confided in the baron, who decided not to mention the five ragged stitches the man now sported on his forehead. The drunken dastard of a doctor deserved the disfiguring scar. Bidlaw ordered laudanum for Miss Henrietta's concussion, and bloodletting for Miss Charlotte's *crise de nerfs*. Having seen more than his share of head wounds and shock, Nick knew both prescriptions were the worst possible. Then Bidlaw decided to unsplint the coach driver's leg, to reset the broken bone. No gentleman could do a competent enough job, he'd sworn, not even a veteran of the Peninsula campaign. Likely the leg would have to come off.

Nick packed the still half-seas-over sawbones into one of his carriages and sent him home to torture other patients, not those at Worth Keep. Now, however, he was at point-non-plus.

"We need help, Salter," he understated. "Send the

other coach for the Mundys' maid. I don't think they should be moved yet."

"The ladies do not have a maid, my lord. They live in rather reduced circumstances, you see. The coach and driver were hired for the night."

"Lud, just what we needed, two genteelly impoverished spinsters. Well, call back our own housemaids. They can take turns sitting up with the ladies until I can find a more competent doctor. I could not find a less competent one, by Zeus."

Salter stared at something over the baron's shoulder. "I regret that our two housemaids are off visiting their parents in Yorkshire. The scullery maid is barely twelve years of age."

"But Mrs. Salter cannot nurse the ladies and cook invalid food at the same time. I would not even ask her to manage the stairs again this morning, except for the emergency."

Salter sniffled and his pale eyes grew suspiciously damp. "I regret, my lord, that we have let you down. My Livvy and I should have retired years ago, with the generous pension your lordship offered. But serving the Nicholson family and taking care of Worth Keep is all we know, nearly the only home we've ever had."

Nick awkwardly patted the man's frail shoulder. "And you shall have it as long as you wish. The fault is all mine, for not giving you warning of my arrival. I am certain you could have had the place fully staffed."

Salter was not so certain. "It's hard finding workers, my lord, especially this time of year."

"Nonsense. We'll simply hire some local girls. A bit of coin never comes amiss, especially at Christmas."

The old butler shook his head. "They won't come, at any price. Superstitions, you know."

Nick knew them all too well. Hadn't he been shout-

ing like a bedlamite at one of them? "Surely there are
a few levelheaded women in the village who don't
believe those ancient fairy tales. Older females who
understand such things as possets and potions. What
do the local folks do for a midwife? There used to be
an herbalist, I recall. The neighborhood lads called
her a witch."

"That would be One-Tooth Mags. She's been dead
these many years."

"Well, think, man. Sending to London will take too
long. Miss Charlotte will work herself into apoplexy
if we don't find a female to aid her and her sister."

"Well, there is Mrs. Merriot."

The name meant nothing to the baron. "Another
witch?"

"Oh, no, my lord. Mrs. Merriot is a gently reared
young lady, a widow. I understand she keeps a well-
stocked stillroom. She made up a tisane for Old Jake's
rheumatics that worked a treat."

"Capital! Hire her. Whatever it takes, just get the
woman here."

"Oh, but Mrs. Merriot is not a servant, my lord. I
doubt she needs the money, and her family would
not—"

"Dash it, we need the blasted female! If she won't
come for the money, then she ought to come out of
Christian charity. Thunderation, I'll go ask her myself.
If she refuses, I swear I'll toss her over my saddle and
drag her here. Now, where can I find the matchless
Mrs. Merriot?"

Salter listened to the tolling bells. "Why, I suppose,
my lord, that you'll find her at church. It is Christmas
morning, after all."

Lord Worth strode down the center aisle of the old
church, his boot heels tapping on the stone floor. The

small building was filled, and the vicar was reading the Gospel, so Nick had no choice but to take his seat in the empty family pew, all the way at the front of the church. The vicar stumbled over his words when he saw the late arrival, and the black-clad woman in the pew behind Nick gasped. The baron did not need to turn his head to know that Lady Rostend's Christmas was now as miserable as his own. He kept his eyes forward, willing the reverend to hurry through the benedictions so he could find Mrs. Merriot and flee, before he had to confront Gregory's mother in public.

At last the vicar was intoning, "Go in peace, my friends. Happy Christmas."

Nick stood up and turned to address the congregation. "Before you leave, I must beg a moment of your time. There has been an accident at Worth Keep."

He could hear the muttering, the word "curse" growing louder and louder.

"Miss Charlotte and Miss Henrietta Mundy have been injured, and are now resting at the castle. Mr. Bidlaw is unable to care for them, and I need assistance. Anyone wishing a position of employment will be considered. A Mrs. Merriot has been recommended to me as a healer, but I am not acquainted with the lady. If she is here, I beg—"

"Never!" Lady Rostend got to her feet and shook her prayer book at Nick. "My niece will never cross your doorstep, you murderer."

"Your niece?"

"Amelia Merriot, nee Rostend, as if you did not know, sirrah."

"Little Amy?"

"Amelia, and she is a decent, God-fearing young widow now, and you shall not sully her with your notice."

Everyone in the congregation was noticing. No one had made a move to return home for their Christmas feast, not with this juicy morsel laid out at church. The vicar was wringing his hands, and his wife was hustling the Sunday-school children out the side door, lest anyone think she ought to attend the Mundy sisters.

No other female would meet his eye. Not a single one was willing to come to Worth Keep, not to save a hundred impoverished gentlewomen. So much for the spirit of the season.

"Is this how you celebrate Jesus' birthday?" Nick spoke quietly, but with enough force to be heard in the last pew. "By turning your back on neighbors in need? Is this what you learn from your prayer books? What happened to His teachings, to doing onto others as you would be done to?" Everyone looked at their feet, except Lady Rostend, who was gathering her fur muff and her ermine tippet. Nick started to walk back down that aisle, saying, "May you never find yourselves in dire straits, and God have mercy on you if you do. For certain your friends and neighbors won't."

Before he reached the third row of seats, a woman next to Lady Rostend stood. She was dressed in gray, and Nick had thought her a servant or a companion. Now she pushed back the hood of her drab cloak to reveal fair curls and a well-remembered, heart-shaped face. "I will go with you, my lord."

Lady Rostend pulled on her arm, hissing, "No. You cannot go with him, Amelia. The dastard killed my son. He'll try to destroy you, too."

"Nonsense, Aunt Viveca, the French killed Gregory. I will be perfectly safe with his lordship."

"Think of your reputation, girl! You cannot go into that place alone."

"You are right, Aunt. You'll have to accompany me."

Lady Rostend sank back against the seat, her mouth opening and shutting like a landed trout's.

Amelia patted her hand. "Never fear, I will take my maid. She can help make the ladies comfortable. And I'll take Sir Digby, too, for protection."

Nick raised an eyebrow as he led Gregory's cousin Amy out of the church past the gawking parishioners. "Sir Digby?"

She giggled, the loveliest sound he'd heard in ages. Church bells ought to chime with such sweetness. She smiled up at him, her blue eyes alight with laughter, and said, "My dog."

Nick drove Mrs. Merriot back to Rostend Hall to gather her things, while he described the Mundy ladies' conditions so she would know what to bring.

"Yes, I have been making an infusion of the foxglove for Miss Charlotte, but I should think she'll need a soothing draught first. Probably chamomile. Willow bark tea for Miss Henrietta, and rose water to bathe her head. Lavender is always a comfort. Laudanum for the driver if the pain grows too bad."

Following the young widow through the entry of Rostend Hall, Nick could not help noting the difference between this manor house and his own castle. Not just the cleanliness and general air of elegance as opposed to mere antiquity, but Rostend Hall was swathed in pine boughs and ribbons, gold bells and pine cones, clove-studded orange balls and holly wreaths. Even the air here smelled of Christmas, full of gingerbread and greenery and spice-scented candles.

"I am sorry to be taking you from your celebrations, ma'am. I fear we cannot offer half the comfort and festive fare you'd be enjoying here."

"Of course, you were not expecting company. Think

nothing of it, my lord. I'll have Cook prepare a hamper so we can be quite merry."

"Mrs. Salter is preparing a goose, I understand."

She smiled again, that enchanting grin that was half girlish and half goddess. "In that case, I'll have Cook pack two hampers."

The quartermaster's office could have used Mrs. Merriot, Nick decided, watching the slight figure efficiently direct Lady Rostend's servants in ten different directions, for food and clothes and medicines and books and a hundred things she thought might be necessary. The way the servants hurried to respond, with fond respect and smiles, said much for the lady's standing in the household, and her own character. She'd always been a winsome little minx, he recalled, wrapping her cousin around her tiny fingers. She had turned into a charming young woman, from all appearances. She must be, what? Five and twenty? Too bad she'd been widowed at such a young age, he thought, wondering about the departed Mr. Merriot, the poor clod. Nick wished he'd asked Salter more questions.

While her maid packed a valise, Mrs. Merriot bid Nick follow her to the stillroom, where she quickly packed jars and labeled packets into covered baskets. When one was filled, she handed it to him and started on the next. She would have passed that one to him also, but Nick had to hold up his injured hand. Trying to sound nonchalant, he said, "Sorry. It's not good for much but matched gloves."

Without the least bit of missishness, Mrs. Merriot took his hand in her own. She bent the fingers, flexed the wrist. "Bad doctoring, I suppose, but at least they saved it for you." Then she went back to collecting her concoctions.

Nick marveled at her. The few young ladies of the *ton* whom he'd encountered had cringed from his disfigured face. They would have swooned at the sight of his ungloved hand with its gnarled ridges and crooked fingers, had he ever given them the opportunity to view the mangled limb. Not even the women he paid for companionship saw his uncovered hand by light of day. Mrs. Merriot, however, might have been selecting wools for her embroidery, for all the notice she paid the hideous scars. What a stalwart little soul she was, he told himself, just what he needed at Worth Keep. He'd make another donation to the church in thanks for sending him such a trooper.

"You're not afraid of anything, are you?" Nick asked now, knowing he was going beyond the line of prior acquaintance.

Rosy color washed across Amelia's fair cheeks. "Aunt Viveca finds me forward, if not an outright hoyden. I beg your pardon if I have given offense."

"Lud, I meant it as a compliment. No mealy-mouthed milk-and-water chit could help me now. If she would, which is highly unlikely. But tell me, ma'am, are you not the least bit anxious about the Christmas Curse on Worth Keep?"

"Fustian. If there were such a thing, which I sorely doubt, the curse would have been used up for the year on the unfortunate Mundy sisters, although I am certain that the care you give them will far exceed any discomfort they might suffer."

Nick bowed his head in acknowledgment of the high expectations Mrs. Merriot held. Her aunt, he supposed, most likely believed him capable of tossing the two old ladies back in the roadway, if not the river. "But what of the ghosts who are supposed to walk the halls at Yuletide?" he felt compelled to ask, giving his rescuer a last chance to back out of an awkward, perhaps awful, situation.

The gray-clad female drew herself up to her full

height, about the level of his chin. "Ghosts?" she echoed. "You think I should turn craven at the silly notion of ghosts? I'll have you know, my lord baron, that I am made of sterner stuff than that." Then she flashed him that grin again. "Nothing so paltry as a disembodied demon can faze me, Lord Worth, not after living with Aunt Viveca for three years."

4

"A Rostend? You brought a Rostend descendant to my home? That base-born churl caused this whole mingle-mangle, or have you forgotten that small detail, husband?"

"How could I forget, my jewel, with you reminding me at every turn?" Sir Olnic was in a fine mood, fencing with the shadows on the walls, lunging, feinting, parrying imaginary sword thrusts. "Ah, what I would not give for a worthy foe."

"What I would not give for a rational thought from you. You are out of practice, sir, out of your mind, and out of your armor."

The old warrior looked down. "Why, so I am, my dear. I suppose I'll have to don my mail. Wouldn't want to give the Mundy sisters lewd thoughts, now, would we?"

Lady Edryth made a rude noise and turned her back. " 'Tis more likely the sight of your hairy loins would give them a disordered spleen. 'Struth, it fair turns my stomach."

"Ah, 'twas a different song you sang that last Christmas. By the saints, 'twas not your gut aching for me, my lady."

If ghosts could blush, Lady Edryth would be a fiery red. "Fie on your memories, you old rasher of wind.

What are you going to do about the widow? If you think to install her here as mistress, I vow I will lay another curse on you. I will not have that whoreson's whelp take my place as chatelaine." She peeked a glance over her shoulder at her bare-assed beloved, sighing. "I will not have that benighted man's blood mixed with ours. I will not, I say."

"Forget about the female, my lady. Mrs. Merriot is of no account. It's the dog we want."

Mrs. Merriot took over the Keep. She could do nothing about the missing servants, but she and her maid Stoffard, a stout, dour woman who held no truck with phantoms, or with flibbertigibbets who took any excuse to avoid an honest day's work, had the sickroom in hand within hours of their arrival. Then they started on the rest of the castle. Amelia Merriot was not about to take up residence in a pigsty. Ghosts were bad enough, but dust balls were beyond the pale. Furthermore, she'd declared to the bemused baron, sending Nick out to care for the horses, dirt was unhealthful for the invalids. Mrs. Merriot, it seemed, considered shoveling manure a chore well suited for a titled gentleman, freeing up the few stable hands for moving ladders and turning mattresses.

The wellborn widow was not above helping in the kitchens or carrying cans of water herself, shaming the lily-livered footmen back from the gatehouse. She even had the baron's valet, Hopkins, performing tasks the gentleman's gentleman had considered well beneath his dignity. Soon the smells of beeswax and lemon oil replaced the odor of mold and mildew. Arrangements of evergreens and holly appeared on occasional tables, and Nick could actually see out the window of his book room, where he escaped with the estate's ledgers, nursing his blisters.

When not directing her small army of servants, Mrs. Merriot was in the sickroom suite, two bedchambers connected by a small parlor. Her presence seemed to reassure the ladies of their safety, so they could expend their energies on regaining their strength—and gossiping. Miss Charlotte's color was better, Miss Henrietta no longer saw double, and Amelia learned more about the Nicholson family history than she ever wished to.

The Mundy ladies were in no hurry to return to their own cottage. What, with no servants to bring them tea or lemonade or a drop of sherry? No fires in the minuscule bedrooms, nothing but bread and butter for supper, no one to talk to but each other, no one to gently bathe their foreheads with lavender water? No, thank you. They were far too weak to undertake the journey home.

Amelia was in no great rush to return to Rostend Hall, either. Here she felt needed, and could see the fruits of her labors in the wondrous old castle. Why, she half expected to see unicorns around every corner, the place was so filled with magic. In addition, no one was giving her orders, for a change. When Lord Worth protested that he had not invited her to his home to be a menial, she just laughed.

"What, did you think I was a lady of leisure at my aunt's house? Aunt Viveca has quite firm opinions on the place of a poor relation. This is a vacation, I assure you. Besides, I enjoy keeping busy, and love uncovering the treasures you own, as Mrs. Salter and I remove the Holland covers. And Miss Charlotte and Miss Henrietta are dears, so appreciative of every small favor." Unlike her aunt, although Amelia did not say so. "I should be thanking you for the holiday."

They were having dinner together, at Nick's insistence. "I would not see you growing sickly yourself, ma'am, eating beef broth and cow's foot jelly in the sickroom."

"No fear of that," she laughingly declared, helping herself to another serving of pork cutlets from the tray Salter proffered. "I am no fragile hothouse blossom that will easily wilt, my lord."

"No, but you are the rose in my garden of thorns, so I need to assure myself of your well-being. Lud knows how we would have managed without you and your maid." He raised his wineglass to her in a toast, and Salter seconded, "Here, here," before backing out of the room.

One dark eyebrow raised, Nick told her, "You see? Even old Salter recognizes the debt we owe you."

Embarrassed, Amelia addressed her plate, but the warmth she felt had more to do with his words than the wine.

After dinner, Mrs. Merriot had to walk her dog, an undistinguished, scruffy-looking brown terrier, with a bushy beard and comical eyebrows. Sir Digby was longer than he was tall, and as fat around as an over-stuffed sausage.

"Named after some country squire, I presume?" Nick asked, following the widow and her dog about the walled garden, where they were sheltered from the winter wind.

"Um, not precisely," she replied, tugging on the small terrier's lead when he would have stopped by a bare-branched rosebush, pulling him behind a rhododendron for privacy. "Here is a better spot, Sir Digby."

The little dog immediately returned to the rosebush, stub of a tail wagging, nose pressed to the ground.

"No, sir, we are walking, not investigating where some rabbit might have passed. Come, Digby."

But the terrier had other ideas, and started pawing at the earth.

Nick stepped back, not quite before his trousers were covered in loose flying dirt. "Ah, now I understand where he got his name."

Embarrassed, Amelia quickly scooped up the animal, dirty feet and all. "We are guests here, you bad dog. You cannot go excavating the rosebushes! My apologies, Lord Worth. I will keep him—"

A crash of thunder boomed through the still night. Nick took her arm. "Did you hear that? We'd better go in before the storm hits."

Mrs. Merriot and her maid took turns sitting up with the patients during the nights. Nick was not happy with the arrangement, not with both women working so hard during the days. They needed their rest, but he had no alternative, since the castle was still without housemaids. On the second night, he offered to keep Mrs. Merriot company on her vigil. "That way I could fetch more hot water or broth if you needed it, so you would not have to leave the ladies or rouse the servants. My man Hopkins can be on call during Stoffard's watch."

"Oh, no, I am sure that won't be necessary. Miss Henrietta's headaches are almost gone now, and Miss Charlotte has not suffered a nervous paroxysm since yesterday. There is no need for you to lose your sleep, too."

He raised one eyebrow. "There is no reason for you to sit up there alone, either, when I am offering. Unless you find my company burdensome?"

"Of course not, my lord. You have been everything accommodating. But I fear . . . that is, my aunt . . ."

"You are worried about your reputation?"

Amelia studied the fringe on her shawl. "I have to live in this neighborhood, my lord."

Nick had to laugh at that. Mrs. Merriot was more

intimidated by gossipmongers than ghosts. "Destroying your reputation would be a poor reward for your assistance, wouldn't it? I assure you, though, that none of the servants except Hopkins venture above stairs after dark, and he is as loyal as your Stoffard, so no one needs to know. Except the Mundy sisters, if they should happen to awaken, of course, but I think you could not ask for better chaperones than those two. We will leave the door open, naturally."

She was still unsure, so Nick added, "Truly, ma'am, I have no designs on your virtue, just your comfort."

Lord Worth's graciousness was making her uncomfortable, and a trifle disappointed, if Amelia was honest with herself. She nodded, though. "Then, I accept your generous offer."

He read aloud while she sat with her mending, then they played a game of chess and a round of piquet. Nick went down to the kitchen and fixed a tray of tea and biscuits. Mostly, they talked. The cozy warmth of the small sitting room and their necessarily lowered voices seemed to inspire companionable conversation, shared memories, and confidences. Soon they were calling each other Worth and Amelia, then Nick and Amy. Eventually, the baron felt they were well acquainted—re-acquainted—enough that he could ask, "Why ever did you agree to come here, to this Godforsaken old place?"

"Why, to spite Aunt Viveca, of course."

She smiled at him over her teacup, and Nick thought her husband must have been one lucky fellow, while he lived, to see that smile at his breakfast table every morning.

"And because it was Christmas," she was going on, "and because you asked." Then she set her cup aside and stared at the low-burning fire in the hearth. "And because I know how the Mundy ladies must have felt, alone and afraid."

"As you felt when your husband died?"

"Before. After my mother passed away, my father went into a decline. He never made provision for my future. I had no home, no income, no dowry. I had no choice but to accept Mr. Merriot, a neighboring widower, a mill owner. He paid Papa's debts, so I was grateful, but he was not . . . not a comfortable husband."

That man who Nick had thought so lucky just moments ago was lucky he was already dead. Anyone who could bring such a note of sadness to Amy's voice deserved to be thrashed. "And then?"

"Then he died, in his mistress's bed, and his son from his first marriage inherited the mill and the house. Alfred Merriot was even less . . . comfortable."

"The dastard." Nick could well imagine what a pretty, defenseless young widow had to endure at the hands of some loose screw of a stepson. "So you fled to your aunt's."

"Only to borrow enough funds to see me through till I could find employment. Aunt Viveca had other notions. According to her, a Rostend did not go into service, not for wages, at any rate. Becoming Lady Rostend's unpaid servant was much more fitting my station and breeding."

It was a tribute to that breeding, Nick thought, that the poor puss hadn't lost her spirits altogether in a life of hopeless drudgery. Despite the evidence of her dreary gray gowns, Amelia Rostend Merriot had not become that shadowy nonentity, the poor relation. She was still a warm, vibrant young woman with a giving heart and a laughing soul. How long her vitality would last in the face of Lady Rostend's bitterness was anyone's guess, but Nick would not place money on Mrs.

Merriot's happy future at Rostend Hall. She'd be better off staying here, taking care of—

Nick had an idea that was as startling as an icicle
on his tongue. He tasted it, swirled it around, and
found the idea palatable, no, not merely palatable, but
downright appetizing. Here was a way to repay his
debt to Gregory Rostend: in return for his own life,
Nick could rescue Greg's cousin. He could marry her.

Lud, marriage.

He could do it, though, for Gregory's sake. Without
puffing off his own consequence, Nick knew he had a
lot to offer a woman: the barony, wealth, three estates,
and a hunting box in Scotland. He owned a town
house in London that was currently leased, but he
could pay off the renters if she wanted to make a
splash in Society with a new wardrobe and a new title.
He would not demand that she live with him, nor
would he insist on his husbandly rights if she could
not bear the sight of his battered body, much as leaving her untouched might kill him.

What he could not offer her, unfortunately, was a
love match. Amy deserved a knight in shining armor,
white charger and all, professing undying devotion,
but she'd have to make do with a weary old warhorse.
At least she would never again be alone and afraid,
or at the mercy of her relations.

"Mrs. Merriot . . . Amy, I have a proposition to put
to you. Would you consider becoming my—"

A great crash came from the old part of the castle.
Amy jumped to her feet. The dog started growling
from under the sofa. Miss Charlotte woke up, screaming about specters. Stoffard came running, brandishing
a fireplace poker.

"No, no, it's nothing," Lord Worth reassured them.
"One of the suits of armor must have fallen over,
that's all. It happens all the time."

5

"Look at them, holding hands like frightened children. You might as well have shoved the girl into his arms, by St. Germaine's garter."

Sir Olnic was shaking his head at the fallen armor strewn about the Great Hall. "Never liked that Sir Harlock anyway. What was he, our great-grandson?" He kicked Sir Harlock's helmet under a table.

"Never mind that pile of rusted rubble. The woman is the problem, husband. Get rid of her."

"Nay, I cannot. Not until I get the dog to find your blessed ring."

"You could not get a foxhound to find a flea. You are wasting precious days of our Christmas season. Again."

"Nonsense. We have more than a sennight remaining. Why, 'tis not even the new year yet. I'd have the ring in the house days ago but for the lady keeping her mongrel on as tight a leash as you try to keep—" Sir Olnic bit back the rest of his words, eternity being a very long time to spend with an angry wife. His beloved was already finding something else to bedevil him about anyway.

"No, you will have to frighten her off, and soon, before she falls in love with him."

"What? After a handful of days, and little enough of that spent in his company?"

Lady Edryth tapped her foot. "I fell in love with you the day we met. I might have been regretting it since, but that is the way of a female's heart. Once given, it is not reclaimable."

Sir Olnic stroked the beard on his chin. "Nay. He is a braw lad, I'll grant you, but all those scars will repulse a tender damsel. Asides, our Oliver Nicholson is naught but a rough soldier."

"As were you, when first we met."

"And so I remain despite your best efforts, and you love me still, no matter what you say." He ignored her *humph*. "Do you think the lad might love her, too? 'Od's teeth, I have been worrying so hard about retrieving the ring, I never thought about t'other, the true love's hand to put it on. Damme, could we be that close to ending this wretched bane, this ceaseless half existence at last?"

"No, no. Do not get your hopes up. The heir is merely acting noble, rescuing the maiden fair from her dragon-like relations. Some notions of chivalry never die, it seems. But, nay, this Baron Worth does not know the meaning of love."

"What man does, until the right woman explains it to him?" He did a little jig over the fallen armor. "He's already interested, I can tell that much. In sooth, what man wouldn't be? Mrs. Merriot is a cozy armful under those stiff, shapeless frocks she wears, with soft womanly curves in all the right places."

"What? You've been spying on the lady at her bath? Why, you—" Lady Edryth took off down the hall after her laughing husband.

Amelia was enjoying herself too much. After five days at Worth Keep, she was too comfortable, too nearly lulled into ignoring the dangers of her situation. There was a snake pit ahead, into which she was blithely waltzing. Doom lay in the direction she was dancing, with nothing but doubt and despair.

She was liking Oliver Nicholson, Baron Worth, too much. She'd always liked him, way back in the idyllic summers of her childhood when she'd visited Rostend Hall with her parents. The Nicholsons and the Rostends were not on good terms even then, but both heirs attended the same school and were fast friends.

Gregory never let his young cousin tag along after them. Neither did Oliver, but he had taken the time to explain that their adventuring was not safe for a mere poppet, and he'd bring her back a treat from the fair, or the village, or the Gypsy camp. He'd never gone back on his word, either. He would not renege on his vow to preserve her reputation now. It was her heart that was in mortal danger.

They were hardly alone; he'd seen to that, with Miss Charlotte's assistance. Now that she was feeling more the thing, the elder Miss Mundy was needing less sleep, so they played three-handed whist during those nighttime hours. Nick let the old dear win his pennies, after paying her pretty compliments on the lace-edged nightcaps he'd fetched from the Mundy cottage. He plied the old woman, and her sister when she was awake, with wine and delicacies he bought at the bake shop in the village. Miss Charlotte and Miss Henrietta would have nothing but happy memories to take back with them to their little house. Amelia would be taking shattered dreams back to Rostend Hall.

Nick would never marry. All the neighbors had said so, and the Mundy sisters confirmed the gossip. His cousin in Hampshire had three sons, and word was that one was being schooled as the next baron. The baron's scars and war injuries were part of the *on-dits* now, although Amelia thought his hand would regain some of its strength if he kept currying the horses and wielding the pitchfork. No, it was the Christmas Curse, the December disasters, that were keeping Lord Worth from taking a bride all these years. That's what everyone said, anyway. Amelia believed Nick was just noble enough to sacrifice his own future happiness to protect his would-be wife from the superstition, despite his own avowed disbelief in the hauntings or the hex.

If Nick would never marry, Amelia should not tarry. She ought, she told herself again as she brushed out her hair in front of the mirror, she really ought to go home before her heart was well and truly lost. "We'll both be happy back in our own room and our own gardens," she told Sir Digby at her feet, knowing that she was lying to both of them. Aunt Viveca's gardeners hated the little dog, and only tolerated him because he kept their tool sheds free of vermin.

How were either of them going to face the prison that was her aunt's home after this enchanted interlude? Rostend Hall was more luxurious, better staffed for certain, more sociable, than Worth Keep. Aunt Viveca held endless teas and encouraged interminable visits between the neighborhood matrons. No one called at Nick's castle, not even the vicar, yet Amelia was far more content with the company and the conversation. Too, too content, she repeated to herself as she got ready for bed in her room across the hall from the sickroom suite. Her maid Stoffard was there now, keeping watch for the last night. The old ladies were well enough to sleep without nursemaids, nearly well enough to return to their own home. Amelia ought to be returning to hers, too, to assist Aunt Viveca with her New Year's Eve party. She could never accept Nick's offer of a housekeeper's position or whatever other charity he'd been about to offer the last time they were alone. No, leaving was her best choice, her only choice. A horrid choice.

Amelia straightened the blanket placed before the hearth for Sir Digby, then climbed into her high bed and blew out the candle. She could hear the dog circling his blanket, then wadding it into a ball. She'd wake up to find he'd jumped onto her bed anyway. Soon she could hear the terrier's soft whuffling snores, but her thoughts were keeping her awake, not the dog's noises. She rolled over, pounded the pillow, threw one of the covers off the bed. No matter what she did, or how exhausted she was, sleep was not forthcoming. Finally she sat up and relit the candle with the nearby flint and started to read from the book she kept by her bedside. She was asleep in minutes.

Amelia had no idea how much time had passed when she heard the noise. The candle had burned out, and the book was beside her. No, that was Sir Digby, curled against her ribs, starting to mutter a sleepy growl.

"Just the old part of the castle settling," Amelia told the dog. "Or another of those ridiculous suits of armor collapsing." If this were her house, Amelia swore, angry at having her hard-won rest disturbed, she'd have the whole row of chain-mail mannequins sent to the attics. She shut her eyes, but there it came again, a soft, stealthy creak, as if someone was carefully opening an old warped door, inch by insidious inch.

Her bedroom had just such an old door, with no lock on it.

Sir Digby was standing now, facing in that direction, gnarling in earnest.

"Stoffard, is that you? Is aught amiss with the ladies?"

Stoffard did not answer. As her eyes adjusted to the darkness, Amelia could see the outline of the door, banded in a lighter shadow from the oil lamp kept burning down the hall. The band was growing.

"Stoffard?" Amelia got out of bed, fumbling for the flint and for her slippers at the same time. She caught the faint scent of cooked meat, similar to the fricasseed chicken they'd had for dinner. "Mrs. Salter?"

She turned to light the candle, and when she faced the door again, she thought she saw a man silhouetted in the cracked opening, a tall, dark-haired man. "Nick? Lord Worth? This is not amusing." Sir Digby barked.

The dark figure in the doorway muttered, "Damme. A pox upon you and your plaguesome pet."

Amelia screamed. Actually, she whimpered, her voice having frozen in her throat. Should she make a dash for the fireplace poker, or simply swoon? No, she was made of sterner stuff. She screamed louder. Sir Digby barked louder. The intruder cursed louder. Then Nick was there, his hands on her shoulders.

"Are you all right?"

"The ghost," she gasped. "I saw the ghost."

"Nonsense. You have been keeping long hours, is all. Your weary mind produced a nightmare."

"No, someone was there at the door, I swear. Sir Digby saw it, too." Sir Digby was cowering under the bed, his fur all ruffled.

"I would have passed anyone in the hall, if one of the servants had come to check on the fires or the hall lamp. I saw no one."

No one had come yet. Her screams hadn't even disturbed the old ladies across the hall, and Stoffard must have drowsed off over her mending. "But I saw him. It. The ghost," she insisted.

"Too much Madeira, my dear. You know there are no such things as ghosts."

Now that her heart had stopped racing and her breath stopped coming in short rasps, Amelia did know it. There were no ghosts. Especially none that smelled of chicken fricassee. But if not a ghost, and not a servant, then who . . . ? For that matter, now that she could think in a rational fashion, how had her host come to her aid so quickly? He wore a white nightshirt, and his feet were bare, but his hair was still neatly combed as if he'd never gone to bed . . . thinking he'd go to her bed.

"Why, you cad, frightening me like that. And coming here! Now I understand what kind of proposition you wished to make me. I thought you'd be offering me a position, and I was right, only I never imagined the position you had in mind was that of mistress." She hauled back her right hand and slapped him with all her might. "I might be a poor relation, but I shall never be that poor! My aunt's charity is cold comfort indeed, but at least I have my pride and my dignity. And my virtue, too, of course. I will be leaving in the morning, while I still have an honest reputation."

Nick staggered back. "What the devil?" Was it he having the nightmare? He'd been going over some papers in his bedroom when he'd heard her dog barking. Thinking to take the mutt down to the garden for her, he'd approached her opened door. For coming to her assistance, he'd been soundly smacked. Thank goodness he'd decided to wait to make his proposal till Mrs. Merriot left his household, thinking that only a dastard would place a gentlewoman in the uncomfortable position of refusing an offer from her host. Perhaps he ought to rethink his decision to offer for the woman altogether, he pondered, if she was unhinged. "I never offered you *carte blanche.*"

She sniffled. "No, but you were going to."

"I was?" Mrs. Merriot did not look like mistress material to him, not with her blonde hair in a girlish braid and her toes peeking out from under the hem in her high-buttoned flannel nightgown. She looked adorable, though, and her bosom was definitely heaving. Of course that was with self-righteous wrath and not burning passion, but, hell, he'd already been slapped for being a rake. He might as well deserve the sore cheek. So he kissed her. And she, despite her scruples and her fears for the future, kissed him back.

6

"She enjoyed it."

"You watched? You moth-nibbled knave!" Taking a page from Mrs. Merriot's book, Lady Edryth slapped Sir Olnic, her hand making a whistling sound as it passed through his image.

"What, you did not?"

"I turned my back, of course. I am a lady."

"A lady who used to be a lusty wench in her day." Sir Olnic waggled his thick eyebrows at her.

The lady raised her chin and changed the topic. "How did you know Mrs. Merriot liked Nick's kiss?"

"Zounds, she didn't slap him again, did she? Asides, she turned all rosy, and her breath came hard."

"Fie, she was merely embarrassed. Confused and upset to be manhandled in such a fashion."

"So confused that she twined her arms about him like a vine? So upset that she had to stroke the back of his neck? So embarrassed she had to hide her reddened cheeks by taking a step closer to him, making sure their bodies touched from tip to toe? I swan, you could have seen the sparks fly between them, had there been an inch betwixt." Sir Olnic held his hands together, as if to show how close Nick and Amelia had been standing, or to give a prayer of thanks.

His lady frowned. "I suppose the heir enjoyed the kiss, too?"

"Hah! His short sword was well out of its scabbard when he left."

"That was lust, you old goat. The Nicholson men were ever a passionate breed."

"Nay, if 'twere only a man's hunger he'd never have left the lass. Mrs. Merriot was so moonstruck, he could have had her for the asking, the fool."

"Why did he not stay, then?" Lady Edryth wanted to know. "Prithee, why did he not ask?"

"What, and dishonor his future wife? Our boy is a motley fool, but a courtly, gentle dunce for all that."

Lady Edryth sighed. "Then, I suppose we shall have to accept her into the family. If she does not flee back to that whoreson's house this very morning, the way she swore she would."

"The lady is not leaving, not if I have anything to say in the matter."

He did not have to say much at all, not even "Boo."

Miss Henrietta suffered a setback. She saw a vision near dawn that next day. Not a double vision, just an apparition, a dark-haired, dark-bearded, hairy-backsided bare man. Unlike Mrs. Merriot's, her shrieks were enough to roust the entire household.

"It was just a bad dream," Amelia said soothingly, pouring a glass of restorative for the trembling woman and shooing the wide-eyed servants out of the room. Miss Henrietta swore the man had winked at her, though, which no man ever had, awake or asleep. "Likely it was some prankster, then," Amelia told her, "using one of the escape tunnels all old castles have, or an ancient priest hole passage. You needn't fear a repeat of his visit, however, for we can all go home to our own houses today." She made sure to keep the regret out of her voice.

Miss Charlotte Mundy had other ideas. She hadn't seen any hairy spooks about, thank goodness, or her heart would have given notice to quit for sure, but she was not ready to return to the penury of their prior existence. "Secret passages?" She moaned, clutched her chest, and collapsed into the baron's nearby arms. It was a good thing his left hand had regained a bit of strength, or he might have dropped her in his surprise.

Nick knew that all the hidden corridors had been closed off ages ago when the modern wings were added to the castle, but he didn't say anything. He'd been trying all night to think of ways of getting Mrs. Merriot to stay, not that he had been wishing illness on either of the old ladies. He could not let her return to Rostend Hall until she was ready to hear his proposal, not until he was certain what her answer would be. He'd been thinking of less drastic measures, like chopping down the causeway bridge, or locking Amelia in the dungeons until she promised to marry him. Miss Mundy's vivid imagination had worked a lot better. Amelia was not leaving. He almost kissed Miss Charlotte as he placed his slight burden back on the bed. "That convinces me. I am sending for a specialist from London. He'll get here in a day or two." Or three.

"But Aunt Viveca's New Year's party . . . ?"

"You'll have to go, of course, Mrs. Merriot." Nick tried to look sincere. "Your aunt needs you. We'll manage somehow."

Miss Charlotte groaned and feebly reached for Amelia's hand.

"No, I'll stay," Amelia quickly replied, relieved to have an excuse, any excuse. "If it's her heart, I'd better be nearby."

Nick's own heart, that closed-up bud, unfurled another petal.

At breakfast the next morning, Nick offered to drive Mrs. Merriot to Rostend Hall to inform her aunt, and to fetch more clothes. The day was cold but clear, and the horses were eager for a run. Amelia covertly admired the way Nick tooled his pair, despite his weak left hand. While he watched the road, she watched him. She could not help but notice how broad-shouldered he was, nor how well-muscled his thighs, not when he was seated so close beside her on the curricle's bench. He also looked more like the carefree boy she'd known than the desperate man who'd marched into church on Christmas Day. Was it less than a week ago? Heavens, it felt like a month, or a day.

She really had no option but to remain at Worth Keep, not when the spinster sisters were relying so heavily on her and Stoffard. The wiser course, naturally, would be to get down at her aunt's house and never return to the castle, to temptation. Even now, in the moving carriage, she wanted to see if those dark curls at the back of Nick's neck really were so soft. She wanted to see if he still tasted like wine, or the chocolate he'd had for breakfast. She wanted absolutely unsuitable things, even for a widow, and unattainable from Nick. What she was liable to get was more heartache and another indecent offer.

Oh, he'd apologized for the kiss last night, swearing he never meant to offer her insult or a slip on the shoulder. But why else would a man be creeping about the corridors, pushing open ladies' bedroom doors? No gentleman came courting in the middle of the night, not unless he was courting trouble. Oliver Nicholson was trouble, all right, from his fairy-glen green eyes to his high leather boots. She sighed.

Nick almost put them in a ditch, trying to get a better look at Mrs. Merriot. The close brim of her gray satin bonnet hid too much of her face, and the gray cloak she wore hid everything else. Deuce take it, the first thing he would do when Amy was his baroness was buy her a new wardrobe. No, the first thing he'd do was take her to his bed, where she wouldn't need a stitch of clothing. That thought was not condu-

cive to careful driving. When he had the horses back
under control, Nick tried to put a checkrein on his
own galloping pulse by concentrating on Mrs. Merriot's clothing, not what was beneath it.

Pink. He'd dress her in pink to highlight the roses
in her cheeks. No, blue, to match her eyes. Springtime
yellow, for her golden curls. Anything but gray. Thunderation, what did he know of women's fashions? He
knew that the less fabric the better. He'd insist on
that, not that Lord Worth wanted every Tom and
Town Tulip ogling his wife, but those ample charms
he'd felt last night when Amy was pressed against his
chest should never be hidden away. Keeping such
bounty behind yards of shapeless gray cloth was a sin
against nature. His wife was not going to be a dasher,
but neither would Amy be a dowd. He sighed.

The question was, was Mrs. Merriot going to become Mrs. Nicholson? Or Baroness Worth, to be
exact. There she was, sitting prim and proper as a
schoolmistress, as far away from him on the bench as
she could manage. What he could see of her, those
soft, sweet lips—he had to regather the reins—were
pursed in a disapproving scowl. This did not seem the
time to tender his proposal.

The more Nick thought of offering for Mrs. Merriot—and he'd thought of little else since the notion
crept into his mind like a gentle breeze that turned
into a tornado—the better he liked the idea. He'd be
rescuing Gregory's cousin, offering Amy a better life
than any she was likely to find living with Lady Rostend. He'd guarantee her future with settlements and
marriage contracts so she would never want for anything. She'd also have his respect and his loyalty, since
Nick did not believe in breaking one's marriage vows.
That's how he'd first seen his proposed arrangement,
as a debt canceled, a lovely young woman rescued and

protected. Now he saw it as a ray of sunshine on a very dark day. He might even be getting the better of the deal if she agreed. Zeus, she'd be getting money and security. He'd be getting a helpmate, a housekeeper, a lifelong friend—one who kissed like an angel and turned his blood to liquid heat.

The horses came to a dead stop in the center of the village high street, thoroughly confused by his hamfisted driving.

"You, ah, mentioned stopping at the apothecary's for more supplies, didn't you?" he asked to cover his cow-handedness. "I thought we'd stop on the way, instead of later, in case the, ah, shop closes or runs out of something you need."

Amelia was relieved to get down and away from Lord Worth's disturbing presence, albeit for the few minutes it would take to complete her shopping. Sitting beside his lordship's buckskin-clad thigh much longer, she very much feared, would see her reaching out to touch it. Lud, she might as well reach for the stars.

Nick handed the reins and a coin to an eager lad, then stepped into the village emporium and went directly toward the jewelry counter. The shop had a limited supply of merchandise, naturally, but Nick wanted to have a ring in hand when he eventually offered for Mrs. Merriot. He'd send to the London vault for the family engagement ring, a monstrous diamond set in a band of alternating emeralds and rubies, if she accepted, but he did not want to frighten the lady off with that hideously ornate and old-fashioned piece. He wanted something delicate like Amelia, yet strong like Amelia, and beautiful, like Amelia. He settled on a slim gold filigree band with a lustrous pearl at the center, and put it in his inside pocket.

* * *

While Lord Worth and Mrs. Merriot were hunting for the items on their lists, Sir Digby was hunting, too. The little dog had finally found an open door, with no one watching, no one to call him back. He raced on his short stubby legs toward a remembered scent in the walled garden, and began to dig. Dirt was flying, the rosebush's roots were being shredded, and the terrier was having a wonderful time. He occasionally stopped to sniff in the hole, and once he watered a nearby chrysanthemum, but mostly he dug. Soon the hole was nearly deeper than he was tall. He almost had what he was after. One more pawful and—

"Here, now, what are you about, you fool mutt, messin' with my roses?" Henry the gardener shouted. "I don't care if you do be Mrs. Merriot's pet. No blasted dog belongs in my garden. Now, get away from there, you, afore I have Mrs. Salter set you to turnin' her spit."

Sir Digby needed one more nose length, one more good dig. He did not heed the yells, for this loud man was not his owner. He was not even the owner of the house. The dog burrowed on.

And found himself dangling by his collar. "I told you to— Here, what's that you've got in your mouth? Drop it. Dang fool little mongrel like you is like to choke on something you'd oughtn't eat, then we'll all be in the suds."

Sir Digby did not release his prize till Henry gave him another shake.

"What the devil? You dug up my best rose for this bit of a bone?" Henry dropped the dog to pick up the fallen white scrap that looked like it could have been a mouse's spine . . . or a man's little finger. "Bloody hell!" Henry would have tossed the vile thing away except for the metal band around one of the knuckles. He scraped it off and rubbed the ring on his dirt-encrusted smock. The ring didn't come much shinier, so the gardener wasn't impressed. Still, he brought it in to Mrs. Salter in the kitchen, to give to the master.

Mrs. Salter's faulty hearing didn't quite catch all the gardener's words, but she took the trumpery bit of jewelry and rinsed it off. Then she decided it would make a perfect token for her to bake inside her Twelfth Night cake. Some traditions had a pea and a bean cooked in the cake, to pick the Lord and Lady of Misrule for the night. Lud knew this old pile had enough mischief for any ten houses. What it needed was a mistress, and if the bacon-brained baron was too blind to see what was under his very nose, well, Mrs. Salter would give him a nudge in the right direction. She'd find a key for opportunity and a coin for wealth to stir into her batter, but she'd make certain Lord Worth got the ring for matrimony.

Meanwhile, so she didn't lose the trinket, Mrs. Salter strung it on a bit of string, around her neck.

Her hearing was so bad she didn't hear the three pots that fell off their hooks along the kitchen wall.

7

"That deaf old biddy is going to cook my ring inside a pie?"

"A cake, dear heart, a cake." Sir Olnic was back in his armor, in a taking.

So was his wife. "A cake, a pie, that makes no never mind. You need to get it away from her before she starts her baking."

"The ring is hanging off her neck, by St. Martin's manhood. I cannot reach between some aged cow's udders, not even to retrieve your blessed ring." The old knight shuddered at the thought, making the metal suit rattle like a bucket of nails. "Asides, she is too deaf to hear me, and sleeps too soundly after her dram of 'medicine' to be affrighted. Should I manage to scare the old girl, she'll only run off to her daughter's in the village, with the ring dangling between her dugs. You go get it."

"You know I cannot move material objects. If I could, we would have had the ring in our possession anytime this past century or more. Prithee, Ollie, what are we going to do? They will not eat the cake until Twelfth Night, the last chance this year to get the ring on the finger of the heir's beloved and end our wandering. Who knows when we'll get another opportunity?"

"Do you think I haven't been worrying myself to a shade over that very thing?"

She did not reply to that bit of irony. "Once they're wed, she'll wear that gaudy atrocity the king bestowed on us. Or they might never spend another Christmas here. What if Mrs. Merriot rejects his suit, when the dunderhead gets around to making her an offer in form? They might never wed at all, but go their separate ways, and our Nick will never find another woman to love." She began to weep.

Never had Sir Olnic wished harder that he still had the ability to take his beloved into his arms. He felt like weeping himself, and could have used her comfort. Knights do not cry, however, so he stiffened his spine, straightened the lance by his side, and said, "I will think of something, my heart's own. By my last hope of Heaven, I swear I will."

At first, Lady Rostend declined to meet with Lord Worth. She was not receiving, and he was not invited past the marble-laid entry hall. Since she'd just subjected Mrs. Merriot to a thundering scold, before that lady fled up the stairs to pack more clothes and stillroom supplies, Nick decided she could deuced well receive him. He walked past the startled butler to the parlor from whence he'd heard her strident voice.

He bowed.

She sniffed. "Barracks manners. I am not surprised."

He ignored the barb. "Lady Rostend, I could not help overhearing your conversation with Mrs. Merriot." Mrs. Salter could have overheard that conversation. "I would have you know that your niece is not compromised, as you declared."

Lady Rostend snorted. "Humph. If you hadn't seduced the gel, she'd be back in her rightful place."

"At your beck and call?"

Now it was the lady's turn to ignore a remark. "I can recognize a mooncalf when I see one. And kiss-swollen lips, sirrah."

Nick could feel his cheeks growing warm. The woman had always made him feel like a grubby schoolboy with fishing worms in his pockets. He'd been wrong to come into her parlor in such a ragtag state then, and he was wrong now. He'd apologized to Amy again, though, after they'd left the village. He should never have kissed her last night, he'd told her, and vowed that it would never happen again. She'd forgiven him again, with one of her radiant smiles. So he'd kissed her again. Thunderation, his wits went begging when she looked at him that way, all sunbeams and shining approval.

"I have not seduced your niece," he was able to utter in complete truth. "Her reputation is untarnished. Other than this morning, when we drove through the village in an open carriage, we have been well chaperoned."

Lady Rostend toyed with the fringe on her shawl.

"You expect me to believe that you never found a secluded niche in that great barn of a place? That you were never alone, when everyone knows almost all of the servants have deserted you? I think not. Amelia's name is already being bandied about. If this were London, the betting books at the gentlemen's clubs would be filled with odds of whether you were going to buy her a diamond necklace or a phaeton in payment for her favors."

His hostess had not invited Nick to sit, so he was leaning against the mantel. Now he pounded his fist there. "No gentleman would dare use my wife's name so basely."

"Your wife's? No, but your paramour's name is already on local lips. You and she will bring disgrace to my doorstep as I predicted. What else could one expect from a Nicholson? Well, I told her and now I shall tell you: do not expect me to take your strumpet in when she finds herself carrying your bastard. I wash my hands of her and her besmirched reputation."

Nick's brows lowered and his hands clenched into fists. The china shepherdesses lining the mantel were in imminent danger. So was Lady Rostend. He growled, "Mrs. Merriot's name will be as spotless as new snow when she becomes my wife."

"Your wife? Hah. Tell me another tarradiddle, Worth, this one won't fadge. You are not about to wed a penniless chit with no title, no connections beside me, and not much countenance. You might be a dastard, but you are not a fool."

He jerked his head to acknowledge the compliment, then simply said, "I think Amy is beautiful."

"Humph. Men. Since when did a gel's looks matter on the marriage mart? My niece is past her first blush of youth, and is not even a good breeder, if those years with Merriot hadn't produced an infant. No, men of your class do not wed widows of inferior standing."

"Mrs. Merriot is inferior to no female."

Lady Rostend continued as if he had not spoken: "They sure as Hades do not marry their mistresses."

"No, they do not. Which proves my lady's honor, when I ask for your blessings on our match. I shall marry your niece, if she'll have me, with or without your nod. That is why I came with her today, to ask your formal permission for her hand. I suppose I could have asked Sir Nathan, but I understand your son is in London."

Lady Rostend reached for her vinaigrette and waved it under her nose, screwing her face into a grimace that looked more like a gargoyle's than ever. "I never saw the like!"

"And you never shall again, madam, if you refuse my request."

"What, you come to my house, bold as brass, after stealing away my niece then ruining her beyond redemption, and ask my blessing? Your arrogance exceeds your idiocy."

"I take it, then, that you do not approve of the match?"

"No, I do not approve, you fiend. You robbed me of my eldest son, and now my companion? No, you shall not have my blessing."

Nick stepped away from the fireplace, taking a seat next to Lady Rostend's chair. He reached into the pocket of his waistcoat and pulled out a ring, not the new pearl ring, but another one, a gold signet. This one was Lieutenant Sir Gregory Rostend's ring, which Nick had taken from his mortally wounded friend's hand on a battlefield in Spain; the ring Gregory's son should have had eventually, and his son's son.

He turned the ring in his fingers, staring at that

dirty, dusty, blood-soaked ground in his mind's eye. Finally he held the ring out to his best friend's mother, who still wore darkest mourning nearly two years later. "Here. It was Gregory's, of course. I am late bringing it, I know, but I could not bear to face you with my own guilt and shame. I should have been the one to step in front of that French marksman's bullet. He was aiming at me, you see, the superior officer. I should have been watching Gregory's back, not the other way around, Lady Rostend, and I have wished I had done so a score of times. A hundred times, my lady, but a million wishes cannot change what happened. Gregory is dead and I survived. I am sorry. So sorry."

Lady Rostend clutched the ring in her hands, silently weeping. "You might be a fool, after all. I never blamed you for that Frenchman's bullet. I know you would have done the same for him, and did. Gregory wrote that you'd saved his life, not once, but many times. No, my lord, what I cannot forgive you for is leading my son off to the army. His place was here, with his family."

Nick blinked back a drop of moisture from his own eyes. "What, do you think I dragged him off by the nose to keep me company in Hell? I tried my best to dissuade him from joining up. My family were all soldiers; yours were not."

"But you and his other friends were everything to Gregory. He'd always chosen to spend time with you rather than with his own family."

"We were young men, my lady, not little boys on leading strings."

"You were Gregory's idol since he was breeched, though, and he'd have followed you anywhere, tried to emulate your every action. You were a year older, supposedly wiser, and should have set a better example, by George. You should have stayed in England managing your properties, raising sons to succeed you, and my son would have done the same."

About to hand Lady Rostend his handkerchief, Nick replaced it in his pocket. His voice was like a knife when he asked, "Are you saying that I have not done my duty?"

"Your duty was here, curse you!"

"I have already been cursed, if you listen to the local lore, and I was born to be a soldier like my father, and his before him."

Lady Rostend shook the ring in his face. "A man's first duty is to his family, not marching off to war, leaving a corkbrained cousin to inherit. Gregory should not have left, and so I told him when I refused my permission for him to sign up. Who lent the clunch the money to purchase his commission?"

"Gregory was six months from his majority and control of his own fortune, and threatening to take the king's shilling if I did not make him the loan. Would you have had your eldest son enlist as a foot soldier? He'd not have lived to his birthday. No, madam, I will not take the blame for Gregory's buying colors. It was his own decision, and he died living the life he'd chosen."

Nick knew that he and Lady Rostend would never see eye to eye on this matter, so he changed the subject. "Now, you have to let your niece live her life as she sees fit."

"She sees fit to live it with one such as you?"

"I am hopeful that she returns my regard," he answered, somewhat evasively.

Lady Rostend glared at him. "And if I do not give my blessing to this misalliance?"

"Then I hope to wed her regardless, God willing. But know this, madam: if you do not approve our union, if you do not acknowledge my wife, you will be the one who is hurt. Mrs. Merriot will be upset, of course, to be on the outs with her closest kin, but she will outrank you in the neighborhood. She'll have a higher title and deeper pockets. You will look no-account, turning your back on Baroness Worth, and your own standing will fall in the eyes of local Society as well as the London *ton*, where I intend to see Amelia take her rightful place."

Lady Rostend was no fool. She could see that she was going to lose her unpaid companion one way or the other, so she might as well get some advantage out of it. "My niece, Baroness Worth," sounded a great deal better than "My niece, Amelia Merriot, mill-owner's widow." She nodded her turbaned head a fraction of an inch. "In the spirit of the season, then, I wish you happy."

"Thank you. I appreciate your good wishes, and I am certain Amelia will also. Meantime, to show your goodwill and to dispel any rumors, would you attend a Twelfth Night dinner party at the Keep on Friday next? I intend to celebrate the recoveries of the Mundy sisters, as well as the house surviving another year of the so-called Christmas Curse. With luck, I will celebrate my engagement to your niece also."

"With luck? Am I to understand that you have not offered for the girl yet? I thought your asking for my permission was in form only, after the fact. If not, you had no business kissing her, Worth. A formal announcement of your engagement is the only way to stop the gossip."

"In my own time." Nick stood to leave, hearing Amelia's voice in the hall. "You'll come, then?"

"I'll come, and I'll hear that announcement or I'll know why." Lady Rostend twisted the ring between her fingers. "You make sure that Gregory's sacrifice means something."

8

"What will we do?" Lady Edryth asked, with a sigh that echoed through the empty Great Hall like a breeze through the pine trees. "It is nigh onto Twelfth Night, the last day of Christmas, our last day this year to affect earthly actions, and the heir has not yet proposed. 'Struth, I am not certain he loves her yet. He still thinks of making a marriage of convenience, saving the widow from a life of penury, and himself a life of hired companions and paid chatelaines."

"He loves her," Sir Olnic insisted, thumping his sword on the ground. "He has to. Have you seen the way he watches the lady when she crosses his path? Like a drowning man who espies a floating barrel. And Mrs. Merriot is beyond smitten, all full of sighs and shy smiles, dainty blushes and lowered lashes, when she's not in an agony of despair."

"I swear she's also taken to lowering the necklines of those funeral vestments she dons."

"No, I tipped a perfume bottle into the drawer where she kept those fichu things. They are in the wash."

Lady Edryth was too despondent to fly into the boughs over the fact that her husband had trifled with a lady's intimate garments. It was all for a good cause, at any rate. "They are sweet together, aren't they, in a youthful way?"

"Youthful, my arse. Why can they not act like the adults they are and simply get on with it? Neither is in their teens, and the days are hurrying past."

Lady Edryth sighed again at the reminder of time's passing. "Nick is acting the gentleman, I suppose."

"If he wants to be a gentleman, he can get down on his knees like a damned courtier and propose." His own knee pieces were badly in need of oil. "The problem is, they are never alone enough for him to come to the sticking point. Every time I manage to get them together, one of the old besoms calls for a lemonade or a cool cloth for her head. Or a servant comes with a question about the dinner. Or the blasted dog starts leaping about and barking as though it had another bone for him. One or two stolen kisses is all they've managed."

"Methinks that is just as well. A man is not so eager to purchase the cow when he can have the milk for free. Certes, if Nick does propose, and the lady accepts, he'd only place that pearl ring on her finger. I do not suppose you can steal it away from him, can you?" Lady Edryth did not mind Sir Olnic messing about with the baron's belongings, it seemed.

The old knight grunted. "It's too heavy for me to move. Asides, he'd only purchase another. Or send for that mound of ugliness in the London vault."

"Then what can we do, Ollie?"

"Pray?"

Lady Edryth removed the gold fillet that held back her red curls, as if she had the headache. "I do not think," she murmured, "that Heaven answers prayers from such as us."

"Then we'll have to rely on ourselves, by Saint Sebastian's sepulchre, and that accursed Twelfth Night cake. The heir will have the right ring in his possession long before the clock strikes midnight."

"The heir? Who knows what he will do with it? Mrs. Merriot should get the ring, betokening marriage. A woman is bound to try it on to see if the ring fits."

"But he has to declare himself. With a ring."

"He has to be nudged along. With the ring on her finger."

"He'll get the ring in his slice of cake, by Heaven. I am the one who has to see to it."

"You were the one who lost it in the first place."

Lady Edryth turned her back on Sir Olnic. They did not speak for another hour, which was not entirely untoward. Sometimes years had gone by without their talking to each other. Finally she turned back and raised her hand to his visored face, as if she could stroke his cheek. "There will be so little time, after they cut the cake and before midnight. What shall we do, Ollie, if we cannot get the ring on the heir's beloved's finger tonight?"

"Do? Why, we shall do what we have done these decades past: wait for the right opportunity. Meanwhile we'll continue to walk the halls, chivy the servants, frighten away bill collectors, that kind of thing." He tried to sound jovial, and failed. "It won't be so very bad, will it, my lady-wife? We'll still have each other."

Without being able to touch or hold each other or share caresses. Without a chance to make love here or find eternal peace elsewhere. "No, my dear," Lady Edryth softly said. "It will not be so bad."

The kitchens at Worth Keep had rarely seen so much company. It was a wonder Mrs. Salter was getting any cooking done at all.

Mrs. Merriot visited first. The baron had asked her to check the menu for the night's dinner, Amelia said, the Mundy sisters' first meal in the dining room. With Lady Rostend due, along with Vicar and Mrs. Tothy, and Squire Morris, Lord Worth wanted everything perfect. Did Mrs. Salter need any assistance? Amelia shouted, claiming that she was a dab hand at cake baking.

Up to her gnarly elbows in flour, Mrs. Salter declined any help. "What's that, a cake? Lord love you, ma'am, you'd do better to help the master with his bookkeeping," she hinted, thinking it was past time for Lord Worth and Mrs. Merriot to come to an agreement. The only way they were going to get together was to be together, so Mrs. Salter tried to shoo Mrs. Merriot out of her kitchen, into his lordship's book room.

The widow declined, however, for Lady Rostend's harsh words had struck home to her niece. Aunt Viveca was right: Amelia could not afford to have her reputation sullied, not over a doomed affair. She could not, therefore, afford to trust herself with the baron. For the most part, Nick had acted the gentleman, to her regret, since her own thoughts were anything but ladylike. To make temptation easier to resist, Amelia knew she had to keep her distance from her too-appealing host.

To that end, Amelia had Miss Charlotte Mundy move into the bedroom with Miss Henrietta, so that neither sister would be alone if the midnight mischief-maker decided to return. Mrs. Merriot and her maid Stoffard took the second bedroom in order to be on hand, yet get some rest, without being alone. The old ladies were well on their way to recovery and did not require day-and-night nursing. In fact, the London physician had declared them fit enough for a short carriage ride, so they could be leaving anytime, after which Amelia could not stay on at the Keep, of course, not without branding herself a fallen woman. Even if the Mundys remained, the Keep's maid-servants would be arriving back at the castle on the morrow, when superstition said the ghosts would be laid to rest for another year. There would be no excuse for Amelia's continued presence after that—no good one anyway.

Stoffard was already packing. They'd go home with her aunt after the dinner party tonight, Amelia had already decided, but she'd take one more lovely memory back with her. After all, those memories were all she would have for a lifetime.

"I know you are baking a special cake for Twelfth Night," she loudly told Mrs. Salter. "I was wondering . . . That is, if you could, do you think you might put this into the cake?" She held out a tiny horseshoe that the head stable man had fashioned for her out of a nail. "It has to get into Lord Worth's slice, to bring him luck. He needs a good luck token, to counteract all that nonsense about the castle being cursed."

"How am I to see it gets in the master's serving, Mrs. Merriot?" the cook asked, frowning at the batter in her bowl, where the ring was already concealed. She hadn't figured how to make sure that bit of gimcrackery got on the widow's dish yet, either.

"Why, I don't see why you cannot insert the token after the cake comes out of the oven, and mark the location somehow for when Mr. Salter slices the dessert at the table."

"Clever, ma'am. I can put frosting on top, so no one will see the knife marks. That ought to do the trick." Yes, Mrs. Merriot would make a perfect match for his lordship.

. . . Who arrived next. He placed two gold coins on the table next to Mrs. Salter, where she was icing a cake. He dipped a finger in the frosting mix and licked it before asking her if she could somehow contrive to get the coins into the cake and onto the Mundy sisters' plates.

"Don't tell anyone," the cook confided, "but the whole game is rigged. In the spirit of fun, a'course."

"Of course. While you are, ah, performing your legerdemain, could you add this to the cake also?"

Mrs. Salter might not know what the long word meant, but she did know what a ring did. Did his lordship? "You know the ring in the cake is supposed to foretell a happy marriage."

"Yes, I know," he said with a smile, having decided that he could ask for Mrs. Merriot's hand tonight, at last. They could be married tomorrow with the special license he'd purchased, if only she agreed. One more night of torture, of acting the gentleman with her so near, was about all his body could stand. "Yes, I do know about the ring."

Mrs. Salter smiled back, showing a missing tooth. "I don't suppose I need to ask whose slice you want this in?" she asked, ready to consign the token already in the cake, under a bit of candied pineapple, to someone else. Mrs. Merriot's horseshoe had a holly leaf on top.

After the baron left, Mrs. Salter added the gold coins under dabs of gooseberry preserves, and the pearl ring under a dollop of peach jam, then finished icing the cake.

She was nearly done when a messenger arrived from Lady Rostend, with a twisted paper in one hand and a coin in the other. "The mistress requests you add this to your Twelfth Night cake." He handed her the paper. "She sent this for your trouble." He handed her a farthing.

Mrs. Salter looked at the completed cake and then at the pittance of payment. "Right generous, your lady."

The footman winked and left, snabbling a cream tart on his way out.

"Now, who's supposed to get this?" Mrs. Salter asked herself as she unwrapped yet another ring, a man's gold signet. She straightened the paper out, to see Lord Worth's name written in a spidery hand. She scratched her head at the ways of the gentry, then stabbed her knife into the pretty cake and pushed the ring in. And the farthing for good measure, and a tiny key that didn't fit anything. The ring got a raisin, and the farthing's spot was marked with a fig, the key's with a curl of icing. "There. One more hole in the cake, and it will fall apart before it gets to the dinner table. So it's the gold under the gooseberry, the farthing under the fig," she repeated to herself, so she could remember to tell her husband. "The horseshoe has a holly and the key has a curl. Lady Rostend's ring got a raisin, the pearl got peaches, and the pawky ring got pineapple . . . or was it the other way around?"

9

"Forsooth," Lady Edryth cried, "I do not think I can stand the suspense."

"For certain the candles cannot stand your fluttering about, woman. Now, light somewhere and be still." Sir Olnic was himself stationed in the corner of the dining room. For once he was wearing hose and a tunic, blue to match his lady's velvet gown, richly embroidered in golden threads by her own hand. Tonight the knight could not afford to clank, to frighten anyone away from the table.

For once his lady listened to him, taking up a position next to the serving board, but the wringing of her hands was cooling the food. "I pray you know what you are doing, Ollie."

"Hush, my love, I have a plan."
Lady Edryth started weeping.

Dinner was a festive affair, despite Lady Rostend's scowls. Aunt Viveca had come, and that was enough for Amelia, proving she was not yet sunk beyond reproach. Mrs. Merriot was pleased, too, with the table she had set with Worth Keep's heirlooms. She was happiest, though, with a dress from before her marriage that Stoffard had altered for her. Seams had been let out as far as possible, and although the bosom was still somewhat confining, the gown was pink, not gray, and pretty. She'd threaded a matching pink ribbon through her blonde curls in lieu of her lace widow's cap, earning her aunt's censure. Nick's smile of appreciation was worth the scold. Nick's smiles were worth almost anything, Amelia thought.

He was magnificent tonight, the first time Amelia had seen him in formal evening attire. The de rigueur dark colors might have seemed austere or forbidding on others, especially with the scar on his face, but Nick only looked more elegant and attractive in the midnight-blue coat and white satin knee breeches. The emerald at his throat flashed as green as his eyes, alive with enjoyment and anticipation.

The Mundy sisters were in alt. Lord Worth had invited them to stay on as long as they wished, since the castle would be too empty without their presence. In addition, they had Squire Morris to themselves, since that strumpet Mrs. Silvers had refused dear Worth's invitation.

Vicar Tothy and his wife Bess were *aux anges* also, after their conversation with the baron before dinner. He'd promised them a new house for their growing family, and repairs to the church, which Lady Rostend had, predictably, refused.

Nick looked down his table to see Amelia at the other end, and thought that this was how things ought to be: good food, good friends, good feelings, and a good woman across from you. His old soldier's heart was warm despite the cool air in the room, telling him that life could be as sweet as he hoped Mrs. Salter's cake was going to be.

The only thing to mar the evening pleasure was the pesky draft that kept the candles flickering in their sconces. The windows were tightly shut, and no cracks could be seen in the walls. Still, when they first sat down, the ribbon in Mrs. Merriot's hair was fluttering, making Nick wish he could be the one to remove it, to spread her golden curls on his pillow. That thought took care of the chill. Squire Morris was too full of the baron's best wine to notice, but the ladies kept their shawls close around their shoulders—robbing Nick of an enticing view of Amelia's entrancing bosom. At his side, Lady Rostend grumbled about the draft, so Nick promised her a warmer reception in the parlor, as soon as they'd had dessert. They could not disappoint Mrs. Salter, could they?

Lady Rostend agreed that one's old family retainers were to be pampered—hadn't she given them each a new handkerchief for Boxing Day?—but demanded they hurry through the courses before the vicar's tongue froze to his fork. "It grows late, anyway, nearly time to leave," she added.

The anguish in Amelia's eyes was met by a gust of wind through the dining room. Nick called for the cake.

Salter came in, regally bearing the dessert on a silver platter. His muttering did take something away from his stately manner, though. "Curl for Miss Charlotte, Holly for Miss Henrietta. The raisin must be for Lady Rostend. Pineapple for the parson, or does he get the peach preserves? Berries for the baron?" It was something like that, the butler thought. But which section had the ring for Mrs. Merriot? The candlelight was too dim, his eyesight was too poor, and his memory was too faulty for him to get the right slice to the right person anyway. "Dammed foolish superstition, just like the ghosts," he mumbled, placing pieces of cake on the waiting plates, willy-nilly, and serving them to the diners.

Old Salter must be feeling the cold, Nick thought as he watched the man stumble, nearly spilling the two plates he held. Then someone must have jostled his arm, but Salter nimbly saved the next two plates from landing on the carpet, so Nick stopped worrying about pensioning the old butler off. Three candles went out just when Salter was about to place the last dishes in front of Nick and Amelia. Lud knew if the old man had managed to get the right piece to Mrs. Merriot. Nick could only pray.

The vicar was the first to find a token in his cake, the key. "How perfect, my lord, for the new house, and the new opportunities your residence at the castle will bring to the community." He lifted his glass in a toast to the baron.

Miss Charlotte and Miss Henrietta both found gold coins in their cake, and both wept tears of joy. Lady Rostend found her own farthing, and quietly tucked it away down her bodice.

"I say," Squire Morris bellowed, "a little horseshoe! Just the thing. Must mean my filly is going to win the Classic this year, what?"

Taking careful bites now that he realized Mrs. Salter had gone whole hog with this silly tradition, Nick discovered a ring in his cake. The dancing candles were enough for him to recognize Gregory's ring, and he knew who had placed it there for him. He put it on his finger and raised his glass to Lady Rostend, too overcome with emotion to express his gratitude for her gift and her forgiveness. He found his voice, however, when Mrs. Tothy uncovered her token, a gold ring, set with a pearl.

"That's not—" he began, only to be silenced by the vicar's wife's tears.

"It is the loveliest thing I have ever owned, my lord," she said between sobs.

"But—"

"We could never have afforded such a beautiful thing. Thank you, my lord, and may God forgive me for thinking you some kind of demon."

What could he say to that except, "Wear it in good health, as a symbol of your blessed marriage."

Everyone looked to Mrs. Merriot. The candles stopped flickering and the draft ceased altogether, as if the very air was holding its breath. Amelia self-consciously dug about in the slice of cake with her fork, not knowing what to expect. At last she uncovered a slender band, and held it up. The others had gathered closer to see, and Lady Rostend, disappointed, glared at Nick and said, "Looks like something the dog dragged in."

Amelia wiped the ring off on her serviette and held it closer. "No, I think it is white gold, or something very old. And there is an inscription inside."

"Let me see," Nick said, taking the ring from her hand so he could step closer to the candelabrum on the sideboard. "It is Latin. I think . . . Yes, it says, ' 'Til Death do us part.' "

"A wedding ring!" Miss Charlotte cooed, and her sister clapped. "That means a happy marriage, my dear Mrs. Merriot, within the year."

Lady Rostend muttered, "A month would be better

to quiet the gossip," but everyone pretended they hadn't heard.

Since they were all out of their chairs, they decided to adjourn to the parlor, the three gentlemen joining the ladies in the warmer room rather than stay for brandy and cigars. The vicar's wife took a seat at the pianoforte, and the others gathered around to sing the last of the year's Christmas carols. They had to sing without Lord Worth and Mrs. Merriot, however, for Nick steered Amelia toward a secluded corner, in sight of the others, but out of earshot.

He held up the ring. "Will you wear this, my dear?"

"Of course. It is my Twelfth Night token. Unless it is too valuable an heirloom, and you need it here for the family coffers?"

"I need it here, Amy. I need it on your finger. And it is much more than a charm. I do not pretend to know where it came from, or how it got into your cake, but if it is a token, my dear, it is a token of my love."

Amelia's heart was in her throat. "I don't understand. What are you saying?"

Nick laughed. "I am trying to ask you to marry me, Mrs. Merriot."

"Marriage? But you cannot—"

"Of course I can, and that ring proves it. At first I thought to offer you a marriage of convenience, since we rubbed along well together and your situation begged to be improved."

"And then?" she asked, hoping for the words she'd been wanting to hear for so long.

"And then I found I could not bear the thought of living without you, without winning one of your glorious smiles at least every hour, like a clock's chime, reminding me that joy and love and springtime still exist. I did not think I could love anyone, but you have proved me wrong, my dearest. Do you think that you could come to have some affection for me in return? Enough to make me the happiest of men?"

"Silly Nick, I have loved you since you walked into the church on Christmas Day, so brave and strong. Nay, I loved you when I was a girl, when you brought me a ribbon from the fair. I can think of nothing I would rather do than become your wife, but only if you are sure you don't merely want a mistress you can discard when you grow weary of her."

He gently kissed her, removing all doubt from Amelia's mind—and from the minds of the others, who were surreptitiously watching from the room's other end, and the ether. "I want you, the only mistress of my heart, today and tomorrow, and every tomorrow after that," he said, slipping the ring on her finger, where it fit as though made for her, " 'til Death do us part."

10

Hand in hand at last, Sir Olnic and Lady Edryth ascended a stairwell of sunbeams, just as the clock in the Great Hall struck midnight. As they climbed higher, their outlines blurred, the knight's shining armor blending into the lady's flowing gown. Just before they faded into the golden light, Sir Olnic turned back to look at his heir, and the future of his house.

" 'Til Death do you part, lad?" he said with a smile and a wink for his own beloved. "That's not the half of it."

A Gathering of Gifts
by *Andrea Pickens*

"Oh, show a little spirit, Charles! Must you always be as cautious as a church mouse creeping past a sleeping tabby?" Without waiting for a reply, the young lady slapped her crop against her mount's flank and sent the high-strung stallion hurtling toward the towering stone wall.

"The trouble is not *my* lack of spirit, but rather *your* overabundance of it," muttered her companion through gritted teeth as he spurred his own horse forward. "I fear that if you don't learn to rein in some of your less laudable tendencies, my dear Emma, it is going to land you in the suds sooner than later."

His jaw unclenched slightly on seeing that she had cleared the obstacle without mishap, but the slip and clatter of hooves on the slippery ground brought a fresh grimace to his face. The fact that a patch of ice nearly threw his stallion off stride as the animal approached the tumble of stones did nothing to improve his temper. It took a firm hand to ensure that neither of them came to grief because of the treacherous footing, and by the time he pulled to a halt beside his cousin, Viscount Lawrance felt his patience about to snap.

"You see, there was nothing to worry about!" Lady Emma Pierson gave a toss of her blonde curls, causing the jaunty little feather adorning her riding cap to brush against the shoulder of her stylish frogged jacket. She then grinned at her cousin. "Ajax and Orion have jumped far higher fences on countless occasions. Come, there's a path up ahead with several more obstacles and a stretch where we can race—"

"Nothing to worry about?" he repeated angrily, drawing to a halt beside her. "The deuce take it, Emma, it was a foolish risk! You had no idea what lay beyond the stones. Why, if the ground had been a trifle more icy, both Ajax and you might have broken your necks." His mouth thinned. "You may have little regard for your own well-being," he went on in a low growl. "But such a splendid animal deserves more consideration."

At the first volley of sharp words, the smile disappeared from Emma's face and her chin took on a stubborn jut. "You needn't lecture me as if you were one of my former governesses. I don't need anyone to tell me how to go on, especially you, Charles, who are only two years my senior." If anything, the tilt became even more pronounced. "I'm *not* a child anymore. In case you have forgotten, I have already had a Season in Town. A very successful one, at that," she added with a decided sniff.

"Then, show you have gained some sense as well as years, Em. You're right—you are no longer fourteen and dragging the rest of us into one bumblebroth after another with your impetuous actions. It's time to stop acting like a headstrong little hellion, with no mind for aught but your own whims."

If she had been standing on the ground, she might have stamped her foot. Instead, she made due with a flounce of her shoulders. "The rest of the gentlemen of the *ton* do not seem to find such fault with my behavior," she retorted.

"Don't be so sure," he shot back. "As a matter of

fact, I had been meaning to broach the subject at some point during my visit, so it may as well be now." There was a brief pause. "An undesirable reputation, once garnered, is not nearly so easy to shed as a gown whose color no longer pleases you."

Beneath the wind-whipped color, Emma's cheeks went very pale. "How dare you imply such a horrid thing! I . . . I had more admirers dancing attendance on me than any of the other misses making their come-out."

"Oh, there's no denying that your beauty—not to speak of your lineage and dowry—attracts gentlemen like honey draws a swarm of bees," replied her cousin, the edge of anger replaced by a note of concern. "People may fawn over your looks and your fortune, but around the clubs, there are whispers that your behavior is not nearly so admirable."

She blinked.

"I may as well be blunt," he continued. "Since your mother's death, your father has indulged in your every whim, and it has done more harm than good. You are in danger of becoming a spoiled brat, Emma. I say such a thing because I know that, at heart, you are no such thing. But of late, your actions do you no credit."

Her lips quivered slightly. "I don't know what you mean."

"Don't you?" he asked quietly.

She turned in profile, but the color that crept back to her face was a shade darker than before.

"Let me remind you of just a few incidents from the past Season. Demanding that poor Palmerston let you drive his team of grays along Rotten Row nearly resulted in Lady Haverstock being seriously injured."

"She should have moved out of the way a bit quicker."

"Lord, Emma, the poor lady is nearly eighty!" He

smoothed at the collar of his coat, though the crease remained on his brow. "Then, there was the poem you composed about Miss Taverhill and recited at Lady Jermaine's gala ball. That was not well-done of you."

"But she *does* look like a Maypole, especially when she is dressed in cherry and white stripes!" Her expression turned more mulish. "Besides, I thought the rhyming scheme was quite ingenious. And everyone laughed."

"Everyone except Miss Taverhill," he said quietly. "I happened to see her sobbing in a corner of the deserted library, and her brother mentioned that it was nigh on a sennight before she had the courage to appear in public again." His lips compressed in a tight line. "If you had stopped to think, you would have realized it was a cruel thing to do."

"It was just a joke. I meant no harm," she replied rather sulkily.

"Perhaps not. But you caused hurt and humiliation to someone who deserved neither. What I am trying to say is that at times you are indeed childish, and tend to think only of yourself. If you wish to be truly admired, you would do well to temper your high spirits with a bit more consideration for how your actions affect others."

Emma turned back to face him, and he was disappointed to see that the momentary show of contrition had been replaced by the all too familiar spark of defiance in her blue eyes. "Christmas is supposed to be a time of good cheer and jolly fun," she said in a brittle voice. "If you find me such a despicable person, I don't know why you bothered to come here for the holidays."

A sigh escaped his lips. "You know that I find you no such thing. If I did not like you so well, Emma, I would not bother to make known my concerns. Trust me, I take no pleasure from bringing this up."

Her hand tightened on the butt of her crop. "Well, now that you have voiced your sentiments, I should hope that you do not mean to go on and on with such nasty criticisms for the entire time you are here. It would be a . . . a dashed bore."

"No, I've said my piece and am done with it. However, I hope you will think on it." He forced a smile. "Now, let us ride on before the horses take a chill." He gathered his reins and quickly sought to point the conversation in a new direction as well. "Your father mentioned that there is finally someone in residence at Hawthorne House. Have you met the family?"

Emma shook her head as they moved off. "No, but I understand that the gentleman is some junior officer who only recently sold out when he inherited the baron's title." She shrugged. "Heddy Tillson says he's brought his widowed sister and her child to stay with him, and by the glimpse she caught of them in the village, they don't look to have much polish or blunt. It is too bad—we could have done with some lively company in the area, but it sounds as if they will prove to be dull as dishwater."

Her cousin bit back a reproach about rushing to judgment, especially when it was based on the observations of such a flighty pea-goose as Heddy Tillson. "Perhaps you will be surprised," he murmured.

Ignoring the remark, Emma urged her mount into a brisk trot. "If we go left here," she called over her shoulder, gesturing toward the fork in the trail, "we shall drop down into the orchards by Hawthorne House. The recent storm has left several fallen trees that make for a bracing ride."

"Let us go right, then, and continue on to the open

fields," he replied. "The ground is too frozen to chance any more jumping."

"Oh, pooh!" Once again, her crop flashed through the air, and Ajax thundered off at a dead gallop. Charles already knew which turn Emma would choose before the stallion was halfway there.

For a moment he was sorely tempted to turn back to the manor house and leave her to face any consequences of such impetuous behavior. However, gentlemanly scruples won out over pique. The weather looked to be turning even worse, and, as he had remarked before, the frozen ground was dangerous in spots. So after letting fly with a few choice epithets, he followed after her, though at a more circumspect pace.

The worst of his anger had been vented along with the curses. It was hard to stay mad at Emma for long, for despite her faults, he considered her the best of friends—smart, funny, loyal, and good-natured, regardless of the criticisms he had voiced earlier. If only she would . . .

Even from a distance, the cry of pain was sharply audible. But by the time Charles had reached the spot where the riderless stallion sidled in nervous agitation and vaulted down from his saddle, there was not a sound coming from his cousin's prostrate form.

"My God, Emma! Can you hear me?" he demanded as he knelt down beside her.

Her eyes slowly fluttered open. "Y-yes." She bit her lip and struggled to sit up. "I think it's just a bit of bruising. To both my rump and my pride. But is Ajax unharmed? I shall never forgive myself if—"

"Yes, yes, he's fine." Charles slipped his arm under her shoulders, but prevented her from rising. "Don't move for a moment. You've had a nasty spill." The breath he was holding came out in a rush of relief. "Lord, another few inches and you might have been killed," he added in a low voice, eyeing the jagged stumps of broken branches poking up from the fallen oak.

"You may go ahead and say that I would have thoroughly deserved such a fate," she said with a tremor in her voice. "I-I—"

"Silly poppet." He cut off her words by burying her face in the folds of his jacket. Her fashionable little military style shako had been dislodged by the fall, and his fingers began to gently stroke her tangled curls. "Life should be sadly flat without my favorite cousin to brangle with."

Emma stifled a sob. "I know that I—"

"Shhhh," he soothed. "We shall discuss that some other time. Right now, do you think you can manage to stand?"

"I think so, if you will give me a hand." With a game smile, she attempted to get to her feet, but as soon as her right foot touched the ground, she bit back a scream of agony and collapsed against his chest, her face ashen with pain. "I-I fear it is worse than I thought," she gasped.

Charles helped her lie back down on the frozen earth. "Hawthorne House is not far. I shall have to ride there to fetch help and to send word for a doctor. Will you be all right for a bit?"

She nodded.

He peeled off his riding coat and tucked it over her chest. "That's the spirit. I knew I could depend on you not to fall into a fit of vapors," he replied with a wan grin. "I'll be back as soon as I can."

Emma shifted slightly on the hard ground, and an unladylike word escaped her lips. Several, in fact. She winced, thinking that if Charles had overheard such language, he would no doubt ring down another peal upon her head. Not, she added with a wry grimace, that it was possible to sink any lower in his esteem.

The uncomfortable thought caused her to move once more, sending a stab of pain through her right ankle. What hurt more, however, was the memory of her cousin's frank words. *Was he right?* she wondered, blinking back a tear. *Was she really the selfish monster he described?*

A part of her longed to shrug off such criticism, dismissing it as childish pique on his part. Perhaps he was merely jealous because she had not spent as much time with him during the whirlwind months in London as in the past. After all, she *had* attracted a goodly amount of attention. Countless gentlemen had vied for the honor of leading her out on the dance floor. They had laughed at her *bon mots,* applauded her performances on the pianoforte, and complimented her on her riding skills. Indeed, in their eyes, it appeared she could do no wrong.

Charles must be mistaken, she assured herself. *Or simply acting out of spite.* Such a conclusion made her feel infinitely better, and so she chose to ignore the tiny voice in the back of her head which whispered that Charles was never petty or mean-spirited. Instead she heard only the echo of all the honeyed flattery and sugared praise that had come her way as she drifted into unconsciousness.

Such sweet reveries were rudely interrupted by a rough shake of her shoulders. "Come, now, open your eyes."

When she complied, what she beheld caused her to blink several times in succession. It was not Charles whose face loomed only inches from hers, but rather that of a perfect stranger. Actually, he was not perfect at all, she found herself thinking. His face was lean and angular, its color unfashionably bronzed by the sun. A shock of unruly black hair fell over his brow, accentuating the sharp, aquiline line of his nose. His chiseled lips looked to be full and well formed, but it was difficult to be sure, as they were presently pursed in a grim scowl. No less grim was the piercing gaze he had fixed upon her person. She squirmed slightly under such severe scrutiny, though it was impossible to break away from the glittering intensity of his hazel eyes. Not exactly hazel, for they had the most interesting flecks of molten gold—

"Well, she appears to be conscious." The stranger looked away, and Emma was vaguely aware of Charles hovering somewhere behind him. He looked back to her and then to the massive tree trunk and the patch of ice in front of it. "Good Lord," he muttered with barely concealed disdain. "How could anyone be so corkbrained as to attempt such a stunt in conditions such as these?"

She managed to prop herself up on one elbow. "I'll have you know, sir, that I am accorded to be an excellent rider."

One brow arched up. "It would appear that such praise is completely unwarranted." There was a slight pause. "You might have seriously injured your horse."

Emma gasped, first at the effrontery of his words, and then at the fact that his hands began to run down the length of her arms and then her legs. "How dare you—*ouch*!"

The stranger leaned back on his haunches. "I don't think any bones are broken," he said to Charles. "But the ankle appears to be badly sprained. I suppose we shall have to move her to Hawthorne House for the present. Fetch her horse while I take her up."

"But—" began Emma. The protest was muffled in the folds of his coat as he lifted her into his arms with one easy motion. To her dismay, she saw that her cousin had jumped to obey the man's curt command.

"Put me down!" she snapped. "I do not wish for you to—"

"Stop squirming," he ordered. "Lest you wish to add to your collection of bruises by taking a second tumble to the ground." His arms drew her closer to his chest. "Though perhaps another thump would knock some sense into that head of yours."

She fell silent and ceased her struggling, though she studiously avoided any eye contact with the stranger. Harder to ignore was the corded strength of his shoulders or the heat emanating from his broad chest. From her precarious position, it was clear that he was at least several inches taller than her cousin and a good deal more muscular. Despite her not inconsiderable height, he carried her through the orchard as if she weighed no more than a feather.

"Odious man," she whispered to herself.

For an instant, Emma thought she detected a faint chuckle, but when she ventured a surreptitious peek at his face, the same hard expression was etched on his features. She leaned back and closed her eyes, praying that one of her father's carriages would soon be arriving to take her home.

Noel Trumbull stared out the mullioned windows and let out a harried sigh. Of all the deuced luck! He had enough to worry about without being stuck dancing attendance on some spoiled heiress, no matter that she had hair like spun gold and eyes as blue as the Mediterranean in summer. His lips compressed in a tight line. Oh, she was attractive all right. And damn well knew it, he reminded himself. Even though he had only spent a week in London on his return from the Peninsula, he had heard Miss Pierson's name men-

tioned in the same breath with other Diamonds of the
First Water. A shame that her beauty appeared to be
only skin-deep. It seemed, from first impression, that
she was both arrogant and waspish, traits he abhorred
in any person, be they male or female. He could only
hope that one of her father's carriages would soon be
arriving to take her home.

Such hopes were quickly dashed by the terse pronouncement of the doctor.

"A nasty twist, Lady Emma," he announced with a
cluck of his tongue. "I'm afraid there is no question
of you being moved until the swelling has gone down."

"But—" began both Emma and Noel at once.

They both stopped short. Noel then clamped his jaw
firmly shut, regretting that surprise had wrested any
show of emotion out of him. He turned toward the
hearth, determined to keep to himself just how unwelcome the announcement was. The last thing he needed
was yet another responsibility weighing on his shoulders as Christmas approached. It would be difficult
enough creating the proper spirit of the holidays without the presence of a conceited stranger in their home.

The young lady appeared no more pleased with the
announcement than he was. "I would not dream of
imposing on this gentleman's gracious hospitality any
longer than I already have," she said with unveiled
sarcasm. "Surely my ankle can tolerate a short carriage ride."

The doctor shook his head. "Absolutely not." He
pushed his spectacles back up to the bridge of his
nose. "The injury should heal without any lasting ill
effects, but only if great care is taken now. And even
if I were to consider the request, it would not be possible, given the state of the lane leading up to the cottage. It has been unused for so long that it is hardly

better than a cart track. Any ride over such jolts and ruts could cause further damage."

"Charles could take me up on Orion and—"

The doctor waved away the suggestion. "Now, don't be foolish, Lady Emma. Why, you are very fortunate that Hawthorne House has lately become inhabited. You will be quite comfortable here."

"Hah!" she muttered under her breath.

"It will only be for a short time," piped up Charles, slanting an uneasy glance at Noel. "That is, if you have no objections, Lord Kirtland."

"It appears there is little choice in the matter," he replied grimly. With a tone designed to match the young lady's earlier mocking politeness, he added, "Though I must warn Lady Pierson that we are hardly able to entertain her in the style to which she is no doubt accustomed."

He watched Emma's lovely features twist into a scowl. "But it's not fair! Robert and his friends are arriving soon for the holidays. And Papa. And your friend Mr. Harkness. Just think of all the fun I shall be missing." Her lower lip began to quiver. "And my ankle is beginning to throb unmercifully."

Noel couldn't help himself. "Dear me, life is not fair, to have heaped such unconscionable suffering upon your poor head," he said with withering sarcasm.

"I shall ride back this afternoon with a number of your things, Em," said Charles quickly, seeking to forestall any further comment from his cousin. "And, of course, all of us shall come visit and spend as much time—"

"No. That will not be possible." Noel folded his arms across his chest and calmly regarded the two startled faces that turned in his direction. "My sister is still recovering from the death of her husband. I'll not have my family and household turned on its ear because the Duke of Telford's daughter imagines she cannot live without constant amusement. One visitor, for one hour a day. That is all I will allow." His eyes met hers. "You'll survive."

Emma's chin came up. "Shall you keep me on bread-and-water rations, too? It is probably what you fed your troops, sir."

He gave a harsh laugh. "If bread and water was to be had, they were infinitely grateful. On the battlefields of the Peninsula, Miss Pierson, liveried servants do not appear at the ring of a bell with silver salvers." Noting she at least had the grace to color, he went on, "Neither will they here. Now, if you will excuse me, I have some rather more important matters to attend to." Turning on his heel, he quit the room, making no attempt to prevent the door from closing with a pronounced thump.

That should make it clear to the pampered little minx that he would not dance attendance on her like everyone else did, he thought as he walked down the narrow hallway toward the kitchen. It was quite evident that "no" was not a word with which she was intimately acquainted. But she did have some spirit, he was forced to admit. He had half expected her to turn into a watering pot or lapse into a fit of hysterics on hearing his announcement. Instead, she had met his deliberate roughness with a show of spunk. A faint smile crept to his lips. Her comment about bread and water showed she had a sharp sense of humor as well. And more than a little courage. Although he had made light of her injury, he knew it was a painful one. In all fairness to the chit, she had born the discomfort with more fortitude than many a soldier would have shown, making no complaint until that moment.

He made a wry face. Perhaps the young lady had more to her than he had first thought. However, that was hardly any concern to him. As he had told Miss Pierson and her cousin, he had a good deal of other things to occupy his mind.

Picking up the hammer and chisel that he had left lying on the scarred pine table, he turned his attention back to trying to loosen a rusted bolt on the door of the iron stove. The house had been sadly neglected by his predecessors, but until he could make a final assessment of the late Baron's finances, he was determined not to incur expenses that he could ill afford. For the time being, most of the rambling structure would remain closed off, save for the small wing where he and his family had taken up residence. It, too, needed a good deal of attention to make it a snug place to live, so he had determined to do much of the menial labor himself in that part of the house. He didn't mind—he disliked being idle, and the work would keep him busy until he could make longer-range plans and see about hiring a proper crew of workmen. Besides, it gave him a sense of satisfaction to see the improvements take shape with each passing day. By Christmas Eve, he vowed, the fires would burn without smoking, the draperies would be free of dust, and the hearths would be polished and hung with greenery. Anna and Toby would have a snug, cheery place to celebrate their first holiday without James.

But try as he might to concentrate on the task at hand, he couldn't keep his thoughts from drifting back to the unexpected guest. She was no milk-and-water miss, that was for sure. He preferred a lady who had opinions of her own, but whether Miss Pierson's spirit was indicative of merely a headstrong nature or other, more exemplary qualities, he wasn't sure. What he did know was that he found no fault with the lush fullness of her lips, even when they were pursed in a pout, and that the spark in her eyes was . . . intriguing.

To his dismay, he found it impossible to banish the picture of a mass of spun-gold curls and the way her chin came up in a saucy tilt when she was angry. He supposed it was only natural to feel the stirrings of physical attraction for a beautiful lady, but his reaction to this particular one only caused his mood to turn blacker. It grew even worse when a careless swing of the hammer caught a sharp blow to his thumb. Swearing under his breath, he gave it a shake, then set his jaw in a grim line. No doubt Miss Pierson already had a legion of besotted young men making cakes of themselves over her. He would not add to their ranks.

And yet, whatever the young lady's faults, she radiated a certain vitality. Lord, if only a spark of Miss Pierson's lively fire might be rekindled in Anne. . . .

The kitchen door opened, and his sister and her young son came in with a basket full of pine boughs they had cut. "Joseph says there has been some kind of accident," she said with some alarm as she fumbled with the knots of her bonnet.

Noel pulled a face. "It's nothing serious. Telford's daughter has taken a tumble from her horse and twisted an ankle. The doctor and her cousin are with her now." He stood up and ran his hand through his hair. "The bad news is that it appears we are to be saddled with the lady until she is well enough to be moved."

"Oh, dear, I had best go see if there is anything I can do to be of help."

"Anne!" His rather sharp tone caused her to stop in mid-stride. "The chit is not at death's door. Much as she might wish it, she's not in need of someone to wait hand and foot on her."

"But I don't mind—"

"That's not the point," he continued doggedly. "You are as much a guest under my roof as she is.

It's bad enough that you must help with household tasks until I see what staff we can afford, but I won't have you reduced to serving as a maid for some whiny brat."

Anne's brow furrowed. "Surely the young lady cannot be as bad as all that."

"Hah," he muttered, then added another expression for good measure.

His young nephew had been listening to the exchange with great interest. "The devil take it?" he repeated. "What is he taking, Uncle Noel? And where is he taking it?"

"Tobias!" warned his mother. "You are not to use such improper language."

"Sorry," growled Noel with an apologetic shrug in his sister's direction. "I shall try to set a better example." Reaching out, he ruffled the little boy's tousled curls. "He is taking me to task for using such horrid cant in front of your mother. Let it be a lesson of what you should *not* say in the presence of a lady. Now, I need another man to give me a hand in fixing the stove. Will you help hold my tools while I work at this bolt?"

Toby gave a grin of delight and took up the hammer.

"I could not wish for a better example for my son, Noel," she said quietly, a wistful smile stealing across her pale features. "Save of course for . . ." Her voice broke off, and she looked away. "Well," she continued after a moment in a brisker voice. "While you two are occupied, I best see about setting one of the extra bedchambers in readiness for our guest."

"I vow, Charles, I should prefer to hop back to Telford Manor on one leg than stay here," grumbled Emma as the doctor left the small drawing room. She looked at her cousin through lowered lashes and gave a long sigh. "Orion's gait is smooth as silk. Surely you could take me up behind you without any trouble."

"Oh, no, you don't." He crossed his arms. "You may wrap half the young bucks in Town around your little finger, but I know you too well to succumb to your wiles, Em. One disaster is enough for the day." There was a fraction of a pause. "And don't look at me that way," he added, taking note of the jut of her lower lip. "You heard the doctor. It would be foolish to risk further damage, so I'll not be swayed by any pleading or wheedling. The baron is right—several days of quiet recuperation here will not be an undue hardship."

"But he is an *odious* man!"

"Because he stands firm in the face of your entreaties?" he countered with a glimmer of a smile. "Unlike any other male of your acquaintance."

"Wretch" came the muttered reply. "So you truly mean to abandon me here with an ill-tempered martinet and a grieving widow? What an excellent way to get in the proper holiday spirit," she said with some asperity. "I can't imagine a less merry Christmas. Whatever shall I do to keep entertained, since Lord Kirtland seems incapable of civil conversation and forbids me any more congenial company?"

"You might spend some time giving thanks for the fact that you were not seriously injured," said Charles mildly. "After all, Christmas is not just a season for frivolity and fun, but a time to consider our blessings."

All the petulance drained from Emma's face, and she suddenly looked very young and very vulnerable. "Do you really think me so . . . shallow?" she asked in a small voice.

"I am beginning to think that *any* female is unfathomable for a poor simpleton like me."

"Please don't joke. It's just that . . . it's obvious that

Lord Kirtland doesn't like me above half. He looks at me as if I were a chicken with three heads."

"Then, I shall bring a pair of spectacles for him, along with your things." Before she could make further protest, he rose and took up his hat and gloves. "That should ensure that he will not try to truss and roast you for Christmas dinner."

"Charles!" Her tone became even more plaintive.

"Cheer up. It won't be nearly as bad as you think."

It was a good thing that she did not say aloud exactly what she was thinking, for her cousin had scarcely quitted the room when another person appeared at the half-open door.

"I understand there has been a dreadful accident," said Anne, venturing a step into the small parlor. "I do hope you are not in too much pain, Miss Pierson. You must tell me if there is anything I can do to make you more comfortable." She bent to fuss with the pillow, propping up Emma's freshly bandaged ankle. "I am Noel—that is, Lord Kirtland's sister, Mrs. Hartley." A twitch of embarrassment played on her lips. "I am still getting used to the notion of his being a titled gentleman."

Relieved that someone was showing a little sympathy for her plight, Emma managed a wan smile. Though the lady before her was dressed in somber black, there was a warmth to her expression, especially in soft hazel eyes that were now crinkled in some concern. She was, Emma judged, some years older than herself, though not far past the first bloom of youth. Indeed, with such lustrous raven hair accentuating her delicate features and porcelain complexion, the baron's sister was likely to be thought a very pretty lady by anyone making her acquaintance.

"How kind of you, Mrs. Hartley," she murmured. "I should very much like a cup of tea and some toast.

Then, perhaps you might spare the time to sit with me and read—"

"No, Miss Pierson, she *cannot* spare the time. I warned you, we are all quite busy enough as it is around here, without having to cater to the whims of one used to being waited on hand and foot."

"Noel!" cried Anne in some surprise. Biting her lip, she then dropped her voice to barely above a whisper. "There is no need to speak so harshly."

If anything, his expression became darker. "I told you, Anne, I'll not have you forced to play nursemaid to our guest." The emphasis he put on the last word made it clear he was, after further deliberation, still no more pleased about the entire situation than Emma was. "I know you are anxious to choose the material for Toby's room, and there is no reason for you to put it off. I, too, have some errands that cannot wait, so I have had the gig brought around for a trip into the village."

Emma took pains to match his scowl as he turned her way.

"Our housekeeper will bring you some refreshment when she is done putting fresh linens in one of the spare bedchambers," he continued. "Later, she will fix you a light nuncheon as well. But from this evening on, you will have to take your meals when the rest of us are served, though the fare may be not to your taste."

Goaded on by his rudeness, Emma made an attempt to rein in her own tongue. "But I shall be frightfully bored if Mrs. Hartley cannot sit with me for a bit."

Noel paused for a moment, then his glance fell on his sister's workbasket. He took it up and dropped it none too gently within Emma's reach. "Bored? Then make yourself useful and mend one of my nephew's stockings if you are bored."

Her jaw dropped.

"Or perhaps you can't manage so much as a simple stitch." He shrugged. "If not, then you will have to think of something else to amuse yourself. Anne, come along with me. Before we leave, I wish to know your opinion on what color is best for the trim in the dining room."

The young widow shot an apologetic look at Emma before hurrying after her brother.

It was all Emma could do to keep from bursting into tears, more from anger than from any physical hurt. *Drat the insufferable man!* Arrogant, sharp-tongued, unfeeling—it was not *she* who should be put to blush for her behavior!

Or should she? Her throat constricted as she thought back on the events of the morning. Her cousin's warnings had been eminently reasonable, yet she had paid them no heed. Indeed, she had deliberately flaunted his advice. She swallowed hard. It was hard to deny that she had acted out of stubborn pique. The consequences could have been a good deal worse. Her horse might have been seriously injured. Or Charles, since he had been obliged to risk his own neck in giving chase to her.

And what about his other chidings? She shifted uncomfortably against the faded chintz cushions of the sofa. Why, it had never occurred to her that any of her actions might have caused pain to anyone else. Surely he must know that she would never consciously seek to hurt . . . Emma's chin dropped and she gave a small sniff. That, she suddenly realized, was exactly the point he was trying to make. As she recalled his little lecture, she saw that he must consider her thoughtless. And no doubt just as arrogant, sharp-tongued, and unfeeling as the odious Lord Kirtland.

A tear spilled down her cheek. It was not a pleasant

thing to have to contemplate, and it set off a warring
of emotions within her. A part of her wished to deny
the truth of his words. Her behavior might be less
than perfect, but it was wrong of him to bring up such
serious matters during a holiday that was meant to be
joyous. Nor did her own shortcomings in any way excuse the cold rudeness of her reluctant host.

Emma felt her spirits sink to a new low. Between
her own depressed state of mind and the overt dislike
of Lord Kirtland, how would she ever endure this confinement? Feeling ill-used and abandoned, she allowed
her gaze to wander around the small room, hoping to
find any sort of respite from such dismal thoughts.
Perhaps there was a book or newspaper that might
offer a brief distraction, she thought, though how she
would fetch it was another matter.

There was, however, nothing. With a sigh, she rearranged the wool blanket over her lap and looked
around once more. The room was, at least, a pleasant
one, with light beginning to stream in through the
large mullioned windows, though the second glance
did make it clear that the baron had not exaggerated—there was much work to be done to put things
in order. The hearth could use another coat of beeswax, the draperies were in need of a good beating to
rid them of the dust, and the planked floor had a dull
scuff of neglect to it.

Perhaps it was no wonder that Lord Kirtland was
not in the best of humors, admitted Emma. Heddy
looked to be correct for once in guessing that he had
not inherited much blunt along with the title and
house. Still, it did not excuse the man's execrable
manners—

The thump of a cricket ball bouncing through the
doorway and up against a side table caused her head
to jerk up. It was followed by a small boy, who was

so engrossed with retrieving his toy that he had nearly collided with the sofa before he noticed there was someone else in the room.

"Oh!" He pushed a shock of tousled hair back, and his eyes grew wide. "Are you an angel sent down from Heaven as a Christmas present?" he asked, staring at Emma's ethereal features and golden curls.

She smiled faintly in spite of her bleak mood. At least one male did not consider her a witch. "I'm afraid not. I am simply your neighbor who is here in your sitting room because of a riding mishap."

He looked rather crestfallen. "I thought maybe you had been sent to cheer up Mama," he mumbled. "She cries a lot, when she thinks I don't see her. Uncle Noel says it is because she misses Papa." His lip trembled. "So do I."

"I fear I am hardly cheerful company for your mother or anyone at the moment." Seeing disappointment spread across the boy's features, she added, "But I will do my best to lift her spirits." That is, she said to herself, if she could manage to lift her own. However, her own misfortune suddenly seemed rather insignificant, and she felt a twinge of contrition on recalling her earlier complaints to Mrs. Hartley.

The boy's face brightened a bit, then his gaze fell on her bandaged ankle. "When I must stay abed, Mama always reads to me. Shall I get one of my books and read you my favorite story? You would only have to help a little with the words."

Emma's lips twitched. "I should like that very much, sir."

He giggled. "I'm not sir, I'm Toby!"

"And I am Emma. Fetch your book, Toby, and let us begin." She usually found her young nieces and nephews rather annoying, but at this point any diver-

sion—even the company of a five-year-old boy—
seemed preferable to sitting and stewing alone.

Charles had to clear his throat to gain Emma's attention. "Well, as usual, you have captivated the attention of every male in your vicinity," he remarked dryly
as he set down several bandboxes on the worn carpet.

She gave a low snort, but before she could answer,
Toby shot him an aggrieved look. "You are interrupting the best part."

"I beg your pardon." He took a seat in one of the
side chairs and grinned at his cousin. "Do go on."

She finished reading the page aloud, then put the
book aside. "We shall start the next chapter in just a
bit," she promised, taking in Toby's mutinous expression.

"Very well," he allowed.

The grin on Charles's face grew wider. "Perhaps
tomorrow I shall bring along some of the picture
books from the nursery to keep the two of you occupied." He gestured what he had brought. "Your maid
packed a few essentials while I took the liberty of
adding a few books." He glanced at Toby. "Though
the offerings from Minerva Press might not be exactly
to your present audience's taste."

"Does the big brown horse I saw this morning belong to you?" interrupted the boy, the awe apparent
in his voice.

Charles nodded. "And if you ask your housekeeper
for an apple, I shall take you out when I leave and
let you feed him the treat."

With a squeak of delight, Toby scurried off as fast
as his little legs would carry him.

"I told you it wouldn't be so bad," her cousin said
after the boy had quit the room. "You have a gentleman hanging on your every word."

Emma made a face. "You needn't keep reminding me that you think me a vain and selfish creature, Charles."

"I don't—just a bit headstrong at times." He toyed with a fob hanging from his watch chain. "Is there anything else you would like?"

"A ride home," she shot back. "Despite your teasings, there is one gentleman here who, I assure you, is not exactly enamored with my presence. I vow, I should not be surprised to find myself relegated to a bed of straw in the stable when night draws nigh. And grudgingly at that."

His brow rose a fraction. "You exaggerate. Kirtland seems quite a solid fellow to me."

She crossed her arms. "I do *not*." He might be solid, she added to herself, recalling his muscular chest and the corded strength of his arms, but he was not very nice.

"Hmmm" was the only answer her cousin made. After a brief pause, he changed the subject. "Robert is expected to arrive by Friday. He is bringing along a Lord Bryson from Devon. My friend—you remember Mr. Harkness, from the Fernleigh's ball—arrives this afternoon. . . ." The conversation continued on for a time on the comings and goings at Telford Manor until Toby, who had been standing at the doorway, could no longer contain his impatience.

"Mrs. Crenshaw has given me an apple," he piped up in a not so subtle reminder.

Charles made a show of consulting his watch. "I do believe my allotted time is nearly up. Wouldn't want to face the firing squad for disobeying orders, would I, lad?" He rose. "Perhaps I shall contrive to coax permission from his lordship to allow an extra hour tomorrow." He winked. "And maybe I shall smuggle in a sweetmeat or two to supplement the bread-and-water rations."

"If Papa were home, he would not make such a joke of my predicament."

"The time will pass quicker than you think. After all, it's only for a few more days."

"It's easy enough for *you* to say," she muttered as he strolled off with Toby.

But indeed, she hardly noticed that the afternoon was well advanced, so intent had she become on reading the latest chapter of the swashbuckling adventure to the boy when he returned a short while later. Toby had climbed up beside her, his small head nestled against her shoulder, and he, too, was listening with rapt attention.

The sight of them together on the old sofa drew a sharp intake of breath from Anne. "Oh, Miss Pierson, I do apologize if Toby has given you no peace this afternoon. I am sure you would have preferred to rest or—"

"Toby has been a delightful companion," she said. "He has helped keep my mind off my injuries." And the rude manners of the lady's brother, she added to herself.

She gave Emma a grateful look. "That is very kind of you to say."

"I read the story to Emma—well, almost."

Both ladies smiled, then Anne cleared her throat. "Toby, you must address our guest as Miss Pierson. It is not proper—"

"It's quite all right. I should prefer it if Toby thinks of me as a . . . friend."

"Mama," continued Toby. "Emma has been great fun." He cocked his head to one side. "Why did Uncle Noel call her a whiny brat?"

Anne turned a vivid shade of crimson. "Toby!" she

gasped in strangled embarrassment. "You must learn not to repeat what you overhear adults saying, for there is much you, er, misunderstand."

"That's quite all right, Mrs. Hartley. Don't trouble yourself over it," said Emma quietly. "Lord Kirtland has not exactly kept his sentiments a secret. I am sorry that my presence appears to be an onerous burden on your household at this time. If I had any choice in the matter, I assure you I would have taken myself off long ago."

Anne's color deepened. "I apologize for my brother's manners, as well as those of my son. I am ashamed that you have been made to feel so unwelcome." She shook her head. "I don't know what has brought on such unaccountable behavior in Noel—he is usually the soul of politeness."

"You needn't apologize for me, Anne" came a low voice from near the door. "I am capable of making my own, if necessary."

She fixed him with an odd stare for a moment, and seemed on the verge of making some sort of reply. Instead she merely turned and picked Toby up from the sofa. "Come, lambkin, it is way past time for you to have your nap."

"But I haven't shown Emma the spillkins Uncle Noel made for me! Or the painted pony he brought from Spain."

"I should love to see such treasures, but I am a bit fatigued right now. Might it wait until after supper?" said Emma, darting a look at the baron that seemed to challenge him to issue an order to the contrary.

"Oh, very well." The boy's eyes were already half closed, and his head was resting on Anne's shoulder.

As soon as mother and child had quitted the room, he took a step closer to Emma. "Do you wish to be taken up to your bedchamber for the evening?" he asked gruffly.

Her chin came up. "Despite your wish for me to be out of your sight, sir, I am not in the least tired and would rather remain where I am. That is, of course, assuming I really do have a choice in the matter."

"Very well. But I warn you that I have a few things in here that I must attend to."

She made a wry face. "Well, I shall try very hard not to get in your way." To her surprise, a glimmer of a smile twitched on his lips. Instead of taking his leave right away, he shifted his weight from foot to foot and clasped his hands behind his back. "I see I shall have to watch my tongue a good deal more carefully around my nephew from now on. I am sorry that he gave voice to a comment that was not meant to be repeated."

Emma gave a slight sniff. It was hardly a handsome apology, but as it clearly cost him some effort to make, she supposed she must accept it, however unsatisfactory. Still, stung by his obvious reluctance, she couldn't resist a gibe of her own. "Ah. You are sorry that Toby repeated it? Or sorry it was said in the first place?"

His jaw tightened. "You may take it to mean what you wish." With that, he turned on his heel and left. In a few minutes he was back again, carrying several rags, a tin of beeswax, and a large wooden box. Studiously avoiding any glance in her direction, he stripped off his coat, rolled up his sleeves, and began a vigorous cleaning of the carved pine mantel.

Emma made a show of picking up one of the books that Charles had brought for her, but try as she might, she couldn't keep her gaze from straying to where he was working and taking in the way his corded muscles moved beneath the fine linen of his shirt. To her acute

embarrassment, he turned abruptly to reach for another rag and caught her staring.

"Gentlemen are not supposed to engage in such menial tasks," she said sharply to mask her dismay.

"As you are well aware, I am not a proper gentleman. At least not the sort of gentleman you are used
to," he answered, taking up another dollop of the fragrant wax and rubbing it into the wood. She couldn't
tell whether his expression was a smile or a sneer.
"But in my mind, a true gentleman would not ask
another person to do a task which he is not capable
of doing himself. I am not ashamed to put an honest
effort into making this house a more cheerful place
to live."

Emma bit her lip as she forced her eyes back to the
printed page, realizing that once again she had appeared rather foolish. The thought of it shouldn't
bother her in the least—after all, why should it matter
what some rough country lord thought of her? But
somehow it did.

He was as different from other gentlemen of her
acquaintance as chalk was from cheese. There was a
certain strength that radiated from him, not just a
physical presence but a sense of character as well. He
certainly made no attempt to hide his true self behind
a facade of charming manners or amiable wit, like so
many bucks of the *ton*. Yet, though he presented a
hard and impenetrable countenance more often than
not, the softening of his features when he looked at
his sister and nephew revealed that a caring, compassionate nature lay within.

Loath as she was to admit it, she found that much
as she wished to dislike him, she found him quite . . .
admirable. And, if truth be told, quite intriguing.

Her fingers turned the page with a decided snap.
Well, she chided herself, there was little need to won-

der what he thought of *her!* He had ignored her presence since making his barbed retort, focusing all his attention on his work. Why, he had even had the nerve to begin whistling under his breath, as if he was enjoying himself.

She slanted another furtive glance in his direction and saw that he was finished with the polishing. Putting the rag aside, he drew the wooden box closer and removed a half dozen oranges, a long length of ribbon, scissors, and a glass jar of cloves. He lay all the items before the hearth, then picked up one of the oranges and began to stick the small, pointed pieces of spice into its thick skin in a willy-nilly fashion. The first few went in without mishap, but the next one slipped and pricked the tip of his thumb.

"Damnation," he muttered, giving his finger a shake.

"Perhaps I should remind you about slips of the tongue, sir," she murmured, "lest Toby keep adding to his rapidly expanding vocabulary."

"I beg your pardon," he growled. After another grimace, his mouth quirked upward into a wry grin. Emma swallowed hard at seeing how the smile brought a certain golden sparkle to his eyes. "Quite right," he continued. "I doubt Anne would appreciate that sort of progress in his learning." He paused to jab another random spike into the fruit.

"Lord Kirtland, those cloves are supposed to be arranged in a certain order, you know."

His brow furrowed. "They are?"

"Yes. You must make sure that the ribbon can wrap around—oh, here, hand it to me."

He hesitated. "You have made pomander balls before?"

"I have," she said rather wistfully. "My brother

Robert and I had great fun making decorations for Christmas when we were children."

"And?"

She thought for a moment. "And then Mama died, and well, I suppose the servants did it."

Still, he made no move to give it to her. "You might scrape your delicate skin or break a nail," he warned.

Emma felt a sharp stab of disappointment. She looked down at her book again, hoping that she might hide the glint of a tear that his casual rebuff had brought to her eyes. "If I did, you need not fear that the whiny brat would complain," she replied in a brittle voice. "But of course it is clear that you do not wish my touch to sully anything in your precious household." Taking great care to smooth a crease from one of the pages, she pretended to turn her full attention back to the volume in her lap.

His tongue seemed bent on creating no end of problems today, thought Noel with a rueful grimace. He sat back on his haunches, twining the length of ribbon around his fingers as he cast a sideways look at the figure on the sofa. The two spots of color on her cheeks and the rigid set of her jaw indicated that despite her show of unconcern, her feelings had been wounded. His lips compressed. He hadn't meant to be cruel. It was just that her offer had taken him by surprise. So, for that matter, had her behavior with Toby. She had been nice to the lad. And patient, which he well knew was not always easy with an energetic five-year-old.

The trouble was, he wanted to keep thinking of her as naught but a spoiled heiress, for to allow even a hint of regard to develop might be . . . dangerous. He slanted another quick glance at her profile—the rich blue of her eyes, the pert tilt of her nose, the lush fullness of her mouth, and the hint of vulnerability in her expression—then looked quickly away.

Lord, she was quite the most lovely lady he had ever met, and if he were not careful, he would find himself reacting like the drab, common moth who finds itself drawn inexorably toward a bright, shimmering flame.

Dangerous indeed.

Uttering a silent oath, he stood up abruptly and held out the orange and the jar of spice. "I'm sorry," he said gruffly. "That was ill done of me. I would be grateful for your help, if you still wish to offer it."

It was Emma's turn to hesitate. "You needn't ask me just because you feel you need be polite."

Noel allowed a wry smile. "As you may have noticed, I am not overly concerned with the social graces."

She gave a tentative smile in return as she accepted the proffered items. "The thought might have occurred to me."

"Actually, I am simply being pragmatic," he added dryly. Uncorking a can of linseed oil, he began to wipe down the dingy wainscoting around the fireplace. "I could use a hand if I am to finish making things cheery for Anne and Toby by Christmas Eve. It is their first holiday without—" The words cut off. "But that is hardly any of your concern."

"Do I really seem so incapable of caring for anyone except myself," she asked in a tight voice.

"I did not mean—" A slight flush rose to his lean cheeks. "That is, I simply did not mean to burden you with my problems."

Emma's fingers were already placing the nubbed cloves in neat rows. "Was your sister's husband a soldier like you?"

"No, he had a small estate near Lymington. When

an epidemic of influenza swept through the area, he and Anne insisted on tending to their servants. . . ."

Though naturally reserved, Noel soon found it was easier to talk to Emma than he had ever imagined. She listened well and asked thoughtful questions. And any doubts that may have lingered as to her character were quickly put to rest by her quick intelligence and lively sense of humor. She was hardly the shallow, conceited young lady he had first taken her to be. As he managed a bit of probing of his own and learned something of her own background, he found she had much more depth to her than that. Indeed, the more they spoke, the more intriguing she became.

Dangerous, indeed.

Noel barely noticed how much time had passed until Anne and Toby returned, followed by the housekeeper who, along with his sister, was carrying a tray of food.

"Since it would be uncomfortable for you to move to the dining room, Miss Pierson, I thought we would join you for an informal supper here," announced Anne, venturing a stern look at Noel as if she expected him to protest.

"An excellent idea," he murmured, standing up and wiping his hands with a clean cloth. "May I fix a plate for you, Miss Pierson? You have certainly earned a bit of sustenance with your labors."

Emma laid aside the last of the oranges. "I am almost done with these, so you had best find me another chore so that I may deserve breakfast," she replied in a bantering tone.

Anne ducked her head to hide a small smile, but tactfully refrained from making any comment on the marked change of attitude in both her brother and their guest.

"Emma, Emma! I have brought my spillkins, and

my pony for you to see." Toby climbed onto the sofa beside his new friend and dumped an armful of wooden toys in her lap.

"Perhaps you would care to dine alone in your room," said Noel quietly. "As Anne said, things tend to be rather more informal here than you are used to."

She was already admiring the gaily painted animal. "I should prefer to stay here," she replied. "That is, if you have no objection to my joining your family meal."

"You are welcome to remain." He handed her a plate, then gathered his nephew in his arms and tossed him up in the air. The little boy shrieked with delight as Noel caught him and turned him upside down. "Here now bantling, you must leave Miss Pierson in peace for a bit."

Toby grabbed at his uncle's knee, giving a yank to the well-worn top of his boot. Noel pretended to trip, and collapsed to the floor. The two of them wrestled for a few moments before the boy emerged from a tangle of limbs and plopped down on Noel's chest with a thump.

"I give up," cried the baron in mock surrender. "I see I shall have to engage in a series of lessons with Gentleman Jackson himself if I am to have any hope of victory in the future." He sat up slowly and brushed a mass of tangled locks from his brow. No doubt after this display of behavior, Miss Pierson would find him to be an odd sort of gentleman—as well as ill-tempered—compared to the polished, well-mannered bucks of the *ton* that she was acquainted with.

And what of it? Giving an inward shrug, he turned and added another log to the crackling fire, trying to ignore the flicker of desire within his breast.

Between Toby's eager chatter and Anne's polite questions to Emma concerning holiday traditions of the area, the meal passed quickly. Noel waved away his sister's offer of help and removed the supper tray himself. When he returned, he brought back her basket of greenery and another box filled with assorted items for fashioning decorations.

Anne hesitated as she picked up a bough of fresh-cut holly. "We could take our work to the kitchen so that we don't disturb you any longer, Miss Pierson. You must be rather exhausted."

"Please don't go," replied Emma. "I should hate to miss all the fun."

And good fun it was, she found herself thinking a short time later, when everyone was engaged in making the room look cheery. Noel had begun to hang the clove-scented oranges from the freshly waxed mantel, while Anne was arranging garlands of fragrant pine boughs in earthenware jugs and along the window tops. Meanwhile, Toby was busy cutting out lopsided paper snowflakes with a pair of blunt scissors. The boy's peals of laughter punctuated the baron's gentle teasing of his sister, and a warmth filled the air—not just from the flames dancing high in the hearth.

How had she thought the baron a cold, unfeeling man? He was certainly neither. Recalling his playful antics with his nephew, his undisguised concern for his sister, Emma was moved by the genuine show of feeling he let show, so unlike the bored ennui affected by many of the gentlemen of the *ton*.

Her fingers paused for a moment in finishing the last pomander ball, and Emma suddenly felt a small knot form inside her chest. There was a palpable spirit of love and kinship around the three other people. Lord Kirtland and his family might lack for blunt, but they had something infinitely more valuable, she realized with a start. Something that many people would gladly pay a fortune to possess.

She bit her lip as she thought of the endless rounds of balls, routs, and house parties she had been a part of for nigh on a year. Between all the attentions of her admirers and the swirl of new activities, she had become nearly a stranger to her father, her brother, her cousin. Not only that, but the prospect of missing a bit of revelry because of a twisted ankle had taken on the proportions of a dire calamity in her way of thinking. She colored on comparing her trifling misfortune to that of Mrs. Hartley.

No wonder Lord Kirtland had thought her a spoiled brat.

Emma watched as the baron paused in his labors to help Toby thread a ribbon through one of his creations. Out of the corner of her eye, she caught sight of Anne staring pensively into the fire, a sad expression stealing to her face in the moment that she thought no one was looking.

"Mrs. Hartley," she said after a moment's thought. "Do you and your brother plan to visit London this spring?"

"Why, I—that is, Noel hasn't . . ." she stammered.

"I daresay you would enjoy it immensely. Though I cannot vouch the same for Lord Kirtland."

Anne looked rather startled.

"No doubt he should be forced to spend much of his time fending off a host of admirers."

"Oh, w-what an absurd notion," mumbled the young widow in some confusion. Her cheeks, however, took on a pretty pink glow. "I-I am much too old to attract a second glance from a gentleman."

"I would love to show you some of the shops on Bond Street," continued Emma, ignoring the other lady's blushes and stutterings. "I know any number of dressmakers and milliners who would delight in the opportunity to fit someone with such a pretty face and lovely figure."

The color on her face deepened to a vivid shade of red. "Y-you are simply being kind," she whispered, though it was clear the compliment had affected her deeply. She cleared her throat. "I have read in *La Belle Assemblé* that to be fashionable, one must purchase a bonnet at Madame Therese?" she ventured.

"Oh, as to that, I should advise you to visit a little shop off of Bond Street where the prices are not only better, but the styles more flattering and the workmanship superb. . . ."

The two ladies then fell into an animated discussion on fashion, which soon turned into a description of the various balls and assemblies that Emma had attended during the Season. Anne hung on her every word, and even Toby stopped with his tossing of the spillkins to listen to the descriptions of the colorful gowns, lavish suppers, and the latest music from the Continent.

"London!" cried the little boy when Emma paused for a bit. "Uncle Noel, can we see the horses at Astley's while Mama and Emma dance a waltz? And taste the treats at Gunther's?"

The baron's expression was hidden in shadow. "We shall see, imp." Before Toby could make any further demands, Noel scooped him up from the floor and tossed him over his shoulder. "Come, give me a hand in fetching more wood for the fire," he said, giving a quick wink at his sister. "I have learned that men are never welcome when the ladies fall to discussing these sorts of topics."

When the two of them returned a short while later, Emma had brought a spark of fun to Anne's eyes and a smile to her lips with a humorous account of some musicale gone awry when the featured singer had imbibed a glass too many of champagne. The sound of their laughter took several minutes to die down.

"Miss Pierson, do tell Noel the story of Mr. Patterson ending up in Lady Chalford's fountain," urged Anne as she stifled another giggle.

"I shall be happy to do so if you are sure he will not be bored by it—but please, you must call me Emma. All my friends do."

The young widow blushed again, this time with pleasure. "I would be happy to do so, if you will do me the honor of calling me Anne."

The intimacies agreed upon, Emma dutifully recounted the incident, drawing a chuckle from the baron and a quizzical look from Toby.

"How can a gentleman be in his cup?" demanded the boy. "Even if he were as small as me, he would never fit more than several toes in such a tiny thing."

"Quite right, lad," replied Noel dryly. "Perhaps in another few years I shall be able to explain to you just how such an odd thing can come to pass. But not now."

"Why—" A warning glance from his mother caused the protest to die on his lips. "Oh, very well," he finished, trying hard to hide a yawn.

Not fooled in the least, Anne rose from her chair. "I think that a certain young man is ready for bed," she murmured, watching her son's chin slump to his chest. "If you will excuse us, I shall take him up to his bedchamber." She flashed a shy smile at Emma. "I am sure that you, too, have had enough excitement for one day. Noel will assist you up to the guest room, and I will be along to help you settle in as soon as I have seen to Toby."

An awkward silence descended over the room once she and the child had left. The baron took up the poker and turned to jab at the dying flames in the hearth while Emma carefully refolded a length of ribbon.

A log hissed and crackled as it fell from the andirons, causing her head to jerk up.

"Well, I suppose I had best see you settled for the night, then." He approached the sofa, hands jammed in the pockets of his coat.

Emma felt her cheeks go as red as the glowing coals at the thought of being taken up in his arms again. Embarrassed by how much the idea sent a frisson of heat through her, she shrank back against the cushions. "M-my ankle is really much better. I am sure I can manage the stairs by myself if you will but steady my arm."

"And risk further injury?" He shook his head, a grim expression coming to his face on seeing her recoil from his advance. "Not a wise strategy, Miss Pierson. I, for one, do not wish to have to report to the duke that his daughter's condition was made worse while under my roof by another act of foolishness that I might have prevented." Like the banked fire, his voice had lost all of its earlier warmth, and the chill of its tone was matched by the rigid line of his jaw.

The sudden change in his manner was like a pitcher of cold water being dashed in her face. So, she thought to herself, he must still think of her as a willful, spoiled brat. No doubt he had been merely feigning the apparent thaw in his feelings in order to please his sister. Although the notion of it hurt far worse than the throbbing in her ankle, Emma was determined to mask her own true feelings as well as he had done.

"As you are no longer in the military, Lord Kirtland, you need not consider yourself responsible for the actions of those under your command. My father would hardly line you up before a firing squad for dereliction of duty, even if you were at fault," she managed to reply quite coolly. "So do not worry. You will not s-suffer for my s-sins." To her dismay, the last words were accompanied by a tremble of her lip and the spill of a tear. "Oh, the deuce take it," she cried, wiping at her cheek with an angry swipe of her sleeve. "Go away, you horrid man! You have already made it clear I am naught but an onerous burden without another lecture to show how much you loathe my very presence in your house. Anne will help me, or I shall stay here on this sofa for the night—indeed, I should crawl to the stable if it meant I might avoid another moment of your grim, disapproving stare!"

Noel's expression, which had indeed been quite grim, changed to one of shocked surprise. "Y-you think I disapprove of you—"

"No—I think you simply despise me." The tears were flowing more freely. "Not that I care at all what you think," she added between watery sniffs.

He took a step closer. "Of course you don't. And why should you, when apparently I have shown myself to be a tongue-tied ass." There was a shuffling pause while he cleared his throat. "I am afraid I have little experience with Polite Society, having lived for the most part in the company of plain-speaking soldiers. Please forgive me if my manners appear rough and unpolished in comparison to what you are used to. I— I meant nothing of the sort."

"Oh, you needn't apologize," murmured Emma, instantly regretting her outburst. No doubt he would now think her more childish than ever. "Rather it is I who should beg pardon for indulging in such a fit of vapors, as well as for becoming a veritable watering pot." A few small drops still clung to her lashes. "I-I am not usually prone to tears."

A ghost of a smile crossed his lips. "I am sure you are not. In fact, you have shown more courage than many of my veteran troops, putting on a brave face with what I know must be a very painful injury."

Ducking her head to hide the blush that his unexpected compliment brought to her cheeks, Emma stammered something unintelligible in return.

"But now I am sure you must be truly exhausted, both from discomfort of your ankle and from being pressed into service as a nursemaid and a lowly laborer." His expression twisted into one of wry regret. "I am sorry you did not land in more congenial company, Miss Pierson. However, I hope you will at least put up with my grim face long enough that I might see you comfortably settled upstairs."

This time when he bent forward, Emma made no move to sidle away. His arms slipped around her and lifted her from the sofa. The baron was right—his manners and bearing were indeed different from all the other gentlemen of her acquaintance. As her head settled against his shoulder, she realized she couldn't begin to imagine one of the dandies of her set doffing his elegant coat to wrestle with a giggling child. Neither could she picture any of them deigning to mess with cloves and oranges in order to create a Christmas decoration for a mantel he had just cleaned with his own hands.

"I haven't enjoyed anything as much as such labors—as you call them—in a long while," she said softly. There was a shy hesitation. "Or such company."

Noel gave a low chuckle, and she could feel the light tickle of his breath on her neck. "You need not go that far in doing the pretty, Miss Pierson. While I, too, find Anne and Toby delightful to be around, I have no illusions about how pleasant my grim visage has been to you." His tone became more serious. "As I have said, my skills are sadly lacking when it comes to playing a proper gentleman."

He pulled her closer to his chest on starting up the stairs, and Emma was suddenly aware of the faint tang of orange and clove mixed with the masculine undertones of bay rum and leather. That, along with the heat emanating through the thin linen fabric of his shirt, made her feel a bit light-headed. "I-I . . ." she stammered in some confusion. "That is, y-you . . ."

The baron appeared to take no notice of her stutterings. "While you seem to have a knack for putting people at their ease," he went on in a low voice. "For weeks I have been racking my brains for a way to bring a smile and some life to Anne's face, yet you managed it so easily. My thanks—that was truly kind of you."

"I hardly deserve much credit—what female can remain blue-deviled when talking of the latest fashions and fancy balls?" she joked, though his sincere praise had brought a lump to her throat.

"Ah, is that the secret?" His tone was as light as hers. "I shall keep it in mind, though I fear such topics will prove just as difficult as fine manners for a rough country farmer to master."

They had reached the doorway of the guest room, and Noel paused to nudge the door open with his boot. It took only a stride or two to reach the narrow bed. He set her down, then quickly stepped back. "Anne will be in shortly," he said, turning to light the candle on the small pine table. "Is there anything else you have need of?"

Emma hesitated. "Just a list of the tasks I should tackle tomorrow, so that I might continue to earn my keep."

"That, at least, is something I can manage with no difficulty at all. They will be sent up with your water and crust of bread." He allowed a momentary grin.

"Good night, then, Miss Pierson. You had better sleep well."

"Good night, Lord Kirtland."

Noel pulled the door shut behind him.

Lord, had he really made such a fool of himself before the young lady? His lips compressed as he recalled each and every one of his stilted words. She must truly think him a bumbling nodcock for his brusque manner and lack of polish. *As if it was of any consequence,* he reminded himself. A Diamond of the First Water—and one of the most sought-after heiresses in all of London—was hardly going to take note of an impoverished country baron, no matter how charming or affable he might strive to be.

Especially one with a grim, disapproving visage rather than the handsome, smiling features of a Buck of the *ton.* His expression grew even fiercer, though the look of disapproval was directed at himself for entertaining, even for an instant, such a silly notion that she might find him . . . agreeable. Just because she had hinted that she had enjoyed the evening, and the company. . . .

Don't be an ass. Of course she had only meant Anne and Toby! And who could blame her, given his offensive behavior? Muttering an oath under his breath, he headed back downstairs. There was still a great deal to accomplish before Christmas Eve, and while he may not have any idea of how to go on in a drawing room, he could at least perform a host of practical skills.

But at the moment, the fact that he knew how to loosen the bolt of a stove and concoct a polish for pine did not afford him nearly the same satisfaction as it had the day before.

* * *

"Oh, Toby, do be careful!"

The little boy barely managed to avoid tangling his feet in the long garland of holly that Emma and Anne had just finished knotting together, though the hop caused him to tumble headfirst into a basket of pine boughs. The two ladies began to giggle as he righted himself, a profusion of green needles clinging to his sable curls.

"Why, he looks the very picture of a Christmas imp," remarked Emma as her laughter subsided.

"And quite likely to wreak some mischief before the day is done," said Anne with a smile. "Come, Toby. If you wish to be of help, you may hold the end of this holly rope while I arrange it over the dining room mantel." She turned to Emma and added in a lower voice, "I am sure that you would welcome a bit of peace and quiet, along with a respite from such mundane labors—"

Emma waved off her new friend's tentative words. "Nonsense! If you will pass me the ribbon box and the pine boughs, I shall start on the garlands for over the windows while you are busy in the other room."

"But the sap is quite sticky. And the needles can be terribly prickly."

"Yes, and the berries from the holly can make a gooey mess." Emma wiped a smudge of red from her nose and grinned. "No doubt I already look as gloriously disheveled as Toby, so I have no intention of missing out on the fun in order to avoid further despoiling of my person."

Anne looked a trifle unconvinced, but as Toby was already tugging on the twined leaves and threatening to undo all their hard work, she let out a small sigh. "Very well, however, I shall not be long."

Once alone, Emma brushed an errant curl from her

cheek and took a moment to survey the small parlor. Its transformation was nearly complete—the woodwork glowed with its fresh coat of fragrant wax, the mantel was festooned with greenery, the brass fender gleamed like a newly minted coin in the reflection of the roaring fire, and the spicy scent of oranges and cloves perfumed the air. The draperies had even lost their coating of dust, though the baron must have risen at dawn to have managed the task. All that was left to do was arrange the swags of pine boughs above the painted casements.

Her brow furrowed. Though the room was hardly larger than the sewing room at Telford Manor, it seemed so much cheerier than the vast formal drawing room where she and her family were accustomed to celebrating Christmas. She looked around once more. The decorations at the Manor were exquisitely tasteful—hothouse flowers spilled from cut-crystal vases, the greens were wrapped with expensive ribbon and arranged in perfect symmetry around the windows, while all manner of exotic fruits filled the silver epergnes. But somehow, in comparison with the lopsided paper stars cut by Toby, the simple stoneware crocks of pine and holly, and the crooked rows of cloves stuck into the oranges, they seemed rather . . . spiritless.

It was, she admitted, as if her home, though perfect in outward appearance, had grown hard and cold with the lack of laughter and sharing. Lord, when she thought about it, when was the last time she and her father and brother had spent more than a fleeting moment with one another's company over the past months? The answer caused her frown to deepen. She had become so engrossed in her own concerns that she had not given a thought to . . . well, to a great many things, it seemed—

"Sorry," said Noel gruffly, on seeing how Emma's

head had snapped up at the sound of the logs dropping into the wooden box at the side of the hearth. "But I wished to bring in another load in case it begins to snow." He brushed some bits of bark from his sleeve. "I trust your ankle is not worse this morning?"

With a start, Emma realized she had forgotten all about her injury. "On the contrary, sir, I have not felt the slightest bit of discomfort."

The corners of his mouth gave a slight twitch. "Perhaps if you give such a convincing reply to Dr. Dumberton, you might be able to persuade him to release you from confinement sooner than expected."

Biting her lip, she forced herself to ignore the pinch of disappointment caused by his apparent wish to be rid of her. "Speaking of confinement," she replied rather sharply. "I was wondering whether you might allow more than one visit by my cousin today—as well as permission for him to bring a friend with him this afternoon."

All trace of humor disappeared from the baron's face, and his shoulders stiffened. "Ah, I suppose it is not to be wondered at, that you have tired of the company of—"

"No!" Her chin took on an indignant tilt. "That is not what I meant at all. What I was thinking was—Charles has invited a friend down from Sussex. A widower, actually, with a daughter only a year or two younger than Toby. Mr. Harkness is a very nice man, and it occurred to me that the two of them might provide pleasant company for Anne. It would do her good, you know, to meet other people and see a spark of admiration in the eye of a gentleman other than her brother." Not, she added to herself, that *she* would ever see the light of such sentiment from Lord Kirtland.

Noel's hand tightened on the log he was straightening. "I—I beg your pardon, Miss Pierson," he said after a moment or two. "It is a most thoughtful idea. If your cousin is agreeable to the plan, he and his friend are welcome to come by whenever they wish." Moving with great deliberateness, he finished arranging the rest of the wood in a neat order, then rose and left the room without a further word.

The pine needles suddenly felt like hedgehogs beneath her fingers. Was the baron always so prickly, or was it her presence that brought out such behavior? Despite the occasional lowering of his spines, he seemed determined to treat her as naught but an unwelcome intruder. Blinking back the sting of tears, she began to fashion a festive bow for one of the garlands, though her spirits had been sadly flattened.

The devil take it!

Noel threw down the chisel and rubbed at his scraped fingers. It seemed he was all thumbs at everything he attempted this morning! Not only was the groove for the larder hinge now looking a bit crooked, but once again he had shown himself incapable of behaving with even a hint of gentlemanly civility.

She must think him an idiot.

Shoving aside the rest of his tools, he rose and stalked toward the kitchen door. Perhaps a spell outside chopping wood might help relieve some of his pent-up frustration—as well as cool the heat that was coursing through his veins every time he thought of the lovely Miss Pierson. It was one thing to ignore her when she seemed no more than a willful brat, but now that she had shown herself to be thoughtful and perceptive and . . .

He swore again under his breath, reminding himself that to let his mind stray in such a direction was unwise.

Thwock. The ax split the log neatly in two.

No, it would be best to keep both his thoughts and his person well away from the young lady. Surely it should not be so difficult to avoid her—or at least feign indifference to her presence. After all, she would be gone from under his roof in a matter of days.

But he feared she would haunt his dreams for a good deal longer than that.

". . . and don't forget, there are a number of things that I want you to bring along when you return with Edgar."

Charles regarded his cousin with bemused amazement. It was not merely the sight of the pine needles sticking to her fingers or the faint smudge of red across her cheek or the scraps of cut ribbon and paper clinging to the soft merino wool of her elegant gown that had rendered him momentarily speechless. Rather it was the striking change in her demeanor since the accident.

"Have Larkins fetch down the box of lead soldiers from the attic, for I know Toby will be in alt at having his very own army to maneuver. Gather up the last few issues of *La Belle Assemblé,* for Anne will greatly enjoy seeing the very latest fashions from Town," she continued. "And ask Mrs. Hawkins for a tin of her special wood polish, along with the recipe, for Lord Kirtland . . ." Her voice faltered. "That is, Lord Kirtland no doubt has his own preferences, but perhaps he might find it useful."

Was this the same headstrong young lady who had sat there not twenty-four hours ago beseeching him not to leave her in such a dreadful place? Repressing a grin, Charles couldn't help but wonder whether she had, indeed, suffered a severe knock on the head as well as a nasty twist of her ankle. If so, he found himself hoping the effects would be a good deal more lasting than the damage to her leg. But he wisely forbore voicing such thoughts aloud. Giving a slight cough, he merely nodded. "Is that all?"

"Oh—have Cook make up a basket of her cakes and perhaps a pigeon pie and a crock of her stewed mushrooms. And why not include a bottle or two of Papa's favorite claret. We are busy enough here without Anne or the housekeeper having to see to making supper."

At this remark, Charles couldn't resist an arch of his brow as he regarded her slightly disheveled state. "Hmm, yes. Busy, indeed."

Emma made a rueful grimace as she brushed a strand of hair off her forehead, then looked down at her grubby hands and the scraps clinging to the folds of her gown. "I suppose I hardly look like the proper lady, but there is much to do to get this house ready for Christmas, and it was clear they could use an extra hand."

"So, it does not appear as if you are suffering from the ennui or deprivation that you feared."

It was true. With a small start, she realized her thoughts had been far too occupied to dwell on her own imagined travails. However, she chose to ignore his comment while at the same time turning to avoid his inquiring gaze. "In fact, you and Edgar will be able to help Lord Kirtland move the cupboard in the kitchen. I overheard Anne say that she wished it might be shifted to the other side of the room, but it needs more than one man. And no doubt there are a number of other heavy tasks that might be done while you two are here."

"I shall warn my friend that we are expected to provide more than just our scintillating presence." He took up his hat and gloves. "Well, I had best take my leave now." There was a slight pause as he tugged the soft York tan leather over his fingers. "How fortuitous for all involved that you landed here."

"*Hah!*" muttered Emma under her breath. It was quite evident to her that not everyone at Hawthorne House would agree with that sentiment.

Noel sat off to one side and stared into the crackling fire. A burble of laughter came from the ladies as Charles finished another humorous anecdote concerning the surreptitious addition of a bottle of brandy to the ratafia punch at Lady Atwater's ball. He forced a smile as well, though he had not really been listening.

It was proving nigh on impossible to ignore Miss Pierson. Throughout the afternoon, she had required his presence as one task after another had been drawn up for the assembled company. Her animated banter and gay laughter had kept everyone in high spirits—including himself. Perhaps tonight, if he kept his gaze averted from her blonde beauty, he thought glumly, he would not feel so much like a lowly moth being drawn toward a flame.

It was, of course, too late to keep his heart from being singed.

Admit it! he cajoled himself. The seasoned officer, who had come through countless battles unscathed by bullet or saber, had been brought to his knees by Cupid's arrow. He was, however, determined to nurse his wound without becoming the object of amusement or pity. No one would have reason to guess at the true state of his feelings.

Another laugh from Anne caused his expression to soften for an instant. The undisguised change in her behavior was cause for silent celebration, no matter his own depressed spirits. Noel slanted a quick glance at her animated face and shy smile. She had clearly made the first tentative steps toward emerging from her shell, encouraged by the kind attentions of their guest and the two affable gentlemen. Why, Anne had even managed a conversation with Mr. Harkness while the two of them had been engaged in hanging one of the swags of pine. Although the talk had been mainly about the sorts of mischief young children were apt to create, it was a start. He took a sip of his wine. Perhaps Toby's innocent observation had been correct—Miss Pierson was indeed a Yuletide angel sent down from the heavens in answer to his prayers.

No matter that she would bedevil his peace of mind far longer than the holiday season.

"I hope that we might be permitted to call on the morrow and offer further assistance," said Mr. Harkness, rising reluctantly as the clock on the mantel chimed the lateness of the hour. "I heard mention of chairs needing to be moved down from the attic, and there is still the Yule log to be cut."

"And you may bring more jam tarts!" cried Toby. "Oh, do say yes, Mama."

Anne ruffled her son's hair. "The duke's cook has been far too generous as it is." She picked at a fold in her skirts. "And I am sure the gentlemen have far more interesting things to do than to—"

"Why, not at all," replied Mr. Harkness quickly. "In fact, the Manor is rather quiet as the duke and Robert have been delayed in London. We would much prefer the company of two charming ladies to another endless round of billiards, wouldn't we, Charles?"

"Of course," chimed in Emma's cousin.

"Well, in that case . . ." Anne turned to Noel.

"I should be glad of any help you care to offer," he replied politely. Then he, too, gave a glance at the clock and rose abruptly. "Now, if you will excuse me,

there are some matters I must attend to before it
grows much later."

"Dear me," murmured Mr. Harkness after the door
had fallen closed. "Did I say something amiss?"

"Oh, it's not you, Edgar," said Emma with a forced
smile. "It's me. I'm afraid Lord Kirtland has formed
quite a low opinion of me—"

Charles coughed. "Well, he did have ample reason."

She shot him an aggrieved look. "—and now he
finds it difficult to be in the same room with me."

"Surely you exaggerate," exclaimed Mr. Harkness
with an odd quirk of his lips. "From what I observed
this afternoon, I would have guessed that Lord Kirtland does not find your company . . . unwelcome."

"I assure you I do not." She wiggled the toes of
her bandaged ankle. "You are quite mistaken—he
cannot wait for me to be out from under his roof."

Her cousin tactfully refrained from further comment. Anne, too, remained silent, though a pensive
expression drew her brows together for an instant as
she stared first at the closed door, then at Emma.

"If you don't mind, I should like to be taken up to
my room," continued Emma after an awkward pause.
Her head was lowered so that none of the others could
discern her expression. "I am suddenly feeling very
fatigued."

Charles was quick to comply with her request and
carried her upstairs without indulging in any more of
his usual teasing. He returned in time to catch Anne's
puzzled sigh as she rose to see the two gentlemen to
the door.

"I cannot for the life of me figure out what has
Noel acting so strangely," she murmured. "He is not
usually given to such unaccountable shifts of mood."

"Emma, too, is behaving quite unlike her, er,
usual self."

Mr. Harkness gave a short cough. "I am, of course, a stranger to them both, but it seemed to me that, well, maybe . . ."

Charles stroked at his chin. "By Jove, do you think it possible. . . ."

"Are you saying . . ." Anne's eyes took on a rapturous light. "Wouldn't that be wonderful. . . ."

"Wonderful, indeed," repeated Charles, a sly grin stealing to his lips. "Though it appears that the two parties involved are being deucedly stubborn about the whole matter." His hand came up to stroke his chin. "Hmmm. We shall have to see what might be done to help things along."

The next few days were filled with a whirlwind of activity that somehow required Noel to spend a good deal of time in consultation with his injured guest. The others seemed to need both of their opinions in making the final decisions for a number of minor details. The result, however, was that the inhabited wing of Hawthorne House was looking more like a true home with every passing moment. Every room had been scrubbed and polished, down to the last nail head, and a profusion of Christmas greenery in gaily beribboned crocks enlivened the freshly dusted chintzes. Even the hallway leading to the kitchen bore a fresh coat of paint, as volunteered by the visitors from Telford Manor. The project had engendered quite a few giggles from the ladies, as it seemed that more of the pigment had ended up on the two gentlemen and their small helper than on the plaster itself. But all agreed that the end result was a vast improvement over the former dingy shade of soot gray.

Charles and Edgar—as all present had been begged to drop the more formal use of his last name—insisted on bringing hampers of food prepared by the duke's cook for when the work was done, so suppers turned into a shared affair as well. Fortified with an ample supply of excellent champagne from the cellars of His Grace, the meals also passed in an effervescence of good spirits. If Noel and Emma were a trifle more sober than the others, it was not remarked upon, at least aloud.

That evening, Toby had been put to bed, and the adults had moved to the parlor for a celebration of sorts. The cast-iron stove had finally yielded to the ministrations of three muscular gentlemen and now burned without filling the kitchen with a cloud of smoke. The baron, as was his habit, took a seat slightly apart from the others and allowed the others to carry most of the conversation, though Charles and his friend took great pains to draw him out.

"Was that Dr. Dumberton's gig that I spied leaving as we were returning with the last load of cut holly?" asked Charles, after recounting the latest bits of news from the London newspapers. His eyes had strayed to where Emma's ankle sat propped up on a hassock, and showing from beneath the folds of fine merino was evidence of a new—and greatly reduced—bandage.

"Yes." She seemed engrossed in studying the progress of the myriad tiny bubbles to the surface of her drink. "In fact, he says that I am recovered enough to return home on the morrow."

"Well, now, that certainly calls for a toast, doesn't it?" he replied with great heartiness.

She raised her glass, a crooked smile upon her lips. "Yes. Of course."

The others joined in with murmured congratulations.

Noel was the last to speak. "What good news, indeed" was his enigmatic comment. He swallowed the contents of his glass in one gulp, then reached over for the bottle and refilled it to the brim.

His sister fixed him with an odd look before turning away. A small sigh was heard from her. "It will seem very . . . quiet without you here. All of you," she said after a moment.

"As to that . . ." Edgar cleared his throat. "Er, seeing as, er, you might have a bit of free time, I thought you—and Toby—might like to go for a drive in the afternoon. My daughter is to arrive from the visit with her grandparents, and I should like very much for you to meet her. Assuming, of course, that you would care to."

Anne's cheeks took on a very becoming shade of rose. "Oh, but I—I would. Very much so." She darted another quick glance at Noel. "That is, if you are sure there is nothing pressing—"

"Not at all." His words were accompanied by a brief smile. Then, as on the previous evenings, he made to rise and quit the room before the others, leaving one of the other gentlemen to assist Emma upstairs. But this time, Charles forestalled his exit by getting to his feet first.

"Edgar, we must be off early," he announced, making a show of consulting his pocket watch. "Uncle Ivor is due to arrive sometime later tonight, and it would be quite rude on our parts if we were not there to greet him."

His friend shot up as well.

"I shall pack up the hampers and help you take them out to the gig. No doubt Cook will have need of all her platters now that the holidays are beginning in earnest." Anne rose quickly and joined the two gentlemen. "It has been a long day, and I am sure all of us are quite ready to retire." With that, she hastened toward the door, the others taking their cue and following close on her heels.

The devil take it! Noel shifted uncomfortably in his chair, his gaze still riveted on the dancing flames. Taken aback at being left alone with Emma, he was still trying to compose his thoughts when she stirred from her seat and lowered her ankle from its resting place.

"It *has* been a long day," she murmured, echoing Anne's words. "I believe I shall follow her suggestion and bid you good night, sir."

"Miss Pierson, just what do you think you are doing?"

She hesitated. "Why, I am going upstairs." Her chin rose a touch. "I trust you have no objection—" Before she could finish, Noel had her up in his arms. "T-that is quite unnecessary, sir," she stammered. "The doctor says I am permitted to move about on my own, if I exercise a modicum of caution."

"Since caution does not seem to be your strong suit, I prefer to ensure there are no further accidents." There was no sting to the words, as they had been uttered with an unexpected gentleness.

Emma's head jerked up in some surprise, then she quickly looked away. "What you mean is, it would be your worst nightmare were a slip to delay my departure." Though she tried to keep her tone light, there was a small catch in her voice.

Hah! The only nightmare that promised to plague his dreams was the thought of never seeing her angelic face again!

Noel knew he would be treading on dangerous ground were he to venture a reply, but suddenly his foot paused on the stairs. Perhaps it was because he had imbibed more of the champagne than he was used to that prompted him to speak. "You think I shall be glad that you are gone?"

"O-of course. You said yourself that my leaving on the morrow was good news indeed."

"We seem to be in the habit of misunderstanding each other's words, Miss Pierson," he murmured, his face only inches from hers. "What I meant was, it must be good news indeed for *you*. I remember quite clearly how, on the morning of the accident, you lamented being forced to miss all the fun. Well, rather than being stuck in this isolated house any longer, you will soon be back in the whirl of fashionable balls and dinner parties, surrounded, no doubt, by a crowd of admirers. All of them a good deal more charming and amusing than a grim-faced ex-soldier."

"Perhaps I have come to realize that it is much more important to be surrounded by people who truly care for each other than by a crowd of fawning strangers." Her cheek came to rest against his shoulder, then she spoke again, in hardly more than a whisper. "J-just as I have come to recognize that you possess a good deal more than charm and *bon mots,* Lord Kirtland. You are all the things a true gentleman should be—caring, compassionate, forthright, and unselfish. Due to your efforts, Hawthorne House has become a special place, and I shall miss . . . everyone here." She drew in a deep breath. "Though I know you still think of me as a nuisance, if not a spoiled brat, but I thought that, in the spirit of Christmas, we might part as . . . friends."

"It has been quite some time since I have thought of you as a brat," he replied slowly, his arms tightening ever so slightly and drawing her closer to his chest. The subtle fragrance of fresh lavender, mingled with a hint of orange, was even more intoxicating than the sparkling wine. And so was the heady notion that her opinion of him was not . . . entirely negative. For an instant, he feared his own feet might slip out from under him. But then again, he thought with a rueful grimace, he had already fallen hard for the young lady.

However, he reminded himself with cold reason, only a lovesick fool would think her words were anything more than a casual compliment. To a friend.

Forcing his features to remain impassive, he went on in a measured voice. "Indeed, you have been all that is kind and thoughtful in regard to Anne, not to speak of all your tireless labors. I am most grateful." Realizing he was still standing like a statue, he forced his feet to resume their climb. "It would be most churlish of me to refuse your generous offer, so by all means, let us take our leave on a cordial note."

"Cordial. Yes. I see." She blinked, trying to hide the flicker of disappointment in her eyes. "No doubt you will be engaged in some task when Charles comes around with the carriage tomorrow, so perhaps we should say our good-byes now." Her head dropped so that it was impossible to make out her expression. "Thank you for your hospitality, Lord Kirtland. You have been most patient in hosting an unexpected visitor."

They had reached the door of her bedchamber. After an awkward pause, Noel set her on her feet and stepped back. "Rather it is I who owe you thanks, for you have brought a good deal of cheer to this place with your presence, Miss Pierson," he replied in a voice that he forced to remain neutral. Resisting the urge to gather her once again in his arms, this time for a passionate embrace, he took her hand and grazed his lips lightly over her fingers. "May you have a merry Christmas."

"And you, sir." Emma reached for the latch, but

the door suddenly yanked open and a small, drowsy face peeked out from behind the polished pine.

"Oh, you've come at last!"

"Toby!" cried both of them in unison.

"Imp, what sort of mischief is this?" added Noel. "It is way past your bedtime and your mother—"

"But she said I might wait up for my kiss!" He pointed at a sprig of green that hung by a slender ribbon from the top of the molding. "Mama and Mr. Harkness gathered a great bunch of those funny looking toes on their walk this afternoon. They said that it makes people who stand under it kiss each other." There was a bit of giggling before he went on. "Mama said I might have a piece of my own to hang where I wanted, and Lord Lawrance helped me with the hammer and nail. I put it over Emma's door so that she would have to give me a special good-night kiss before she enters."

"And you shall have it." She bent down and hugged him close, then planted a long kiss on each cheek. "Sweet dreams, lambkin."

Until that moment, Noel would never have believed it possible for a grown man to be jealous of a five-year-old.

"Now, off to bed with you, young man, lest you fall asleep on your feet." She gave him one last squeeze before directing him toward his room. After watching the little boy disappear around the corner, she started to rise, but her ankle buckled slightly, drawing a sharp intake of breath.

Noel was at her side in an instant, his arms slipping around her waist to steady her progress as he lifted her up. "Have you reinjured yourself?" he asked with some concern.

Emma forced a wan smile. "No, no. It was just a momentary twinge."

"You are sure?" As Noel looked searchingly at her face, he couldn't help but note an elongated shadow shading her cheek. Somehow the two of them had come to be standing directly under the suspended mistletoe, and the silhouette of its delicate leaves and berries flickered across her alabaster skin. He leaned closer. "P-perhaps you should allow me to carry you the rest of the way."

"Oh, that is not really necessary, sir. As I have said, I have been burden enough on you." Her mouth, just inches from his, gave an odd little quirk.

For once in his life he decided to throw all caution to the wind.

If a five-year-old could so easily request a kiss from the lady of his affections, then surely an experienced officer should be able to muster the courage to do the same. After all, if he had not enough spirit to take the chance of declaring himself, he deserved to have her walk out of his life without a backward glance.

His lips came down upon hers with a gossamer touch.

For an instant he feared she was about to use her good foot to boot him head over heels back down the stairs. But then, with a muffled sigh, she tilted her head back and allowed her mouth to soften under his.

It ended all too quickly for his liking, as Emma drew back in some confusion. "B-but, sir, you don't even like me! You think me . . . a . . . a . . ."

"A sweet angel," he finished. "One who has touched all of us with your warmhearted spirit. But most of all me."

Her lashes dropped. "Y-you are just being gentlemanly—"

"If I were a true gentleman, my dear Emma," murmured Noel, "I should not be doing this." He kissed her lightly, first one cheek, then the other, then full on the mouth, where his lips lingered for a lengthy interval. "But I can no longer keep my true feelings hidden away and risk having you walk—or hobble—out of my life. Do you think you might come to feel some regard for a grim-faced country farmer, with no—"

This time it was his words that were interrupted as Emma placed her hands on his shoulders and drew him into her embrace.

It was some minutes later before he recovered his equilibrium. "You realize, my love, that I have only a modest inheritance and this small manor to offer you—"

She silenced him by tracing a finger along the line of his jaw. "I am well aware of what you have to offer, Noel Trumbull. And it is infinitely more precious than any of the things of which you speak."

"Still, I would be remiss if I didn't remind you that it will be rather crowded here, compared to what you are used to," he continued. "Anne and Toby do have a home here as well."

A twinkle came to her eye. "Their company would always be most welcome, but judging from how Mr. Harkness behaved while helping your sister hang the mistletoe in the front hall, I have a feeling they may be well on the way to having a home of their own again."

Noel grinned. "Why, that would be splendid news indeed. He seems a fine fellow."

"Very fine. There is, of course, no need to mention to either of them that they neglected to shut the door while engaged in their . . . efforts." She brushed back a shock of dark hair from his forehead. "I trust you are not going to suggest any other drawbacks, else I might start to think you are trying to drive me away—"

He hoped the ardor of the embrace that followed put to rest such a ridiculous notion. "Good Lord, no," he said softly as his lips reluctantly raised from hers. "I just want you to be sure you don't mind that I can't offer you fancy gowns or glittering jewels for Christmas. Only my love."

"That, my dearest Noel, is the most wondrous gift I have ever received."

"Well? What's happening?"

Edgar edged a little farther around the corner of the house and craned his neck so that he might see up to the dimly lit window. "Nothing—no, wait! He is . . . bending toward her."

"Thank goodness!" sighed Anne, her breath turning into puffs of white in the chill night air. "I thought he would never admit, even to himself, that his heart was engaged."

"Now what?" asked Charles with some urgency.

"I can't quite make out . . . Or is she? . . . Yes! She is kissing him back!"

"That's the spirit, Emma," murmured Charles. "Always knew that despite your penchant for taking occasional tumbles, your innate good sense would prevail." He pulled a fresh bottle of champagne from inside his coat and popped the cork. "Now we truly have something to celebrate." After a prolonged swallow, he passed it to Edgar.

"To friends and family, old and new!" exclaimed the other man, giving a wink in Anne's direction as he took a generous nip and handed the spirits back to Charles.

She repressed a laugh on watching the two of them become increasingly unsteady on their feet. "It appears that it is going to be a very merry Christmas indeed!"

EXPLORE THE WORLD OF
SIGNET REGENCY ROMANCE

EMMA JENSEN

"One of my favorites, the best of a new generation of
Regency writers." —Barbara Metzger

LAURA MATTHEWS

BARBARA METZGER

"One of the genre's wittiest pens." —*Romantic Times*

To order call: 1-800-788-6262